Avalon Wishes

Alexa Whitewolf

Avalon Wishes
by Alexa Whitewolf

Copyright ©2017 Alexa Whitewolf
ISBN 978-1-9994499-7-1

Cover design by **Y. Nikolova at Ammonia Book Covers**

Fourth Edition

"To exist is a wonder.
To grow is a necessity.
To learn is a challenge.
To understand is a blessing.
To teach is a privilege.
To love is a miracle.
To die is an adventure."
-Merlin

ACKNOWLEDGEMENTS

I have to first and foremost give credit to all the literature and fantasy that exists out in the world on King Arthur and the characters in the Arthurian legend.

Where would we be without the principles Arthur teaches, of equality and loyalty, that every growing boy wants to follow? I don't know about everyone else, but my childhood was spent with many a story read on Merlin, Lancelot and Guinevere, shaping my own ideas of life in general.

The take on these well-known characters is all entirely mine, and for that surge of inspiration I have a huge thank to give to Zeus and Achilles, my furriest of babies ☺ They've been my loyal companions for nine and four years respectively, and their enthusiasm and canine behavior is much reflected in Alistair's own.

As always, I have to give a huge thank you to my husband, Steven, for his encouragement and never-ending faith in me. A bear hug to my mom, for being a role model and the best parent one could ask for!

And last but not least, to everyone who gave their input and contributed to the edits, cover (Y., you REALLY rocked this new cover! ☺) and overall look of *Avalon Wishes*.

I would be remiss if I did not thank my loyal readers as well. Please believe I appreciate each and every one of you to the utmost! You are the reason I write, and I thank you for the time you put into reading these words.

PART 1

FRIENDSHIP

CHAPTER 1

Eons ago…

Heavy lays the burden on the one who wears the crown…

Except of course, in this case, there was no king – only a pantheon of deities passing judgment on criminals. *Or so they would have you believe.*

Eyes of onyx surveyed a circular room, actively searching for a way out. All that could be observed were high ceilings, ornate walls, marble floors in multiple colors such as were never seen on Earth. Large, thick columns supported a dome, giving the room a grandiose air. In the middle of it all was a throne step, with three golden seats in its midst.

The reason for the gathering was to pass verdict for a felony that had been committed. The judges were three gods that made the trinity, head of the pantheon. Sadly enough, the drama that had unfolded passed right over the heads of the mere mortals worshipping them, but it was nonetheless real.

The three wardens sat, immobile, on their perched seats of glory. In front of them, chained and on their knees, were three other deities: one woman and two men.

Their crimes? Greed. Ambition.

The three each had their wrists shackled. The metallic binds could not actually put a stop to their powers – they were supreme beings, after all. It was all a show, to humiliate them before the punishment.

The woman, Deasa, had blonde hair, curly, a tattered robe on her. Her face, ravaged by tears, still remained beautiful: all soft lines, a rosebud mouth, and large blue eyes. Long lashes covered them as she sobbed silently, her shoulders turned inwards, her dignity hanging by a thread.

Next to the woman stood a man, Faitus, only slightly taller than her. He was wearing a grey, dust-covered toga. He would be considered striking in the mortal world with his blonde hair and blue eyes, tight jaw and muscled body.

He would have been deemed handsome even amongst the gods, were it not for the company he kept. Indeed, the last of the three accused, kneeling slightly ahead of them, was the head of their little triangle. Atrox was his name, and he surpassed them all in looks and charisma.

Proud though he knelt, his head was raised, chin defiantly pointed to the ceiling. He met the gazes of his three judges unflinchingly. His midnight black stare was one few dared to challenge. The dark head of curls was, like everything about him, sensuous, down to the full lips, which curled in disdain. Though he was restrained and on the floor, he held his back straight, looking blankly ahead – as though past their mere presence.

The trinity facing the accusers could have been models, in today's modern world. They were all dressed in navy togas, held by shiny brooches. Each piece of jewelry was designed to a specific animal, which represented their beastly form – the one they took when crossing realms, to protect the less resistant human-like bodies.

The man to the far right, Vulper, had a head of red hair, eyes of molten gold, a firm and unwavering gaze in a face set of stone. His brooch was in the shape of a fox. He was the seer amongst the trinity, the one meant to warn them of incoming changes. He had not failed in his role, and his reward would soon be plucked from the trio of sinners.

In his hand, Vulper toyed with the Orb of Sight. About the size of a baseball, it was a perfect circle. When one peered within, they could see the universe itself – until the mist defogged into a vision of the future.

The object of power used to be Atrox's. A long time ago, it had been gifted to him by their parents, and stolen by Vulper. It had been the only way they had caught on to his plans, and managed to subdue him. After causing the rebellion, Atrox had lost the Orb to the winners: the gods currently facing him.

The Orb itself, even now, pulled his gaze away from nothingness. If only he had it, he would be able to harness his vision powers and figure a way out. The circle was the only thing potent enough to cut through magic, and see everything as it was – even if someone was trying to hide it.

As if he can wield it properly, Atrox snorted at Vulper, then looked towards the other two judges.

The second man, on the far left, had dark hair that came to

his shoulders, and eyes the color of pure emeralds. His name was Aequus, and he was scowling at the head of the sinners, his large fists clenched in anger. His brooch was in the shape of a panther, glinting oddly on the shoulder as though moving. His role was of the warrior, to protect their pantheon.

Lastly, the woman, Ardea, was their head. She had the tallest chair in their midst, and the most somber robe. Her brooch was in the shape of a hawk, though her hair half-hid it. The long, straight hair was raven-black, stunning in most instances. But her most striking feature was her eyes: one green as the emeralds, one black like coal.

She leveled that uneven stare onto the trio, her mouth setting in a thin line – the only show of her anger.

The judges' faces were meant to be impassive. They knew the penalties spoken tonight, under a full moon, could never be reversed. They had to be just, but incontestable, in order to avoid another revolution.

Yet Ardea could not help herself from letting her wrath out of control – just a bit. Her thin hands grasped the handles of the throne, and she had to bite down the screams she wanted to hurl at the man facing her.

Why would you betray us!? She wanted to unleash, but pushed it all down for the sake of their future…and his.

Ardea knew the three supposedly deserved the punishment. Vulper had shown them proof of Atrox's disobedience, his rallying of the smaller deities, how the three had planned to overtake the current trinity.

And for what? Ardea's scowl deepened. *All for more power.*

According to Aequus, they would have taken the lesser

gods' powers and absorbed them for their own. They would have invariably kicked the current authorities out. They were not the first, nor the last to attempt to do so, but they certainly were the first who had gotten so close.

The middle one, Atrox, had still not learnt his lesson. Ardea could tell from his conceited stance – one she knew well enough by now to decode.

Despite it all, The Cardinal Rule – laid before they had ever existed, by their forefathers and those before – forbade the three judges to kill other deities. It had taken a long time, but Ardea believed they had found a suitable consequence. One good enough to teach them humility – and a lesson they would not soon forget.

"Is this your idea of a court of justice?" Atrox spoke, his thunderous voice echoing across the empty surface. His words were followed by a sneer. "Even humans can do better."

"Silence!" The rumbling warning from Aequus only earned him a laugh. "You are not here to speak, lower –"

"Cut through the *shite*, brother," Atrox taunted, enjoying the sudden quaintness, as though no one dared to breathe. "Let's face it, you and my dear sister want me out. You have ever since you let Vulper into our little trio."

Atrox turned a flaming gaze to the red-haired man, before meeting Ardea's bi-colored eyes. "You know what I mean."

The tone was accusing, but she refused to rise to the bait. Lifting her chin in a gesture that truly showed their familiar liens, Ardea stated, "You were never pushed out."

Eons earlier, the three siblings had been thick as thieves. Though they had their internal squabbles, they had always been united. Vulper had joined their pantheon from afar, and it was after his arrival that Atrox changed.

Ruthless, the god did not like competition – which he had plenty with Vulper. Cunning like him, the newcomer had gotten into Ardea and Aequus' good graces, and slowly but surely made them see him differently.

"You let him poison you against me," Atrox rumbled low, even as the sparkle in his opaque eyes burned more intensely. Despite the assailing anger, he remained calm – deceptively so. "You thought I was too ambitious."

"And you were!" Aequus burst, standing up as though to step towards him. "This is all your fault, and you know it!"

Atrox rose to his feet, though not as quickly. He lifted one knee, then the other, and stretched himself into a standing position. Every movement was feline, full of power and grace, unhurried. Even captive, he outranked them all.

Ardea's hand on Aequus' quieted the god down and he sank back on the chair, pouting petulantly. He glared, as Atrox remained unmoving.

"Back on your knees," he ordered, pointing a finger at his brother. "Where you shall stay when faced with your superiors."

Atrox stared back, enjoying Aequus' ever more frustrated expression. Then, he smiled. "Yes, we are all quite aware you outrank us," he continued in the same insolently bored tone. "Can we get it over with or is our punishment to stay here being ogled at forever?"

Ardea met his arrogant gaze, the midnight black eye firing shots of poison, the emerald one almost steely with wrath. "Did you really believe there would be no consequences for your actions?"

"We all know this has nothing to do with dispensing justice," Atrox scoffed, unperturbed by the fury he could feel emanating in waves, "but rather with establishing power. And control over me."

"Enough!" Vulper spoke, waving a hand dismissively towards the group. "Atrox has a point: this has taken too long already. Let us bypass the internal squabbles, and put an end to it."

Atrox turned to the god, features twisting momentarily in contempt. "You *would* want this over with, and me gone, wouldn't you?" he growled.

When Vulper leaned forward eagerly, as though itching for a fight, Atrox looked away. *I will not give him the satisfaction of losing control.*

Ardea bit back a sigh of annoyance – after all, they had to show unity – then said, "Very well. Atrox, Deasa and Faitus, you have been charged with the sins of greed, ambition and malice. You conspired against our backs and had your plans succeeded, it would be you sitting in our places. Those of us who had not met your criteria for 'proper' divinities would have been banished – or worse."

"Pity," Atrox muttered under his breath, knowing full well his voice carried across.

He felt a tug on his hand and looked to Deasa, his blonde partner. He did feel bad – slightly – that she had to endure this, after all the joy she had brought him. If it had been a decision he could influence, she never would have paid the price.

I have been trying to end eons of corruption and indifference in the pantheon and this *is my reward?* His lips curled in disgust.

Meanwhile, Ardea kept talking. "For these crimes, you are all three banished to the underworld."

Cue the collective gasps, Atrox rolled his eyes.

There were none, since the six of them were the only ones present. Atrox guessed the rest of the pantheon was probably aware of the failed coup d'état. Cowards as they were, each was biding their time to see who would come out the winners – and the losers – before they showed which side they were on.

He was pulled from his thoughts by Faitus' undignified whimpers. "Please," the god begged the three judges, "not the underworld."

Atrox, for his part, stood up straighter. They would not hear a single pleading from him. True, for beings such as them, to be around demons and half-spirits might not be exactly a walk in the park.

For one, they would be limited, chained to the darkness below to do its bidding. For another, their powers would be less, making them prey for the numerous beasts that lived underneath.

In the end, it would beat being incarcerated like the Titans had been, before their time. Plus, the underworld did have one advantage…a particular plant whose properties would be of much use to him, once he could his hands on it.

Well, that and these blasted chains. They may not impact our powers, but they can sure as hell cut through a deity's body.

A movement to the side had Atrox shift to better keep an eye on Vulper. The fox-god met his icy gaze, then with a confident smirk turned to Deasa.

"Darling, you do not have to join them," his voice was

sweet as honey. "Just say the words, and I can save you."

Atrox could not stop the primal snarl erupting from his throat. Vulper had long since coveted his beautiful but naïve partner, and he would not let Deasa be taken advantage of.

Vulper glanced to him briefly, recognizing Atrox' agitation, then smiled broader. He stood up and approached the trio with slow, purposeful strides. Atrox's stare was glued to his every step – a predator ready to strike to defend what was his.

When Vulper was near Deasa, he put a hand under her chin and lifted it up. "Do not be foolish, you are yet so young for a goddess…"

Atrox snapped before he even knew what was happening. He moved his shackled hands, throwing them around Vulper's neck, at the same time dragging him away from Deasa. He had the god in the grip of the icy steel, reveling in the knowledge it could kill him.

"You actually thought these chains could restrain me?" Atrox hissed, no longer caring of the consequences.

Ardea and Aequus rose to their feet, mouths agape at the sheer violence displayed by their brother.

"You will leave Deasa alone," Atrox snarled in the man's ear, "otherwise your life will pay the price."

"You…cannot…kill…" Vulper was trying to re-state their Cardinal Rule, but Atrox pulled on the chains, cutting off his air supply.

"Try me. Give me an excuse," he taunted.

And for a brief moment, Atrox considered it. Snuffing out Vulper's life would end his problems and his siblings' – though they were unaware of the danger courting. Vulper was a viper in their midst, one waiting to strike when the time was right.

The Cardinal Rule clearly stated that he could not take a deity's life without giving one in return. And yet, the temptation was alluring, if only to have the slimy fox gone.

Atrox tightened his grip some more and had the satisfaction of seeing Vulper's eyes widen in fear. Then a soft cry to his left made him turn his head, to meet the pleading in Deasa's eyes.

"Let him go," she whispered softly.

Atrox hesitated, hands white-knuckled from the force he was applying. He warred with himself for a few moments, but Deasa's unflinching blue eyes were his undoing.

With a disgusted sigh, Atrox released Vulper. Stepping back, he watched smugly as Vulper fell to his knees, then crawled back to his throne.

Only then did the dark-haired god stride back to his original place, this time holding Deasa's hand in his. Faitus had remained unmoving from his prostrate position the entire time – once more, Atrox wondered why he had ever thought the man had strength.

Ignoring his siblings' raging cries, he turned to Deasa and met her gaze. "I will keep you safe."

Her blue eyes met his, and he saw a pure love shining within. Deasa had always been his opposite, gentle where he was hard, loving when he was ruthless. The only one he had ever given his heart to – and ever would for his existence.

It was why Atrox never forgave himself what happened next.

One moment, Deasa leaned her lips towards his, kissing

his anger away. Just as he prepared to deepen the kiss, her body jerked unnaturally. Atrox pulled away to see her eyes glazing over, death in their depths.

He looked down, not comprehending what had taken place, even with the evidence presented: a silver blade protruding from her robe.

Unwilling to live in the underworld, Deasa had stabbed herself with the one weapon that could kill her – a dagger Atrox had gifted her, for self-defense. A blade created out of the very crater their pantheon's entrance existed at.

Atrox grasped Deasa in his arms and removed the offending metal. Red blood, the color of dark rubies, flowed out of her body. With one hand, Atrox tried to staunch it, using his powers. But where they should have healed, they did nothing. He narrowed his eyes, then turned to Ardea and Aequus. "Help her! She is an innocent in all this!"

His siblings were speechless at first, in shock at what had taken place. Then Ardea spurred into action, attempting to move towards Atrox.

"No."

The word had come from Vulper, whose Orb of Sight was already glowing. It took Atrox only moments to understand that the god was absorbing their powers.

Being condemned felons, the trio's status as pure gods was reduced. As such, their abilities were up for grabs, and Vulper knew it. The Orb of Sight had already started collecting them for his own use, which was why Atrox was left unable to heal his partner.

He held Deasa's body tighter to him, before turning his head to the side towards Ardea.

"I have never asked you for anything," Atrox murmured hoarsely, "since my childhood years, but now I do. Not for me, but for another. I no longer have the strength to aid her, but you do. Help Deasa!"

Ardea moved closer, but Aequus' hand restrained her. She looked to her brother in shock, but met only stone in his expression. "No. Punishment was already doled out. It must be the fates' command Deasa dies in this way."

The raven-haired woman hesitated, then yanked her arm out of his grasp. She walked over and knelt next to Atrox. She reached over the wound, then Deasa's face.

Atrox was about to thank her when, under his astonished gaze, Ardea closed Deasa's eyes and stood up.

"What are you doing?" he whispered, almost not believing it until their glares clashed.

"Aequus and Vulper are right. The punishment is set."

Atrox clenched his jaw, then bent his head over Deasa to kiss her soft lips one last time. He only vaguely noticed their coldness, as numbness overtook him. Because of her act, Deasa would not be granted entrance to the paradise of the gods. She had simply ceased to exist... Despite the fact she been driven to the brink of desperation, the laws that governed the realm of the deities were crystal clear.

The wolf god's heart stuttered in pain, and a whimper of anguish threatened to escape him. It took all his willpower, but Atrox pushed it down. He inhaled Deasa's soft fragrance one more time, then let her body lie down gently on the marble floor. It rippled as water would and swallowed Deasa's body within, where it would become one with the earth once more.

Atrox then stood up to face the three, with Faitus still

kneeling next to him. His face was a mask of stone. Whatever emotion had once ruled him, whatever mercy he had once been capable of, was extinguished from him the moment Deasa took her last breath. Instead, all Atrox had left within was a black pit of anger – and a need for vengeance that demanded to be satisfied.

"I have but one question," he stated unflinchingly, staring at a spot above the three judges' heads, removed from their presence already.

"Speak," Ardea commanded.

"Will you let us have the powers that go with the underworld?"

It was not a fool's request he voiced, for his new home, though a lesser realm, was filled with darkness. At his command, it would be a tool to be reckoned with. And there was more... For within the most secluded mountains, beyond the most somber crevices, existed a flower filled with obscurity, whose nectar could kill any god.

And that, Atrox had decided, would be his reward for all he had endured. If he was to be given the abilities that belonged to the realm of the dead, then with them came immunity to the flower's nectar. He would be able to use it – and never once pay the price.

The god kept his expression blank, refusing to let them see his trepidation. The plan was his, and his alone. *Let them have my visions, my powers, and the control of the elements. The last laugh shall be mine....*

There was a pause as the three wardens consulted, then Ardea stated, "Yes. You will have demon lord status."

A brief flash of victory passed his gaze furtively, before

dying in its depths. *Fools! You have no idea the power you turn your nose at.* Dimly, he became aware of Vulper stepping slightly closer.

Vulper chose that moment to intervene, a slight smirk on his lips. "Your tasks should suit you: plenty of conspiracy and malice in the human world. You are to feed it to a certain extent; always ensuring the balance does not get tipped."

"Though you are shunned from this pantheon," Aequus continued, meeting his brother's gaze, "the Secondary Rule remains: do not engage with humans outside your duties. Do not speak directly to them or otherwise form relations, upon pain of losing what little you still have. Are we understood?"

Only Atrox's stone stare answered them – and Faitus' moans of fear.

"One more thing," Vulper added mockingly. He could not stand the humiliation he had suffered at the captive's hands, and how close he had come to dying.

The fox-god waited to see if Atrox would acknowledge him, but only a silence of stone answered him – despite the fact his muscles were so tense they seemed ready to snap. "Since you have so well demonstrated the beastly qualities we all hide within… You will only be able to enter Earth in your animal form, never your human one."

Ardea glanced to him in surprise, but the words had been spoken and the spell cast. Whatever she had meant to say was lost, and Aequus' indifference confirmed it was a concluded battle.

Save me your pity, sister. When it counted, you did nothing! Atrox raged internally, but did not show it in his countenance on the outside.

With a shared glance, the trinity joined hands to open the portal that would take the two sinners to the underworld. A void opened between the two parties, and grew larger still with every moment. It rippled with darkness and echoes of silent laments in its depths.

Atrox threw a look within, sensing the fire – and power – awaiting. Once the portal was fully formed, he turned to Vulper and his Orb, where his forces of the old now glinted – as did Faitus' and Deasa'.

Atrox spoke only once in a low tone, cold in its fury – a promise veiled. "You will pay for this. Mark my words."

Not deigning a single wasted breath to his siblings, he then stepped willingly into the portal, whereas Faitus had to be thrown in.

A thunderous roar erupted as they disappeared within, and the portal closed with a bang. In its place was the marble floor once more, as though it had never been disturbed.

CHAPTER 2

Many years and centuries later – a town, in the Welsh countryside.

A tiny house, broken down and barely standing, was his home. Born to non-magical parents, he had been a source of discord between them as of his birth. He belonged nowhere – not at school, not at church, not in the community, small as it was.

His name was Emrys, and he was a prodigy with no support.

* * *

The sixteen-year-old young man entered his usual meadow, eyes checking around to ensure he was alone – and not followed. These were basic security measures he had learned to take, as his kind was not kindly accepted.

A bitter frown tugged at the corners of his mouth. Year after year, Emrys grew, as did his powers. And inside him, something became harder to control.

It was a barely restrained fury, as he wanted to shout to the world who he was, and what he could do, not hide away like some shunned secret.

Somewhere, sometime, I will belong...

Sighing, Emrys took a spot on the grass by one of the trees.

His hair was long and shaggy, of a muddy brown. His frame was tall and lanky, but muscles could be seen under the beige tunic and trousers he wore. Holes and a worn color were clear indication these were old garments, probably since he was a child.

In truth, his parents had not deemed it wise to attract attention to their boy any more than he already did. They mainly pretended he did not exist – except for the rare times his father *did* notice him, and those were best kept to a minimum.

As though his thoughts brought back the sudden pain, Emrys absent-mindedly touched the bruise on his shoulder, where his father, Niell, had last shown his *affection.*

The young man's wry smile turned into a scowl. *One of these days, he will not beat nor abuse me any longer...*

With that in mind, he lifted a palm in greeting to the earth beneath him and to the entire meadow that served as his only source of solace. With his other free hand, Emrys reached behind and touched the tree's trunk, the roughness of the bark, to ground himself.

He could have sworn, within moments of him doing that, the branches tilted just so, blocking the sun's rays and bathing Emrys in a welcome shade. The summer was pulling to its end, but the heat was just as horrible to withstand.

With a grimace, the young man removed the palm and instead focused on his breathing. He emptied his mind of everything that would otherwise cause disturbances – parents, schoolmates, stares, unfounded hatred – and breathed in the fresh air, the grass scent.

Exhaling, Emrys let go of all distractions and existing pains, inhaling rather the scents that empowered him.

Moments later, he was ready. He opened his cerulean blue eyes, shining of an unnatural glint, and lifted his hand. The magic within him, which he always felt as a fire, flared to life, and a small circle of light emerged from the earth.

Emrys grinned.

* * *

Atrox stirred in the depths of the underworld. He slowly extricated himself from the silky bed – all in black, of course – and headed out his room.

The underworld was nothing like he had pictured. It was better – much, *much* better. The last centuries alone, with his demon lord status, he had built a mansion. The realm itself was not literally underneath the Earth, as the current Church tried to teach all sinners – Atrox had to snort at mortals' naiveté.

Rather, it was a universe on its own, a realm accessible to deities and demons only. A portal opened every time Atrox wanted to return to Earth, and the same process repeated as he wanted to return home.

Lost in thoughts, Atrox walked bare feet through the palace, his skin not even registering the coldness of the marble floor. His mind was focused on the young man he had dreamt of, and the magic he wielded.

The negative forces of the underworld that led everything that happened there were already hard at work, tugging at him in the shadows. They were only whispers, shadows of what could or would be, but they were powerful…

He needs to be turned…

Accursed one…

He sees too much…

Manipulate him, make him see this is where he belongs…

"Enough!" Atrox growled, stopping in his tracks.

The shadows froze, then retreated under his glare. He may have been only a demon lord when compared to the chaos reigning on this land, but his word was still law.

"I will take care of this Emrys," Atrox stated for the benefit of the darkness lying in wait, always awaiting weakness and treachery.

Atrox might be lord, but he still had to answer to the wraiths – always at work, always spurring him on. Without them, he did not have full use of the abilities he could otherwise. Indeed, teamwork was the name of the game.

Gritting his teeth, Atrox headed on a new mission.

* * *

The sun was setting, hours later, and Emrys was still in the meadow. He now had not one, but over fifty of the small light balls floating around, like fireflies. His mind was at peace, as was his body, unaware of the approaching storm.

He was so busy playing with the magic, he did not hear the voice until it was close by.

"Emrys!"

Startled, the young man lost hold of the energy and it dropped to the ground. The patches of grass the balls fell on immediately caught fire. With a muttered curse, Emrys took off his tunic and put the flames out before they spread.

When he turned around, his mother had her hand to her mouth, frozen in shock. Her eyes were wide, staring at the burnt patches of grass.

Emrys sighed, then pulled his tunic back on, watching out of the corner of his eye as she slowly breathed in – as though to steady herself. Feora had been beautiful, once. Her long, wavy brown hair was now dull, white locks sparsely emerging through it. She was thin, and the brown eyes that used to smile with laughter were somber and unseeing.

His father had transformed her so, blaming Feora for putting on earth a devil's spawn, as he affectionately called his son. Both son and mother had been victims for far too long.

Straightening himself as best he could, Emrys faced his mother again, sadly noticing that she was keeping a wary distance between them.

"Niell is looking for you." Feora murmured, barely audible. For some reason, she never called her husband 'your father' in Emrys' presence. Still, the young man was used to her soft-spoken tones, especially lately, and his attuned ears caught the urgency in her voice.

"You have to come!"

Emrys thought back to his last *talk* with his father and winced, massaging his bruised shoulder again. Feora's eyes followed the movement, and the look in them told the young man she was recalling the same incident.

She turned her head to the side, unwilling acknowledge the truth, and whispered, "Please come back home, before Niell gets upset again."

Emrys stepped closer to her, slowly, as though she was a frightened doe – and in some ways, she was. "Mother, why do you stay with him?" he asked gently, noticing even now how he towered over her.

Feora glanced up at him briefly, before pursing her lips in an attempt to appear mad. "Stop saying such things. It will do neither of us any good to think we have a way to escape, you hear me?" She turned to leave, muttering under breath, "As if we had anywhere else to go!"

Emrys hesitated for a brief moment, taken aback by her outburst. It was not the first – nor would it be the last – time she had gotten upset at him for suggesting a way out. Feora was a non-confrontational person, and his father had beat into submission any remnant of strength she had.

It saddened the young man to no end, and was the main reason why he stayed. If he was not there to protect his mother, who would?

Sighing, his eyes took in the meadow one more time, then followed in Feora's footsteps. Outside the quietness of the forest, it was night now, but their decrepit house was near enough that he arrived shortly after his mother.

As Emrys stepped through the door, he only had a second of warning before a fist struck him in the face. The force behind the blow, as well as the angle, threw him off his feet, onto the ground.

"You been out doing the devil's work again, boy?"

Emrys looked up from the ground, blue eyes burning in hate. Niell stood over him, a burly bulk of a man – three times his size. He could smell the alcohol coming off the man in waves, if the red nose and glazed eyes had not yet alerted him to the drunken state.

"No," Emrys retorted in answer to the question, before spitting out blood. "I finished all the chores and the field work, and went for a walk."

"As if I'd believe such lies!" Niell growled, then kicked his son in the gut.

Emrys curled up in a ball, coughing to catch his breath, before pushing back to his knees. He inhaled deeply, trying to gather that same peace that had filled him only hours before.

The young wizard knew it was best to stay quiet and avoid Niell's glare, but the desire to rebel was stronger than him. Emrys glanced behind the man to see Feora in a corner, cowering in fear. No help would come from her.

A movement above him got Emrys to focus on the man in time to register the wooden stick in his hand. Thicker than a staff, almost as wide as a board, it seemed heavy enough to inflict damage.

"If I can't get you to listen to me, maybe this will teach you to leave magic alone."

The words alone confirmed what Emrys already feared. He bowed his head to protect his face and tensed his back, even as Niell brought it down with all his strength. The wood hit to the left of the spine, and Emrys lost his breath once more, flattening back to the ground.

He gritted his teeth, refusing to give the satisfaction of showing pain. Instead, he gathered what force was in his young body and pushed himself back up, this time settling an infuriated gaze to Niell.

The man had stepped back to take another gulp of beer. He noticed Emrys staring and his face turned a nasty shade of crimson.

"How dare you look at me!?"

Niell slapped the mug down on the table and lifted the wooden board again. The stick came down hard, and Emrys held back another groan of pain, but did not bow down his head.

Another blow followed. And another.

It seemed his unsettling blue eyes only angered Niell even more, as the blows became stronger every time.

Emrys refused to break the stare. In doing so, he caught sight of Feora's downturned eyes, even as she busied herself with cleaning a dish, well-versed in the art of denial.

It was that instance, more than the beating he was taking, or the soring of his back muscles, that hit the boy the hardest. The realization that Feora's weakness would never change, and Niell would always hate him. And this would be the rest of his life, unless Emrys did something to stop it.

Now.

When Niell raised his hand to strike again, Emrys moved.

He pulled back from under the burly man and out of his reach. On wobbly feet, adrenaline pumping through him and holding the pain at bay, Emrys stood to face his abusive bully of a father.

Niell was gaping in shock, unable to comprehend how his son could oppose him. Feora had stilled, eyes wide open, silently begging Emrys not to make any trouble.

"Sorry, mum," the young man whispered.

He lifted a hand up and drew a circle in the air. The round shape grew until it enveloped Emrys in a slight silver glow of protection.

Niell stepped away in fear, sputtering, "Evil!"

Emrys turned disdainful eyes to the man he used to call father.

"You are done striking me. I will not apologize for this gift I have."

"Get out of my house, boy! You're the devil's son! You are not mine!"

Emrys' eyes flashed of lightning, and Niell was thrown into a wall as a burst of air hit him full force. His unconscious body fell to the ground. "You are quite right, I cannot be yours."

He turned to Feora, watching her closely. His eyes, once gentle, now demanded explanations. "I have asked you before, and I know you lied to me. This is the last chance you will have to tell me the truth. Whose son am I?"

Feora gulped, meeting his determined gaze, before whispering, "One night, on a full moon, your father was working late. I thought it was him... A man came, he had his appearance, but he was different."

"How different?"

"He was softer, well spoken. Looked at me as though..." Tears streamed down her cheeks. "As though I was worthy, and loved, and beautiful."

Emrys raised a hand to caress her cheek, "And you are."

Feora shook her head, "No, I am not. You wanted the truth, so let me tell it. He shared my bed that night, and was gone by morning. When your father returned in the morning, drunk, I realized the trickery...but it was too late."

"Did you ever see him again? The man who fathered me."

"Once." She took a deep breath, eyes shining with regret

and shame. "I wanted to kill myself, after realizing I carried his baby. I went by the cliffs, but he appeared."

"What was he like?" Emrys questioned, unable to keep the pleading out of his voice.

Feora smiled in a way he had never seen. For that moment, Emrys could almost envision the beauty that had once been. Then he shook the pity out of his thoughts, and focused on her words.

"He was beautiful. Long, silver hair, the face of an angel, and eyes... Eyes the color of the bluest sky." She looked at him. "Like you... He begged me not to take my life, or yours. He admitted that he had been lusting after me, but had not considered the consequences, thinking only of the immediate pleasure."

Feora shook her head derisively, unhappy with herself. "He also admitted being Fae, and warned me you would be a strong child, with magical potential. He begged and pleaded with me for hours, going so far as to name you. In the end, I... I could not finish what I started, and so decided to keep you."

Emrys was silent for a moment, absorbing everything, before asking, "What happened with my father?"

"I do not know, my son. It was the last I saw of him."

Emrys turned to the man who had raised him, sparing him one last look. Then he moved to his mother, extending his hand. "This is my last offer: you can leave with me, or have your life with him."

The fear in her eyes was unmistakable, as was the desire to agree and shed their horrible past, putting it all behind. In the end, Feora turned her head to the side in silent refusal.

Emrys gave a tight nod, half expecting her answer already.

He stepped to the corner by the fire, where he had slept for the last few years – on the floor like a dog. In the wall, he had carved a little hole that hid his meager possessions: some herbs, plants he had gathered, stones, and stale food.

He packed it all quickly in a small string bag, then stood.

"I have one last question," he said to Feora. "What was my real father called?"

"Merlyddus."

Emrys nodded, as though expecting an exotic name. "And the name he had wished for me?"

Feora bit her lip, and for a moment he thought she would not divulge it. In the end, she whispered, "Merlin."

The young man inhaled deeply, before declaring, "Then I shall forgo the cursed name of Emrys, thus going forward. I will be known by what my father wanted… Merlin. If ever you have need of me, seek me by that name."

He took one last look around him, then stepped out the door and left his old life behind – forever.

* * *

Atrox, in his animal form, watched the young man as he walked off into the forest, where hours before he had been playing with his magic. Yes, the demon lord had watched in consternation as the mage possessed more power than he had seen in a century.

It was only during the fight with the father, that the answer came to him: Emrys was part Fae, a fact confirmed with the mother's words.

Interesting indeed… Atrox knew it would not be as easy to influence a Fae. They were too pure, and manipulative as well, to allow themselves to be strayed away from their own path.

Faes had come to be at the same time as demons and gods. They were Elementals who could wield the powers of air, water, fire and earth to their liking. Formidable beings with great abilities, some had become warriors and even fought deities they saw as obsolete – or too greedy.

In the end, as humans took over the land, Faes went into hiding. Some created their own realms to live in, parallel to the Earth. They were governed by no laws, but their very being implied their actions had to be at all times one with nature. It was the price to pay for the power they could wield.

Thus, Faes could not eradicate the mortals that used the land, for fear of upsetting the balance. It had been the same rule that had stayed their fatal hand when they had fought the Great Wars with the gods.

One thing about these blasted Faes is at least they can live for centuries. This means I have all the time in the world to corrupt the Halfling.

Atrox followed the wizard, newly baptized Merlin, as he walked through the forest. The demon's animal form, a wolf dark as night, blended well in the shadows. Day upon day, he trailed the Halfling, until Merlin reached a little village.

It was there Atrox left him in a cottage, where he seemingly intended to remain unseen.

* * *

Years later, Merlin had traveled through most villages in Wales, and some in other places. He had self-taught himself the art of magic, offensive as well as defensive spells. He ran into shamans, magicians, and mages. Most of them were fakes, but some, every once in a while, surprised him.

From those few, Merlin absorbed all the knowledge he

could, before moving along. He never stayed in the same place longer than a few months, for fear his skills would attract unwanted attention. Furthermore, he was always seeking what he would never find: someone who knew about Faes.

In between villages, in his twenty-second year of life, Merlin found a cavern, dug deep into a mountain. It immediately appealed to him for its privacy and location, and after ensuring it was not inhabited by some type of animal, he put a protective charm on it and made it his own.

Maybe here, I could stick around for longer than a year.

He would have stayed there, were it not for the king that happened to cross his path one cloudy morning...

* * *

Merlin awoke to the sound of hooves – and men. Wary after his last few encounters, which almost always ended in a brawl, he stepped to the entrance of the cave and observed the outside. The charm he had set upon the entrance would keep anyone from noticing him, but still allowed a perfect view of the landscape.

A consortium of knights and soldiers seemed to follow one man. He was old, in his seventies, with a long beard. The golden crown on his head, visible even in the dark fog of the morning, was enough to inform anyone of his royal lineage.

A king, on my own doorstep? Merlin chuckled. *Now this, I have to see.*

Muttering a spell to hide his form, the wizard then pulled on a cape to protect against the chill of the air, and walked outside. As he neared the men, he gathered bits and pieces of conversations, enough to realize what they were seeking: a place to build a fortress, one the king could have be his greatest legacy.

Merlin walked unseen through the soldiers until he was near the royal's horse. He noticed the man was looking at the rather large hill sitting between them and the next village, and could almost see the wheels turning in his head.

There was only one problem.

"It will not work," Merlin announced, dropping the charm and appearing out of thin air next to the king.

He rolled his eyes at the yells, threats, and swords immediately shoved in his face – even as he immensely enjoyed the monarch's shocked expression.

"The fort you plan to construct cannot be built there," Merlin stated firmly.

The king looked to the hill, then back to the odd-looking young man. Though his features were hidden by a cape, two of the bluest eyes he had ever seen glinted from within. There was something almost feral about the newcomer, causing the man to gulp in slight fear.

"Why not?" he finally asked.

Merlin smirked, registering the fact the soldiers were edgy enough to impale him. With a flick of his wrist, he could have them on their backs, but he much preferred to control the situation with words – for now.

"Get your soldiers to remove their swords, and I may choose to answer."

The king waved his hand and the soldiers dropped their weapons, though the horses uneasily neighed.

"Now, will you tell me?" the elderly man questioned after a few moments of silence.

"This hill is ancient beyond belief, sire. No fortress can be erected on it, because of the turmoil living underneath it. At its deepest heart, two dragons hide: one white, one red."

Gasps were heard all around, and Merlin nodded patiently. "Yes, one a symbol of the Romano-Celtics, another of the Saxon powers. They have been cursed and caught underneath since before this country existed."

"How can we fix this?" the monarch questioned.

"There is but one way: they have to battle each other."

The soldiers burst into laughter, but the royal did not seem to find it amusing. Eyes narrowed in thought, he assessed Merlin once more.

"And your name?"

"Merlin," the wizard bowed, barely an incline of the head. At the same time, with an easiness that amazed even him, he plucked the man's name from his own mind. "King Vortigen," he warned, "feel free to dig, and prove me wrong. But beware of what you may find."

With that, Merlin recast the charm and disappeared under their stunned gazes. He walked over to his cave to enjoy an early breakfast, whilst the king bellowed orders to start the excavation.

* * *

The roars woke Merlin up.

He exited his cave in a hurry, worriedly taking in the blood-red night sky. It did not take a genius to grasp something had shifted in the world, and needed to be set right.

"Those fools!" the mage growled, already sensing the soldiers' and horses' uneasiness.

Grabbing a cape, Merlin made his way over to the encampment where advisors were briefing Vortigen. Their restlessness was well apparent, and he struggled against the urge to roll his eyes.

"Perhaps I can help."

When Vortigen turned to him, Merlin noticed the slightly wary look in his eyes – but also his relief.

"You were correct," the leader admitted. "Two dragons have been found… And it seems we have awakened them from a deep slumber."

"I could have told you as much," Merlin scoffed. "I can put them back to sleep… Or I can let them out, so that you may build your fortress."

The king seemed to consider both options, then slowly nodded. "Let them out," Vortigen ordered.

He followed Merlin as he stepped close to the hill and lifted both palms to face it. The mage could feel within it the large barrier that had been put there, and wondered if it might be something past his skills.

Determined, he closed his eyes and latched onto the shield mentally. It took close to an hour, but finally a great thunder was heard as it fell away.

Moments later, two blurs shot out of the hill: one white, one red.

The humans gathered nearby watched in fear as the two dragons fought in the sky. Only Merlin realized the danger they were in, and extended a shield of protection over the entire encampment.

Then, he focused on the battling beasts. Their large wings spread as they faced off, glinting in the moonlight. Bursts of fire escaped their inhuman jaws, shining like beacons in the night sky.

For a moment, they stood frozen in time. Then with roars loud enough to wake the dead and shake the earth itself, they launched at each other. They became blurs, grappling at inhuman speed, until the humans could only gape in amazement.

Only Merlin, with his Fae vision, could still distinguish them. He watched in reverence as their jaws drew blood, as the fire scorched their wings. He kept observing as slowly, the red one defeated the white. When the white surrendered with a roar, he started to fall from the sky.

The red watched him, supreme ruler of the sky, then plunged in flight after him. He caught the white dragon in his claws and both disappeared into the night, as though they had never existed.

Merlin blinked, pulled out of his daze, and turned to the king. "You can build your fortress now."

"What of you?" Vortigen asked as Merlin turned to walk away. "You should be compensated."

"I have already received my payment," Merlin muttered, disappearing once more.

None of them could understand how rare a sight they had seen – or how lucky they were to have witnessed it and not die.

Merlin, having protected them all, was ready to sleep.

* * *

Atrox scowled, watching the mage sleep from his spot in the underworld. *A few years, I let him stew, and he becomes more of a pain in my ass...*

The energy of the underworld was unhappy, and that made *him* unhappy. It was time Atrox went back to Earth, before Merlin touched further things that needed to be left to rest.

Groaning, the former deity stood and stretched. Yes, it was time to call darkness to him, and do what he should have done years ago – turn the wizard to his use.

CHAPTER 3

It was a dark night, all fog, clouds and eerie vibes – a storm was underway. Thunder rumbled across the heavens as though the gods themselves were fighting.

Merlin reached the new village just as the skies opened and rivers of rain poured down. He hastened his step, heading to the nearest pub he could find all whilst cursing the impulse to help that king.

After Vortigen, many had come seeking his counsel and a certain rumor had started to spread of his wisdom. The blue-eyed mage, they called him. The influx of people had become too much, enough so that Merlin had reluctantly left his cave and gotten back on the road.

It had been three years since. He was now getting close to being three decades on Earth – though in reality, only twenty-five – and still had not found any further information on his real father.

Reaching the pub, the wizard pushed the door open and welcomed the stifling heat, smells of freshly baked goods, ale, and sweat.

Ignoring the stares he got – the cape easily hid his features, but probably did not inspire confidence – Merlin headed to the bar.

"What can I get ye?" a voluptuous woman headed to ask him.

Merlin raised his gaze towards her, watching as she blinked in shock – they all did, when they got closer. Through the years, his face had gotten stronger and being outside gave him a sun-kissed appearance.

His unnatural-blue eyes shone that much brighter, and more than one woman had fallen for what they called his rugged good looks. None knew it was the Fae in him that attracted them, as the males of the species had done for eons before.

"A mug of ale and one of your pies," he responded shortly and placed a few coins to cover the cost.

As the barwoman headed to get his order, Merlin stared unseeingly at the plates and mirrors across from him. He found his reflection easily – it was the one everyone was turned towards, though he barely recognized his own features.

Underneath the hood, the youthful appearance was gone, now replaced by steely brawn. His frame was still tall and lanky, but muscle had built underneath from the work he had done in fields on his journeys, as well as the constant walking. His face had lost all softness, now only angles and hard jaw. The blue eyes shone like sapphires – easily his best feature.

Merlin had noticed that with each use of his powers, the

clarity of his eyes intensified to levels never seen before in a human. Further, his hair had changed from the muddy brown color to black with purple reflections. He kept it shortly cropped to his head, if only to avoid more ogling from strangers.

Merlin sighed, stopping his observation and instead surreptitiously glanced around. For days now, the feeling he was being followed was nagging, but he could not recognize a single presence out of bounds.

"Here you go," the lady came back with the food and a shy smile.

Merlin muttered a thank you, pushed the coins towards her and proceeded to wolf down the food and ale.

* * *

The sun's rays hit him in the face, eliciting a groan. Merlin blinked – almost angrily – before sitting up with a sigh.

He looked behind at the naked form of the barwoman with whom he had spent the night. Her offer had come as a surprise, but the wizard was not one to deny himself a warm body, in an even cozier bed, for the night.

Though no emotions were involved, Merlin felt strangely at odds with himself, as though he was lacking something. He got off the bed, put on his tunic and trousers, and stepped out the door without further dallying.

He was barely out of the pub when he noticed three youngsters heading his way in determined strides. One of them, the leader, had the same blonde hair as the barwoman.

"That's my sister you just left," he spit out, confirming Merlin's suspicions. "You think you can just up and leave after a night?"

"Correct me if I'm mistaken," Merlin smirked, "but she was *very* willing."

The boy clenched his fists and was about to attack when one of the friends grabbed his arm. "Wait, Michael. Look at his eyes!"

The one called Michael peered closer and saw lightning dancing in the deep blue depths. It seemed to only infuriate him further. "You put a spell on her!"

Merlin laughed humorlessly as the boy moved to attack, and his entourage followed suit.

* * *

Atrox watched from a distance as Merlin evaded their punches and repelled their poor attempts with only defensive strikes. *He is barely trying, and still winning!*

The demon lord could admire skill such as the mage's. It seemed it was not only his magic he had fine-tuned over the years, but also his body.

Time to push his limits…

In his wolf form, the demon lord inhaled deeply, then exhaled a black cloud of smoke. He watched as the mist, filled with bad intentions, neared Merlin and was absorbed by him.

It was only moments later that Merlin's punches became harder, aiming to injure. Atrox continued observing until blood was drawn. Only then did he feel satisfied enough and turned to leave.

A sudden silence, as though nature itself paused to watch, brought Atrox to a stop. Growling low, he circled for a second look.

Merlin had the brother of the woman by the throat, hanging in the air. His free hand was clenched in a fist, ready to strike. And yet, the blasted wizard was hesitating.

Atrox tried to breach his mental defenses, but found only a solid wall. He growled low, annoyed at the sudden turn of events – but it was too late.

Merlin let go of the boy as though he had been scorched. He scoured the surroundings, but not even his all-seeing eyes saw anything. Despite it, the feeling of being watched persisted.

Shaking his head, the mage picked up his bag and took off on a run, before the attackers were any wiser.

Next time, then, Atrox vowed, his midnight eyes glued to Merlin's disappearing form.

* * *

Merlin spent a few months away from the public eye, sleeping under the starry skies and eating whatever he could hunt or find in the forests. After his last encounter and the sudden fury that had filled him, he was afraid of hurting people.

One night, as he lay half-asleep, he sensed something in the woods. Merlin stood from his spot on the ground, ears perked for any sounds. "Who goes there?"

Nothing answered except the howling of the wind. Unable to shake off the sensation, the mage cast a protective circle to protect his body and mind. He did not register the two red eyes, glowing in the darkness as they assessed him quietly.

Months passed by and soon it was winter. It made it harder for him to find food or spend time outside, despite the magic that kept him more than comfortable. Having not felt the uncontrollable wrath for ages, and with the memory fading away, Merlin felt it was safe to go into the next village.

Unbeknownst to him, Atrox skulked in the shadows, lying in wait for that exact moment.

* * *

Merlin towered over the old man who was now on his knees.

The burly man had insulted him and gone so far as to attack his patronage, calling him evil, a spawn of the devil. It was all so reminiscent of Niell, that Merlin lost his poise.

He had left the pub before doing anything rash, but waited almost eagerly. When the large man exited, Merlin followed him into a dark alley and his fist struck before he knew what was coming.

The man was now wiping blood off his chin, looking up in fear.

The mage raised his palm, a glow forming in it. *Teaching him a lesson, just this once, would not be a bad idea.*

Hidden in the forest, only a few feet away from them, Atrox's large wolf form snarled low. *Yes... Kill him!*

In some deep corner of his deity soul, Atrox wanted to see the magician succeed. Something about his force, the character underneath the tough exterior, commanded respect. And yet, his new nature as a demon lord was binding. He was as much a slave to the dark forces of the underworld as they to him.

Kill the human.

The magic in Merlin's hand grew brighter, then he froze and looked around. Blue eyes met dark over the distance and widened in disbelief. Stricken, Merlin dropped his hand and the energy within it.

"Stay here," he growled to the man, who whimpered in fear, cowering in a corner.

Then, he stepped closer to the forest's edge, angry for a different reason. "So, it is you who has been following me around."

The wolf pranced out of the forest, his large body more apparent in the dim moonlight. Merlin stared at him, refusing to take a step back, despite the fact that with his head reaching his shoulder, it was by far the largest wolf he had ever seen.

The animal refused to speak, but Merlin could tell by the fire in his eyes that it was angry.

"Well. Will you tell me why?" Merlin pressed.

Atrox squinted at the human, then the full force of his mental power hit the mage.

Kill him.

Merlin gritted his jaw, fists clenching at the authority in the voice even as he fought against it. It was like a wave, trying to push him past the forbidden limit, and he felt the sway.

Why did I not see this coming? Merlin wondered dimly. He had been assailed by odd visions, but none had warned of this being's surveillance.

It was then, in the dimness of the moon, that it hit him. "You're a demon!" Merlin forced out, even as his fists tightened in an effort to oppose the onslaught of the mind attack. "That is why you follow me. *That* is why I could not see you coming."

Very well, Halfling. You see past the illusions of my kind, not that it will be of much help to you. Now, kill the human.

"No!" Merlin growled. "I will not take a life."

Atrox paused in his efforts, opaque eyes widening in disbelief. He had expected some resistance, but a flat-out rejection was unheard of. Arching his back as though to pounce, he commanded, *Kill him!*

The mental defenses, which had held strongly until then, crumbled, and Merlin's body was no longer his own. He watched as an outsider, not in control of his muscles or movements. His body turned around, walking back to the man kneeling in the dirt.

A dark fury passed over his face, and the wizard was unable to disassociate the man's features from Niell's. The two faces overlapped until they became one.

Remember how he beat you... Humiliated you... Hurt you... Now is your chance to strike back!

In a corner of his mind, Merlin knew this man was not Niell. But it was useless to fight the overwhelming mental prowess of the demon. His hand grasped the old man by the collar of his shirt, and his fist struck. Once. Twice.

The body went limp, and Merlin let him fall to the ground. The man was still breathing, but barely.

The mage's palm lifted, a glow forming within once more.

"Please don't do this," Merlin pleaded in a whisper to the demon.

The wolf, relentless, kept at it, until the magic increased in brilliance, the spell ready to hit the man and put him out of his misery.

KILL HIM!

Atrox's last roar would have done the trick, were it not for Merlin's other powers.

Unbidden, he was assailed by a vision. His eyes grew blank and his body was as though paralyzed. Atrox, deeply linked with Merlin's mind to control it, was dragged into the trance, as well.

They were walking, side by side, to a scintillating blue lake. Within its depths, a hand rose, holding a glinting sword. It absorbed the sun's rays, before shooting them in reflection.

A melodic voice spoke: "A young boy born by the mage's hand shall lead. Two guardians to protect and raise him. Do not fail the child, defend him. The world is at his mercy, at his need."

They were snapped back to reality brutally as the image faded away. Merlin was on the ground, panting. Atrox, further away, shook his head in confusion.

He stared at the mage until Merlin looked over his shoulder at him. The blue eyes, filled with lightning, met the midnight ones of the demon lord, filled with fire.

Until next time, Atrox warned.

Then, he released his hold and retreated, leaving the panting Merlin on the ground. The beat-up man, registering he would not be killed, rose to shaky feet and ran away.

Merlin remained unmoving until the first snowflakes fell all around him. As they melted on his face, the wizard pulled up the cape to cover his features and got to his feet. He took one step, then another, until he was running to put as much distance between him and the village as possible.

As he did so, Merlin went over the event in his mind, over and over. *Yes, until next time, demon.*

* * *

The day came to an end as Merlin reached the tavern. It was now spring again and he had enjoyed the last few months, free of any presence following him – or demons trying to get in his head.

And yet, now, the sense of unease beckoned him.

Listening to his instincts, the wizard bypassed the tavern and instead went around it, to the back. A large forest loomed in the dark. In its shadows, he could discern the wolf's shape, the midnight eyes glinting in the dark.

"You again," Merlin greeted, his tone devoid of emotion.

Atrox was stunned – his abilities alone should have kept him from the mage's sight, like they had done in the past. Eyes narrowed in suspicion, he walked into the light. *You can see me?*

"Should I not?" Merlin tilted his head in question.

Not when I use my powers.

Merlin hesitated, before pointing out, "Then perhaps you should stay out of my head. Whatever you did last time seems to have affected us both. I was not able to see you before, yet now I am."

A dead silence was the only answer.

"What is your name?"

What makes you think I would tell you?

Merlin shrugged, taking a seat on the ground itself. "You seem less inclined to turn me into a murderous sorcerer, for one."

Atrox tilted his head slightly, then stepped closer and sat on his hinds. *I am Atrox.*

"Ah… Fitting name. You know it means 'bloodthirsty' in Latin?" Merlin mentioned offhandedly, then grinned. "And you are a demon?"

A demon lord.

"Wonderful," the grin slipped off, as Merlin realized how much trouble he was in.

In his quest for knowledge of Faes, he had learned of the deities governing the different realms – and the demon lords that associated with the underworld. Atop the food pyramid, they represented everything that was nefarious in existence.

And yet, this particular one did not meet the idea he had of such creatures. Realizing this was his one chance to find out more, Merlin pressed forward with questions. "Why me?"

Because your powers are grand, and it would be a fitting use to darkness to have you work for them.

"You say 'them'," Merlin pointed out. "You do not count yourself amongst the dark, then?"

Atrox took a moment to think about it, then shrugged. He had not felt a need to speak to a human, let alone explain himself, for eons. Since his own exile, if he was to be honest. Yet something about Merlin inspired confidence, and he felt less…alone.

No, I do not, the wolf finally admitted.

Merlin knew it was a gamble, but he figured the worst that could happen would be his death. Using gentle magic, he probed around the demon lord and the aura surrounding him.

Atrox felt it and growled low in warning.

As he was not immediately mauled, Merlin continued for a few moments, before admitting, "You are no simple demon lord. I feel an old power within you. Almost…" *It cannot be!*

The wolf tilted his head, scanning the wizard facing him. The Fae blood had truly honed his skills, if he was able to sense the divinity that had been.

You should not be able to perceive that, Atrox rumbled again. *Then again, I suppose with your Fae abilities, it is only normal that you would.*

"What do you mean?"

Faes wield magic, but they do so always with a purpose. Their energy finds answers to things normal magic does not. Being as old as the most ancient of deities, that is why you are able to perceive these things.

Merlin took a moment to analyze the words, then his eyes widened. "Are you telling me you're a *god*?"

Atrox stood up, getting ready to leave. Before disappearing into the forest, he turned around, opened his mouth, and the large canines shone in the night. Merlin felt a flash of fear momentarily, then it registered that Atrox was grinning.

Was.

As oddly as he had appeared, the beast was gone, leaving the mage to his ruminations.

* * *

What is it about Merlin that created this link?

Atrox was pacing further in the forest, annoyed at having started the conversation and even more irritated for wanting to continue it.

Since their spirits had met, he had found it easier to locate Merlin.

A shimmering to the side made him stop pacing. His paws tightly gripped the earth in simmering anger – he had recognized the scent. Moments later, Aequus appeared in full deity form: all navy-blue toga, brooch and as human as one could look.

"You are breaking rules even now, brother."

Bite me.

Atrox turned to leave, but found the forest was blocked

off. He turned back to his brother, shaking his head in frustration. *What do you want? I am in no mood.*

"The Secondary Rule is clear. You are not to engage with humans. Yet here you are, talking with one."

Atrox was silent, knowing full well Aequus had come for more than that.

"You might have been right about Vulper," the god finally admitted, sheepishly rubbing the back of his neck. The accusing tone was gone, replaced by contrition.

Hmm, was Atrox's only comment.

"Will you not come to our aid, if I tell you he is trying to overthrow us?"

Atrox could not help it – he burst out laughing, his roars filling the forest around them. *You are truly something, brother,* he finally stated. *After eons of keeping me at bay, nothing less than a servant in the underworld, you expect me to lift a finger?*

He turned as if to leave, deceptively calm. Instead, he whirled around and with all his strength lunged at Aequus. They tumbled to the ground, rolling over, until Atrox's wolf form was atop him.

For a moment, he savored the feeling of supremacy, of triumph. Aequus had always been the weaker of the two, though he was bulkier. Always, Atrox had been able to beat him in hand to hand combat, a prowess he could evidently still replicate.

The wolf inhaled deeply, enjoying the upper hand, before snorting one word out.

Never.

Aequus stared for a beat, willing his brother to change his

mind. When Atrox only stared back, his claws digging into Aequus' shoulders menacingly, a resigned glint passed in the god's eyes. With a dejected sigh, he looked away and conceded defeat.

In that same moment, Atrox felt the barriers surrounding the forest drop, and knew he was free to leave. He departed without a backwards glance.

"You are making a mistake!" Aequus yelled out from behind.

And it will not be my last, Atrox muttered.

Before disappearing back to the underworld, he hunted down Merlin, who was getting ready to head back into the tavern.

Merlin, Atrox called out from the forest.

The mage turned around, scrutinizing the forest, before his eyes fell on the wolf.

I suppose the fates will it so, this link created between us. But what it is you are searching for, human? Another fight? Testing the limits of your endurance?

Merlin scowled at the mutt, his face darkening at the truthful words. After a few beats of silence, the demon snorted. *You will not deal with your father issues through constant brawls. Take it from someone who knows.*

"Why do you care?" the mage asked, sounding more like a sourly teenager than the wise wizard Atrox foresaw he could become.

Make no mistake, I do not. I am simply trying to avoid more of your clumsiness causing a mess for me to clean.

Shaking his head, Atrox disappeared for good.

CHAPTER 4

In his palace of the underworld, Atrox paced, his body tightly wound up in tension. A change was happening within him, and he did not especially enjoy it. Not after Aequus' fateful warning.

And yet, his encounters with the mage happened more and more, ever since they had both seen the vision of the young boy at the lake. He was able to sense Merlin's presence, and easily portal in and out of the underworld to his exact location.

As if that was not enough, Atrox no longer felt compelled to corrupt the wizard. He wanted to help him, despite the fact the words themselves tasted bitter on his own tongue.

A demon lord was supposed to wreak havoc, corrupt souls, and lead humans astray. Instead of doing those exact things, Atrox was narrowing his sight on this one Halfling, all because of his Fae parentage. To make it worse, he felt no incline whatsoever to do either of the things he was supposed to.

Exhaling heavily, Atrox had to admit that he *was* changing. And it had not truly started with Merlin, but with Deasa. Her innocence and kindness had spurred him to be a better god.

As a result, he wanted to take that same concept and apply it to the mysterious child that was to be born. With the sliver of his former deity powers, he could feel it had been an important vision Merlin had, the kind that changed the fates of worlds.

This meant, if he wanted to be part of it, Atrox had to keep a close eye on the mage. And unless he wanted the child to be a pawn of darkness, it also meant he had to keep Merlin out of trouble...

Or did he? Was what he wanted truly for the child to have a light destiny? Frowning at the turbulent thoughts, Atrox kept pacing.

You are turning away... from us...

"I am not!" Atrox scowled at the darkness. Lately, it was on his case like a nagging human housewife, and he had reached a limit.

"I have done your bidding, have I not?" he challenged, turning in a circle, glaring at the shadows. "I have tried to influence Merlin. He is incorruptible!"

No one is...

No one...

You lie...

Atrox turned away in disgust, ready to return to Earth. If he could not find peace in his own realm, then perhaps he could there.

* * *

Merlin stepped out of the modest hut and started walking towards his own cottage towards the edge of the woods. Daylight had waned, night only moments away, and the way was clear.

As he neared the small house, he slowed down. An unnatural shadow lengthened the long of it, one that was not always there.

It is only me.

Merlin relaxed at the voice, even as Atrox stepped closer to the light. He glanced around, ensuring no one would see them, then opened the door to the house. Keeping the inside dark – one never know who would be watching – he took a seat on a worn chair and turned to the large wolf.

"What brings you here?"

I should be asking you that. Why stop here of all places, on your travels?

"The family I just left had a sick child. I was able to heal her, and in return they offered me food."

Atrox threw him a quizzical look. *You already have food. You have everything.*

Merlin shrugged in response, taking a fresh loaf of bread out of a small satchel. "Perhaps."

What is it you seek, mage?

"It is not the first time you ask me, and you already should know the answer. Are you trying perhaps to find weakness to exploit?"

Atrox growled ferociously and the house itself shook. Merlin seemed unsurprised.

I did not travel between realms to hear your human accusations.

"Then why *have* you come?"

Atrox pondered the question for a moment, head tilted to the side. The answer, if he was to be honest, was that he had wanted to escape the underworld. But he could not admit it to the wizard – not in a million years! The reason came to him in a flash, and it was not a lie in itself.

To tell you about your father. Is that not what you keep searching for?

Merlin stood straighter, the loaf of bread forgotten. His blue eyes shone with curiosity – and pain. Atrox fought back a grin of satisfaction.

One way to keep Merlin behaving and stay on the right path was to teach him about his parentage. Without fully being aware of what he had been gifted with, he would never be able to tap into his Fae potential, and in turn would become easy prey for other forces.

"How did you…"

The legend of Merlyddus is not so lost that I cannot remember it myself.

"So you know who he was? You had an idea, from the beginning?"

Atrox did not deign to comment on the last part, instead declaring, *You have to know a few things of Faes, to better understand your own nature. All the powers you possess come from your heritage. The visions, controlling the elements, magic in its purest form… At some point, you may learn how to open portals, get better at reading auras even.*

He let it all sink in, before continuing. *Faes did not divulge these things to mortals. Thus, if ever someone comes to be an apprentice of yours, be careful you do not share what is not yours to do so. If they are Fae −*

"You mean more Fae exist?" Merlin interrupted, a light of hope shining in his eyes.

Until then, Atrox had not fully realized how lonely the wizard was. He thought to be the only one of his kind, and had no one to share things with. Ironically, the demon lord was discovering he felt much the same towards his own predicament.

Though he did not intend it, the wolf was quickly becoming a type of ruler of the underworld that had never been seen before. Whether that was a good or bad thing, would remain to be seen.

Yes, Atrox answered, snapping out of the morose thoughts. *Not pure, as your father was. But half, like you. Many Fae took humans as lovers. Thus, if a Fae comes to you, you can teach them. But be careful of humans; their fickle hearts will want to partake in certain aspects of the magic.*

"Such as?"

You are able to distinguish between good and evil magic. Not many can. Human mages are more attracted to the dark.

"Because it is more powerful."

Atrox snorted. *It is their belief, at least.* He stared at Merlin for a moment, before pressing, *Do you understand?*

"Yes. But what of my father?"

Your father was lord of the Faes in this part of the Earth. The realms of Fae were divided in provinces, each answering to the highest king. He ruled fair and wise, for as long as he could, before returning home.

"Home?"

Where you cannot follow. The Faes have a land − a realm

separate from this one – between worlds. Only pure Faes can gain entrance because it demands a blood sacrifice. You will never be able to join him. Furthermore, once a Fae is there, they can never return to another plane of existence.

"So I will never see him again?"

No.

Atrox let Merlin come to terms with the idea, waiting patiently. Moments later, the mage spoke. "Thank you, for all this. One last question... Why tell me? Aid me, at all?"

Because I need to keep an eye on you to make sure you do not blow this world apart with your blind stumbling about.

Atrox kept the thought to himself, though he yearned to voice it to the wizard. Instead, he expanded his mind far and wide, to corners of the world not even Merlin would be able to attain. Between realms, the demon lord traveled with only the power of thought, searching for the one thing he knew Merlin would need.

The brilliance of the object finally drew him like a magnet, and he caught onto it mentally. With a tug, he ripped it from the reality where it existed, and transported it back to Earth.

All Merlin had observed of the entire phenomena was Atrox's eyes becoming oddly glazed, as though a veil had been thrown over them. His immobility was shattered when the air between them blurred.

Atrox inhaled deeply, then blew some smoke. A mist formed in the air and moved about until it took the shape of a staff. It was made of silver oak and had a large, clear crystal atop it.

This was your father's, and I have managed to secure it

back to you.

Reverently, Merlin took the gift, caressing it. He muttered under his breath, casting a spell to hide the crystal and give the illusion of a normal staff until such time as he needed it.

"Why?" he asked again, meeting the demon lord's gaze.

The vision you had, of the young boy and the sword. It implied you and me work together, to mentor and raise him. This staff will center your magic when you need it to be more potent than normal. If you are to protect the boy, you will need it. And... I wish to help.

"You are a demon. Do you really think that falls in your duties?" Merlin mocked.

Dancing flames appeared in Atrox' eyes. *It will, if I choose it so.*

With the cryptic answer, he turned and stepped out the door, paws silent in the night.

* * *

Merlin decided to head out of the village, to the East. It was high time he searched for a place to establish himself. Even as he packed, the nostalgia of what he would never have – a family – gnawed at him. With a strong will, he pushed it away.

As he exited the house, Merlin did not look back, instead focusing on each step forward. Staff in hand, every mile hiked took him further away from the past, and into the future.

Hours later, deep in the forest, he heard horses nearby. Moments passed by, then human voices followed.

"Halt!"

Merlin stopped in his tracks, waiting as the riders and their horses surrounded him.

"Take off your hood."

Without touching it, Merlin used air to blow it off and lifted his chin defiantly. He was surrounded by five riders, but only one seemed brave enough to approach.

He dismounted off the horse, taking off his helmet. Brown hair, calculating hazel eyes, in a strong, handsome face. Broad shoulders pointed to the warrior side of the man.

"Are you Merlin?" the stranger asked, sizing him up.

"Depends who wishes to know."

"Watch your tone!" one of the riders admonished, but the newcomer lifted his palm, silencing him.

"We have followed your trace far and wide, Merlin," he said. "I am Uther Pendragon, and I wish you to be in my service."

* * *

I know what you are thinking, and you should not accept the king's offer.

"Again with the unsolicited advice," Merlin sighed.

He was outside, lying down on the grass under the starry skies. Though he was close to being asleep, it was hard to miss the slight trembling in the atmosphere when the portal was opened. Thus, the wizard had felt the demon lord approach from far away.

You listen to no one, Merlin. How will you guide the young boy we both saw when you have not dealt with your own demons?

The clenched jaw of the wizard was indication enough of his refusal. Groaning, he half stood and turned to face Atrox.

"Uther admits having followed me this far. It is a tempting offer."

To be his advisor and servant?

The disdain in Atrox's voice was more than apparent, and Merlin winced. "It will not be thus…"

You clearly do not know the kings in your region.

"And *you* do? You live more in the darkness of the underworld than here above!" Merlin scowled.

I may, yet I know the race of man. Uther is not who you think he is.

Merlin shook his head and walked off a few paces, before retracing them. "What is it you wish of me?"

To stay away from corruptible people. To remain as you are. To help me find that boy!

"You forget part of the prophecy, Atrox. It said the boy would be borne by *my* hand. What if this is how?"

There can be only chaos, following in Uther's path.

"Why do you hate him so?"

I have no time to hate, nor the energy. There is something about the man, whispers of the underworld. In the end, it is your choice, but –

"Exactly! *My* choice!" Merlin growled.

Atrox remained silent in the face of his fury, waiting for it to pass. Once the mage took a deep breath and exhaled, he knew it was gone.

"There is anger within me," Merlin admitted. "I cannot… I do not know how to extinguish it."

Perhaps you need not extinguish it, as you say, simply learn to use it as fuel.

When Merlin stared blankly, Atrox snorted ungraciously, then added, *You need a woman.*

The instant the words escaped him, a vision assailed the

mage with such force he fell to his knees. Atrox stepped closer, but in doing so retied their link and saw what Merlin did.

In the garden, a young woman walked. She had long, raven hair, eyes the color of dark clouds, a saddened look. She smiled suddenly, and it was more beautiful than all the suns of the world combined. A man entered the picture, and she ran to his arms, embracing him. When their passionate embrace ended, the man opened his eyes... blue like the sky, shining with love.

Merlin gasped and came out of the trance as though he had been drowning underneath. He was still catching his breath when Atrox got up in his face, his muzzle much too close for comfort.

Stay away from Uther's daughter!

Merlin's gaze widened as he read the indignation – and panic – within Atrox's. "What was that? A vision of my own future?"

You cannot dream of your own future, wizard. It is not a perk that comes with your abilities, no matter how much you may want to! Whatever it was, you need to stay away from her, Atrox pressed, more urgently than he meant to. *Swear to it!*

"I've never even met her," Merlin mumbled, astonished at the twinge in his heart. It was as though something had been missing from his life all along, and he was only now coming to realize it.

Which is why it should stay that way. The demon lord tried to push down the sense of dread spreading, to no avail. He knew what he had seen, and what Merlin missed – the look in her eyes, so similar to his own.

The mage remained pensive for a moment, then nodded.

"I shall not touch her, I swear."

Little did he know, at the time, how useless that promise would turn out to be.

* * *

Atrox watched as Merlin left with Uther, following him back to the castle. It would only be a matter of time before he encountered Morgana... And whatever would follow.

"My, my, what a tangled web they weave!"

Atrox turned around, savagely roaring at Vulper's smug expression. The god still had the scent of betrayal trailing behind, a fact that did not escape his notice.

"Your wolf form suits you," he cackled. "Much better than your deity one ever did."

What do you want? Atrox snarled, refusing to rise to the bait, but having to fight down the urge to throttle the god.

"Merlin and Morgana," Vulper sang, "what a beautiful couple they will make!"

Atrox stopped his snarls, tilting his head to the side. *You have seen with my powers, inside the Orb.*

Vulper's silence was admittance enough.

Will you tell me, or do I have to pry it out of you?

"Tsk, no need to be so beastly."

I will show you beastly!

Like a wave unleashed, Atrox lunged at the god, catching him unawares. They tumbled to the ground, and it shook with the force of their powers smashing together.

Vulper managed to throw Atrox off him, trying to retreat behind a shield of protection. Before he had a chance to, the wolf jumped again and with a sickening crunch, caught hold of his foot.

"You beast!"

What. Did. You. See!?

When the god only glared furiously, body rigid with agony, Atrox tried a different tactic. *The Cardinal Rule forbids killing a god. Nothing in it mentions anything about* mauling *one.*

Vulper clenched his jaw, but as the wolf clamped the force of the canines tighter on his leg, he gulped. His eyes widened, evidently realizing the truth of Atrox's words. In the end, he nodded abruptly in agreement.

Despite his show of good faith, Atrox did not let go, causing Vulper to laugh. "I see. I spill first, then I am freed. As you wish."

He waited for a minute, building up the suspense, then grinned, "Morgana is Fae."

The shock hit him like a wave of air and Atrox let go of Vulper, stepping back. *So I saw true...*

"Yes, even you recall the old legends of the Fae. You know how tumultuous their relationships can turn, if soured," Vulper laughed. "And Merlin is no romantic. Damaged goods, is he not?"

Atrox had to ignore the meaning behind the words. If two half-Faes, burdened by the past, got together in a romantic relationship... Well, the last time he had seen it happen, Troy had been burned to the ground.

You lie, he shook his head adamantly. *Morgana cannot be Fae!*

"And yet, you sensed in the vision there was something about her, something your precious Merlin should stay away from... Something that would turn her akin to a toxic drug for him, perhaps?" Vulper stood up as he spoke, dusting himself off.

You lie! If it was true, there had been no point in gifting Merlin the staff. The energy they would generate together would be enough to unbalance *all* the worlds...if it became unstable.

"Why would I? I came here specifically to see the havoc this would wreak." At Atrox's growl, Vulper rolled his eyes. "Fine, she is half-Fae, if that is any consolation."

It was not, he could tell by the wolf's pacing. Happy to have thrown a wrench in his plans, Vulper continued, "I did not drag myself in this forgotten realm only to discuss those two. There are other matters... I know Aequus was here not too long ago, trying to get your help."

I am not interested, Atrox glared.

"Join me instead, and you can regain your role by my side, not this demon lord status you were given... Think about it –"

I am not *interested,* Atrox repeated, smacking his paw on the ground, and it vibrated with the power at his command.

Vulper scowled, then muttered through pursed lips, "Very well. Enjoy the chaos with the Halflings, then!"

Atrox glared daggers towards Vulper, even as the god disappeared back to the realm that remained forever inaccessible to him.

He turned back to where Merlin's shape was disappearing in the distance, and exhaled heavily in frustration.

If Morgana is truly Fae, then all the more reason for him to stay away.

CHAPTER 5

Merlin woke up as the sun barely peaked over the horizon. He blinked sleepily, then stood up, glancing around the bedchamber.

Uther treated him like a worthy guest. He had been settled in a room three times the size of the cottage he had grown up in. Thick sheets covered the bed, beautiful baroque furniture everywhere. No expense was spared.

In a few hours, the servants would come to bring him a tray of food, as the mage usually ate his meals alone.

For three days now, since he had arrived, he had settled into a routine. Waking up in the morning, testing the boundaries of his magic in one of the lovely gardens, then meeting with the king to advise him on whatever was needed.

Uther kept hold of Britain, and the country was peaceful under his rule. Yet the occasional skirmish, or lord too greedy for his own good, arose. It was those matters that Merlin had been tasked to help him with.

Or so the story went to the outside world…

The truth was, Uther was getting old and, more than anything, he wanted an heir. Merlin had gathered that for whatever reason his daughter Morgana was not fit. He had yet to meet the maiden, considering Atrox's warnings were prominent in his mind.

The king's imminent desire was to get a male heir, and Merlin was tasked to find a solution.

Sighing, Merlin stood, pulled on a fresh pair of trousers and a shirt, wrapped a cape about his shoulders and was out the door.

His bare feet made no noise on the marble tiles, even as he passed through endless corridors unseen – a shadow in the early morning. Servants were barely waking up to tend to their masters' needs.

Merlin followed the path to the outside gardens, aimlessly crossing through rooms and antechambers – more so than he had ever seen in his entire lifetime.

Uther's castle was immense, surrounded by large stonewalls. On the northern and southern corners, two barbaric-looking towers stood against the sky, angrily defacing the otherwise peaceful landscape.

The building itself was surrounded by a moat, dug deep into the earth and filled with water that looked menacing at best with its dark pits. A drawbridge that appeared to have seen better days, but was still in working condition was lowered most days.

On the outside of the castle was a thick forest with trees that blocked the sunlight and let no one go in or out – or so the superstitions claimed.

The mage himself felt an old power within, one he was willing to test as of yet. As he walked down the stairs in the tower, Merlin glanced out to the forest, before continuing on his journey.

He passed through the last of the barriers, and out the servants' exit, finally entering the peace and quiet of the gardens. They were rectangular, about the size of his room, with flowers of every type sparsely across. An oak tree, older than the castle itself, stood in the middle.

It was towards it that Merlin headed, his hands tingling at the prospect of touching magic again. In these three days, he had not had as much time as he wanted, and it was akin to breathing: a need, potent and inquisitive.

He took a seat by the oak, hidden in the tree's shadow, and pressed both hands to the earth by his side. Imbued by the power of the nature surrounding him, Merlin breathed in deeply. On his second exhale, his hands began glowing, and a faint vibration animated them.

Soon, Merlin was lost in the magic, the back and forth between him and the earth. It felt as though his entire body was re-energizing, replenishing with an elixir far more potent than any human beverage.

He could feel himself reverting back to primal needs, carnal desires, to a part of himself that wished to be freed.

"You must be the new advisor."

The soft, melodic voice penetrated Merlin's haze, and he blinked. As he came to, her scent assaulted his senses: sweet, almost overtly so, like a nectar he craved to sample.

Merlin caught the woman's presence out of the corner of

his eyes, and turned his head slowly to the side.

Morgana.

She had not introduced herself, but every fiber of his being felt it. Her alabaster skin was almost translucent in the early morning. Long, straight black hair fell to her waist, cinched by a belt. Her soft blue gown did little to hide the curves of her body, something his eyes lingered on.

"I did not mean to interrupt," Morgana spoke again, and his eyes settled on her rosebud mouth, and the lips moving ever so softly.

Merlin gulped, then looked away. He could not, would not. A promise had been made, one he had to keep. Something within was emphasizing that he *really* needed to uphold it.

"You did not interrupt," he replied hoarsely. His throat felt as though it had been force-fed sand.

Extinguishing the magic, Merlin reluctantly let go of the earth and stood. He had no choice, now, but to turn towards Morgana.

The princess moved a few steps closer, as though pulled closer by the same force he was fighting against. *This is not good.* Merlin could sense the unseen atmosphere literally yanking him forward, like a magnet unwilling to let go.

Their eyes met – and held – cerulean blue to silver. Then Morgana's gaze roamed over the wizard in a way that did nothing to appease his unsettled body.

What is this!? Merlin fumed internally.

Such weakness had never struck him around a woman – especially not one as young as her. For though Morgana was very much of age at her two decades of life, there was an innocence still within her eyes that drew him in like a moth to a flame.

"I am Merlin," he cleared his throat, bowing in greeting. "The new advisor, you are correct. And I presume you are Lady Morgana?"

There was a brief hesitation, as though she wanted to try lying, then Morgana inclined her head in assent. "I am."

Their gazes locked again and Merlin cursed the fates for putting him on the path of this temptress. Her eyes were not so innocent now. Instead, a burning look shone within, one he very well recognized, for it was surely the same one reflected in his own.

Lust, pure and simple.

"I was surprised," Morgana spoke again, drawing his gaze to hers, "to hear my father sought you out. Apparently, tales of your exploits reached him from afar."

Merlin was silent, unsure of how to answer. Morgana peered at him for a few moments longer, before smiling briefly. "At ease, Merlin. I shall leave you to your secrets."

As she turned to leave, the mage could not help his eyes from roaming her form. He turned away, cursing against his own impulses.

* * *

Merlin watched from his seat in the corner as Uther dismissed the lords. The king was sitting on the throne, head in his hands, evidently more tired than anything.

It had been a week since the encounter with Morgana, and still he found himself constantly thinking of her. Every morning as he woke up, every night as he fell asleep, her face was at the back of his mind, out of reach – yet so tempting.

"Merlin," Uther called, and the mage walked over.

"Yes, sire?"

"How goes the search for a solution, for an heir?"

Merlin hesitated, mulling over an answer, before admitting, "Not, sire. It would help if I knew –" He stopped, unsure of how to continue.

"Knew what?" Uther asked.

"Of Morgana's mother."

One had nothing to do with the other, but Merlin was curious about the young woman's past, and everything about her. *This is bad,* he had the lucidity to realize, but still did not take back the words.

Uther narrowed his eyes, even as his entire body tensed. "She was a witch, let us leave it at that."

"Why do you say such things?"

Merlin turned at her voice. Engrossed in their talk, neither had noticed Morgana walk into the throne room. She was dressed in a dress the color of darkest emeralds, hair loose, eyes shining with anger.

"Why do you accuse my mother of such things!?" she stepped forward, hands clenched in fists.

Uther barely looked her way, even as he snorted, "It is the truth."

"*Liar!*"

As Morgana yelled, her palms developed a shine. Uther noticed and his eyes widened in panic. He looked to Merlin for help, but the wizard could only stare in shock.

That power! He could not understand how it was possible for the aura around Morgana to resemble his own. Uther had accused her mother of being a witch, but a sorceress would not have the kind of potent energy he felt.

Neither would an enchantress, for that matter. And if Morgana's parentage was related to neither, then that left only one other possibility…

"Get her out of my sight!"

Merlin was snapped out of his thoughts and turned a stricken face to the king. It was not the command that shocked him, he was used by now to his comments and tone towards Morgana. But there was something else in his voice now, a new type of indifference and anger born out of fear.

Merlin clenched his teeth, then moved towards Morgana. He grasped one of her hands in his and pulled on it to get her attention. She raised incensed eyes to Merlin's and he noticed, not for the first time, the unnatural glow of her grey eyes – much like his.

Whatever Morgana had been about to say froze on her lips, as the fire within her met his cool ice.

"Come with me," Merlin asked softly.

Morgana's entire body seemed paralyzed, but she did not fight him. Instead, she leaned towards him like a plant towards water, calming down. Merlin could read the confusion in those deep, silver orbs, as well as the hurt at her father's words.

"I said get her out of my sight!" Uther yelled, breaking the spell.

Morgana snapped out of the trance, and removed her hand from Merlin's grasp abruptly. "Do not touch me!" she hissed, then turned angrily to the king. "It was you who seduced my mother, not the other way around! Then once you'd bedded and had her, you could not stand that she was Fae!"

So my suspicions are correct, Merlin mused. He could now understand better the connection between them, but was still at a loss on how to deal with it.

Adding to the mix, Morgana turned her blazing fury to the wizard. "You best know the kind of king you serve, Merlin. He has no loyalty, no mercy. Not even for his own wife – let alone his daughter."

With the bitter words echoing behind, Morgana whirled around and left.

Left alone with Uther, Merlin noticed his pallor and ragged breathing. For a moment, he half-feared the monarch was about to give his last breath.

"I cannot have her take my place," the king whispered hoarsely. "Do you not see? She will destroy this kingdom!"

The mage did definitely not grasp what the king meant, so wrapped was his mind with Morgana. Despite it, he thought it wise to hold his tongue. He waited until Uther left for a horse ride, then went to hunt down Morgana.

* * *

"Morgana," Merlin called out softly, but it was as though he yelled.

She turned away from the forest's edge, a lost look in the eyes, unfocused. Then, she seemed to recognize him. "Coming to do my father's bidding?" she asked sarcastically.

Merlin was surprised at how much it hurt to have her ire directed at him. "I am not," he reassured the princess, taking a few steps closer.

She watched him, unmoving and suspicious. Her body was tight with tension but as the wizard neared, her shoulders slumped, all fight gone.

Merlin could see in Morgana the same loneliness that had plagued him for years – different, unique, their kind did not fit in with the rest of the mundane world. A need to wipe out her desolation, to return the smile in her eyes filled him.

"I am sorry," Merlin whispered, raising a hand to caress her cheek.

Morgana froze, then hesitantly lifted her face up to his. The grey eyes, smoking in their intensity, searched for something in his expression. "For what? You did nothing wrong, except follow orders."

"I do *not* follow orders," Merlin growled, annoyed that she was right. "I never have in the past. Nor will I start now."

Morgana was pensive in her observation, as though expecting him to turn away and leave her. It only took a tiny probe of the mind for Merlin to see she had not been dealt the tiniest affection since her mother had passed away.

Rather, she had been shunned, sequestered, sat aside. Uther did nothing to include Morgana in the castle's events – only when it suited him to charm the nobles. Then, he took advantage of her radiant beauty to distract them, getting them to agree to what he needed.

As he read this in her, Merlin's free hand closed in latent anger. "Why does your father…"

"Hate me so?" Morgana finished wryly, as though guessing he had been looking within her. When Merlin was about to deny it, she continued, "Do not bother trying to appease me. It is the truth. He hates me for being a half-breed, for being more than he is. He hated my mother because all men wanted her, and she was weak – she gave her love to him."

Merlin wanted to contest the words, and retort that love was not a weakness. And yet his own mother's trial with his father stopped the words on his tongue.

"What happened?" Merlin asked gently instead.

"She died," was the finite response.

At whatever memory assailed her, Morgana turned her head abruptly and broke the small contact they had between them. She then moved away from his touch, to become a solitary figure in the shadow of a desolate castle.

* * *

Deep in the forest, Atrox shook his head. *Stupid!*

He had monitored Merlin and Morgana's encounter in their entirety with a growing sense of dread. The demon lord had sensed Merlin's surge of protectiveness, and the irrational desire to defend the princess from any and all dangers – at the peril of his own life.

Little did the mage know, he was the one in need of shielding…

Unfortunately for him, Merlin believed it was only his Fae nature that lusted for Morgana. He did not realize it went much deeper than that, a spell as old as time that could never be broken. *Love is fickle, indeed.*

"You truly *do* care," a voice came from behind.

Already annoyed, Atrox refused to turn. He knew his sister's voice from memory, and did not need confirmation that Ardea had finally deigned to come down to Earth to lecture him.

"I thought it was only Vulper's machinations, but in this, he seems to have told the truth."

Ardea's tone had a certain surprise in it, as though she could not believe that him, Atrox, lord of the underworld and her sibling, could actually feel.

What are you here for? Atrox growled low. *I am in no*

mood.

"I had hoped…" Ardea stopped – a hesitation very unlike her. It did not take a genius to figure out she wanted something.

If you came here to enlist my help to fight Vulper, you have wasted your time. I am not interested. The other two have come already.

"I see…"

When only silence came after, Atrox gave in to pure curiosity and faced her. To his surprise, Ardea was still there, her bi-colored eyes pleading.

"Will you not reconsider? We *are* your family, after all, the only one you have…"

As if that ever served me.

Ardea pursed her lips, evidently not liking his snippy tone. "I understand why you do not wish to get involved, after how we treated you. But this is truly a matter me and Aequus cannot achieve on our own."

Treated me? Atrox growled, stepping closer inch by inch. His large body was tense, eyes glowing red fire, even as large canines protruded from his jaws. *Did you forget you let Deasa die in my arms, rather than save her?*

"I could not –"

Lies! Anger fueled Atrox, pushing him close to the breaking line. To think she had the nerve! *You could have saved Deasa, all it would have taken was standing up to those two! But you chose to let an innocent die, all to punish me further!*

Ardea watched, frozen in shock by his words, then her façade dropped. Her eyes shone brightly with tears she refused to shed, even as she murmured hoarsely, "I am deeply sorry, brother. Yes, I was angry at you, but I realize now, more than ever, the pain I caused you and that you still carry with you."

I do not need your sympathy.

Atrox snorted in disgust, but Ardea continued, "I understand that. But we need *yours*."

I do not care.

Ardea sighed, and for a moment – a brief instant – Atrox regretted the acerbic reply. But he would not feed the hand that stabbed him, familial duty be damned!

Anything else?

The wolf did not truly expect Ardea to stick around, but her words surprised him. "Yes, as a matter of fact. I came to warn you about the two Faes."

Atrox focused a warning glare on the goddess – his patience was running thin. *I have heard it all from Vulper. Whatever else there is cannot be new.*

"But it is. Merlin and Morgana *will* be drawn together," Ardea spoke rapidly, as though afraid he would interrupt again. "Theirs will be a love like not many know – consuming and everlasting."

Do I look like a romantic type to you, dear sister? These details are meaningless.

"I say this because of Deasa, whom I know you loved dearly –"

Do not dare *talk about Deasa!*

Ardea was taken aback by the feral note in her brother's words, as well as the force with which he projected his voice inside her head. She winced when Atrox continued, on a rant.

She died because of your *cowardice. She was an innocent, who could have been saved, were it not for three gods with no hearts.* He paused, midnight eyes flaming red.

For eons now, he had kept the anger under control, not willing to lose his life unless he was taking Vulper down with him. But as his sister stood there, contrite and pitying him, a raging frenzy rose within the demon lord. One that came very close to shattering the last of the control he had.

And you expect me to help either of you? Atrox continued, stepping towards Ardea once more. His thunderous laugh echoed in the forest, causing her to shiver. This was no longer the brother she had known, but indeed a creature of the underworld.

The chaos emanating from Atrox was affecting nature itself. The sky above darkened, the wind started beating wildly in the trees. Leaves fell to the ground, then lifted in the air to be twirled like puppets.

At first, Ardea thought it was related to his underworld status. After all, the punishment they had dealt to Atrox was bound to have some consequences. But then the real source of the discontent stemming from him registered: madness for losing Deasa.

I said it once, and I will say it again, Atrox snarled wildly. *You can all burn in the pits of hell, as far as I am concerned!*

Ardea stepped forward, as though to touch him, but Atrox was past reaching out.

Leave me BE!

The force of his spell, filled with the strength of the underworld, struck her head first, and the goddess flew back into a tree. When she wobbled to her feet, Ardea could not see the wolf anywhere. Tears streaming down her cheeks, she disappeared.

It was only once the shimmering was gone that Atrox stepped into the light from the shadows. The constant meetings with his brethren were a constant frustration, even as they vividly made him recall powers he had lost long ago.

Ardea's nerve, to have brought up Deasa, whom he had loved as much as he could love anyone… Atrox growled low, the fury unleashing within once more at the perceived manipulation.

The beautiful innocent had been the purest deity he had ever come across, and she had brought out the best in him. Losing her had truly taken away his emotions.

His thoughts turned back to the mage and Morgana. Despite everything, even Merlin's own stubbornness, Atrox hoped Ardea's words would never come to pass. He would never wish upon another to suffer the kind of deprivation he had, after Deasa's death.

CHAPTER 6

Morgana was brushing her hair and staring in the mirror, a certain magician in her thoughts.

Since arriving, Merlin had been a source of distraction – and confusion. During the times they had come together, he was either elusive or incredibly intense. When his blue eyes settled on her, Morgana was lost for words.

Never had she felt such a rush of emotions for a man, sheltered as she had been. It was hard to breathe even being around him, but when he showed her love, attention, respect, the princess could feel herself fall for him.

It more than just lust that pulled Morgana closer. Every time their eyes met, something deep within roared to be heard. Each time they were near, her palms itched to touch him. He was a magnetizing force and she, the willing captive.

The more Morgana tried to fight against it, the more demanding the need became. It was a yearning within her blood, to the point she lost all sanity when near Merlin. Lately, she had kept a distance, if only to catch a break. Still, the wizard was in her mind day and night, and she woke up panting, longing to be with him.

The young woman's rational mind had no place in the feral, primal longing growing within. In fact, it was pushed completely to the side, only there when Uther came in the picture. And even so, it was to point out all the other ways Merlin was an equal, a friend, a protector almost.

When Uther dismissed her, Merlin had been there, a steady presence to hold on to. When the king ignored her, he was attentive to her needs. When she was lost and lonely, he responded with compassion and kindness.

This is dangerous, the royal mused, observing her flushed reflection.

Morgana had seen it with her mother, Elysia. She had grown up in a lonely household with Uther mostly away, waging some war or another to gain control of the lands. Her mother had loved Uther blindly – and it had destroyed her.

The king had conquered Elysia easily, as he always did what he put his mind to. She was a means to an end – a magical creature that should have been able to give him the male heir he was entitled to.

Instead, what he got after marriage and nine months was a daughter. A *magical* one, to boot. From the moment of Morgana's birth, Uther had done nothing but ignore the young woman, much preferring his hunting parties and any activity that excluded her from his sight.

The king had not even come to his wife's bed afterwards, instead finding others to assuage his manly needs. He had easily betrayed Elysia, the vows of marriage broken without a second thought.

Morgana was convinced her mother, after years of neglect, indifference, and hurtful words, had died of a broken heart, in shame of not giving Uther a son. Her words, that last night before her fateful passing, still resonated within her.

Do not let a man own you as I made the mistake to let Uther, my daughter. Play them, always, and never let your heart be theirs.

Despite the warning, Morgana firmly believed Merlin was no Uther. He was just, loyal, fierce – the kind of man she could allow past her walls.

I can trust him.

* * *

A month had passed since Merlin first stepped in Uther's employ. In that time, he had become increasingly tortured by dreams of Morgana, and the more he wanted to stay away, the more they nagged at him.

To top it off, they grew in intimacy and detail every night. From visions of kissing her soft lips, Merlin had now gone to the point of having heated fantasies of her body naked against his. Every morning, he woke up with Morgana's moans echoing in his mind.

One such day, unable to push the images out of his head, he felt the need to go for a swim.

Near the castle rested a river, deep in the nook of the forest. It suited the mage, for not many regular humans neared it and he found it cleared his mind. Lately, he had needed all the help he could with that particular issue.

After shedding the shirt and trousers, Merlin kept on his

undergarments and jumped in the water. The coolness of it cut his breath – after all, it was early fall. But he swam back to the surface and with long, powerful strokes, moved against the current.

The river itself was a few feet in width, something normally Merlin could cross in a few minutes. Beating his body up in this manner had become a new regimen, if only to give it something else to focus on besides Morgana.

As he swam, Merlin let all thoughts drift freely. It was evident, even to his clouded mind, that the fact they were both half-Fae contributed to the attraction.

Morgana was the only half-Fae in the kingdom, as far as Merlin knew. In reaction to her nearby presence, his primal urge to procreate – much more alive now that he had met an equal – was elevating out of control. Nonetheless, there was something more underneath it, an underlying sensation as though they were fated together.

The wizard refused to entertain the notion, not willing to accept that his destiny was out of his control. Since he had left his parents' house, Merlin had sworn that never again would he under someone's thumb – and especially never like his mother had been.

And yet there he was, unable to sleep, incapable to function without craving to be with Morgana. She was a slow burn, a flame he longed to get closer to. The searing would be a price he was willing to pay for just a touch of her lips.

With a disgusted shake of the head, Merlin sank under the water. He let its coolness attempt to clear his head, before resurfacing. What still eluded him was why he could not fight the allure, despite his better judgment.

It is not a simple lust problem, mage. Have you not realized it yet?

The familiar voice in his head made Merlin stop moving. The river lashed, unruly waves assaulted him, and he went under. Within moments he re-emerged, sputtering clear liquid.

"Some warning would have been nice!" he yelled above the noise.

Merlin had not seen Atrox since arriving at Uther's palace. At first, he thought the demon lord was upset for ignoring his advice. Then, as he got more and more drawn to Morgana, he realized it was more likely that he did not want front seats to the havoc that would soon be unleashed.

Lifting his head slightly above the water, Merlin could now see the large wolf on the opposite shore. He was deceptively immobile, an odd glint in his eyes.

I have given you plenty of warnings. Perhaps a more lethal one is needed.

Merlin had no time to prepare as the river rose against him, fighting him off like a wild horse. The current inflated, the water became harsher, and then he was being tossed like a helpless twig from side to side.

"Stop this!" Merlin commanded, but had to stop speaking as he gulped more water. His overwhelmed lungs ached in protest and his limbs quickly grew numb from trying to oppose nature itself.

Under he went, this time losing sight of the light of day. The liquid rushed around Merlin like venomous vines, unwilling to allow an escape. The mage did not have his staff, and his thoughts were too muddled to grasp onto the magic that could save him.

The thought alone stilled him. Ignoring the combative water, Merlin closed his eyes. He fought against the burning lungs and the body that wanted to shut down. Instead, he lifted his palms to feel the water.

I am your friend, he whispered to it, trying to grasp control.

It was a lost cause, something Merlin soon became aware of. If anything, the river became even more abusive. There was no winning the battle, at least not by wrestling it into submission.

Before running out of air, the mage attempted once more.

His palms clenched and this time, he focused on one thought only, letting it fill his entire being: *Let me escape. I am no enemy of nature.*

Merlin's body shone brightly for a split of a second, and the river released its hold. He was let – almost spit– out of the river and onto the opposite shore.

Coughing and spluttering, Merlin looked around, but the demon was nowhere to be seen. It was only once he was able to breathe properly that he stepped from the shadows.

Do not bother trying to harm me, Atrox glared. *You needed some help to regain your focus.*

"Were you *trying* to kill me!?" Merlin sputtered, turning to face him, still on his knees – and panting. "Because if you were not, I cannot fathom the need to drown me!"

Really?

Merlin paused in the rant, trying to read between the lines.

You truly see no reason I had for forcibly trying to clear your head? Nothing that has kept it occupied lately?

Merlin gritted his teeth, seeing where Atrox's train of

thought was headed, the sarcasm more than apparent in the wolf's tone.

"That is none of your business."

It is my business! Atrox snarled. *Two half-Faes, falling in love, in a kingdom at peace. You have no idea how perilous this liaison can be.*

"Why?" Merlin muttered. "Why would it be so dangerous? Can we not be only two people, falling in love?"

You do not have the luxury of such a choice, not when both your powers combined can erupt a volcano, let alone unleash all the elements!

Merlin's eyes widened. Yes, he had known Faes powers were grand, as they tapped into the elements, being Elementals themselves. But to control nature as such, to make it do his bidding...

"And what if we could use that force for good?" he murmured.

Fae magic is unstable, wizard, or have you not realized it? Do you not remember the fury that used to plague you?

"That was your doing!" Merlin accused, eyes flashing.

I only augmented it, but it was already there. Whether you want to accept it not, Fae energy is and always will be rebellious. What you try to dominate will turn against you, or do its own bidding in the end. It is foolishness to believe you two can be together with no consequence.

"I cannot accept that...We could do something together, even remove Uther from power and –"

The wolf moved swiftly, soon within an inch of the mage's face. *Listen to yourself! Morgana clouds your mind like a toxic poison, and you have not even been involved yet!*

Merlin knew it was useless to deny it. After all, the demon lord could read him as well as an open book. The anger disappeared out of its midnight eyes, instead replaced with pity.

Morgana will be your doom.

"What has she done, to deserve this judgment from you? From Uther?"

Nothing yet...

When Merlin raised his head again, the wolf was gone.

* * *

A week later, Merlin was returning from yet another swim when he heard stifled sobs at the edge of the forest. His heart clenched in pain, enough to realize the owner of those tears was none other than Morgana.

With Atrox's warning forcibly present in his mind, the mage regretfully moved away. It was not his place to comfort the princess – she was not his.

A yelp of pain made him turn around, running in the direction of the crying without thinking twice about it. "Morgana!"

He arrived by her side only moments later. The young woman was on the ground, clutching her ankle. With one look, Merlin concluded it was broken and resolved to help out.

"Leave it," he murmured, stepping closer.

With deft hands, Merlin reached out and picked her up in his arms. He turned to head back to the castle, but her pained voice stopped him.

"No, do not bring me back, please," Morgana pleaded.

Merlin glanced down at the silvery eyes filled with tears, the trembling lips. He gritted his teeth against the urge he had to kiss her, and instead willed himself to look away.

"Why? What happened?" he asked, directing his feet to take them instead to a meadow close by.

"My father truly hates me," Morgana whispered, leaning her head against his shoulder.

Merlin could smell the soft floral fragrance coming off her, and every fiber of his being begged to be allowed nearer – closer than he already was.

This is not good.

Even his subconscious realized it would be unwise to give in to impulsive instincts.

Settling Morgana on a rock, Merlin knelt at her feet. Pointing to the swollen foot, he asked, "May I?"

She hesitated, though there was an almost eager glint in her eyes. "I can do it myself," Morgana whispered. "I am, after all, a magical creature."

The disdainful tone as she said the words made Merlin cringe.

"Let me, please," he entreated.

When Morgana inclined her head in assent, Merlin reached for her ankle, allowing one hand to settle on it gently. The responding vibration made them both gasp, their gazes locking in stunned awe.

There was a palpable connection between them, one harder to ignore in the privacy of their surroundings. When Morgana leaned forward, getting closer, Merlin focused his attention back to the healing, purposefully.

"I will have it mended shortly," he whispered, even as he allowed a lingering touch.

* * *

Morgana watched as Merlin bent over the broken ankle. There was no doubt in her mind the mage desired her, but why was he keeping at bay?

Though it was true she had run away from the castle, and her sorrow was not faked, the Halfling had purposefully stepped askew to wound herself. Morgana had felt Merlin nearby – it was his energy that had attracted her towards the forest in the first place.

After she had angrily run away from Uther, her feet had carried Morgana to the one place solace awaited – in Merlin's company. She had watched as the wizard passed by, and saw the hesitation in his step when he turned away.

Morgana's next movements had been a blur, as though it was not truly her that hurt herself, ensuring the ankle was broken, then crying out for help. Merlin's words snapped her back to the present and his soft touch.

"Why do you speak of yourself in such a way?"

His question took her unawares, leaving Morgana at a loss for words. Her eyes unwillingly took in his earnest expression, the dark-violet hue of his cropped hair, the jaw she wanted to run her fingers across...

Believing she had not understood him, Merlin peered at her and rephrased, "Why do you believe being magical is to be ridiculed?"

Morgana turned away to hide her own anguish – and hope. Could she have truly met someone who not only understood her, but also strove to ease her pain?

Do not hope... If you hope and fail, it will destroy you...

Elysia's voice at the back of her mind was a warning, the conscience she refused to listen to more often than not these days.

The young woman breathed deeply, revealing, "You could not possibly grasp the meaning. You use your magical abilities to heal, to be good and wise. I was never taught to do so. From the moment I took my first breath, I was something shunned, put aside…dismissed."

When Merlin frowned, she cut off the rush of words.

"Do not stop, please," he pleaded, grasping one hand in his. "I understand that part, more than you may know. My father hated what I was and what I could do."

Morgana wanted to believe it. She desperately wanted to believe this man in front of her was not like others.

"Uther is the worst," she confided. "I cannot understand how he sees what you do as good, but what I do as evil. We both wield magic, do we not? How much different are we?" She trailed off, looking away pensively.

The words were true, but what Morgana was not divulging was the utter hate she had for the man that had fathered her. She waited only for the day he would die. Elysia had warned her long ago that she could not use magic to affect the balance of nature, and it was the only reason Uther was still alive.

For months after Elysia's death, Morgana had dreamt of killing her father in a thousand different ways. When he had fallen sick from the ill will she sent his way, the young princess had no choice but to cease and orient her thoughts otherwise.

A tug on her hand had Morgana glance down.

"I understand your contempt," Merlin murmured. "But you should not listen to him. What you are, what you can do, is beautiful, wondrous…magical."

His reverent tone stirred something deep inside, a part that had been buried as of when she was a child. Something that had been starved of affection and Morgana wanted – craved – more of it.

Noticing the ankle was healed, she stood. *I cannot give in. This can end in disaster.*

Merlin followed suit, towering slightly over her. Her gaze again hooked onto his blue eyes, noticing their unlikely hue, something she had not seen in humans before.

"I…"

Morgana paused, lost in that unwavering stare, and lost her train of thought.

Merlin raised a hand to her cheek, unable to deny himself another touch. "Why did you run away from the castle?"

Remembering what she had overheard, Morgana had to push down the fury trying to unleash itself. It was a lost cause, and she could see the mage took note of it – she was a poor master of hiding emotions from his perceptive eyes.

"My father plans to write me out of his will," she hissed. "He would rather this country be split among the nobles, or governed by a trinity, than allow *me* to lead it!"

Merlin was silent, but could not help gritting his teeth. *So that is what all the secret meetings were about…* He had not had time to join, believing they were political games and nothing more.

"He cannot do that," he whispered. Even as the words were spoken, Merlin knew it was wrong. He should not be siding with the daughter, not when it was Uther that had come to him.

Morgana stepped away, as though hearing his thoughts,

and Merlin had to drop his hand. "This realm, once my father is gone, is all I have left of her – my mother. You would not be able to understand what it means, to have roots in a place, to have it mean so much…"

She trailed off again, her gaze lost in the distance. What Merlin divulged next hit her like a storm.

"I may understand better than you think."

Morgana lifted an eyebrow questioningly, unsettled by the cryptic declaration. Merlin seemed to struggle with something, his expression more hesitant than she had yet seen it. In the end, he grasped her hand to flip it over, and passed a palm over it.

A ball of fire appeared between their skins, burning brightly. Under Merlin's mastery, it took the shape of a small dragon, then of Morgana's own image.

Mouth agape, the princess could only stare in disbelief. Merlin's following confession had the effect of a train wreck upon her.

"I am half-Fae, like you."

* * *

Atrox was returning to the underworld when the shadows came in front of him, blocking the way.

"What is this?" he enquired aloud.

You have shunned us….

Disobeyed us….

Forgotten us…

"This is not humorous!" Atrox growled, clenching his fists. "I have done nothing of the sort!"

You consult with the mage…

You help a human….

You do not corrupt him…

"He is too pure! I have already explained that!"

No one… is… incorruptible!

The shadows hissed at him like vipers preparing to attack.

"You cannot keep me away from the underworld! It is *my* domain!"

Atrox's bellow was loud enough to boom across the entire realm. Savagely, he struck the cavernous wall to the side and a rumble went through the floor.

"I am lord of this place," he stated firmly. His dark eyes shone with flames, his muscles rigid, barely dominating the rage attempting to escape. "You *will* allow me entrance."

The wraiths slithered, resisting him. Gritting his teeth, the demon lord slashed the air with his palms, producing a sword of fire. He pointed the tip towards the entities in silent menace.

After tense moments that left Atrox panting, his nostrils flaring wildly, they moved aside and allowed passage.

Yet even so, as Atrox made his way back to the chambers, their echo followed him, and the walls whispered continuously.

Traitor…

Traitor…

Traitor…

CHAPTER 7

Merlin watched in silence, seething as Uther pushed suitor upon suitor on Morgana. It had been a week since he had revealed their shared parentage and she had run away, denying it all.

Now, looking at her weaving a particular brand of magic, at the suitors eating out of her palm... They surrounded Morgana in a circle, coveting her, oblivious to the fact she played them like a master puppeteer. Merlin could not understand why the princess was unaware of how special she was.

She is *aware,* the voice of conscience whispered.

Merlin glanced to the corner and the dark shadows giving onto the garden. He could almost discern the midnight eyes watching him – and the princess – from within.

He clenched his jaw and started to move outside, but was interrupted halfway.

"Are you leaving us?" Uther intervened, pushing a goblet of ale towards the mage.

"Yes, my liege," Merlin inclined his head slightly, declining the drink with as much a semblance of respect as possible. "Unless you need me…"

"No," Uther denied, eyes locked onto Morgana. "Not unless you can make her bed one of them and give me a male grandson in next months, before my imminent death."

The wizard froze at the offending remark. If Uther was a regular man, he would have pummeled him into the ground without a second thought, maybe even used magic upon him. Such an act, seeing as he was king, would only get him captured. Still, the possibility was enticing, buzzing in his mind like an annoying fly.

Merlin bit back the curses on his tongue, instead managing to utter, "No, sire. I am afraid not. With your permission…"

He left the king's presence before temptation won and he gave in to baser impulses to throttle the man. Tonight, whether he wanted to or not, he would guard Morgana. He would not put it past Uther, drunk as he was, to cross limits that should not be crossed.

At the exit door, Merlin threw one last look over his shoulder, ensuring Morgana was still within the public eye. Satisfied, he turned away and crossed in long strides to the garden, where he was soon covered in darkness as well.

"Where are you?" he called out to the surroundings, knowing the demon was in the vicinity.

When will you stop lying to yourself? The monstrous wolf half-stepped out of the shadows. *It is about time you realize Morgana is no innocent.*

"How would you know?" Merlin hissed. "Would you be able to recognize innocence, if it stared you in the face?"

Atrox watched him in silence for a few moments, before giving a disgusted shake of head. *You are truly something, mage.*

"You do not understand," Merlin insisted, stepping closer. There was a frenzy in his voice Atrox had not heard before. "Morgana barely knows how to use her powers. She is as strong as me, but has been given no magical training! This puts her in danger."

Atrox glanced past him into the ballroom, then back to Merlin with a meaningful look. *She seems to be doing just fine enchanting every male in there.*

"Because her father is using her! She is making use of her female charms, nothing else. I have been in there for hours watching, thinking she might use magic, but *nothing*!"

What is it you are getting at?

"I want to train her."

No.

"I am not asking for your approval," Merlin scowled. "I was merely informing you."

I doubt that. You remember as well as I do my warning about whom you will be training. You knew I would have something to say against it.

"Fine then. What are your objections?" Merlin taunted, folding his arms defensively.

Morgana is unstable. I know to your eyes she seems fine, but there is hurt and pain within her that goes deeper than you can heal. That is my objection: she will use what she learns to her own benefit.

"And would that be so bad, if it can help her against Uther?"

Will you abandon her, once she is fully trained? Atrox countered.

"What?" To say Merlin was stricken was an understatement. The demon lord could sense that the idea had never even crossed his mind.

You say she needs to learn about her magic in order to protect herself. Once she does, will you leave her?

"I..." The wizard glanced behind, then back to the wolf, undecided.

Atrox gave him a pitying stare. *You are playing with forces you do not understand, Merlin, same as with those two dragons.*

"If all you have to contribute it riddle-filled advice, then please abstain," Merlin retorted. The desire was too grand and, unable to sit still, he looked towards the inner ballroom again.

Atrox could easily read his emotions. *Even now, you want to go to Morgana.*

Merlin's head snapped back to him, fire lighting within the blue glare. "Stop it!"

"Merlin?"

The alluring voice froze the mage, his thoughts churning as he tried to find the right course of action to follow. Impulsively, his body did not listen and instead turned around.

Morgana stood barely a few feet away, clad in a pale blue gown that wrapped her body and showed off its lovely curves. Her jet-black hair was adorned by a crown of white flowers, enhancing the beauty of her face – and the innocence that shone through.

No wonder they run to her like moths to a flame.

Merlin did his best to ignore Atrox's words, sensing the demon had once more withdrawn into the shadows.

"Morgana," he bowed, then looked over her shoulder. "You should not be out alone. Your father...."

"I am aware," she admitted, her mouth twisted in a bitter smile. "He expects me to be married and bedded by the end of the night. Or, at the very least, bedded."

When the wizard was silent, Morgana added softly, "Not even you will defend his actions?"

"Defend?" Merlin half-growled, eyes lighting up in response. "I dare say not!"

Morgana blinked in shock at the words, barely daring to believe it. "Are you saying you disapprove?"

Merlin's almost bared teeth were enough of a confirmation, even as he muttered, "Yes."

The clipped answer was not lost on the princess. The mage was angry, and it was directed at Uther. Yes, the more Morgana focused on his features, it was as though she was attuned to Merlin's aura, becoming immersed in him...

"Why did you run?"

His question took her by surprise and Morgana had to blink again, trying to understand. "Run?" she frowned.

"When I told you I was half-Fae. Were you scared...repulsed?"

Atrox groaned, watching the entire scene and helpless to step in – unless he wanted to be discovered by the witch.

"No," Morgana was replying, stepping closer to Merlin and raising a hand to his cheek. The fool only leaned in closer, to feel her touch. "Never repulsed. I was afraid, yes. Of my own emotions, of what I feel towards you." She peered at him as though searching for the meaning of life itself. "I cannot understand this attraction, this need to be near you, to get lost in you."

Merlin opened his mouth to speak, but Morgana only stepped closer, barely an inch away. Her soft lips opened close by, begging, pleading...

Stop it! The growl tore in his head harshly enough that Merlin pulled away brusquely.

Morgana watched in shock as the wizard shook his head, almost as if to rid it of something unpleasant. She could have sworn catching a glimpse of darkness around him, as though something had intruded upon him. The feeling had been brief, but powerful, and she wanted more – so much more of it.

She stepped closer, but Merlin retreated. "We cannot do this, Morgana. Let me help you. I can get you out of here, away from Uther. But please do not ask me to be what I cannot be."

Morgana tilted her head to the side, considering his words. The mage was a fool if he truly believed he would not succumb. All men eventually did, when it came to her charms... And he would not be the last.

Soon, Merlin, she promised, even as her lips turned into a hopeful smile. "Yes. I will think on it."

With a slight curtsey, Morgana returned into the ballroom and was soon lost amongst the crowd.

Atrox stepped out of the shadows once more, trying to get through to Merlin. *You need to stop this. Get away from her while you still can.*

Merlin turned a haunted look towards him. "She needs

me. I cannot leave here until Morgana is happy and safe."

With a disgusted shake of the head, the demon disappeared. He did not catch a whiff of the other darkness, his brethren, lying in wait. It was there for an entirely different purpose, to seek the one out of the two Faes that would listen to its whispers of corruption.

In trying to protect Merlin, Atrox had only egged it on further.

* * *

Merlin looked around, trying to see past the mist, but could not detect anything. His eyes were as good as blind in the surroundings.

What is this? A dream, but of what?

The mists swirled around him into a tornado, throwing dust and debris towards him. Merlin protecting his face with a raised hand, but to no avail.

Recalling the elements were at his control, the wizard lifted a palm in the direction of the agitation and imposed his will on it. "Stop this. Show me what you will, or else let me be."

The fog hesitated, then increased in speed until it stilled and became limpid as a mirror. Only then did Merlin see the shapes within.

A beautiful brown-haired queen, giving birth. A boy with hazel eyes. Merlin, presenting the child to Uther. The boy growing by the king's side, becoming a ruler... And leading the country to war.

"No..." Merlin whispered, stricken at the image. "This cannot be. The boy cannot be a warrior, he is meant to be a ruler of peace!"

A pause, then the reflection became blurry once more. Round and round it turned, showing the passage of time, then the future was shown – a different one.

The beautiful brown-haired queen gave birth. The boy had hazel eyes. Merlin took him, and on a horse brought him to an old couple. The boy grew to be strong, wise, and just. A true ruler...

Merlin's eyes snapped open as he came back to reality. He now knew what lay in waiting – a future that had no need of Uther. His own presence at the castle was not meant to lead the king to the just path. It was meant to protect the son from his father's ruthlessness.

With that realization, came another. *Perhaps, then, I can also protect Morgana...*

* * *

"I hate you!" Morgana screamed, storming out of the throne room.

Merlin stared in shock at the blasted doors, then moved within to find Uther getting to his feet. It was evident the king had been on the floor, as though hit by something. The mage could not believe Morgana was the cause, yet the evidence was unquestionable.

Barely a few moments earlier, he had been unable to find sleep. His feet had led him to the garden, but shouts from within the castle had rerouted his steps to the throne room. Even from afar, he had sensed Morgana's mounting rage as one would notice incoming storm clouds, and had been helpless to keep away.

Merlin redirected his gaze to Uther. The monarch was red in the face, scowling furiously. "That girl is a menace!" he shouted, his index pointed to the now empty hallway.

It was a good thing it was nighttime and no servants around, thus no one had borne witness to Uther's embarrassment.

"Sire, what happened?" Merlin tried to ask politely. Lately, it was all he could muster around the ruler. His repeated verbal abuse of Morgana, as well as the plans to use her somehow, had succeeded in disgusting the half-Fae to no end.

Uther wiped at his mouth, removing the thin line of blood that had been trickling down his chin. "Morgana lost control. Came in here demanding the right to rule this kingdom, and I told her she never will, not while I live!"

Merlin stared in anger and despair at the king. There truly was no hope, no way to make him change his ways.

"You need to help me," Uther turned his wrath to Merlin. "I brought you here for a reason: I need a male heir. You have seven days to come up with a solution, or the price is your life."

Merlin barely held back the taunting words wanting to escape past his lips. Uther could do him no harm, but he still had power over Morgana. Before the wizard embarked on a new journey, he planned to put a stop it.

Thus, much as he wanted to bash Uther's face in, Merlin inclined his head in deference and left the royal to his anger.

* * *

Morgana was seething at her father's behavior, hitting the pillows in a frenzy. She only stopped when a music came to her ears, a lullaby of sorts.

She stood and walked towards the window, wiping at her

cheeks dismissively. Tears would not rule her, and they would not be the last she shed because of Uther.

Her eyes fell on the darkened grounds and Merlin's shape walking by the forest's edge. The wizard seemed deep in thought and though she could not see his face, hidden as it was by the cloak he wore, Morgana felt an undeniable urge to be by his side.

Go to him... He needs you... You want him...

The voice of darkness whispered seductively and she could no longer ignore it. Without even bothering with a cloak, Morgana made her way through the castle, taking secret passages where none would see her.

She escaped soon enough into the fresh air and nearly ran towards Merlin, eager to bask in his essence.

As though sensing someone in the vicinity, Merlin stopped pacing and whirled around.

"Morgana, what are you doing here?" he demanded, eyes raking over her heatedly. The nightdress Morgana wore was akin to translucent under the moon's light, and a fierce throbbing flared up in his blood.

The enchantress took a deep breath, noticing Merlin's stare fall to her chest. She drew a certain satisfaction as his gaze grew in intensity on her opulent shape, before returning back to her face.

"I saw you from my window," Morgana murmured, moistening her lips. "I could not sleep."

Merlin's eyes fixated on her luscious mouth. Thoughts churned in his head, but the turmoil that had assailed him before Morgana's apparition was now gone, replaced by an intense craving.

It was a yearning to hold her in his arms, to respond to those wishes buried deep within her eyes and show her true loving.

As though reading his mind, Morgana stepped closer. In a bold move, she stood on her tiptoes and pressed her lips to his.

Fire and ice detonated at once in their bodies, and what started as a soft peck turned into a languorous embrace within seconds. Merlin wrapped his arms around Morgana, pulling her tighter and molding her body to his.

Nothing existed except her lips, her soft sighs as they parted, his own groans as he took possession of her mouth. Nothing else mattered except the need to be closer, to feel skin upon skin, to...

"We cannot do this," Merlin pulled away from the enticing kiss, panting heavily. His glazed eyes met Morgana's and he noticed the foreign gleam in them, which was reflected in his.

The Fae in us... It is an illusion, an attraction of the same genes. It has no meaning... A full moon...

Excuses drifted in his mind, an explanation for what was happening, for the despair filling him, for his sudden empty arms. There was no explanation for the wretchedness cast over him once there was distance between them – nor the feel of being ripped in half.

Morgana's silver eyes darkened, her lips parted, her features echoing the wizard's anguish. "You feel it too. We cannot be apart!"

Merlin shook his head in an effort to deny what was happening. "We cannot."

"Why not?" Morgana contested, arching her back and

pressing closer. "I need this, Merlin. I need *you*."

Merlin knew not what broke his will – the pleading in her gaze, the softness of her mouth, the yearning growing within... With a groan, his mouth dropped to Morgana's and then they were kissing until two were one, and he never wanted to let her go.

He did not even realize, in their heated embrace, that both had teleported themselves to the princess' chambers. Neither noticed as their clothes came off in rapid movements, pushed by the need to be skin to skin. Only once Merlin's fingers touched Morgana's soft alabaster skin, and he felt the electricity run across, did he truly catch on to what was happening.

By then, it was too late.

Touches turned into caresses, whispers into moans, and then Merlin had Morgana lying on the bed, his own frame looming over her. He touched her innermost corners, tasting her nectar as he had dreamt to for ages, basking in her pleasure.

When she begged, pleaded for him to assuage his need, Merlin buried himself deep within her. Time stood still around them as their gazes locked, their bodies joined in the most intimate of ways.

Morgana's eyes lighted with an inner sparkle, and that same passion responded within him, hungry for more. Only then, did Merlin move, causing the dam of emotions to break loose, and the wave of bliss crashed upon them both.

* * *

The next morning, Merlin escaped Morgana's bed like a thief in the night, leaving before a handmaiden found him in his lord's daughter's room. He went to wash up and walked at length, ending up in the forest.

Churning emotions filled him and he punched one of the trees repeatedly, alternating between blows like a boxer. Finally, knuckles split and bleeding, the wizard fell to the ground with a cry of despair.

Atrox waited in the shadows, searching the warlock's mind for something to use. He was methodical, purposefully ignoring the man's darkening emotions, instead trying to understand the rage.

As he caught on, the realization made him step out of the shadows. *You love Uther's daughter.*

The statement made Merlin's head snap up, eyes narrowed in suspicion. Atrox had been against the relationship from the beginning but, in that moment, all the wizard could detect in his stance were peaceful intentions. As if to confirm the fact, the wolf sat down and tilted his head to the side.

Would you like to talk about it?

Merlin was pretty sure his jaw hit the ground as he stared at the incongruous question. For once, the demon was not trying to warn him, or lecture him, but rather understand him?

This is new...

Atrox snorted, then continued, *You amuse me, druid. What can I say? I promise not to kill you as you unburden your heart.*

Merlin stayed quiet, considering the request. Then, the words came out in a torrent. "I do love her. And I should not, as it will mean both our dooms."

What makes you say that?

"Besides all your warnings? I do not have to foresee it...

We are not good for each other. A love such as this can only end in misery on both sides." The young man suddenly looked much older to the demon's eyes than his mere three decades of existence.

Your powers are not all omniscient, wizard. You could be wrong.

Merlin threw him a look so filled with pain that Atrox got up and walked closer. With a lick of his tongue, he healed the Halfling's bleeding hands.

"Why do you still try to help me, when I fail so?"

Because I was omniscient. And even I did not see everything coming. And things I thought I did... ended differently.

Merlin frowned at Atrox's nostalgic voice in his head, so unlike the malicious one he was used to.

As for why I healed your wound... I am not heartless, though I must seem it. You have done what few humans – or Faes, for that matter – ever have: intrigued me. It is not often I see one such as you readily give in to emotions.

At Merlin's furrowed brow, Atrox continued, *You are right about one thing. You must be careful. Morgana is fragile of mind, yet strong of magic. More so than you can guess. She has burdens, though she might hide it well.*

The demon paused, realizing he was saying too much, yet wanting to help the wizard. *It is too late to undo what you have started. Do not betray her, whatever you do.*

With that, he left Merlin to his ruminations.

CHAPTER 8

Merlin stepped in front of Uther, watching as the king sent the advisors away. These days, he found it easier to look the man in the eye, despite the nights in Morgana's bed.

In the end, we are both adults, and this concerns only us, was his reasoning.

As Uther rubbed a pensive hand on his chin, Merlin addressed him.

"You wished to see me?"

"Sit."

The wizard did as he was bade, forcibly unclenching his jaw. Until Morgana made up her mind, he would stay – for love of her, if nothing else. But listening to Uther was harder every day. He did not make it easy.

"I need an heir," the king announced – or rather, repeated. "And the week I gave you has come and gone, still with no solution."

Merlin met his stare unflinchingly. "You have Morgana, sire."

"She is a woman," Uther waved a hand dismissively. "I need a *male* heir. And while you were busy doing who knows what, I found the lucky one to bear him."

I guess he forgot about my head being the price for incompetence, Merlin mused sardonically.

"And you will help me get her."

At Uther's words, Merlin's mind pulled him in a vision – another prophecy. It had the effect of being sucked into a vortex, and losing one's grip on reality. Though the wizard remained sitting, his eyes glazed over slightly and his body became more rigid.

Then, Merlin focused on what only he could see:

It was the same brown haired-woman giving birth. And Morgana's tear-ravaged face, in this kingdom, looking at someone accusingly.

Merlin returned from the trance to Uther's lecture of Morgana's faults and why she was not fit to be a ruler. He interrupted the monarch with a single word: "No."

Uther's mouth opened and closed, his face reddening. "What do you mean, 'no'?"

"I would have thought that was clear," Merlin retorted with a tight-lipped smile. "I will not aid you in this scheme."

Uther's veins seemed ready to pop with the mage's every word, until he finally spit, "You *will* obey me."

"I am not bound to you, *my liege,*" Merlin hissed and got up to walk away. Uther's next words stopped him in his tracks.

"You can have Morgana."

Merlin turned back to Uther, clenching his jaw painfully

to the point of breaking. "*What* did you say?" he challenged coldly, anger lacing every letter.

Uther smirked, though he paled a bit at the lightning reflected in Merlin's eyes.

"You are interested in her, are you not?"

Merlin refused to answer the slimy snake, instead wanting nothing more than to take Morgana far away from there. As he was about to leave, Uther raised his voice.

"I will give her to another!" the king threatened.

Merlin paused again, not at the threat, but at Uther's sheer arrogance. The man actually thought he could control the fate of not one, but *two* Faes, and play them as pawns!

The wizard took a deep breath, desperately trying to rein his emotions in check. In spite of his best efforts, the rage that had always been at bay, since he had last fought Niell, rose to the surface. It was a tidal wave, as unyielding and unrepentant as the love for Morgana. It filled Merlin without mercy, flaring up his temper…then the dam broke.

He marched to Uther in two long strides and punched him in the face. The king fell down, clutching his jaw and groaning in pain. He raised outraged eyes to Merlin at having been brutally assaulted in such a way.

Reading Merlin's shocked expression, Uther started laughing maniacally. "You have signed your death warrant. If you try to leave with Morgana, I will hunt you at every corner until you are both dead. Not even your magic will save you."

Merlin growled, about to strike again, when Uther held up a hand. "Or, you help me."

The mage froze, once more assailed by the image of the boy-king. Though Uther's behavior was despicable, his fate and the child's were linked.

* * *

In the palace of darkness, Atrox awoke, blood pounding in his veins. A sense of foreboding filled his every fiber and left a bitter taste in his mouth, shadows in his heart.

An image of Uther and Merlin floated in his subconscious, and he knew it was time to step in and stop Merlin from making the biggest mistake of his life.

He stepped out of the room and walked down the hall towards the portal. Atrox had taken the corridor many times, and not once had he met an obstruction. The underworld had an odd sense of humor and, on that same night, chose to challenge him.

As he rounded a corner, Atrox hit a wall on the way. He raised both fists, pounding on it, then scowled as he realized it was unyielding crystal. The demon lord stepped back, then joined his hands to create a ball of energy. He threw it towards the barrier, but still it remained immovable.

"What is the meaning of this!?" he raged at the surrounding shadows.

You betrayed us…

Traitor…

"Not this again!" Atrox growled. "We settled it once. I will not have you command me as you did previous demon lords. I am my own master!"

We do not command…

We work together…

You shun us…

The old deity barely refrained from rolling his eyes, yet at the same time realized he was wasting time. "Let me through!

I need to intercede."

It is not yours to change…

The mage makes his own choices…

Let him…

Atrox barred his teeth, in a frenzy to get out of the realm and reach Merlin before it was too late. Out of patience, he thrust his fist forward, projecting a burst of demon magic at the darkness nearby. It was enough to shatter the wall, whose remnants dissipated into nothingness.

The demon lord rushed to get to the portal, but sensed it was too late. As his spirit was sucked in, he made one last attempt to reach Merlin.

* * *

"Give me the son I deserve," Uther was saying, slowly standing up. He could tell he was winning ground by the slight tilt of Merlin's head, and pressed on. "And you can have Morgana. I will allow you both to leave."

Panting heavily, Merlin wanted nothing more than to refuse. Him and Morgana could depart either way and it would not affect anything. And yet… *The boy, the prophecy.* None would come to pass and he would not be able to mentor the child if Uther did not father him first.

Which meant, for better or worse, the king had not yet served his purpose.

Do not do it! Atrox's voice commanded. *What is fated to pass will take place, even if in a different way than you foresaw.*

Can you guarantee it? Merlin questioned. Only silence answered.

He looked down at Uther, and schooled his face in a mask.

"I want it written in blood."

Uther paled at the implications – a blood oath could not be broken, even someone as un-magical as him knew it.

Merlin produced a scroll and ink from thin air. The king took them and spread the parchment on the table. With one hand, he unsheathed his sword partly and pressed the left hand on the blade, wincing as it cut through.

As the blood poured off his palm, and onto the floor beneath their feet, Uther grabbed a writing quill and dipped it in the red liquid. With one glance at Merlin's immobile face, he started writing.

As soon as Uther's attention was fully focused on the scroll, Merlin's eyes glowed with the unrestrained lightning of magic at work. If he had to stick around, then he would make damn well sure Morgana was out of the king's grasp and forever untouchable.

* * *

You should not have agreed.

Merlin was in bed by Morgana's side, her sleepy form half-spread over him. The voice had interceded in his mind barely hours since the meeting Uther. This time, he had no choice but to go to him.

With a stifled sigh, he left Morgana's embrace to follow the angry energy in the outside gardens.

"He would have sold her to anyone!" Merlin hissed, meeting Atrox's eyes.

Is it any better that you bought her?

Merlin's palms lighted in fury. "Do not dare say that! I love her. With all my heart."

That may be so, but it was your pride that guided your

hand and pushed you, as much as love did. You could not resist being the one in control of the young prince's destiny.

Merlin's shoulders slumped and he looked away, unwilling to admit how truthful the words were.

The wolf wanted to feel sorry for him. But the half-Fae had made a mess – and Merlin still did not yet realize to what extent. Only moments after emerging from the portal on Earth, Atrox had sniffed out the change in balance.

Through his simple act of Fae magic, Merlin had shifted something essential. Good and evil always battled in the background of the world, on a plane of existence not many were aware of – especially mortals.

Due to his godly lineage, Atrox' subconscious was open to the never-ending energies that surrounded every being. He was able to clearly distinguish when something changed, for better or worse.

With Merlin's new spell, the future that been set was irrevocably altered. Though Atrox was no longer a seer, the remnants of the energy dispersed were enough to clue him in.

"What is it you propose I do?" Merlin's question, barely a murmur, brought the demon lord out of his ruminations.

Nothing. After a moment, he added abruptly, *You had to have it written in blood, didn't you? On a parchment that is now proof of what took place... And which cannot be destroyed unless it is to break the oath. There is absolutely nothing you can do now! Once the deed is done, it cannot be undone.*

A disgusted snort escaped him, and he looked away. Disappointed at the turn of events, Atrox wanted nothing more than to leave Earth in that moment.

"Not even if I charmed the agreement?"

The wolf froze, not believing his ears. Noticing Merlin's serious expression, he growled in confusion – and warning. *What more have you done?*

"When Uther wrote his promise to give me Morgana in exchange for a male heir that would follow him, I asked the elements to protect Morgana. To help her succeed in her utmost wish."

Atrox whined this time in a way that gave Merlin chills.

"What is it?"

You do not realize what you have done... You truly do not.

It was a statement, but the way the demon said it made it seem more like a question.

"I do not follow," Merlin said.

You are half-Fae, Merlin. Atrox pointed the fact out wearily, for what felt like the thousandth time. *This means any spell you create, especially one affecting another Fae or Halfling, is bound to be tricky. You have ensured with your words that Morgana becomes who she is meant to be – an enchantress to be reckoned with.*

"How can that be? I only wanted –"

For Morgana to be happy, I know. You may not yet have grasped this, as blinded as you are by your love for her... But the key to Morgana's contentment lies in having the power to dominate everyone else around her, including her father.

"No, that cannot be true!" Merlin denied. But already he could see a terrible vision, of a gorgeous sorceress with the world at her feet. It swirled around his head, not quite a prediction, but a hint of something to come.

Merlin's face crumbled and he slipped to the ground on

his knees. "What have I done?"

The demon was silent for once, only looking at him pityingly.

"You have no advice for me? None at all?" Merlin pleaded.

Only one.

At Merlin's expectant gaze, he delivered, *Morgana must never find out. If that cursed paper ever comes in her possession, you will lose what semblance of trust she has given you. What will follow if that moment ever comes, believe me, you would not wish it on your worst enemy.*

Dismissing the mage, Atrox turned and left, weary of human minds and their politics.

* * *

Atrox had barely left Merlin's presence and entered the forest, when he sensed someone nearby.

You again, Aequus?

He turned around, meeting his brother's gaze.

What is this, are you all taking turns to seek me out?

"Brother, you truly are too full of yourself," Aequus snorted. "I come here with a decree. You have not met our expectations as demon lord."

Atrox did not react, merely stared indifferently.

"Darkness complains you do not do your part to maintain the balance, to corrupt the innocents, and so on..." Aequus paused, then continued, "You will not be allowed to return to the palace, as it is meant for those who take the duty seriously."

You cannot do this, Atrox growled. *I was given a fair trial, and it was my punishment!*

"Do not see this as another penalty, brother," Aequus stepped closer, peacefully extending his hand. At the snarling coming the wolf, he quickly withdrew it. "You can roam more of Earth, with your same abilities and continue…whatever you wish."

I have no purpose on Earth alone.

"Do not think of it that way. I expect soon, you will come to your senses." His emerald eyes glinted with speculation, "And perhaps even help your siblings."

So that is what this is all about, Atrox caught on. *Your petty war with Vulper.*

"I would not call it petty," was all Aequus responded.

At the god's offended expression, Atrox laughed. *You truly believe there would be a single chance that I help you, when you have done nothing but create chaos in my own life?*

"Can we not move past that, being a family? We all made mistakes at one point or another."

Some more so than others… Atrox growled warningly.

When Aequus only pursed his lips, refusing to apologize, Atrox snorted. *Right. Either way, I am not in the mood for this.*

"When you make up your mind, simply call my name on a full moon."

There is nothing to decide! Atrox growled, but the annoying god was already gone.

The demon was left to pace, ruminating dark thoughts, groaning at the laughing fates that would not leave him alone.

Hoping against all that Aequus had been jesting, he tried to reach the portal that usually awaited him in the forest. When his powers tapped it, a force blew him into the air and he fell to the ground.

Groaning, Atrox stood up and shook his head. *Damn them all!* he rumbled, then took off on a sprint in a halfhearted effort to clear his mind. There was nothing he could do now that the entrance was blocked. He was truly stuck on Earth, forced to witness Merlin and Morgana's fallout.

* * *

Morgana turned to Merlin in her sleep, blinking sleepily when she met the cold sheets. She stood up, drowsily looking around, and noticed him up by the window.

It was not the first time the enchantress had stirred up in the middle of the night to find her lover awake and in deep thought.

He is hiding something, the voice of corruption whispered. It had gotten stronger now, more forceful, and Morgana found herself listening to it more. More often than not, it suggested ways to deal with her father or some lord that was trying to become too friendly.

And then sometimes, it revealed things she did not necessarily want to know. Lately, something – perhaps a womanly instinct – told her Merlin was indeed hiding something.

But what? Morgana wondered, taking in his tense shoulders and the way he was staring at the moon longingly as though it could provide answers to soothe his worries.

Something important...Something deceitful... Doubt was quick to answer.

Enough!

Morgana shook her head to clear it and the movement was enough for Merlin to notice. His eyes widened in surprise to see her awake.

"I am sorry if I woke you," he whispered, contrite.

Morgana pushed away her own dark thoughts, smiling and endeavoring to appear inviting. "You did not, it was the empty bed that did."

Merlin attempted to return the grin, but it felt forced and did not reach his eyes in the way she liked. Morgana did not enjoy the clenching of her own stomach, the uneasiness filling her.

Elysia's warnings, which she had been ignoring these last few months, were now pushed to the forefront of her mind. Resolutely, Morgana cast them away.

She was happy with Merlin; he truly understood her, and brought her happiness she had never dreamt of. Somehow, as well, her powers strengthened. In the last few days alone, Morgana had discovered new things she was capable of, new abilities that surprised in the most exciting of ways.

By no means did she credit it all to Merlin. However, the fact they were both half-Fae and literally shot sparks when around each other – whether in bed or outside – was bound to play a part in the latest surge of magic she could tap into.

On that note, Morgana pushed off the covers hiding her body and stretched. She smiled languorously towards Merlin, drawing satisfaction at his sharp intake of breath.

"Will you return to bed, darling?"

Merlin moved as though in a trance, eyes fixated on her. "How could I resist such temptation?" he murmured and stepped ever closer, until he was lying down by her side.

Morgana chuckled softly, touching his cheek tenderly. "Whatever worries keep you awake, forget them for tonight," she whispered, locking her gaze onto his. "Let me take them away."

As she spoke the words, Morgana sent a gentle nudge in Merlin's mind. Distracted by her curves, he did not register the fact his muscles relaxed and he was becoming more pliable. Even as his hands roamed the enchantress' body, and her moans answered in response, Merlin was letting go...

The walls he had erected around his mind since Atrox had come into his life weakened. They had kept him safe for ages, kept others' at bay – even Morgana. Despite the fact he loved her, Merlin was not ready to share everything. In the throes of desperation, wanting to let go of everything weighing on him, those same barriers trembled.

Merlin placed his lips by Morgana's ear, biting gently on the lobe. Triumph surged through him at her moans, then he surrendered to the enchantress' curves. He moved down her neck, to her shoulder, then collarbone, breasts, and lower still.

Through it all, Morgana writhed underneath him, feeling the waves of pleasure rise. And still, she kept the gentle assault on Merlin's mind, probing deeper.

When his talented touch brought only ecstasy, Morgana begged for more. "Please, Merlin, please... I need you..."

The mage lifted himself on his elbows, peering down at Morgana. His features reflected the intensity of the love he felt, the depth of the connection uniting them.

Morgana smiled and opened her arms, welcoming him within her, wanting nothing more than to forget the outside world, together.

The fates were not so gentle.

As she reached another pinnacle of satisfaction, and Merlin followed shortly after, Morgana got a glimpse of the secret he hid. A stark image was thrust in her mind, shining as brightly as a comet across the night sky. Though it was brief and disappeared within instants, it was enough for Morgana to realize what it was.

A will, with my father's writing!

Exhausted from the lovemaking, Merlin was already dozing in her arms, but Morgana was wide-awake. She slipped from under him and stepped away from the bed. Her gaze never left his dormant form, though it was no longer soft and loving, but calculating.

The memory in Merlin's mind was now engraved in hers, and Morgana fixated on it like it was the solution to everything. She had hoped the warlock's turmoil came from something insignificant, but this was proof there was more going on.

It was time she stopped being blinded by her affections towards Merlin and instead focused on her needs.

After all, I am the one who has my own best interests at heart.

Part of Morgana was undecided, wanting nothing more than to crawl back in bed and comfort herself with Merlin's heat. But the larger part that had been waiting for such a thing to happen was now relishing the satisfaction.

I need to find it, Morgana decided resolutely.

Yes... The treacherous voice answered. *Find it...*

CHAPTER 9

It was night when Merlin met the king in the throne room. It had been difficult leaving Morgana's arms, and she had not easily accepted the excuse of an urgent meeting. It was as though she knew something was afoot, and did not want him involved.

For weeks now, the warlock had been in meetings with Uther, devising a way to bring him the son he desperately needed – and that would gain their freedom. Of course, Uther did not know that Merlin planned to the take child and raise him with Morgana.

Neither did Morgana, for that matter.

Merlin had to shake his head to clear it of Morgana's eyes, brimming with tears as he left. It had not been easy, but he would make it up to her later, as soon as the ugly task at hand was complete.

Though by no means dark magic, it was not a spell Merlin

was particularly inclined to perform – especially not for Uther. The morality of it alone was enough to crush him, if he had been a normal man preoccupied by where his soul would end up after death.

As it was, Merlin was not. Despite his less than stellar morals, he took his time walking to the throne room. The magician's reluctance stemmed from what would follow, but also the fact that Uther would actually benefit from it. The last thing he wanted was to gift the monarch happiness, when he had stolen it from Morgana.

The king was pacing in the room, but turned eagerly towards Merlin when the doors opened. "You take your time, wizard. Let us get on with it!"

The plan was simple. Uther's crush, a lady Ygraine, was married to a man named Gorlois. He was a duke, one of the many under the king's command. At the beginning of the week, Uther had sent him on a mission with some soldiers, thus ensuring the wife would be alone.

Merlin had come up with the rest of the solution. He knew Ygraine would never betray her husband, but if it was Gorlois that came to her in the middle of the night.... She would be unable to resist. He had his mother and real father to thank for the stroke of genius, in the end.

Though he detested the trickery, Merlin had to push past his own conscience. It was time, if he wanted to truly have a hand in the birth of the child.

Shaking all doubts off, Merlin pointed his staff towards Uther. He could see, reflected within the crystal, the mirrored face of Gorlois, the Duke of Tintagel. The image shimmered and with his free hand, the mage projected it onto Uther.

Within moments, the king's features started to change, becoming the other man's. The simplicity of the plan would ensure its success, as Merlin had already foreseen. Just as he had, only the night before, dreamt of the birth of the young king once more.

When the spell ended, Uther was no longer. In his place stood a replica of Gorlois. Merlin could not help the satisfaction coursing through him at the spell having succeeded.

"Very well done!" Uther grinned. "Now, send me to her!"

With a wave, Merlin teleported the king to the duke's castle, where Ygraine was asleep. He knew what would happen next: she would believe Uther was her husband, accept him in her bed, and by morning, be pregnant with his heir.

Merlin fell in a trance, watching that exact scene playing in front of his eyes...

* * *

Morgana stretched in bed, noticing Merlin had not yet returned. She was not pleased with his absences, especially when they were because of Uther. And always, when he was away, the voice of darkness was swift to act.

Even now, it whispered, encouraging her to seek what she had last seen: the scroll.

It is hidden... You can find it...

"Leave me be!" Morgana ordered the shadows, though her voice did not have its usual fierceness. She sat in an upright position and hugged both knees to her chest. At times like these, the enchantress still felt alone and knew nothing had truly changed.

Her hand went of its own accord to her flat stomach,

where even now she felt the life brimming to the surface. Yes, an heir indeed... But not one that Uther would corrupt. The child would be raised with her and Merlin alone, she would ensure it.

A sense of restlessness came over her, and Morgana stood. She grabbed a cape to cover her naked form and paced back and forth, until she finally settled by the window.

As she stared down, the glass reflected her own image. Yet as she peered closer, it showed something else.

See the truth... Look....

A man and a woman, intertwined in bed. The man was old, with a beard and brown hair, no one she knew. Lost in passion, he turned his face to the side and Morgana gasped.

Uther's face appeared for a split of a second, overlapping with the other's man. And the lady... Looking closer, Morgana almost recognized her. It was Ygraine, one of the women she had seen numerous times at feasts Uther threw.

In fact, last time she had been there, her husband had stood up to the king and accused Uther of coveting his wife. And now...

"What is the meaning of this?" Morgana murmured, her hand reaching out to touch the glass.

Merlin betrayed you! This unscrupulous farce originated from him, and him alone.

"No, that cannot be!" the young enchantress hissed, but already doubt was taking root in her spirit.

It is the mage who made it possible... Using his father's own trick.

Morgana's face transformed, all softness gone as anger overtook her. She turned away as Uther finished his coupling, disgusted by the deception. In that same instant, a sharp pain struck, starting deep within her stomach.

The princess bent over, biting her lip in as the affliction moved lower. *No...*

Morgana opened her mouth in a silent scream, but only an animal moan came out as she fell to her knees, cradling her womb.

When the pain subsided, she lifted her hands to see them drenched with blood.

"No!" Morgana screamed, feeling the life that had been growing inside leave swiftly, like an overflowing river retreating. Hot tears cascaded down her face as she curled up in a vain attempt to hold on to what was already lost.

Sensing with her magic, she could detect the faint heartbeat. The rhythmic sound slowed down, fainted, and then came to an absolute stop. Morgana shrieked in pain as the hopes of the future were shattered in front of her eyes.

"Curse you, Uther!" she shouted in rage. "May you die forever alone!"

Her entire being trembled as a red aura seized control, then left her in a dark cloud. Morgana collapsed fully onto the floor, sobs wrecking her body. Above her, the mist dissipated to find the person mentioned in the curse and achieve its aim.

It must have been an hour, maybe two later, that Morgana stood. Her expression was blank, eyes sunken, cheeks hollow. She moved as a ghost would, with numbness in every muscle.

Only one thought existed in her mind. *Find the scroll...* Reaching deep within, Morgana touched magic and let it guide her on the quest. Fortified by her despair and rage, the Fae energy rose to the surface and listened to its mistress' unspoken desires.

Underneath the bed, she came upon it: a chest, cloaked with magic to avoid a breach. It was no match for what was fueling the enchantress and she broke it with one sweep of her palm. Then, Morgana reached within and grasped the parchment.

With one sharp nail, she broke off the seal and rolled it open. Her red-rimmed eyes dried with every read word, until all that was left burning in their depths was the fire of vengeance.

* * *

Merlin walked into the castle feeling like an old man, despite being only in his early thirties. After Uther had returned, grinning like a fool, he had felt sick to his stomach, unable to return to Morgana.

Instead, he had stepped outside to the ever-dark forest, to drown his sorrow in nature and the surrounding elements. When Merlin was ready and walked back to Morgana's chambers, it was still the middle of the night.

Weariness spread over him and the pain that had started deep within his chest only hours earlier seemed to get worse with every step. Lost in thoughts, Merlin did not register another person was in the hall.

Only when he was close by and Morgana's energy touched him, did Merlin look up. A faint smile spread on his lips and he went to embrace her, not noticing her rigidity and odd behavior until their eyes met.

It was then he felt the scorching ire shooting off her in waves, the pain within and the resentment. His heart plummeted as Atrox's words rang clearly in his mind: *She must never find out.*

"What is wrong, beloved?" Merlin tried to caress her cheek, but Morgana moved out of his reach.

"Is it true?"

"Is what true?"

"Do not take me for a fool!" Morgana screamed, eyes flashing in anger. "Is *this* true!?"

Merlin noticed the parchment in her hand, the seal he had set on it broken. He gulped, his throat suddenly dry.

"Morgana…"

She stepped away as he neared. "You traded me like cattle!"

Merlin flinched at the anguish and wrath in her voice.

"It was not like that."

"Really?" Morgana enquired in a flat tone.

"Please. I love you. I was protecting you!"

She narrowed her eyes, then laughed. "Right. By buying me. Because, what, Uther would have sold me to someone else if not?"

At Merlin's stunned gaze, Morgana shook her head in disgust. "I cannot believe I trusted you! What a fool I have been, and now I have lost everything. My father will declare that bastard his son!"

"Morgana, we can build another kingdom together," Merlin entreated. He made a move to get closer, but she backed away.

"You think this is about land?" she scoffed, mouth twisted in bitterness.

Something was eluding him, Merlin could sense that much amidst the chaos emanating from Morgana, but he could not place it. He frowned, trying to see past the barriers she had set up – *When did she become so strong?*

It was then he noticed the bloody gown. Merlin froze, staring with wide eyes.

"Yes," Morgana confirmed coldly, "I was pregnant."

Merlin felt the shock of the admission in the stomach, like a powerful blow had been dealt. He stumbled backwards, unable to take his gaze off the stark red now tainting the otherwise white nightgown.

All this time, I was trying to create another child, and my own was growing inside Morgana!

And now…

"What happened?" Merlin whispered, taking another step. He wanted nothing more than to hold and heal her, to no avail. Once more, Morgana eluded him.

"You did. Your actions. Your magic!"

Shock spread on the mage's features and he stared in horror. "No…"

"Half-Fae magic has a price, or did you not know?" Morgana taunted. She did not care of the hurt she was causing, nor anything else except her own pain. "You asked for a life that was not meant to be given, at the urging of my father. And in exchange, the life that was meant to be, *our child,* was taken away."

Merlin gaped in horror as the immensity of what he had done threatened to drown him. He crumbled to the floor at Morgana's feet, bowing his head. "I am *so* sorry, beloved, I did not know."

"Clearly."

The dismissive tone had him look up, but already she was

walking away.

"Morgana!" By the time Merlin snapped out of his stupor and followed, the enchantress was gone. "What have I done?" he muttered, leaning against the wall for support.

Created a monster, was the response within.

* * *

How could you have been so stupid!?

Morgana berated herself, running down secret passages, even as her heart broke and turned to stone. She saw nothing through the tears that escaped her eyes anew. Deep in a pit of despair, her mother's words came to her. *Never let a man own you.*

Why did I not listen to you, mama? Morgana sobbed, then placed a hand on her mouth to stifle the sounds escaping.

Unable to keep moving, she stopped to lean against a wall and let loose the emotions. A lovesick fool – that had been her role, for the past months. Without the veil of love covering her eyes, Morgana would have seen through Merlin's machinations and perhaps could have stopped what he had set in motion.

Morgana had loved Merlin with a passion. A scorching love had tied them from the beginning. Fueled by their Fae bond, it had been enough to get past her own defenses, and allow trust to build between them.

As the tears stopped, that same fire turned cold. Merlin was at fault for having caused the loss of the most precious gift they had been entrusted with. Morgana lowered her hand to her womb and what was no longer there.

She inhaled deeply, begging the magic within for the strength to go on. Alone, like she had always been meant to.

The darkness had been right all along, and Merlin had betrayed her, much like Uther. Unlike her mother, she did not lose her life; rather, her kingdom, her lover and their child.

I can get past this. I will get past this, Morgana swore. *And Merlin will pay, if it is the last thing I do.*

She stepped away from the wall, continuing on the path. With every step, her determination grew – as did the need for revenge. With every tear that dried on her cheeks, her heart became more untouchable. With every breath that escaped her, Morgana resolved to never again let a man reach her so.

Before she had even gotten to the bedchamber, the grey eyes once full of laughter were cold mirrors staring back. Morgana grabbed the packaged bag and returned to the passages, this time heading to the stables.

Fury now fueled her. The princess had never been alone – but the wrath building would be her salvation, and magic would become her protection. She could feel it brimming under the surface, yearning to be used.

Merlin had taught her about their common powers, yes. But he was a fool, a scared one. He only used Fae magic delicately, as though it was something to be cherished, revered and slightly feared. Morgana had no such restraints. To the power waiting to be unleashed within, she vowed to use it as it never had been – unrestrictedly.

As Morgana rode into the night, she let wave upon wave of magic wash over her, cleansing the pain – enough so that she would no longer crumble. In the same breath, she forever let go of the young woman she had been and embraced the sorceress awaiting.

* * *

Morgana had been on her own for two weeks when she was ambushed in the forest by three men. Smelly, tall, burly and drunk, they took one look at the beautiful maiden passing by and moved to stop her.

One grabbed the reins of the horse as it neighed, restraining him.

"Bonny lass," he rasped. "Stay here and have a bit of fun, will ye?"

Morgana curled her lip at him in disgust, "I think not."

"She thinks she's better than us," another muttered.

"Let's see how she feels when we be done with her," the third added.

Morgana was petrified – for all of two seconds – then she raised her palm, index held high and muttered, "Fools."

The darkness at their feet was hers to command. It covered them, slithering up their bodies like a blanket and feeding on them.

Stop!

The voice made Morgana pause, and she turned to see a wolf come out of the shadows. The energy around him was powerful and the sorceress recognized it as what had flickered over Merlin that one night, when he had tried to stay away.

At last, I meet the mysterious presence...

"Did *he* send you?" she sneered, sensing Merlin's energy around the wolf.

No, Atrox looked at the men, then back at her with pleading in his eyes. *Do not do this, Morgana. You could be good, it is not too late to turn back.*

Morgana laughed, and it was brittle as though she had no reason to. Atrox looked at the former enchantress in pity, and

Morgana sobered up.

"Do not give me that. You know what they wanted to do to me!" she yelled, features contorted in fury.

Atrox stepped nearer, trying to get in her mind.

"If you come any closer, I will snuff out their worthless lives like candles."

Why, Morgana?

"Because Merlin betrayed me. Because he took away our most precious gift, and ruined our future!"

These three do not have to pay for his mistakes.

Atrox knew it was the wrong thing to say the minute Morgana stilled.

"No," she smiled coldly. "But they will regardless."

Morgana could have left it at a warning. But seeing the men's repulsive faces, sensing what they had planned to do to her... She gritted her teeth and watched as the obscurity consumed them.

Atrox, seeing it cover the bodies in their entirety, tried to get the shadows to pull back, to save their worthless lives. The writhing mass did not listen, egged on as it was by Morgana's Fae magic.

The demon lord was forced to conclude it no longer listened to him, only to its new mistress.

As the wolf disappeared, Morgana cackled, "Go, and run to Merlin! Make sure you tell him all that you have witnessed!"

* * *

Atrox appeared near the castle, where Merlin was pacing in the forest. Since the enchantress had left him, the mage was more and more turning into a hermit.

The boy will be born in a few months, Atrox muttered as he approached Merlin.

The wizard looked to have aged ten years since they had last met.

"I know."

And you will let Uther raise him?

The king was already planning the wedding to Ygraine, now that her husband had died in battle. He had admitted far and wide the child she carried was his.

"No," Merlin answered unequivocally. "The boy shall grow far from this man's kingdom, where he will be unaware of his nobility until he is of age."

Very well.

Merlin was silent, lost in his own turbulent thoughts. He thought back to the previous night, and the nightmare that had woken him up. Of Morgana with her pale face, bathed in sweat, screaming in agony. There had been a stillborn baby on the bed, and she had died in his arms shortly after.

It had not been a vision, that much was evident. But why the fates saw fit to torture him with more images of what he had lost, the mage could not figure out.

"Morgana is gone," Merlin finally mumbled.

Yes, I saw it all.

"Where is she, do you know?" He hated asking, but she remained hidden despite his numerous searches. Merlin could not stop replaying their last meeting in his head, hating himself for what happened.

You could not have foreseen it, Atrox tried to console. *The future that concerns you will always be clouded in mystery and fog, for yourself. We have lost a lot of history pertaining to the magic of Faes, but this is true for every seer. As for Morgana, what use would it be if I revealed her location?*

Merlin turned to him, a feverish look in his eyes. "Tell me!"

Atrox shook his head determinately. *She is beyond reason, and you cannot undo your actions.*

* * *

Eight months later…

Merlin was outside in the hallway, watching the twinkling stars. The night was quiet, but a sense of expectation filled the air. The waiting came to an end soon enough: there was a noise like a current vibrating throughout the structure, followed by a shooting star across the skies.

The mage turned to the doors behind at the same time as a baby's cries were heard. With a burst of magic, he pushed in to see a nursemaid holding the newborn.

Merlin picked him up and when his blue eyes met the child's hazel ones, he smiled. Something in his heart tugged – a feeling of rightness, as though the world had been given its most precious gift.

The nightmare he had had of Morgana giving birth was forgotten. Merlin turned to the mother, Ygraine, to find her pale, unconscious form on the bed. The nursemaid hesitantly raised her arms. "I can take him."

"No," Merlin barked, his steely eyes meeting hers. The poor woman flinched and cowered away in a corner.

Without a second look, the wizard left with the young child, not stopping his horse until he got to a farm far off the king's lands. Uther's wrath would be terrible, but he would be forced to accept the loss.

At the farm, Merlin gave Arthur to the gentle old woman and her husband. He had sought far and wide for a couple worthy to raise the leader of the new world and their pure hearts had won his approval.

"I will return for him when the time is right," the warlock warned. "Raise him well."

In the distance, the demon wolf observed the scene and the young boy.

CHAPTER 10

It had been years since Morgana walked out of Merlin's life. Half a decade, to be exact. Rumors started of an enchantress turned sorceress, a woman of such grace and beauty all men fell to her spell.

Merlin was busy keeping an eye on the young heir, Arthur. He used the task as an excuse to ignore the whispers, and the dread filling him.

Arthur was growing, past a young toddler now, and already he seemed well beyond his years. The mage could not help but feel satisfied at the decision he had taken.

After giving Arthur to the old couple, he had left on a journey to get Morgana out of his head and forget his own mistakes. Even more so, it was to ensure his former lover could not track down her half-brother. Leaving behind protective barriers fit for a king, Merlin went on his way.

Through traveling, he soon became aware that Uther had

passed away and the hunt for the child he had fathered was laid to rest.

It gave Merlin much joy to think of the old man dying alone, and he saw it a fit punishment for all the hurt inflicted upon Morgana. Had Uther considered her worthy, loved her as she deserved, perhaps events would have played out differently.

The thought of Morgana still brought Merlin to his knees, even as the months and years passed. The depth of their love, the strength of their Fae bond was something he constantly had to fight against to keep from reaching out – or worse, go to her.

His heart ached remembering their good times, the smiles, the laughter… Every night he dreamt of Morgana, and every morning he struggled to forget. Each waking moment was spent dismissing memories of their past and locking them in a far corner of his mind, out of sight.

Merlin blamed himself for the changes in Morgana, and his actions that had contributed to the disaster. Atrox had been right, in the end, warning him to stay away.

I should have listened. It was not the first – nor would it be the last – time when Merlin thought so.

The idea the rumors he was hearing were related to Morgana assailed him with despair. He was not naïve enough to believe the loss of their child would have left the enchantress unscathed, especially not after how things had ended between them.

And yet, he had hoped.

The day came when Merlin was no longer able to ignore the rumors. The decision act came in the shape of his old confidant, the demon wolf who had once shadowed his every step but whose own path had taken him far away.

* * *

Merlin was hunting not for pleasure, but for food. His quest had brought him from village to village, and he had been reduced to killing small animals with magic in order to avoid going into towns.

Meeting people was something to be avoided, women especially. It had started as a way to keep hidden from Uther's men but, in the end, had become part of a routine.

Seeing the rabbit prepare to run, Merlin lifted a palm, about to hit him with a ray of light. A wolf pounced out of nowhere and, in one swell bite, swallowed the animal. Still ravenous, the animal became aware of a presence behind and turned to continue his meal.

Merlin gaped in shock at the midnight eyes sizing him up, unflinching and unfeeling.

"You!" Merlin pointed a finger, recognizing the demon.

The beast tilted its head to the side, but the booming voice did not come as it usually did. Frowning, Merlin lowered the defenses of his mind enough to probe into the wolf's. Within moments, he concluded the old Atrox had somehow reverted back to a more primal self, letting the intelligence within go dormant.

Despite the threatening snarling, the wizard took a step closer. He pushed past the animal's aura and encountered a barrier. Underneath it was where the consciousness of Atrox lay, removed from the world.

Frowning, Merlin lifted a palm and intoned a spell, ignoring his agitation. With the passing years, alone once more, his powers had evolved as he learned to tap deeper into the Fae heritage – and to stop fearing it.

When the light escaped his fingertips, Merlin exhaled heavily and watched as it surrounded the animal. It turned into green butterflies, which then swirled around him in circles until the separate specks became a continuous string, tying the old Atrox like a rope.

Sparks of red shot off where the magic touched the demon lord, attempting to breach his mental barrier. At first, the wolf struggled against it, but after futile moments, he collapsed to the ground.

"Atrox?" Merlin called out, unsure of what to expect.

For a moment, nothing happened, then the wolf grunted. Slowly, he got back up, shaking his head furiously. The opaque stare met the mage's. *I suppose I owe you a thank you for that.*

"None is needed, merely repaying an old debt," Merlin declared, masking his relief. Warily, he continued, "What exactly happened to you?"

For my interference with you, for failing to corrupt you, I lost access to my palace in the underworld.

Merlin raised his eyebrows in surprise.

When I was thrown from the pantheon of gods, specific rules were in place. I was to interact with humans only as the voice of corruption, not to actually change things. Or affect people.

The wizard thought back to all the advice Atrox had given him, to the times he had tried to intervene, to the riddles masquerading as solutions – and winced.

With a loaded look as though guessing Merlin's thoughts, Atrox finished, *My punishment was being stuck on Earth. After a time, I let the wolf, the primal part of who I am, take over. It was much simpler than constantly berating myself for things I could not alter, even if I tried.*

Merlin was pensive, pondering the words. After a few moments, he tilted his head to the side and enquired, "What if I can change it?"

Change what?

"The punishment holding you. Let me remove it. I may not give you access back to the palace, but you would be able to attain more power, and move across realms as you used to. Your original penalty was decided in the land of the gods, and despite my Fae magic, it is not something I can intervene with. But the more recent one…"

As the warlock trailed off, Atrox finished for him, *It was handed here, on Earth.*

"Yes," Merlin nodded. "If I do something, at least you would no longer be tied to this realm. It is something I can directly affect."

Atrox sized up the mage with his inner sight, noticing the atmosphere surrounding him and how the energy reacted to his presence. Unsurprisingly, Merlin was telling the truth. His powers had expanded, and what he promised could be delivered, if only the wolf agreed. But at what cost?

What is it you wish in return?

Merlin's expression sobered with sadness. "Retribution for what I did. A good deed may not wipe out a bad one, but perhaps it is a start."

Atrox hesitated for a brief moment, before inclining his massive head. *Agreed. Release me of these chains.*

Merlin lifted both palms to face Atrox and the staff

appeared in his left hand. He stared blankly ahead, retreating deep within to touch the well of power that could war with that of the gods.

When it was in his grasp, Merlin's blue eyes shone of an unnatural light, reflected into the staff. The energy flew off in a mist, descending the length of the supernatural object until it covered the ground.

As water would, it crossed the short distance and covered the wolf's entire form like a sparkling, cloudy blanket.

"Elements at my command," Merlin intoned, "release this demon lord of the entrapments the gods chained him with. Let Atrox feel the magic he once had, allow him to break the cage set upon him. Though he was shot from the heavens, grant him freedom to move as he chooses."

As he was engulfed in the fog, Atrox howled, then stopped as he felt the Fae elements at work. For a moment, the image of his human form overlapped with his beastly, both warring for a place, until the wolf was a wolf once more.

Panting, he watched as the fog retreated back to Merlin, and into the staff.

"Well?" the mage arched an eyebrow questioningly.

Atrox opened his jaws in a grin, then scratched at the ground. Power rumbled underneath his paws, a vibration in the pads. He smacked one of them onto the grass and the entire area shook ferociously. The shadows at the edge of the woods hissed in discontent at the demon lord powers and the new freedom he had gained.

Does he realize what he has done? Atrox mused, before putting the thought out of his mind. Whatever else Merlin's Fae magic had affected would remain his secret, and his alone.

Truly, I thank you, Atrox stepped towards the mage, going so far as to let him scratch behind the ears. *I can give you one thing, in return, to help your quest for retribution.*

"What is that?"

A warning. One of my abilities, a specific one to me as a god, was being able to see the future to an extent even you cannot.

When Merlin remained quiet, the wolf nudged with his muzzle. *You look older. Wiser. Yet missing something.*

A flare of hopelessness came and was quickly extinguished in the Merlin's eyes. "Your warning?" he enquired.

The former deity paused for another moment, then said the words he had dreaded. *You heard the rumors?*

"Yes."

It is *Morgana.*

Merlin glanced away, clenching his jaw. "And what is it to me?"

Do not play games with me, wizard. You still care for her. Try to save her... before it is too late.

"And if it is?"

Do what you must. Only a Fae can kill another Fae, because much like with gods, they are immortal. With the energy she has tapped into, Morgana is incredibly powerful at the moment. The stars speak of turmoil to come in the shape of a terrible beauty. She must be stopped... One way or another. Whatever happens, do not fall to her charms.

With the fated words, Atrox was gone in the blink of an eye.

Merlin debated for days, before giving in to his heart's

desire. He took from a treasure chest the necklace Morgana had once gifted him. He ran a palm over it, magic faintly escaping, doing what he had sworn never to do: use their Fae bond.

No blinding light escaped the wizard, no shifting of nature, not even in his own mind. Simply, he kept his eyes open, but no longer saw the confines of his habitat. Instead, the gaze went first cloudy, then clear, until it was fully white. Images came forth at first hesitant, barely discernable, like outlines of things and shapes.

In Merlin's hand, the necklace glowed softly. His hand tightened over it, the rest of his body wound with tension. His breathing slowed down....

She lived in a fortress, far from Uther's kingdom. Her skin was paler, almost translucent. Her slight frame even thinner. She was in front of a fireplace, features frozen in a sad expression, tears falling down her cheeks.

Merlin wished so much to bring her comfort, his heart squeezed at the sight of the anguish depicted – pain he had caused.

"Morgana," his lips whispered.

Immediately, she stood up, looking around wildly. Merlin broke the trance, understanding now what the demon meant.

I have to try, or I will forever wonder.

* * *

Merlin stood in front of the fortress, fists clenched at the darkness he could feel escaping it. Guilt tore at him for being the reason she had turned to the dark arts, and helpless at being unable to stop her.

Sighing, Merlin trespassed into Morgana's realm. There

was no barrier he had to fight against, no minions to dispose of. Only an eerie silence, a sense of loneliness like what he carried around every day. He walked numbly down the empty, barren halls, until he found the room he had seen her in.

Morgana was still in front of the fireplace, though the tightness of her back indicated she was aware of his presence. Had she seen him coming? Had she felt him watching the night before? Merlin could not tell, nor did he care. His world was set right by simply being in her presence, and the ache in his chest eased ever so slightly.

"Morgana." The name rolled off his lips effortlessly, as it always had.

"So I was not losing my mind," was the breathy response. Morgana's voice was throatier than normal, as though she was no longer used to speaking to people.

She stood up, turning to face him, and the full impact of his actions hit Merlin like a punch to the gut. Oh, she was beautiful. Gorgeous in her grace, but so cold. Unattainable.

The grey eyes that had once glittered at him with joy and love were now cold and narrowed suspiciously. The mouth he had kissed lovingly was downturned, as though she no longer smiled. Morgana had not aged a bit – but the years passed were still visible in the haunted look she settled on Merlin.

"Do not pity me!" Morgana hissed, her own inspection now finished. "What do you want?"

"To apologize."

"It's a bit late for that, no?"

She tilted her head, sneering openly. "But let us hear it, regardless. What would you like to apologize for, hmm? Breaking my heart? Losing my inheritance? Helping my father ruin a perfectly gracious and innocent woman?" Morgana curled her lip, but the anguish in her eyes had Merlin out of breath. "Or causing my miscarriage with your magic?"

Merlin's swallowed past the lump of sensations threatening to overwhelm him. *I have one chance.*

Without hesitation, he crossed the small distance and pulled Morgana in his arms, holding her tightly enough to crush.

"I am so sorry, beloved. Please. Let me try to help you."

Morgana shook in his arms, trying to push him away, then collapsed. Huge sobs wreaked her body, and Merlin only clutched her tighter, his own tears sliding silently down his cheeks. Their energies mingled and the despair, the sorrow they had not had a chance to deal with together was there, palpable in the air around them.

"It was our child!" Morgana sobbed.

"Our loss," Merlin murmured back, squeezing her more. Never could he forgive himself for having caused their fallout, for not having foreseen the consequences of his selfish acts.

"I never meant you harm," the warlock whispered, knowing she probably did not hear him through her crying. "I still love you, and always will."

Clutching Morgana in his arms, Merlin let the tears he had controlled for all these years escape. He cried the loss of the child that would never be, the deprivation of the future, *their* future. In the barren room, amidst old, broken furniture, the dam of emotions broke.

When Morgana calmed down, she pulled back just a bit, looking into his eyes. Merlin saw a glimpse of the young woman she used to be, and fiercely wanted to bring her back.

The Fae in him reacted to the wish and a yearning for more than just a hug took over. Before Merlin could decide otherwise, his mouth descended on hers hungrily, and he grabbed onto her waist to pull her body against his.

Whatever rational thought Merlin had left warned that Morgana would for sure push him away, but instead her arms wrapped around his neck, silently pleading for more. Her mouth opened and he devoured what she gave.

The warlock's hands found the back of the corset and started undoing it, until Morgana stood naked, the gown pooling at her feet. She stepped out of it, tilting her head back enticingly, smiling the smile that drove him crazy.

Merlin was gone before she even reached out. Touching her was an addiction, a need as much as breathing. Naked as well, he laid Morgana down on the bearskin in front of the fireplace.

He hesitated for a bare moment, searching her gaze, wanting to feel the connection of old. For a split second, he saw the triumph reflected in Morgana's grey orbs and almost stopped. But then her eyes closed and her body arched towards his in silent supplication.

Merlin could not have denied the silent invitation even if he tried. Groaning, he slid inside her, taking her, desperation in his every movement. It was a long shot, but also the last chance he had to fight...

For him.

For her.

For their love.

* * *

The cold woke Merlin up. He glanced around, but there

was no trace of Morgana. As he dressed and exited the castle grounds, Atrox approached him from the shadows, snarling in anger.

What the hell have you done?

"None of your business!" the warlock snapped, confused as well at his actions.

It is when the fate of this world has been influenced!

Merlin focused on the words, but before he could address the accusation, he fell into a trance.

Morgana in pain. Her body in sweat, screaming out. A baby's cries. Later, a young boy with dark hair and grey eyes. A perpetual cold look on his face. A young man, brown hair and hazel eyes, facing off against him. And a prophecy.

> *He born of hate*
> *He born of lies*
> *Two dragons to fight*
> *Only one to survive*
> *And bring them all*
> *Into darkness or light.*

Merlin gasped, snapping out of the vision as though having been underwater.

"The boy!"

Yes. Yours and Morgana's.

The pain in his heart was aching as Merlin realized the sorceress had tricked him. Shoulders slumped, he dropped to the ground on his knees. "You did not see this…?"

No. Atrox stepped closer, his massive head above Merlin's. *I saw the one course of the future you were on, when you wanted to save her. The other, when you gave in to your baser impulses, changed everything.*

Merlin was barely listening, lost in his own self-pity. None of it had been real. He had truly lost Morgana, and now... "My boy!" He raised a haunted look to Atrox. "Will he...wield magic?"

The demon's gaze was full of pity. *Strong,* dark *magic, yes. As of his eighteenth birthday.*

"And Arthur?"

None.

"What am I to do?"

Atrox did the only thing he could, and let his words be imbued by demon lord magic, the kind Merlin was not impervious too. Only a strong, compelling charm could aid him in making a decision – now that he had ruined it all.

Forget Morgana. Focus on Arthur. And find someone who wields enough light to be his salvation. He will not succeed without some help.

Merlin nodded, getting up from the ground like an old man would, with the weight of the world on his shoulders. The wretchedness at being away from his child was too much, and he wanted to rebel against it. But a wiser voice warned it was a lost cause, and he needed to focus on what he could indeed change.

And then the warlock realized the voice itself was coming from Atrox. As he did so, Merlin caught another intention. A murderous one. *He plans to go after Morgana!*

"No," Merlin responded, choosing his words wisely. "I cannot forget what we have done, nor the harm that could come to pass. Let me take responsibility."

The wolf stared in shock.

Responsibility?

"I will track Morgana down. And ensure this mistake is erased."

You were not able to hurt her before.

"Yes. But now I know there is nothing left to save."

The demon was more than happy to let the wizard clean up his own mess. The last years had tired him – and he had unfinished business that he could now take care of, thanks to Merlin.

Be it so. But this is where I leave you. I can no longer remain on Earth, as I have done – intervened – too much. I need the quietness of the underworld.

"I understand. Thank you…for everything." They shared a long look, then Merlin left to track Morgana down.

* * *

In the little cottage in the midst of the woods, Merlin watched from afar as the sorceress sat in front of another fireplace, as though she could never get warm enough. He was about to step closer, his decision made, when her features changed. They softened as she caressed her stomach in a gesture so pure, so like his Morgana of old.

It was enough to cause Merlin to hesitate.

A shimmering presence in the woods wanted to warn him that this was the one and only chance he would ever have.

Do not hesitate, it tried to communicate. But it was no use. The mage's heart was soft, pained, and full of despair. Atrox turned away in anger, frustrated at the Halfling's own weakness, and his for caring.

Because he had, Merlin had tricked him and he had believed. Now, the warlock would not act and cross the line that needed to be crossed. In so doing, he doomed them all.

Humanity, Atrox snorted in disgust. *What a waste.*

He left on a run, paws pounding the ground, leaving it all behind. Already, his new powers were opening a portal ahead, one through which he jumped into another realm.

The destination was simple: distance. As far away from Earth as possible.

At the same time, with a cry of rage, Merlin turned from the little house and the scene he desperately wanted to be a part of. With trembling hands, he left behind enough hidden magic to keep Morgana safe, for as long as it would last.

He spared one last moment, one final thought, to the son he would never see grow up, and the lover that was forever out of his reach. Inhaling deeply, Merlin then forced his feet to move.

With each step, his heart weighed less, until he could no longer feel it. The Fae magic within rose to the surface to protect its master, removing the ache little by little. No one would use love against Merlin ever again.

EPILOGUE

Months later…

Atrox glanced around at the forest in which he had spent years trying to keep Merlin in rein, advising him. *Time to move on.*

As he formed a portal to hop into the next realm, he caught a shift behind.

He turned to face a smirking Vulper. "Running away?"

What do you want? Atrox growled.

"I do not know why you waste your time with these humans, and then suffer the consequences from Aequus as you did. Truly, Atrox, if I did not know better, I would admit you have mellowed down."

A snarl, followed by, *I have no time for this.*

Atrox turned to leave, and his back was fully exposed. Without remorse, Vulper struck him from behind with a ray of light. Yelping, the wolf fell into the portal.

Vulper grinned widely. "Now, you will truly not hinder my plans of killing your siblings."

The god was about to leave, but a cord of fire shot out of the portal and grabbed hold of his ankle, yanking him inside.

Vulper yelled, but it was too late and the void closed around him. In the darkness, he was left confronting an Atrox in full deity form. The red-haired god's eyes widened in shock.

"This cannot be!"

"Oh, but it is." Atrox chuckled darkly, clenching and unclenching his fists. "It feels good to finally be on equal footing, so to speak."

"You cannot do anything to me," Vulper tried. "The Cardinal Rule forbids it."

"Right…"

Atrox pretended to think, then in a flash, hit the god with double the energy, burning his chest as he landed. Walking over, he grabbed Vulper by the throat and threw him further away.

"You see, there is one thing that breaks the Cardinal Rule. Or rather, allows someone to contour it."

Vulper spit blood, shrinking back from the demon lord. Something was different about his opponent, as though he had nothing to lose – and would go to whatever ends necessary to hurt him.

"Fae magic." Atrox's words echoed around, and Vulper whimpered.

"Faes are dead, you are bluffing."

"Yes… There was that great war long ago between them and us," Atrox reflected, before smiling coldly. "However, Faes were known philanderers. And you see, they happened to have had children. Lots of them. With humans. And these half-Faes, once they tap into their powers, are just as powerful."

Atrox paused for the fact to sink in, watching as realization dawned on Vulper. The god grew incredibly pale, in stark contrast with the redness of his hair.

Unhindered, Atrox stepped closer and continued, "You all were wondering why I did not corrupt Merlin. You all wanted to know why the hell I *cared*. Well, now you will – not that you will leave this place alive to tell anyone. Merlin's magic was much more use to me light than dark. I did not seek out to get this, but it was my ultimate reward, I suppose."

"I don't... understand."

Atrox, now merely inches away from the god, bent and gripped him by the throat, lifting him in the air. They froze, as though suspended: the prey and the predator. Vulper could no longer breathe as Atrox's fingers closed in for the kill.

"He healed me," the demon lord revealed. "And in so doing, Merlin used certain words in his spell. He gave me freedom to choose. His Fae magic, the only thing that can contour a god's, gives me the power to *choose* to do this."

Atrox watched in satisfaction as the god's eyes, full of fear, tried to beg for mercy. "This is for Deasa," he whispered coldly.

"You...will...pay..."

Atrox laughed, his thunderous bark echoing all around them. Then he lifted his free hand and conjured a flower. It had white petals with black edges and a burgundy center. Its leaves glowed silver, the stem a stark black.

"It...cannot...be!" Vulper's eyes nearly bulged out of their sockets. The tiny contraption, which he guessed Atrox must have stolen from the underworld, would not affect him due to his connection to that realm. Despite the fact he no longer had access to it, Atrox was immune. Not a god, per se, to be affected by the silly plant.

"The flower of the underworld...Yes, it truly is," Atrox confirmed his suspicions. "As for me paying? I am truly sorry to dash your hopes, *god*," his fingers constricted, "but I will not. Because after this, I shed myself of my immortality as a god, and embrace the life of a nomad demon lord. My immortality, my life, given in exchange for yours. The Cardinal Rule stands, brethren. It is something I can *choose*."

Vulper realized he was truly screwed. If Atrox shed his immortality, then that was a godly life given in exchange for another. The Cardinal Rule would be fulfilled, its price paid, and no one would be the wiser, because the demon lord would no longer exist. Instead, he would be a new version of himself, as though reborn.

Noticing the hope die out of Vulper's eyes, Atrox grinned. "Finally." He lifted the flower and brought it between them. Murmuring ancient words of the deity language, the plant dissolved into pure silver dust.

Inhaling deeply, Atrox blew it towards Vulper, watching as the dust scattered all over him and got absorbed into the skin. His tanned hue became an ashen grey, the brightness of the hair dimmed, the eyes dulled.

"Please..." Vulper whispered one last time.

Atrox, now satisfied the god had been turned mortal, only clenched his jaw. Then he squeezed the throat until the god expired. Atrox sighed in satisfaction. He let go, and the man dissolved into dust.

Atrox then stood straight, his chest jutting out in defiance and pride. He conjured a knife made out of the only silver that could harm divinities, and cut into his palm.

Drops of blood spattered into the nothingness, even as he declared, "I purge myself of my deeds, and cleanse myself of my sins. I leave this immortality behind, my name and my identity."

A mist rose, shapeless, opposing Atrox. The demon lord watched it, unafraid. He opened his arms wide, and the energy passed through him. He shuddered at the coldness gripping him, then it was gone. The deed was done and sealed.

Atrox turned back into his wolf shape and hopped into another portal. A new life was beginning for him. Now that vengeance had been achieved, he could perhaps find what had truly eluded him all along.

* * *

In the cottage in the woods, Morgana screamed. She was on the bed, feet wide apart, hair plastered to her face in sweat. Her baby, hers and Merlin, was on the verge of being born.

Outside, a storm brewed, furiously hitting against the walls, nature itself at war. The skies opened and down poured thick balls of ice. The sound alone made her jump, then Morgana laughed maniacally.

"It is too late! You will not stop this baby being born. No one will!"

With one last pained shout, she pushed and fell back onto the pillows.

A cry resounded when the baby took his first breaths, and nature stilled. Even the forces of good knew when they had lost the battle – but not the war.

Outside, the moon was covered by clouds, darkness taking away the last remnants of light.

* * *

On the same night, at the exact same time, another woman was giving birth in the kingdom of Elsior.

Vevila had her husband Adrien by her side, holding her hand as she pushed, a handmaiden helping her.

"You are almost there, my lady!" she encouraged.

Vevila gathered her strength and, gripping Adrien's palm in hers, pushed one more time. Amidst her own shouts of pain, a baby's scream echoed.

"Is it a boy?" Vevila asked.

"A beautiful girl," Adrien smiled tenderly as he took the little bundle the nursemaid gave him. He looked upon his daughter's beautiful green eyes, besotted already.

Outside, a comet passed by, illuminating the somber sky with its light.

"That is a good sign, my lady," the nursemaid said.

Vevila grinned at her husband, then her daughter. "I know. It is an omen of a powerful destiny."

End of Part I

PART II

LOVE

CHAPTER 11

The boy was walking back to the cottage, putting one foot in front of the other, when a noise jerked him to a stop.

Though young – no more than nine years of age – his hazel brown eyes shone with intelligence and wisdom, and his gentle demeanor had long gotten him good graces amongst the village people.

Arthur did not consider himself special, simply someone who tried to help as much as possible.

He had been on the way back from the manor, where he had helped Sir Ector, the town's patron, by sparring with his son. The elder man was a lord in the surroundings, and had taken a liking to Arthur. He let him learn sword fighting alongside his heir, though Ken was no fan of Arthur.

Arthur frowned, recalling the other boy's derogatory comments, accusing him of being inferior and his parents of being akin to slaves. With a shake of the head, he forced such rudeness out of his mind and instead tried to concentrate on the noise.

He turned his head, realizing it was coming from the forest at the border of the village line. His feet hesitated – the last time he had gone in, his mother had been very upset, cursing about superstitions and demons hidden within.

Despite the fading light, it did not seem dangerous at all. The trees leaned apart ever so slightly, as though inviting him in. Soft, wilderness sounds echoed around – and then were disrupted once more.

It was the pitiful whine that snapped Arthur out of the daze. Before his mind caught up with the action, he was already running towards the forest.

When he entered, laughter could be heard – the snide, human type. His eyes, quickly adjusting to the darkness, met the surprised stares of two older boys. They were friends of Ken's, and much stronger than him physically.

Behind them was a small dog, limping on a paw. By all appearances, they had decided to torture the poor beast.

"Why do you feel the need to inflict pain?" Arthur asked directly, looking between the two.

"Get out of here, squirt," one of the boys ordered. "This doesn't concern you."

Arthur shook his head determinately. "I am not leaving. But you should."

The poor creature lifted its face towards Arthur, hope shining within the haunted eyes.

"Last warning, squirt," the boy warned, moving closer.

Arthur stood his ground, balling his fists up in response.

When the boy moved to attack, Arthur ducked under his

arm and jabbed him in the side of the jaw with his fist, like Ken's trainer had taught him.

The boy went on his knees, and his friend rushed to help. With an awed – and slightly fearful – look to Arthur, they took off. Evidently, they had not expected a real fight and were cowards in front of the strength displayed.

Arthur stepped towards the dog, whose tails wagged ever so slowly. Unable to stand, the animal could only stare in silent pleading.

"You poor creature," he whispered. "I wish there was some way I could heal you."

"Perhaps I can help."

Arthur turned to see a man contour a tree, then cautiously approach. He was old and young at the same time, with blue eyes that sparkled with an odd light and shaggy dark hair with a violent hue.

He wore simple clothing, and a cape draped over his shoulders. A curved staff was in his hand, but the stranger did not seem as though he needed to lean on it. Despite the semi-youthful appearance, Arthur noticed lines around his eyes and mouth, similar to what he was used to seeing in his own father.

"Who are you?" Arthur enquired, having learned from his parents not to trust unknown people.

"My name is Merlin," the man declared with a smile. He knelt next to the dog and passed a hand over its broken limb, quickly healing it.

Arthur watched in surprise as light escaped the man's hands. It was a soft golden glow, and it surrounded the animal in swirling wisps. The young boy did not turn away in fear, as most would have. He had heard of magic, but had not witnessed it to this day.

Exalted at what he witnessed, he stepped closer, not wary in the least. Aside from his sharp curiosity, something about the man inspired trust.

When the dog was able to stand, he walked over to Arthur and sniffed his feet, wagging his tail furiously.

"His name is Cavall, and he belongs to you," Merlin announced.

"How do you know the dog's name?" Arthur asked.

"All creatures have a name, and if you listen carefully enough, you can hear it on the wind, in the water, in the sky itself."

As Arthur endearingly – but confusingly – tilted his head to the side, Merlin chuckled. "Do forgive an old man for his poetic side. I fear my long voyage has brought out the worst in me."

Arthur bent down to pet Cavall, not once taking his eyes off the wizard. "What brought you here?" he pressed.

"You have, Arthur," Merlin admitted. "I am here to teach you and be your mentor."

"But I am only a peasant," the child protested. "I am not allowed such things, and my parents have no money."

"There is no price for the knowledge I can impart on you. I do so willingly and without expecting anything in return."

Arthur sized up the man, then nodded solemnly in agreement. Merlin had to smile at the serious expression, so odd in someone of his age. His young protégé had grown in the years he had been away.

As they walked out of the forest, Cavall trailing behind, Arthur gave Merlin an account of his sword training to that point. His nonstop chatter gave the warlock plenty of time to observe and notice the changes in him – qualities that already spoke to the leader Arthur would become.

The boy was eloquent and carried himself with a grace few men, let alone children, possessed. He spoke well, but not full of himself, and listened attentively to anything Merlin added. Every now and then, he would stoop down and pet Cavall, who was already enamored of his master.

Though Arthur was still a young boy in age, already his body was developing. The sword fighting had kept him in shape, causing his shoulders to broaden and his arm muscles to expand. He was not buff by any means, but an outline of the man he would become could already be envisioned.

After a rather long talk, they ended up at the cottage where Arthur resided.

"Would you please get your parents for me?" Merlin enquired politely.

After a slight hesitation, Arthur nodded and went inside with Cavall.

The wizard could hear the parents' exclamations of surprise at the dog that appeared, then their murmurs of agreement. Love surrounded the place, and he was satisfied with the choice he had made long ago.

When the old man and his wife stepped outside, Merlin saw the wariness on their faces be replaced by sadness as they recognized him.

"I am not here to take him away," he reassured them in a low voice. "I simply want to guide him, to help in things which you may not."

"Is he magical?" was the first thing the mother asked.

Merlin shook his head, remembering Atrox's words from long ago. "No, he is not. At least not like me. Arthur has a magic of his own, an innocence and wisdom that make up who he is."

He paused, trying to choose his words, then revealed, "Eventually, I will have to take him away and bring him to Camelot where he belongs."

The elderly couple shared a look, then nodded in resignation.

"There is not much we can say," the father admitted. "You can come and train him as you please. All we ask in return is you try to give us more time with him."

"I will do my best," Merlin lied, already knowing the years they had left with Arthur were counted.

When they returned back inside the home, Merlin walked away. Once he was far enough, he stepped off the road and back into the forest. His search began anew to find a spot he could call home for the next few years.

* * *

Inside her cottage in the woods, Morgana got up from the bed where she and Mordred slept. She had lived with little for so long, using magic to get what they need, that her years of living as a princess were long gone from her mind.

As soon as Mordred had been old enough, she had left the meager place where he had been born and traveled a long way to find something further, and better hidden. Supernatural barriers protected the tiny house in the middle of a forest, at the head of a triangle whose base formed a direct line between Elsior and Camelot.

There, in her little haven of peace, Morgana had set about

giving Mordred what she could. In order to truly showcase to him the errors of his father, she knew they had to live with little. Having nothing would spur the young boy to want more and build his character. It would strengthen him against the weakness that love could be.

Even more important, it would fuel the hate for Merlin. And that, Morgana wanted most of all. For she had sworn long ago that she would cause the warlock pain, and this was the one way she could – for now. Until Merlin loved again. And then, the sorceress planned to truly hurt him.

In the midst of the night, as she blinked at the darkness that was now her friend, Morgana was wide awake. A nagging sensation pushed her on to the basin of water, to search for *him*.

It had been years since Morgana had set eyes on Merlin, and she felt no regrets at hiding Mordred's existence from him. She glanced at the sleeping boy, smiling at the treasure she had and which her former lover would never touch.

Mordred was more like her, already. His black hair and features were mirrors of Morgana's, giving him a faintly Fae look with the translucent skin. His body was growing, already showing bursts of magic. Only his eyes, now closed, reminded her of Merlin each and every day – but it was an agony worth having.

As Morgana passed a hand above the basin, it caused waves to roll over, then smoothed until it was limpid. There, she could see Merlin speak with a young boy, a dog trailing behind. She frowned and tried to probe the child's aura, but found she could not.

"What secrets are you hiding now?" Morgana murmured

hoarsely. "What else have you figured out how to do, Merlin?"

The sorceress knew their powers were a match, and this simple quest should have been easy. The fact it was not was a hint as to the significance of the newcomer.

Morgana peered closer and something struck her as familiar about the boy, though she could not put her finger on it.

"Mama?"

She turned to see Mordred by her side, rubbing his blue eyes sleepily. "Who is that?" he yawned, pointing at the basin.

Morgana looked at the image, her heart clenching once painfully as it settled on Merlin's face. Gritting her teeth in pure refusal to feel, she pushed the emotion aside.

"Your father, darling. Would you like to see him closer?"

When Mordred nodded eagerly, Morgana lifted him up in her arms. All she had told him – for now – was that Merlin had shunned them and did not want them. It was enough for the child to understand, but he still desperately wanted his father nearby.

Morgana knew that in the future, once he grew into a teenager, he would be less forgiving. And then, she could reveal more about what exactly Merlin had done to hurt her, and Mordred, and how he had failed them both. For now, she would simply be satisfied with slowly breaking down the hero image he had of Merlin.

With a faint smirk, Morgana brought Mordred nearer the basin. He glanced within, then made a sound of discontent. He followed it by passing his small hand over the water. There was a zap in the air like electricity and the water froze, then the image zoomed in. As Mordred removed his hand, the liquid rippled, and Merlin's face now took the entire space.

"Why is he not here?" Mordred asked softly.

When Morgana did not answer right away, he looked up into her eyes, noticing the tears within. He lifted his hand to her cheek, "Mama, don't cry."

"Your father is not here because he hates us," Morgana whispered back, kissing his forehead when she saw his face fall. "But do not worry, darling, one day in the future he will pay for what he did."

"But mama, what did he do?"

Morgana glanced down at the precious treasure in her arms, and the tears disappeared as though by miracle. "He took everything from us."

At his slight frown, the sorceress squeezed Mordred tighter. "You are too young for this, my son. When you are older, I will tell you everything."

"Promise?" he yawned, already sleepy.

"I promise," Morgana vowed, embracing him gently.

Then she stepped away from the basin and rocked her toddler to sleep, before closing her eyes as well.

One day, Merlin, vengeance will be mine.

* * *

The demon lord was busy stalking his prey – a grizzly. He had chosen for this earthly encounter the body of a massive black dog, knowing it would withstand against any predator. It had been years since he had stepped foot on Earth, but the land and its inhabitants had not changed. In a way, he was grateful for the familiar surroundings.

The bear was still far away, and he enjoyed the chase, taking his time, feeling the relish that the meat would soon be his.

Once, he had gone by the name of Atrox, but since leaving the Earth last, he had shed his identity, regrets, and all that tied him. Now, he was no more than a beast with certain abilities, forever searching to belong.

And to think, eons ago, I was a powerful deity... The dog snorted, disgusted at the nostalgia filling him. It was not worthy of him, not when his goal was to wreak havoc on Earth... Supposedly. His job description was not as clear anymore, since he had been shunned from the underworld, as well.

It was the singing he heard first. The voice was young, soft – a child. The demon would have ignored it, but then he felt a deep pull within his soul. Before he realized what he was doing, he stepped towards the noise. He reached a small meadow and kept to the shadows of the bushes.

The voice grew clearer, and then *she* stepped in. The girl could not have been more than four years old, with long dark hair and huge green eyes. She seemed so frail, delicate even for a human, but there was an unbidden strength in her eyes.

As he watched in surprise, the demon lord saw her twirl one hand graciously and a butterfly appeared nearby. His eyes widened. *The child is magical!*

The dog probed in her mind, as open as a book, and the name floated easily enough. *Vivienne.* She was a princess in the close realm of Elsior, only daughter to the king. More than what appeared hid beneath the soft exterior.

Even more importantly... *Yes, that is definitely light magic I feel.* He peered at Vivienne through his own unearthly senses, astounded at the discovery. Her aura shined brighter than any sun's. The demon lord, for the first time since he had been exiled, felt a warmth enter his chest.

It was not magic, but a sensation as though he was pulled into her orbit, finally belonging. *This cannot be...* The dog tried to deny it, despite the apparent truth of the situation.

Then a growl echoed, and he realized they were not alone. The grizzly had heard the young child, too. And he was now entering the meadow, muzzle turned upwards, catching her scent. Vivienne stopped her song and turned to the bear in amazement.

Yet she did not scream or run, rather stared in surprise, as though transfixed. The demon lord did not hesitate. When the grizzly charged at her, he jumped out of his hiding spot and lunged for him, a ferocious snarl tearing through his throat.

He landed between the animal and the young princess, body tensed protectively. The grizzly took one look at the massive dog, his defensive stance in front of the prey, and turned away, disinterested.

The demon lord ensured he was gone, then turned to meet Vivienne's eyes. She stared back and as their gazes locked, he felt a click. Something within him snapped into place, as audible as a chain around his neck. It did not feel restraining, but incredibly right.

One thing was sure in his mind: leaving Vivienne was no longer an option.

The young girl smiled and held a hand out to him. Like a tame kitten, the large dog pressed closer, bowing his head and snorting softly.

"Cute doggie," Vivienne giggled. "You are mine now."

Truer words have never been spoken.

* * *

The palace was in uproar when the princess brought home a huge dog that was more the size of a small bear than of an actual pet. More than one man tried to take him away, afraid for Vivienne, but they met the flame of his eyes and cowered away.

Even as men as strong as tree trunks neared him, warily, the princess alone was able to hold him back.

One such daring valet tried to grab the demon lord from behind. The beast had him on his back before he could get closer, his ferocious jaw inches from the man's face. The poor servant gulped in fear, but already Vivienne was tugging on the dog's ear.

"No, puppy," she spoke softly. "They are all friends. Leave them."

With an almost annoyed look, the dog turned away and let Vivienne scratch behind his ears. He could not understand this sudden urge to protect her, to be by her side, but he was powerless to fight against it.

The castle staff watched in awe as Vivienne, with her new pet trailing close behind, walked into the throne room. Her father, King Adrien, stopped mid-meeting with his advisors and stared at the beast.

"Vivienne…" Adrien held out his hand, afraid for her safety. "Step away."

"But father," Vivienne pouted, "he is my friend. I found him outside by the forest and he saved me from a bear."

At the magical words, the king waved everyone away. Then, he stepped towards the large beast, eyeing him warily.

When Adrien gave Vivienne an imperious stare, willing

her to move away, she shook her head stubbornly. "He has no home," she whispered.

The demon lord threw her a shocked look. *How could she have known?*

Adrien's jaw nearly hit the floor at his daughter's statement, but he caught himself in time. Of course, he knew Vivienne had his deceased wife Vevila's powers, but it was not something he was particularly well equipped to handle, seeing as he had no magic of his own.

"And, err, how do you know this?" he asked, scratching the back of his head in puzzlement.

"I feel it," Vivienne murmured, lifting a hand to her heart to illustrate her meaning. As her bottom lip quivered, Adrien had to look away.

The king's shrewd eyes sized up the massive dog. If he had seen him from afar, he would have easily hunted him down, believing he was a bear. Yet there was intelligence visible in the beast's eyes, not an animal trait one saw often. As it held his stare, red flames danced in the dark pupils.

"You are no normal dog," Adrien declared warily. "What do you wish with my daughter?"

The demon lord assessed the king, almost tempted to tear him to shreds. He was stopped by the newfound goodness filling him, a bitter taste in his mouth. The young princess' light was already causing changes within – for better or worse. With a mental sigh, he projected his voice in Adrien's mind.

I wish Vivienne no harm, only protection and guidance with her abilities.

The king narrowed his eyes at the words. "How do you know what she can do?"

Your daughter was dancing through the forest, alone and without a guard, waving her magic freely. Anyone could have seen, anyone could have acted. The dog let the words sink in, before continuing, *I truly mean her no harm. She is too pure, and I want to protect her.*

Adrian hesitated, debating on what he knew of magical beings – which was not much. But did he have a choice, in the end? Someone had to instruct Vivienne, as he did not intend for her to grow up unable to control the wonderful gift she had been born with.

In the end, it was for Vevila's sake that he agreed. "Very well. She is yours to protect."

The dog inclined his head, and the princess jumped around his neck, hugging him fiercely. She had not fully understood what happened, but the fact her father accepted the animal was enough for her.

"Come, I can show you my castle!"

And like a bouncing ball of energy, Vivienne was out the door. With an almost irritated look to Adrien, the dog followed close behind.

"Sire," a servant came to the king within moments of their departure, "we can wait until the princess is asleep, then tear him from her side. She will not know."

Adrien turned cold eyes to the man. "That dog will not be touched, by you or anyone else, upon pain of death. Spread the word – he is under my protection."

The servant gaped, but nodded and fearfully scurried away. The king turned back to his daughter's disappearing shape and the new companion trailing behind.

He is under my protection, as she is under his.

CHAPTER 12

"What is it you wish me to do?" Arthur asked again, staring at their surroundings with a doubtful expression.

Merlin had brought him to a courtyard where a sword stood embedded in stone. It did not appear like much from afar. All Arthur could see was the tip of the pommel and the beat up old stone.

"When the old king Uther died," Merlin started, ignoring the question, "he did not leave behind an heir. As a result, everyone fought over the land. One day, this sword appeared along with an engraving. It says that only the person worthy to be the next king will be able to pull it out of the stone."

Arthur glanced up at his mentor in shock. "You're not saying –"

"Look, a newcomer!" someone yelled from close by, and it was enough for the crowd gathered around the stone to turn.

They all assessed the young man eagerly, even as he

inched closer to Merlin, slightly afraid. The wizard merely gazed back calmly.

Arthur was now grown, with long hair reaching just under the chin in brown waves. His eyes were gentle and his frame broad. Merlin, by his side, could have been an older brother, if not for the difference in their eyes. People avoided his piercing look, but they seemed drawn to Arthur.

Best this way, the mage mused.

"Pull the blade out," Merlin finally ordered, pointing to the boulder.

Arthur looked down to Cavall, always faithfully by his side. "He's joking, right?" The dog, as though understanding the question, snorted in response.

With a shake of the head, Arthur shrugged and went to stand in line. Ahead of him, three other men tried to yank the metal out, but nothing happened.

I will fail, like all of them, the young man thought wryly.

Nonetheless, when it was his turn, Arthur stepped closer. The boulder the sword was buried in reached his hip, and it was of a dull gray color, beaten by the elements. At its base stood the engraving naming the person that took it out the next king of Britain. The letters were misshapen, almost blurry, but the meaning was very clear.

Arthur lifted a hand towards the hilt of the sword, then hesitated. The pommel was long, longer almost than his own grip, and wrapped in leather. What he could see of the blade shone in the sunlight of a cold steel.

"Get on with it!" someone from the crowd yelled.

Arthur glanced up, looking at the weatherworn faces – some hoping he would be the one, others wishing he was not –

then he gripped the handle of the sword, and yanked. At first, it did not budge, but on his second try, it smoothly slid out, scraping the stone.

Gasps were heard all around and Arthur himself gaped at his hand, before turning startled eyes to meet Merlin's knowing stare. The warlock had left one part out of the story: that it had been him who had enchanted the sword and created the engraving at the bottom of the stone.

* * *

Arthur looked around in wonder, taking in the opulent throne room, the stuffy chairs, the tables full of food. And around the tables, every pair of eyes was set onto him, a young fifteen year old – a would-be king.

When Merlin had first told him, a year earlier, the young Arthur could not believe it. "I am a simple boy," he had maintained, even when the mage explained to him about Uther and his true lineage.

Mere hours after pulling the sword from the stone, Merlin had divulged the full story. How, after Uther died, the country had fallen into chaos, and something was needed to put them all in line.

How due to his magical abilities, he had asked the elements for help; how nature had responded by taking the sword and keeping it prisoner. It was Uther's sword, Merlin explained, and only the next true king of the country could get it.

Apparently, the nobles believed the tale as well. Within days of him acquiring the sword, Arthur was back in his father's old castle, once again filled with joy and people.

It had previously been held in trust by a group of

chieftains Uther had ruled over, and now they were deferring to the new king. Though Arthur would not be crowned yet – he had to undergo training first, until he was of age – it was evident everyone was relieved to have a symbol again.

The young fifteen year old looked around at the advisors and knights, all of whom expected him to lead them now that he had the magical weapon.

"They are here for you, sire, to help you going forward," Merlin stated at his side.

Arthur looked to him in panic. "Why do you speak as though you are leaving me?"

"I am not, never," Merlin assured. "However, in order for you to be the king you are meant to be, it is time for me to step back. I will always be here, in the background. But you now have advisors who will come to you and an entourage. Plus, your faithful Cavall."

"I am too young for this," Arthur whispered.

"It is precisely because you acknowledge that, and have the wisdom to see the truth, that you will be such a great leader, Arthur," Merlin beamed.

He watched as, for the next hours, the young boy slowly gained in confidence and charmed each and every noble, who in turn swore oaths of allegiance to him.

Merlin then pulled him aside. "I will be gone for a few months, but will return. If you have need of me, simply say my name out loud and I will come."

Arthur nodded bravely, then hugged him tightly. "You have been a great mentor, Merlin. Please be safe, I still require your wise counsel."

Merlin grinned as he pulled away, and then he was gone.

Moments later, one of the nobles stood and asked for a toast. After they all saluted to the health of the new leader, the man asked, "What would you like us to do, as one of your first actions?"

Arthur looked around, taking in all the different types of people: nobles, and peasants, and knights. Then, he spoke from the heart, "I would like to build a round table. If you are all equal, then there should be no head of table, like before."

The man seemed surprised, but as the elders nodded at the wisdom of the request, he inclined his head. "It shall be done."

Arthur grinned, then bade his leave for the night to take occupancy of Uther's old bedroom – the man he had never known.

As he turned one of the corners of a hall, he almost ran into a young woman.

Glad to see someone his own age, he blurted, "I'm Arthur," to the brunette and gentle-eyed girl.

"Elaine," she curtsied with a shy smile.

Arthur immediately liked her sparkling blue eyes and felt an odd protective urge. He was about to speak more, if only to hear the lovely sound of her voice, when someone interrupted them.

"Sire?"

Arthur turned to see the same handsome noble who had spoken with a younger boy by his side. He was also the same age as Arthur, and the two assessed each other curiously.

"I am Sir Wright, and this is my son, Lancelot."

Arthur shook Lancelot's hand, grinning at the powerful grip. "Would you care to train together, sometime?"

"The pleasure would be mine, sire," Lancelot beamed.

Sir Wright watched pleasantly as the two boys chatted, with Elaine dropping a word in here and there. When it was time to depart, he addressed Arthur respectfully.

"We live in Elsior for the most part," Sir Wright continued, "but if you ever need our services, you have but to call."

Arthur nodded, satisfied he had already met two prospective friends. "I shall."

This may not be so bad!

* * *

Six months later, Merlin was traveling, forever on the move and running from the past, when he entered the realm of Elsior. As though meant to be, he heard rumors of the young princess Vivienne's gifts. Unbidden, his feet took him to the palace, where he was brought to Vivienne.

Green eyes stared at him quizzically in a heart shaped face, with long locks of raven hair framing it. It was the intelligence visible in her stance that stunned Merlin into silence.

"What is it you seek?" Vivienne asked in a voice tinkling with innocence.

Pushed by invisible threads, Merlin knelt in front of the young princess. "To teach you that which is yet unknown to you: magic."

Vivienne stared at the stranger for a few moments in silence, tilting her head to the side.

"Will you ever betray me?" she asked.

"Never, Vivienne."

She continued her unwavering observation for a beat, then a large smile illuminated her features. "Then you shall teach me."

A faint grin played on Merlin's lips as well. The child's radiance was not lost on the warlock, who was already thinking of the young boy that could grow attached to her.

A shadow moved out of the corner of his eye and Merlin stood up, ready to protect the young princess, his hand raised with magic.

Instead of danger, the wizard was faced with none other than the largest dog he had ever seen.

"Put that away!" Vivienne demanded sternly. "You could hurt Alistair."

Merlin choked on the name, even as he stared in shock at the beast – whose midnight eyes were very much recognizable.

So. We meet again, the latter stated, none too welcomingly.

Merlin looked between Vivienne and Alistair, then enquired aloud, "Princess, this animal is not to be trusted lightly."

The green eyes meeting his were not those of a child, and neither were the words. "His soul wishes me no harm, and neither does his body. Alistair is my defender. If you wish to mentor me, you shall have to accept him."

Merlin stared at the young girl, trying to read past her aura. He saw, for a flicker of a second, different lights, different faces overlapping each other. Then, all that surrounded her was the golden light.

"Very well," he agreed, still uncertain as to what he had observed.

The princess beamed at him, and her smile lit his hardened heart.

* * *

It was only later in the night that Alistair found the wizard at the stables.

Merlin.

"Demon lord. Again, we meet."

When Alistair was quiet, Merlin scowled. "Care to explain your change of appearance and name?"

Not particularly.

When the half-Fae merely stared back in annoyance, Alistair sighed, *If I must… In order to move on, I had to shed a lot of who I used to be.*

"And how exactly did you come across this young prodigy?"

The same way you did. I sensed her magic, and it pulled me in.

Merlin hesitated, before voicing what he truly feared. "I am afraid, much like it attracted you and me, that it will bring others…"

Like your former lover, Morgana?

"And your old pantheon."

It will take them time to find me, and once they do, I will ensure they stay away from Vivienne. The Secondary Rule prevents them from intervening with her fate and, after all, they are sticklers for the rules…

"Unlike you," Merlin pointed out.

Alistair snorted, then fixated his glare on the magician. *What you did with Morgana is not the end. Those acts still have consequences, to this day.*

Merlin shoulders slumped slightly, as wariness crept over him. "I am aware. I sensed her eyes on me, which is why I kept my distance of Arthur in the past few months."

I do not want Morgana's focus on Vivienne. Tell me why you want to teach her – the truth – and then we can speak.

Merlin hesitated – to what extent could he trust Alistair, especially considering his past and the corruption that had haunted him?

"I had a vision of Vivienne playing a large part to protect Arthur. And the world."

Alistair squinted at him, trying to see past any deception. In the end, he inclined his head. *Very well. You may impart on her your knowledge, gods know you will teach her better than I could. But you cannot live at the castle as the king suggested,* he rumbled.

"I am aware. I have spent the last hours masking my presence here to ensure she does not find it. Morgana must not find out about the child. She will not from me, I swear to you."

The dog looked at him sharply, sensing the unspoken emotion the mage was trying to keep under wraps. *You still care for her?*

Merlin remained silent, looking away.

You best be ready for action if she ever comes near Vivienne. I let you once finish it, and you failed. This time, I will not hesitate to take Morgana out if she lands on my path.

"You have nothing to fear," Merlin vowed, eyes ablaze with indignation. "Vivienne will be safe with me."

Do not get ideas of using or manipulating her, either, Alistair warned with a growl.

"She has a great destiny awaiting."

Yes. And the fates are the best qualified to handle it, not you.

That night, they came to an unspoken truce for the sake of the princess. And Merlin found a cave within the woods, which gave him the tranquility needed to keep an eye on Arthur through his visions, and to train Vivienne when needed.

* * *

In the following years, Merlin went back and forth between Vivienne and Arthur, dispensing magical learning to one, and advice to the other. In that time, Arthur was crowned king, and Vivienne grew each passing day.

Vivienne was ten years old when her grandfather, the old king Mihail, was on his dying bed. King Adrien brought his daughter up to the man's room to speak to him one last time.

Thus, she was there when Mihail pulled Adrien close, whispering with his last breath, "You have another heir – a male, son from the kitchen maid."

Shocked beyond words, Adrien called Merlin and commanded him to find this son he had not been aware of.

It took Merlin less than a day to find the decrepit cottage where a young woman with her young teenage infant lived. The boy was only a few years older than Vivienne, but the darkness surrounding him touched Merlin before he even stepped into the house.

In the middle of the night, the boy was curled up in front of a fire, the mother on the bed. The house itself was a mess – no food to be seen, garbage everywhere.

As Merlin looked around, he felt a trance coming, and slipped in.

The young boy was grown, in his twenties. His heart was full of hate, rancor. He found his father and sister, and battled her. Vivienne fought back, but the male heir had much anger in him, and the magical potential within him that had been untapped rose to the surface, destroying everything – and everyone.

Merlin came to, noticing the child was now awake, wide eyed and watching him. The mage was now faced with a choice and he had to find a solution.

He could make him forget, but that alone would not save Vivienne. If he was aware of the energy within, it would be even worse, unless…

"Shh," Merlin lifted an index to his lips, motioning for the boy to be quiet. "What is your name?"

Hollow eyes stared back, unfeeling, and the magician sensed a shiver creep up his spine. When he spoke, it was soft and devoid of emotion.

"Carleigh. What's yours?"

"My name is Merlin," the wizard revealed, "and I am here to grant you a gift. You are a special boy, do you know that?"

"My mum says I'm evil," Carleigh mumbled.

Shocked at the admission, Merlin questioned, "Why would she say such a thing?"

The words tumbled past his lips in a torrent, as though they had been held back for much too long. "Because she's evil too, and the devil's powers don't let her be. The pastor said so, at the church we go to. We're both evil, and there is no salvation."

The lifeless tone of the boy got to Merlin, as did the words. Niell had once said similar things to him. The memory of those days threatened at bay, and with an effort, he pushed it away.

"No," Merlin denied, "you are not evil. On the contrary.

You are very special, and sometime soon, you will come to me to teach you."

"Teach me what?" Carleigh narrowed his eyes suspiciously.

"Magic," Merlin grinned, and raised his palm. A blue fire appeared, dancing on the palm, forming shapes and sparks.

Carleigh gasped and stepped closer, unable to take his gaze off the orange glow.

"Are you interested?"

"Yes!" Carleigh nodded excitedly, thinking of how such a power could help him beat the kids that always bullied him.

Merlin had expected the answer, and motioned towards him. "Then come here."

Carleigh crawled nearer and the warlock touched his temple, intoning a spell softly. He placed a suggestion in the boy's mind to forget what had just happened, but to come find him within five years' time in order to receive a reward.

In that time, Merlin knew he could instruct the young boy about magic and perhaps take some of it away, in order to protect Vivienne. It would be worth a shot, and at the very least he would know how to control it.

The mage then stood and as the boy fell to the floor, asleep, he stepped to the mother. He touched her mind, implementing a suggestion that Carleigh was the product of a love affair with a womanizer, not the king. He made the woman forget everything in exchange for the pouch of gold he left behind, for them to leave town.

This would ensure that when Carleigh came to seek him, he would leave what little family he had behind, and never go back looking for answers. He also implemented a suggestion that the boy was special, and not to be told he was evil any longer.

Just because I suffered all my young years, does not mean he should. If there was one small thing Merlin could do, it was to help Carleigh grow up with at least some semblance of love.

Satisfied with the solution, Merlin left the house and returned to Elsior empty-handed. To Adrien, he deplored he could not find anything, and that the boy must have been lost.

When Vivienne came to ask Merlin about her brother, the wizard ensured Alistair was not around and touched her mind. With a wish of the senses, he ensured the princess also forgot what she had witnessed the grandfather say.

Merlin had plans for the young royal Vivienne and nothing would disturb those, least of all a bastard child whose soul was already corrupted with envy and jealousy.

CHAPTER 13

The years passed, and soon Vivienne was fourteen. Her beauty was renowned, her kindness popular, and wisdom fearing.

Merlin took great pleasure in teaching her, and could not help but feel she would be best suited as Arthur's queen. His ruminations on the matter came to a head on the day his romantic matchmaking brought results.

Vivienne was roaming the lands on Shadow, her esteemed stallion, when another horse's neigh caught her attention. She squinted at the newcomer, as the sun seemed to angle on the head of the young man, blinding her.

Then, the horse stepped forward and the stranger's face was visible. He had dark brown hair, gentle hazel eyes, broad shoulders and an easy grin.

"Kind lady," he started in a strong voice, "would you point me to the castle?"

"What brings your near?" Vivienne enquired, assessing him.

As his horse stepped closer, the young girl inside her, not yet a woman, recognized the appeal. The man's charm was easygoing, and a responding smile tugged on her lips.

"My friend Lancelot works there, and I came to see if he was free for a bit of sword playing."

Vivienne bit back a laugh, thinking back to the maiden Lancelot had been with last she had seen him. "You may find him otherwise…occupied," she chuckled.

Arthur stared back at her for a moment, then the meaning dawned on him and he shook his head.

"That would be him, yes," Arthur muttered. "I seem to have wasted my time coming here."

"Not at all, milord," Vivienne entreated, pointing towards her home, "you can still go by the castle. You might want to start your search by the stables."

Arthur nodded, then lifted his hand in goodbye. "Thank you for help. Might I know your name?"

"Vivienne," the princess murmured, and saw his eyes widen as he realized she was the royalty in the place. "At ease, Arthur," she grinned, "I am not offended in the least."

"You knew who I was from the beginning?" he asked, intrigued by this young girl who seemed so much older than her looks implied. Something in the depth of her green eyes held an appeal that echoed within him.

Vivienne felt it the minute Arthur's gaze sized her up, and she took the opportunity to observe him in return. Something was stirring under the surface, and at first she thought it was what all the young girls at the castle chatted about: a crush.

Yet when their gazes locked, she felt no overwhelming attraction, no awareness of the world coming to a stop. The only pull was an odd sensation of wanting to comfort Arthur, as a friend or sister would.

He is not the one for you, came a voice deep within.

Vivienne started at the clarity of the words, so different from her own consciousness. She maintained a calm demeanor and instead replied to Arthur, "Of course. I have heard enough from Lancelot to recognize you, sire."

The king hesitated, as though meaning to say something else, but finished with, "Thank you again, Vivienne."

Wordlessly, she watched as Arthur departed with a salute, his horse carrying him swiftly across the plains of Elsior.

That was interesting, she mused.

Left to her own devices, Vivienne frowned as she analyzed the short encounter.

Something wrong, princess?

Vivienne glanced down to Alistair, whose wise eyes were focused on the horizon where Arthur had disappeared. She had not heard him approach, but that was not new as the companion was constantly around, even when at times he remained invisible.

"Not sure," she admitted honestly. "As I was speaking with Arthur, I heard a voice. It told me...that he was not the one for me."

Alistair tilted his head to the side. *A voice?*

"Yes. I could not place it."

Some things are best let go, princess. If it is important, it will come to you. Deep down, the demon dog held his rage. This type of meddling had his sister written all over it – and

Merlin.

* * *

You have no right! Alistair roared at the moon that same night, expanding his mind until he felt contact, breaching the divine portals until someone answered. *Leave. Vivienne. Alone!*

He was outside the castle, by the lake nearby where he could find peace and quiet and not disturb Vivienne. Within moments of his constant bellowing at the skies, a form shimmered on the waters.

"Who calls on me?" a haughty voice enquired, and the mist took the shape of his sister.

You know who, Ardea, Alistair growled.

"It has been a long time, brother."

Long enough.

"Since Vulper disappeared, in fact..."

Alistair did not rise to the bait, instead switching topics. *Why are you contacting Vivienne?*

"My, my. One could really say that exile from your former pantheon has made you cranky," Ardea laughed. "Have you forgotten your place, demon lord?"

No! Have you?

Ardea smiled mysteriously, as though she knew something he did not. Alistair had trifled with her occasionally in the skies, but never to his liking. The infuriating goddess had too much nerve – noble as she may be compared to others.

What is a goddess such as you doing touching the consciousness of a princess far away from usual roaming lands? Alistair growled.

"I can see why you became her protector, truly. Vivienne

is...special."

And not yours to play with!

Ardea scowled, losing some of her calm countenance. "How dare you! I am a goddess, entitled to –"

Not. With. Vivienne.

"And what can *you* do?" Ardea hissed.

Alistair stepped into the water until his front paws were fully submerged. Then he lifted one limb, clenched the claws in the clear liquid, and yanked towards him.

With a yelp, the goddess found herself in front of the dog, no longer at a safe distance. Alistair moved closer still, enough to touch, his muzzle inches away from her beautiful face. He stared into the bi-colored eyes unflinchingly.

You forgot that by banishing me to the underworld, you gave me access to the one weapon that can destroy you.

Ardea was no fool. She knew her brother was referring to the flower that grew deep within the confines of the underworld, and whose elixir could kill any god.

"You would not dare!" Ardea retorted, but Alistair could see a glint of fear in her expression.

Try me.

"What do you want in exchange for your promise no harm will come to me?" Ardea scowled, glancing down at the water – something he should not have been able to do any longer. "I know the mage helped you, took some of our punishment off. He never should have meddled."

Perhaps. But as half-Fae, Merlin was the only one who could. You and I both remember the war we had with his kin eons ago, and how we were almost all destroyed.

"There were losses on both sides," Ardea admitted with a

shrug, before narrowing her stare. "Your promise, now."

No harm will come to you from me, if you stay away from Vivienne. This means you do not meddle, from close or afar, with her destiny.

Ardea hesitated, then at his burning glare and low growl, nodded. "Agreed. I do not know what, of her, touches you so, brother, but I only wish you had shown this same loyalty to us, your family. Perhaps you would not be in this predicament if you had." With a last irked scoff, she shimmered and disappeared.

Alistair shook his head in disgust, then continued his pacing. Only moments later, he froze as he sniffed another presence. Oddly enough, his brother walked out of the woods.

"I will ensure she does not bother Vivienne anymore," Aequus announced.

And why would you do that? We have our differences. Last time we met, you banned me from the underworld as well.

The god looked around warily, before admitting, "Perhaps. You know that when you were demoted to the underworld, your abilities and possessions passed to us." A pause. "I looked into the Orb of Sight."

Only Vulper had access to it, did he not? Alistair pointed out. What had his siblings been up to? The web he sniffed was much too tangled.

Aequus shrugged. "He did, and since his disappearance…" He threw a side look to Alistair, before continuing, "I find it easier to trespass on his territory. Regardless, the Orb wanted to show me something, and it did."

Alistair tilted his head to the side in question. Objects such as the orb had been created to be used by the gods. If it came to a point where the item itself asked the god to look within, it could not be for a good vision.

"Your charge, Vivienne, holds the weight of the world on her. None of us can intervene as she goes about her destiny. The smallest thing could alter an entire course, and set it awry. However, her essence is pure, her lineage unbroken."

Alistair stared at Aequus in confusion, waiting for more to follow. When nothing did, he snorted.

What am I to make of these riddles?

Aequus frowned, trying to speak clearer. "Your charge has inherited the lightest magic here. But it is not the reason I came."

Then why?

"To warn you. The druid has made a mistake."

Merlin? At the affirmative nod, Alistair snorted. *He has made many. As half-Fae, they tend to make messes that are harder to clean.*

"This is worse. Atrox —"

I no longer go by that name.

Aequus sighed, then started again, "Alistair, then. This mistake, it will be matured at the next solstice."

It?

"The Destroyer."

Alistair stepped closer, but already the man was turning to leave.

You owe me an explanation.

"The Destroyer's fate will affect both Vivienne's, and Arthur's. I have said as much as I can."

No. I need more.

"Speak to Merlin, he will tell you. Ask him about the

young boy he has been tutoring on the side."

Alistair waited until Aequus was gone, his form no longer on the earthly realm. It did not take him long to realize that if his brother had seen fit to deliver the warning in person, then the issue was grave.

Reluctantly, he ran to the mage's cave, paws pounding the ground and getting more anxious with every moment.

"What brings you here?" Merlin greeted him, already waiting outside.

What have you done?

"Done?" the warlock pursed his lips. "I thought we were past accusations, after these last few years."

I have received warning a destroyer will be made at the next solstice, putting Arthur's own fate in danger. Alistair paused. *And Vivienne's.*

Merlin's eyes went blank, even as he tried to understand the words.

Is it one of your tricks gone wrong? Alistair persisted, trying to breach his mind.

"No!" Merlin denied. And yet, as he tried to look past mere actions, realization dawned on him. Just a few months earlier, he had stopped Carleigh's teachings after finding out he was dwelling into the realm of the dark arts.

It had disappointed Merlin immensely, but he could allow such foul actions to continue. Carleigh had left in a rage, the last time they had met. As he recalled the incident, the mage could not help but wince.

Only once had Alistair seen Merlin look so defeated. Once before, years earlier…

Morgana. He uttered the name, and Merlin started. *I never lectured you for not having killed her, nor the child you had with her. But though that will come back to haunt you, this is not related. What* else *have you done!?*

When Merlin only stared vacantly, the former deity lost his patience. With an aggravated grunt, he jumped in the air and landed on Merlin. His claws dug deep within the magician's chest, even as he stared back in shock.

"You would attack me?" he murmured.

For Vivienne's safety, I would tear you apart if it would fix this! Now speak. What or who is the destroyer?

Alistair's growl snapped Merlin out of his musings and he divulged, "King Adrien sent me on a mission to find a child." The warlock kept the facts summarized, without admitting the full truth of Carleigh's parentage. "When I did, the child had magical potential...but he was dark, corrupt. I had a vision that if he did not know how to control it, he would destroy all of Elsior."

Please tell me you did not intervene.

Merlin's eyes closed in despair. "I did. I have been teaching him how to use the magic for the last few months, but he has angled towards the dark arts. I stopped, and—"

Let me clearly resume this, Alistair snarled. *You took in a stray, corrupt child, taught him how to use magic in order to avoid a catastrophe, and instead enabled him on a path of destruction!?*

"I was trying to do right!" Merlin's eyes blazed, even as he futilely attempted to defend himself.

Alistair moved off and the wizard stood to face him.

Then perhaps you should stop! The lecture came tumbling. *This is not the first time your interventions have caused havoc.*

Merlin tried not to react, but the words stung. Too much had gone wrong, in too little time. "I can fix it," he admitted.

It is too late. The child was born with a predestined fate that cannot be avoided.

"Then what can be done? I do not wish Vivienne nor Arthur to pay for my mistake."

We shall both be vigilant, and when this new plague shows, we will help them fight it.

Merlin nodded, before returning into his cave. As he entered it, the demon dog threw one last thought his way.

And stop trying to play matchmaker with Arthur and Vivienne. Their destiny is their own.

* * *

A few days later, in Camelot, Arthur and Lancelot were sparring in the courtyard, away from prying eyes.

The young king had gone to Elsior in person to extend an invitation to his castle, and Lancelot had been only too happy to oblige. Though he was part of lady Vivienne's entourage, he had dreams of being a knight.

As they sparred, Arthur noticed his opponent was quick on his feet and creative in strikes. Lancelot was truly a great adversary, enough so to work up a sweat.

With a last blow, Arthur dropped his sword and extended a hand to the other man. "Good game."

Lancelot grinned and shook it, clapping Arthur on the back in a friendly way. "You too."

His eyes then glanced at something over Arthur's shoulder, and Arthur immediately recognized the look. With a chuckle, he taunted, "Not again! Another conquest?"

"Mayhaps…" Lancelot murmured.

At his quizzical look, Arthur turned to see Elaine waving his way. He returned the gesture, before turning back to Lancelot.

"You know her?"

"Aye," Arthur admitted, clenching his jaw in reflex. Something within him wanted to punch his friend for even looking at Elaine, let alone considering her on his list of conquests. With a deep inhale to calm down, the monarch admitted, "That is Elaine."

"Introduce me," Lancelot demanded.

Stifling a sigh, Arthur led him to Elaine. No sooner were they feet apart, that she threw herself at him, hugging him with all her might. Arthur wrapped both arms around her, burying his head in her neck. For years he had known Elaine, and not once noticed how heavenly she smelled.

"You did good," Elaine whispered in his ear, before pulling away with a wide smile, her blue eyes sparkling.

Despite the fact his arms felt oddly bereft without her in them, Arthur could not help but return the grin. As a second thought, he grasped Elaine's hand in his, enjoying the warmth and soft grip – and ignoring her confused stare.

Arthur did not know what came over him, but something pushed him to make it clear to Lancelot that she was under his protection, and he was not to hurt her.

Since they had met, Elaine had done nothing but be an amazing friend and a great supporter. She was a great listener, always had a soft touch, good advice, and an easygoing attitude.

The young maiden unequivocally brought out the best in

him, and Arthur was truly happy at having her around. Camelot – and him – would not have turned the way it had in her presence. Elaine was truly the most selfless person he knew, and the man who would marry her would be lucky indeed.

A nudge from Lancelot brought Arthur out of his thoughts, and the good mood evaporated. With a brusque nod, he let go of the hand he had been possessively holding, and muttered, "Elaine, this is Lancelot. Lancelot, Elaine."

His friend bowed, then kissed her hand in that charming way of his. It bothered Arthur that Elaine's cheeks became rosy and that her eyes shone of a different light when they settled on Lancelot.

What the hell is wrong with me? Arthur mused darkly.

Muttering something about needing to feed the horse, Arthur stepped aside and let the two talk. He willed himself not to look behind, convinced that Elaine was a smart girl and would not fall for a pretty face.

Of course, he could understand what attracted Lancelot to Elaine. With her long brown hair, sparkling blue eyes and heart-shaped face, she was lovely. He had noticed it... Yes, Arthur had noticed as she grew from the young, scrawny kid he had met only years earlier into a woman with very attractive curves.

Why not claim her as your own?

Arthur ignored the voice of jealousy within. He did not love Elaine, not romantically, and could not hold it against her if she fell in love with Lancelot. After all, it was none of his business if his blonde-haired, blue-eyed friend fancied her. Or if he ended up marrying her. Or if they had loads of blue-eyed babies with brown hair.

A snap made Arthur jump, and he looked down to see he had broken a wooden sword into two. Startled at the outburst, he let go of the two pieces and walked into the stables. Truly, he was in an odd mood.

On the outside, Elaine watched Arthur disappear around the corner, frowning at his rather weird behavior. She turned to Lancelot, contrite.

"I am sorry, I missed that?" she enquired, realizing he had been speaking all along.

Lancelot tilted his head, then glanced to where Arthur had gone, before settling his inquisitive gaze Elaine. The king's demeanor now made sense, and his brow smoothed as realization dawned.

"You are in love with him," he grinned easily.

"What?" the young woman gaped, shocked. "No, that is absolutely not true. I mean –"

"It is no use denying it, Elaine," Lancelot chuckled. "Do not fret, I shall not tell Arthur any of it. He truly is a lucky man."

Elaine blushed, before looking away. "Please do not mention it to Arthur. He does not feel the same way, and it would make our friendship awkward."

Lancelot raised her chin with his finger, looking solemnly in her eyes. "I give you my oath, Arthur will not hear it from me. But as for his feelings, I would not dismiss them so easily. He seemed awfully upset when I asked to meet you."

Elaine could not help it, but her heart soared.

CHAPTER 14

The wind rushed through her hair, the strength of the horse's back between her legs, the breeze in the air lifting her spirits.

King Adrien's daughter enjoyed freedom a little too much on the sunny day, celebrating her twenty-third birthday. Riding astride on her faithful steed, Shadow, satin gown billowing in the wind, she was acutely aware her behavior was entirely un-princess like.

The princess joyously opened her arms, welcoming the wind, while the stallion neighed and kept galloping.

"Lady Vivienne!"

Shouts came from behind, and she glimpsed a group of guards following from far away, evidently trying to catch up. The closest one pushed his horse on, heading for the monarch.

Vivienne chuckled at his disheveled appearance, and threw a mischievous smile his way, emerald green eyes glinting. Shaking her midnight colored hair loose, she bent over the horse, clutching onto the mane, and laughingly commanded, "Run like lightning, Shadow!"

His sturdy muscles bunched under her legs, picking up speed and leaving the knights in the dust. The royal gleefully giggled along, eyes closed in delight.

* * *

"You summoned me, father," Vivienne curtsied in front of the old king, then straightened up and beamed at him.

King Adrien could not help returning it, despite the hour spent attempting to calm down the head of the palace guard, and the guards themselves. They had been beyond furious after Vivienne had, once again, run off with her stubborn horse, and had to give up the chase across the vast plains of the realm Elsior.

Vivienne was his only daughter, and after Vevila's death, Adrien's beloved wife, he had raised her freely – perhaps a bit too much. The young princess was so full of life and laughter, he simply could not restrain her, cringing at the thought of imposing limits. And yet, the challenges awaiting her, especially once he was no longer of this world, would be worse for wear without protection.

Thus, much as the king hated to, he had listened to the reports and finally given in. Adrien landed a severe stare on his young daughter, trying to impress the gravity of the situation.

"Yes, dear daughter," he finally acknowledged out loud. "You are driving your guards quite mad, so I have taken the liberty of hiring a new one. He is knighted, and comes highly recommended from various courts across our land, where he has secured his charges to the satisfaction of his employers.

Please, meet Sébastien Dubois."

Vivienne tilted her head in the direction king Adrien was pointing to, but the haughty reply died on her lips when their eyes met. Green met midnight, and the instant connection was impossible to miss. The grand throne hall disappeared, the only thing existing was his unflinching stare.

The new guardian was a bit taller than the royal, with broad shoulders that were intimidating, if not enticing at first. The look was completed with hair as somber as Vivienne's, and eyes of pure onyx, still fixed on her.

Sébastien broke eye contact first, and inched forward. He kept a respectful distance, less than an arm's width, before kneeling at her feet on one knee. "My lady," he began in a deep, hoarse voice, a delicious caress of the senses.

His hand gripped Vivienne's gently, rough pads grazing the skin. When his lips pressed to it in greeting, the princess' knees wobbled. What was it about this man that stirred her to the core, when none had ever managed to before? He had spoken no more than two words, yet she was left without speech.

"Rise," Vivienne rasped, and cleared her throat at the breathless tone, keeping her features as impassable as possible.

Sébastien did as he was bid, and towered over the monarch momentarily, before retreating a few steps. Vivienne tried to ignore the scrumptious new guard, instead glancing back to the king.

"Father, is this truly necessary?"

"Yes, my dear. I appreciate your independence and I do not wish to limit anything from it, but he will be traveling with you during your lessons with your mentor, and anywhere else you wish to go."

"How is it I am supposed to get some time to myself?" Vivienne argued, eyes narrowing.

"You still will... But he has to come everywhere. Please do not push this issue any further, Vivienne."

The princess was about to protest, but the king's tired tone hit her. For the first time discerning it, she frowned at the pallor of his skin, and replied softly. "Father, as you wish," and curtsied again.

She was about to depart, when a shadow emerged from the corner of the throne room and came to her. Everyone present in the throne room gasped at the size of the animal, and Sébastien's hand automatically went to his weapon. When he realized neither the king nor Vivienne were fazed, he remained immobile, observing silently.

The dog, if he could be called such, nuzzled Vivienne's hand, until the royal peered down at him. His head passed her waist, the rest of the body as large as a young bear. The black fur which had permitted him a seamless blend with the shadows, now stood in contrast with the whiteness of the floors.

The dog's eyes traveled to the new guard, whose hand still gripped the sheathed blade. With a dismissive snort, he strode to the king, walking up the stairs to the throne, and set his huge head in the old man's lap. As if preparing to yawn, the massive jaws opened, and a breath came out in puffs of white smoke, which Adrien inhaled.

The king's cheeks regained some color, eyes now glowing with resolution. Vivienne retained a relieved sigh: Alistair, her familiar, had done it again, invigorating Adrien with life essence, when his was failing.

She could not help but glance towards Sébastien – curious at his opinion of all this – to meet his fixed stare. Before even deciding to, the princess stepped forward, back in his vicinity, drawn to the new knight against all odds.

Alistair retreated from the king, and came to his mistress' side. "Thank you," Vivienne murmured to him, before turning to the king. "You should have told me your health was getting worse," she chastised, half reproachful.

"My dear," he extended a hand out, which Vivienne hastened to grip. "You are aware I will not be long for this world. Old age cannot be avoided, which is why I need you safe, at all costs."

She bit back the tears threatening to escape, before nodding. "If it will bring you happiness and ease your burden, then I shall accept this new guard."

Sébastien knew not what happened – whether the monarch's words, kindness or beauty did it – but his next actions stunned even himself.

He unsheathed his sword, and progressed towards Vivienne, as if incited by an invisible hand. Alistair sharpened his gaze on him, but foreseeing the intent, did not intervene. The princess, however, aimed a confused glance towards him.

Clutching the blade, Sébastien kneeled at her feet once more. He uplifted it, on the flat of the palms, and the words escaped his lips with a rushed intensity. "Lady Vivienne, I swear to you on this day my arm and body to protect you. I will let no harm come to you, and will be there to prevent any perils coming your way. Please accept my oath and bless my sword."

Interesting, Alistair rumbled in his mistress' head.

Comfortable with his telepathic messages, she did not react visibly. However, Vivienne could not agree more with the assessment. Sébastien had taken a basic oath of allegiance, and transformed it into the promise of a lifetime of defending.

As she extended a hand to graze the metal, some magic seeped into it, without her actively willing. It gleamed, before being absorbed, the metal shining brighter for a few moments. "I bless it," she declared, "and accept your oath, Sébastien."

Their eyes met again, and this time the guard's stare did not waver. Something passed among them, and Vivienne became aware of a yearning deep within, as if it had woken up after years of lying dormant. She was the one to break contact, curtsey to the king, and saunter away, Alistair following close behind.

"She is stubborn, but will get attuned to you," king Adrien maintained, noticing the guard's rapt expression.

Sébastien absently agreed, still endeavoring to clear his head. He had come to the castle for duty, but upon contemplating his charge, already control over his emotions was slipping.

The oath was not one the knight had ever given, and it weighed upon his soul now that Vivienne was gone. A sweet citrus perfume assailed his senses, lingering in the air. If he was not careful, this assignment might become more complex than intended.

* * *

In her cottage, Morgana glimpsed into the basin anew, noticing Merlin in a banquet hall, surrounded by the new king. Arthur, they called him, as the talk of his goodness had reached even her ears.

Recalling how she had thought him familiar before, the sorceress focused on the image of his face. Something about the way he laughed, carried himself...

It dawned on her like a dam breaking. "You *bastard*!" Morgana yelled to Merlin, well aware he could not hear. In a rage, she went on a rampage around the house, breaking everything.

Mordred returned in the midst of it, to find their house in shambles. "Mother!" Panicked, as he had never seen Morgana in such a frenzy, the young man stepped and grabbed hold of her hand.

Morgana raised pain-filled eyes to his, unfocused, glazed as though she was in a different time and no longer truly present with him.

"Mother," Mordred tried again, softer. "What happened?"

Shaking her head, Morgana refused to answer. Instead, she took a deep breath and sat back near the basin. Mordred followed her, glancing over her shoulder to see his father and a young man by his side.

Before Mordred could ask who it was, Morgana spoke in a venomous tone he had yet to hear her use.

"So this is my dear half-brother you helped conceive, Merlin. The one thanks to whom I lost our child."

Mordred's eyes widened, and then he focused on the man next to Merlin. *My uncle...* Of course, he had heard the story from Morgana growing up. How his father had chosen to play politics and help his grandfather, and how the price had been his unborn brother.

Mordred noticed how Morgana held herself upright, with

a fragile will as though anything else would make her crumble.

The pain of that night, when she had lost her baby, washed anew, and Morgana was decided not to let it go this time. Over the years, she had learned to use it as a fuel, but always kept it at the back of her mind. Now, she held onto it like a talisman and lifted a hand to the basin.

"You are twenty-seven, well of age to find a queen, are you not?" the sorceress addressed Arthur. "So let me find you a proper bride, brother... You will be your father's true son indeed."

* * *

Days later, Arthur was having a banquet with his advisors and Lancelot, whom he had asked to serve at the Round Table with him. He was about to send a message to Merlin to invite him over, when the door to the hall opened.

Talk came to an abrupt stop, and all eyes turned to the cloaked figure entering, mud on its boots. They could not recognize if it was an enemy or ally, but were held in a trance as the stranger approached the king.

"That's close enough," Lancelot warned, his dagger drawn and pointed to the newcomer when it was only a few feet away.

There was a tense silence and everyone held their breaths, waiting to see if an attack would happen. Then the cloak dropped, and Lancelot's dagger lowered.

Arthur's heart stopped beating, only to restart at a faster pace. He half-rose out of his seat, but had to sit back down for fear of falling over.

The young woman standing before them had to be Fae. Nothing else could explain her beauty: long, wavy blonde hair, cascading down her shoulders. A body the envy of the gods, with a waist he could wrap his hands around. Blue, almost violet eyes, shining under long eyelashes. Soft, plump rosebud mouth, made for kissing.

She wore habits of the common people, but nothing could hide her gorgeousness from their eyes. More than one man fell in love, and almost all fell in lust that night. Not a sound could be heard in the entire hall as everyone's eyes were on the three.

"My lord," the lady spoke liltingly, with a slight accent that sounded exotic. Her gaze skimmed past Lancelot, and met Arthur's straight on. "May we speak in private?"

No one thought to object as the king stood and walked to one of the adjacent rooms. The newcomer followed, as did Lancelot.

"Wait," Arthur held onto his friend's hand as he headed into the room. "I will go in alone."

"But sire, what if this is a trick?" Lancelot tried. He wanted to protect Arthur, but more than anything, he currently wished to keep staring at the young lady.

"No!" Arthur said harshly. When Lancelot stepped away, he shook his head. "I apologize, I have no idea what came over me. But I will be fine."

Lancelot stepped outside the doors, merely advising Arthur, "I will be here if you have need of me."

The monarch nodded absentmindedly, his gaze glued to the young woman who was entering the room. He did not notice as Lancelot's eyes latched onto the new arrival, unable to let go as well.

When the door closed behind them, Arthur faced her. He could not help his eyes from roaming her form, but finally forced down his manly instincts and settled on her fine features.

"I am Guinevere," she spoke softly. "My father sent me to beg for help."

* * *

Merlin had entered too late, he could tell by the tense silence in the hall and the uneasy expectation. He noticed Elaine by the doors and headed her way.

Over the years, the young girl Arthur had first met had grown into a beautiful, kind woman, and Merlin was amazed by her grace every day they met. Elaine's parents had died when she was young, leaving her the sole beneficiary of their estate.

While she stayed at Camelot, Elaine also took care of the manor she had inherited, hoping that one day she would go back there to form her own family. But lately, Merlin had noticed her side-glances to Arthur, and sometimes wanted to smack the king for his obvious blindness.

Someday soon, Merlin would have to do something to push the two together, if nothing else. After all, Arthur did need a queen, and who better than Elaine?

Reaching her side, Merlin asked, "What happened?"

A vision had driven him here, but it had been unclear, only a sense of dread – and Morgana's face.

"Arthur is fine," Elaine reassured, sensing his worry. "A beautiful maiden came by, asking for a private audience."

"An audience?" Merlin frowned, and turned his gaze to where everyone else's was. Lancelot was guarding a door, and within the wizard could sense Arthur and another person. Much as he tried, he could not probe past her aura.

I do not like this one bit…

"This maiden," he addressed Elaine, "did she have dark hair and grey eyes?"

Elaine threw him an odd look, before answering, "Nay. Blonde and blue."

Her short tone clued him in that something was amiss. Just as Merlin was about to ask for more, Elaine pointed, "There they are."

Merlin glanced towards the door where Arthur and a young woman exited. He was struck by the girl's beauty, but even more so by Arthur's enamored state. Already, she was smiling, chatting with everyone on their way to the table as though she was their new queen.

Arthur helped her take a seat by his side, Lancelot on her other, before announcing, "We will send a convoy to Guinevere's village. She has travelled far and wide to deliver a message from her father, who fears an attack. I will not let my people be slaughtered when I can offer help."

Guinevere smiled gratefully, and everyone breathed in relief.

Merlin could not make up his mind. He wanted to believe the girl's story, but something about her, the vision he had, the easiness she had with everyone… It did not rest well with him that this Guinevere already had Arthur eating out of the palm of her hand – and the rest of the court, as well.

It seemed the only one who did not was Elaine. Merlin noticed it as he turned to the young maiden, whose pain-filled eyes were glued to Arthur.

"What troubles you?"

"Nothing, Merlin. I only wish Arthur's happiness…"

Elaine murmured.

"As we all do," the mage muttered. Another glance to Guinevere, then, "But something *is* bothering you. Is it this Guinevere?"

Elaine tried to hide it, but the confirmation was in her eyes.

"The way she appeared, if I did not know better, I could swear she is a witch," she elaborated, before pressing a hand to her lips. "I am sorry, Merlin, it was incredibly rude of me to say those words."

"I do not think it was, Elaine, especially seeing as there may be some truth to them. I know you care for Arthur."

"Does everyone?" Elaine glanced away, unwilling to meet his all-knowing scrutiny.

Merlin peered down at her, surprised by the comment, but then noticed her aura showed embarrassment.

"Darling Elaine, those feelings are nothing to be ashamed of." Merlin lifted her chin with his index and looked deep in her eyes. "Believe me, it is something you should be proud of. As for what you mentioned about this Guinevere being a witch... I had a vision that tasked me to come here, and I find this? There is something abnormal about the situation."

Only silence answered as Elaine closed her eyes in a futile attempt to hide the pain in her expression and the depth of her love for the king. Merlin was not fooled in the least, as both emotions radiated off her in waves. With his sensitive Fae senses, he did not even have to probe further.

"Guinevere will be gone soon, Elaine," the warlock tried to reassure. "Arthur does not belong with her, and he will realize it."

"What if he does not?" Elaine questioned softly, and the mage winced at the anguish in her voice.

Damn, Morgana, if your hand is in this…

"Was anyone else with her?" he asked instead.

"Not that we noticed," Elaine answered, before turning away to hide the tears. "Please forgive me, but I need to be alone."

With that, she ran away, and Merlin was left behind trying to make sense of the whole debacle.

CHAPTER 15

There was a knock at the bedroom door. Vivienne jumped off the bed, opened it, and threw herself in his embrace. "I was afraid you were harmed."

Tears of relief escaped from behind closed lashes. Sébastien's arms went around her waist, gathering his beloved close to him and whispering comforting words, promises of a future to come.

Still maintaining his hold, he maneuvered Vivienne back in the room and locked the door behind. In the obscurity, their mouths found each other, hands roamed through clothing, anxious, seeking more.

"We do not have much time," Sébastien withdrew and murmured, darting a swift glance towards the entrance, but Vivienne yanked his mouth back down.

Bodies pressed together, desperate for contact. A touch of skin, breaths quickened, until finally, they landed on the bed.

Vivienne!

The royal opened her eyes, startled from a slumber in the middle of the day. She sat up on the bed to detect Alistair nearby, head tilted questioningly. Interpreting her aura, the jaws opened wide in his version of a doggy grin. *I see your new guardian left a lasting impression.*

Vivienne blushed crimson, before throwing the closest pillow at her protector. Alistair ducked it, barking out a laugh.

* * *

Sébastien had been at the castle for two weeks and it had been an education, to say the least.

First and foremost, he learnt the mentor Vivienne visited most mornings was none other than Merlin, the renowned mage. He had accepted Vivienne as a pupil, and so most mornings, she would wake up and, accompanied by Sébastien and the fair Lancelot, would go to Merlin's to practice magic.

Cue the not so large surprise: Lady Vivienne was no ordinary lady interested in knitting and dancing. Her mother, Vevila, a common born, was a descendant of the Celts, daughter of an influential priestess, Kyna. When Kyna's husband, Vivienne's grandfather, died young, she sent Vevila to live with a distant relative who happened to be working at the castle of King Mihail, in the realm of Elsior.

A happy king, Mihail had one son, Adrien, a frail young man since birth. Vevila, a kind young woman, came into his life like a tornado, and filled him with a newfound vigor. With her, Adrien grew into a robust man, made his father proud, and inspired the people.

It was only natural that when his father got too old, he withdrew from power and Adrien became king, and chose

Vevila as queen. Unfortunately, the young queen died while Vivienne was still in diapers. But from her mother, Vivienne received her skills, which she was learning to use and dominate to safeguard her land from various threats and to perhaps create a proper alliance with the Pendragons line, and its current leader, Arthur.

And lastly, Sébastien was none too bewildered to find out Vivienne's pet was a demon dog, appeared out of nowhere. No one knew his story, only that he became the princess' companion as a child. According to the stories, one day the young Vivienne had gone out – and come back accompanied by the demon dog. He had never left her side since.

All in all, Sébastien was intrigued, but conducted himself as a proper guardian to the lady, knowing full well there could never be anything between them – despite the obvious attraction and deeper sentiments he felt.

What also killed him, however, was Vivienne's overt fondness Lancelot, out of all the other defenders. A player and carefree man, younger by a few years than Sébastien, he was interested in anything with a skirt.

Sébastien had kept quiet on the matter and from what he had detected, there was no intimacy there. But considering the knight was about Vivienne's own age, the new guard could perceive the appeal. Although half-afraid sooner or later he would have to act to secure her heart, in the meantime, he had no choice but to observe and serve.

* * *

Vivienne snuck to the stables before one of the lessons with Merlin, smiling at Shadow as she let him out of the stall. "Let's go for a ride, you and me."

She had barely mounted when Sébastien strode out of the shadows with his own mare, Illyria. "May I join you on your ride, my lady?"

"No, you may not," Vivienne scowled. "I am in the mood for some alone time."

"I apologize, but I cannot allow that."

"Allow?" She leveled a smug look at him. "I can get rid of you with a wave of my hand."

"So why don't you?" Sébastien countered.

Vivienne was left speechless. Clearly, the reason she could not was because her conjuring light was only used for good. The small victorious gleam in the new guardian's eyes implied he knew it, yet the monarch was not prepared to give in.

With a small shrug, she kicked Shadow's shins and the horse ran forward. Sébastien got out of the way in time, and she was gone.

The royal enjoyed her ride for a total of five minutes, before perceiving a presence behind. She swirled around to discern Sébastien following at a close pace on Illyria, evidently not having lost him.

"Go away!" Vivienne yelled.

"Can't do that, my lady."

His tight smirk infuriated the princess even more than the fact she could not escape him. Did the man never lose his cool?

Sensing fury boiling under the surface, Vivienne bent over the horse and clutched onto his mane. "Run like lightning, Shadow!" she commanded in his ear.

Despite the lengthening in his stride, and the rapidity of

the landscape passing by, she still could not shake the stubborn guard – his mare being smaller than Shadow, her stride matched him easily.

They raced across the plains, speed no object, until they arrived by a stream, and Vivienne ordered the horse to a halt, mindful of his thirst.

In the short moment Shadow came to a full stop, Sébastien was already there to help her dismount. He extended a hand out, and she ignored it, instead sliding down on her own. Vivienne learned the mistake too late, as when she turned, the knight was pinning her at the front, with Shadow at the back.

The young woman contemplated the guard, incensed, but Sébastien was just as furious. Nostrils flaring wildly, his eyes smoldered in fury, jaw taut with the force clenching it.

"Your disregard for your own safety is quite astounding, my lady," Sébastien gritted out. "But you will not shake me, no matter how hard you endeavor to. I have played all these games before, and I am good at them. So, please, play on."

When he backed away, it left her taking in deep breaths to calm a racing pulse, his nearness affecting Vivienne more than she preferred to let on. Still furious, she stalked off to the stream, Shadow following close behind.

In the moments passing by, as he drank his full, Vivienne cast an unbiased judgment back to her father's tired expression, and the whole reason behind needing protection. With a muffled cry of annoyance, she headed back to where Sébastien stood. Shadow continued to drink until finally satisfied, then trailed behind his mistress.

Sébastien was patting Illyria down, whispering soothing words, yet the tautness of the back muscles spoke of his mood.

"Very well," Vivienne kept a level voice, as she conceded. "You win."

His back remained frozen for a few long moments, before he whirled around, features still stormy. Vivienne compelled the rest of the words out.

"I do not wish for my father to worry more than he already does, so… You win."

Sébastien inclined his head, graciously accepting her defeat. "Thank you, my lady."

He offered a hand to mount, as a sign of peace. Vivienne gripped it, and gasped at the shock running right through both of them. She peeked at Sébastien, to see the same astonishment reflected in his gaze.

For a moment, the briefest of instants, he stared at her as a man to a woman. But it was soon gone as he helped her onto Shadow's back, and went to mount Illyria.

* * *

The lessons had been going fairly well, or so Sébastien concluded. Merlin had brought Vivienne in the midst of a meadow for the day, to teach her the art of illusion by way of water.

The princess knelt next to a pond, hands extended towards it, and practiced the mage's exercises. Merlin sat on a boulder next to her, while Sébastien stood a few feet behind, keeping an eye on the area and ensuring their safety.

The knight had been unable to keep his eyes from returning to Vivienne every few moments, drawn by an invisible force, unable to stay away. It was due to the close observation that he noticed her demeanor changed, radiating tension.

Sébastien cast an eyeful at the wizard and noted Merlin's peculiar scrutiny, before inching a few steps closer. The old man barely spared him a glimpse, disclosing nothing as he concentrated on the royal.

"Vivienne, I gather that is enough for today," Merlin advised out loud.

She ignored him, fixated on making the incantation work.

"My dear, it is fine. We will pick it up tomorrow."

With a grunt of frustration, Vivienne dropped her hands from the liquid, and stood up. She gasped upon noticing Sébastien so close, and a slow blush spread across her cheeks.

He bowed, then extended an arm gallantly, glad beyond words Lancelot was not around today. The joy of strolling by her side would be his alone.

"Ready when you are, my lady."

With one last glance to Merlin, they parted ways. Vivienne clutched the guardian's arm as they walked the short way back to the castle.

Sébastien was prompt to notice her frown. "Forgive me if I am too bold, but is there something bothering you?"

Vivienne shrugged, and for a moment he dared not presume an answer, though it came in a whisper.

"You would imagine that as the precious daughter of a king, I would be happy. Yet there are nagging doubts tugging at me. It is not easy being different, and I am afraid that some things which are coming, I am not prepared to tackle."

Sébastien frowned, wondering if any of it had to do with Lancelot. "I am sure you will figure it out, my lady. You have a bright head and compassion, and those two things are enough to ensure you decide the right thing at all times."

Vivienne swirled around, smiling for the first time that day as their eyes met. The breath caught in his throat at her radiance as she replied a sincere, "Thank you."

Sébastien's heart constricted and the longing within was almost agonizing. He craved nothing more than to kiss her, wipe away the shadows and make the princess happy. However, he knew her affection was with another, and she was out of his league.

Lancelot was of noble blood, and if Vivienne so desired, she could have him. Sébastien, though knighted, was of common blood and not suited for a lady such as her.

The cavalier bowed his head, fighting against the rising sentiments, and murmured, "My pleasure."

They continued the rest of the way in silence until Vivienne was securely back at the castle.

* * *

Once his pupil was gone, Merlin was quick to head to Camelot. It was not the first time he returned since Guinevere had appeared, but each time, his senses went haywire around the maiden.

Arthur was much too taken with her, as was the rest of court. Yet in her eyes, Merlin grasped a calculating side very different from the innocent demeanor Guinevere portrayed outwards.

Entering the gates of Camelot, the wizard kept the cloak up to hide his face. He was here to see the one person who could shed some light on the matter, and wanted his presence to remain unnoticed.

As it was nearly evening, Merlin probed with magic and caught the essence of the person in a bedchamber upstairs.

Quickening his step, he got closer and slid past the doors, inside the room.

"Elaine."

The maiden turned away from the mirror where she been brushing her hair, and gasped. Her hand was up to her throat in fright, as though ready to scream.

"It is only me," Merlin tried to reassure, letting the cloak fall off. He frowned in thought as Elaine calmed down, registering she was much more rattled than she should have been.

"Forgive me if I speak out of line, and for frightening you," the mage started, "but are Camelot's streets not safe?"

"Of course they are," Elaine murmured, looking away.

"Then why do you seem so scared?"

Instead of answering, Elaine glanced over his shoulder to the door. Understanding her uneasiness, Merlin lifted a palm and murmured a small incantation.

"No one will hear us, I give you my word," he stated once the spell was cast.

Elaine sat down on the bench, evidently much relieved. "I cannot explain what I feel, Merlin, perhaps it is my own envy of Guinevere that is starting this paranoia. But something is watching me, my every step. I..." she trailed off, muttering, "I must sound insane to you."

The warlock stepped closer, kneeling by her side. "No, you do not. I too, sense something in this woman. And I do not believe Arthur is himself, either. Lately, he seems much too subdued and unfocused, not the king I watched grow."

"Can you not fix this? If Arthur has been bewitched, is there nothing that can be done to undo it?"

Merlin hesitated, before admitting, "Spells that play with love are hard to undo, because they can harm both sides. This particular one, if my hunch is correct, has been cast by a powerful sorceress. If I try to undo it, I have but one chance and I do not believe I can do so now."

"Then, what are our options?"

"Try to speak to Arthur, be there for him. Your love and innocence might be able to break through to him more than my wisdom ever could."

"Guinevere is *always* around him," Elaine complained. "And Lancelot."

"I will arrange to have some time with her, leaving Arthur to you. This is not the end, Elaine. He needs us more than ever."

With a nod, she watched as Merlin left her room, and sighed.

* * *

The next day, Vivienne spent it in a meadow, playing with magic. Surrounded by quiet, the monarch was carefree as she let the charm flow through, while listening to Alistair's tales of his own world. Though usually fairly hushed on his past, today he was in a talkative mood, and she was happy for the distraction.

Letting spirit flow through her, Vivienne imbued the ground and the flowers with her essence, helping them bloom.

At the sound of a twig snapping, Vivienne whirled around. She scoured the forest, and breathed a sigh of relief when Sébastien advanced between the trees.

"My lady," he bowed in greeting. She beamed welcomingly, her pulse beating a frenzy at the sight of him.

At Alistair's quaintness, she glanced down, frowning at his fixed stare on the guard. Sébastien met and held it for a few moments, unaware the demon dog used his otherworldly vibes, and viewed the two humans' interaction for the first time via different eyes, paying special attention to their auras.

"That is truly odd," Vivienne said out loud.

"My lady?" It came as a question.

Still intent on her protector, she answered distractedly. "Alistair has never been so subdued around a man before. It is unusual."

At Sébastien's silence, Vivienne looked up with an almost evaluating glint. After a moment, she shook her head slightly and enquired politely, "Was there something I could help you with?"

"Not particularly. I intended to keep my distance and not disturb you. As you recall, I have to be with you at all times."

"I am almost done," Vivienne assured, releasing the hold of magic on the earth.

"Please, my lady." Sébastien stepped forward, hand extended, but stopped at the wariness in her countenance. "You were so carefree. I would rather not be the reason you stop. I can go back to the shadows, until you are prepared to retreat to the castle."

He bit down the words threatening to escape of the love blooming and his inability to stop thinking about her.

And yet Sébastien could not help but wonder, was that another blush spreading across her cheeks? He was not quite sure as Vivienne turned away, but her rushed words floated on the breeze.

"If I could figure out why I block the spells, sometimes

subconsciously, I would have a better idea of how to work them. Not many people grasp the occult, and being one among few, I have learned it is not always easy. I am either feared or revered, from one extreme to the other."

"I cannot imagine the complications of your life, princess. But your strength and purity will prevail, no matter what."

At the rough timbre of his voice, heavy with unspoken sentiments, Vivienne concentrated on the knight with a sad little grimace. "It must be ironic to think I do not have everything I desire, is it not? To be a defender of my realm, I constantly use enchantments, yet I cannot enjoy... Such basic pleasures..." She trailed off, the corners of her lips trembling. "Forgive my ranting. You may retreat, Sébastien."

The words stuck in his throat, so he simply bowed his head and went to the woods. There, he watched the royal in silence, only her back visible as she conversed with Alistair.

The demon dog, who had been observing the exchange the entire time, was now done with his examination. Disregarding Sébastien, Alistair turned to his mistress.

His energy is different than the others, princess, his loud voice boomed telepathically.

Vivienne inclined her head, noticing the flicker of red in the familiar's eyes. "Yes, it is," she exhaled wistfully. "But I cannot afford distractions, Alistair. You understand better than anyone. It was you who warned me I would have to be apt to confront the risks on my own."

Perhaps I was hasty in my predictions, majesty. Alistair approached, nudging one hand until she began petting him automatically. *There is something between you two, and I have witnessed it rarely in my existence. Do not close your heart to the man just yet.*

Vivienne bit her lip as the words sank in, and finally joined Sébastien. Alistair on their heels, they headed back to the castle in silence.

Before dropping his charge off at the main entrance, Sébastien grazed her arm and she glanced up. "My lady, please feel free to talk to me. I may be only a knight, but I promise I will keep your confidence and make an effort to ease your burden."

Vivienne smiled at the words and stood on her toes to peck his cheek. "Thank you," she murmured in his ear.

The trace of the princess' citrus perfume lingered in the air long after she was gone. Sébastien was left bereft, wishing for more – always more.

CHAPTER 16

The night was silent as Sébastien was on his rounds. Though the grounds were hushed, he perceived a presence following and pulled his weapon out, shifting to confront it. He was met with the midnight eyes of Vivienne's demon dog.

Sébastien hesitated: he could not well attack the monarch's familiar, could he?

Lower you weapon, knight, a deep voice rumbled in his head.

The tip dipped to the ground, as did Sébastien's jaw. He caught himself and, unsure of what to add, sheathed the sword, surreptitiously glancing at the dog – he really was massive.

"Forgive me, but I am unsure how to address you," Sébastien spoke out loud, feeling ridiculous as the words echoed in the night.

Alistair will do, the voice in his head came again.

Sébastien nodded, but a horrible presentiment hit him,

envisaging the dog might have a reason for being present. "Is Vi—Is my lady alright?"

Yes, she is resting. I came to join you on your rounds tonight.

When Sébastien did not answer, Alistair advanced to his side. Together, they stepped back out onto the grounds, the dog trotting next to the man, silent at first.

After a few moments, the voice came again in his head, *I am not an evil demon, knight. If I was, I would not be finding nicknames for you, and engaging in conversation. You can stop fearing I will eat – or otherwise harm – you.*

Sébastien gaped down at him, bewildered once more. "You can read my mind?"

Not easily, but when the thoughts are as loud as yours are, it is fairly simple to tune in.

Sébastien walked in silence for a few moments, then wondered, "If you are not evil, then what exactly are you? You are most certainly not a dog."

Alistair formed a sound like a cough, and the guardian realized it was laughter. *No, I am not truly from the canine family,* he finally admitted. *I simply chose this body for its usefulness. Eons ago, I used to be a divinity.*

"You were a god?" Sébastien tried to mask his astonishment, and failed.

Yes. There existed different realms, governed by different gods, some more influential than others. I was amongst the middle ones. Unfortunately, some gods grew greedy, and commenced playing politics. The resulting wars were worse than you've ever experienced in your few human years. I fell amongst them, and instead of doing good, as I was mandated, I became cunning. After the wars, when some gods established their rule over the others, they punished those who had disobeyed.

Alistair paused for a few moments, surveying the inky sky, and shook his colossal head. *I was one of them. They cast me out of the skies, and sent to the underworld, where I became a demon lord, forever intended to influence for evil, never interfere. For eons, I did this, but I grew tired. The more I interacted with humans, the more I assessed them as pawns, too easy to manipulate.*

They rounded a corner and wordlessly agreed to head on the outskirts of the castle grounds, to ensure the sentries were standing guard.

It was during these incursions, Alistair continued his story, *that two things occurred. First, I came across a wizard going by the name of Merlin. He was young at the time, but still formidable. I tried to influence his decisions towards evil, as I was supposed to, but found I did not have the soul for it. He noticed my presence, and over time, we spoke.*

"You did not attempt to kill him?"

No, for I found him entertaining. At the guardian's surprised look, the old god laughed again. *Yes, the young version of the wise man you now see was truly something else. Regardless, I also eventually realized that Merlin would play a big role in the future of humanity.*

At Sébastien's silence, the dog went on, *There is a prophecy of a young boy who will lead humanity out of the dark ages. His name is Arthur, and he is intended to be a leader the likes of which man has never experienced.*

"I know of him," Sébastien said, "whispers in the

countryside I always presumed were rumors or old wives' tales."

Yes, everyone is under the same impression. But he is very much real, living in Camelot, already on his way to becoming a great ruler. Merlin will be the one to lead him to his glory.

Sébastien pondered the words for a moment, and wondered, "What about the other one? In your incursions, the second thing that happened."

I met Vivienne. Her pure spirit drew me in like a moth to a flame.

"I can relate," Sébastien sighed, barely keeping the longing out of his voice.

The demon dog ignored him, continuing, *And I have been her guardian and protector as of when she was a little girl. Until you came along.*

"I am sensing a threat coming," Sébastien muttered.

Alistair stopped dead in his tracks, peering with a menacing flame in his eyes. *No, knight. A promise. Just as you swore an oath to Vivienne, I have one for you: if you ever hurt the princess, you will pay with your life.*

Sébastien inclined his head in assent, declaring, "I will never hurt her. I fear I might be falling in love with her, and it is not something I planned to let happen."

Alistair did his odd cough-laugh again, sauntering away.

"What's so funny?" Sébastien scowled, hurrying to keep up.

You humans are. Love cannot be limited, nor planned. I have learned that much in my eons of existence. It was, still is, and always will be, the only thing which fights evil, over and over again.

Sébastien was silent and the dog left him to his musings. That night, they roamed the grounds for hours in companionable silence.

Over time, it became a habit, and a bond of friendship forged between them. For the most part, the rounds were spent chatting about security and the past.

* * *

One night, the full moon was witness to a disturbance by the castle. The cloaked figure stood by the border of the forest, looking upon the majestic fortress. His eyes stared in hatred at the opulence it displayed, hating the symbol itself.

"Are you ready, my son?"

Mordred turned to Morgana as she stepped by his side, and nodded. "Yes, mother. I only need the sacrifice."

With a flurry of her hand, Morgana produced a cage. Within it was a wolf cub, barely three weeks of age. "This will send a message as much to the princess as to her protector," she smiled cruelly. "Do me proud."

Grinning, Mordred covered his face, grabbed the cage, and was off towards the castle.

Morgana watched him go, excitement in the pit of her stomach. It had taken years to track down Merlin's steps and find out his little secret. This girl he tutored was a worthy pawn on the side of light, one that had to be crushed.

A full-on assault, she knew, would draw the attention of the warlock – and the entire pantheon behind the wolf god – onto herself. Punishment would surely be swift. What Morgana had conceived instead was a simpler way.

She had found out about Carleigh and his darkened path. Much as Merlin had started to teach him, she would finish his education – from the shadows. The sorcerer would not know he was being helped, but would grow in power until he was ready to battle Vivienne.

And then, Morgana could have her vengeance.

She smiled again, thinking of the panic in the wolf when he would see the blood magic Mordred was bound to create, and sense the evil within. The energy that would emerge from the sacrifice would go straight to Carleigh, without him ever recognizing where it came from.

Chuckling, Morgana withdrew into the shadows and the circle of protection. It would not do for Merlin to find out she was there...not yet, at least.

* * *

Sébastien and Alistair were doing their rounds, in the midst of a discussion, when the demon dog paused. He looked around, his nose up in the air, then a low growl started deep within his chest. Without a warning, he took off on a run.

Sébastien followed him and ended up in the prison tower. Alistair was pacing from one end to the other similar to a caged lion, snarling like the hells of fury.

The defender watched in growing amazement as the dog sniffed the ground, his entire body arched in tension. The enormous jaws opened and he blew out a mist, staring with obvious intent as it spread over the ground. It was an icy blue, thin like fog almost, and the temperature in the tower dropped by a few degrees following its apparition.

Alistair waited as it covered the entire ground and lighted every bit of sorcery left behind, until the entire area seemed carpeted by blue fireflies. He sniffed again, this time tasting the malevolence in the specks. Having gathered enough, he shook his head and the mist dissipated, along with the fireflies.

Blood magic was used here for nefarious purposes, Alistair mumbled at Sébastien's approach, an uneasy glint in his opaque eyes. *Go check on Vivienne and stay by her side tonight until I join you.*

After the knight turned his back, the demon dog squinted at the moon and thundered, *Damn full moon!*

Sébastien was already racing across the grounds to his mistress' quarters, body tightly wired for a fight. Noticing the door to her chambers open, he burst in just in time to glimpse the shadow bolting out the window.

He unsheathed his sword and ran after it, but by the time he looked out the window it was gone.

Vivienne, startled out of sleep, jumped up in bed and dragged the bedclothes to her chin. "Sébastien! What is the matter?" She observed the blade in his hand, the fury on his features, and decided to wait until an explanation was given.

Sébastien tried to survey one more time the grounds, but it was useless. Despite the full moon, there was an unnatural gloom enveloping the castle. His human eyes were no match for it.

He stepped to Vivienne, attempting to calm his breathing – and ignore the sight of the princess in bed, hair a tumbling mess and a vulnerable look. He craved nothing more than to bring her comfort in ways other than as a knight.

Sébastien met her confused stare and began explaining the night's events. It was done both to distract from his errant thoughts and remove the anxious glint in her eyes.

Alistair showed halfway through the explanation, placed his head on the bed by the royal's feet, and waited.

When Sébastien was done, Alistair's voice echoed in both their minds. *You must have learnt by now that whenever used, the occult drops traces of magic behind. In the tower, the black art throbbed still. I am not sure whom it was, or what they intended, but I will be keeping an eye out. Meanwhile, Vivienne, you should use defensive barriers around your bedroom each evening. It is useless to pretend this was not an attack aimed towards you.*

Though pale, Vivienne had reined in her original reaction and was now much more in control. She agreed to the protector's suggestion without flinching. Noticing this, Sébastien realized his presence was no longer required.

He was about to depart, leaving the royal in capable paws, when her voice stopped him, emerald eyes trapping his.

"Thank you, Sébastien," Vivienne spoke softly.

"My pleasure, my lady," he mumbled hoarsely. Through it all, it took his entire will of character to keep silent the rest of the churning emotions – at an extreme price.

You did well, Alistair mentioned for his ears only. *We will catch him, whoever this menace is.*

Unfortunately, the demon dog had a good idea who had set the trap. Why they had, he could not guess. He waited until Vivienne was asleep and, afraid to leave her side, chose to meet Merlin in his dreams.

Alistair closed his eyes and expanded his senses in the realm of possibilities until he found the wizard's aura. Latching on to it, he then tugged and pulled them both into a place of his choosing.

"This is a first," the mage mused as he emerged in a meadow, facing him. "Why not come see me yourself?"

There was an attack at the palace earlier today, Alistair growled. *I could not chance leaving Vivienne alone after it.*

"An attack? Was Vivienne harmed?"

She was not. Blood magic was performed in one of the abandoned towers. A sacrifice of a wolf cub.

Merlin was immediately alert, a sober look on his face. "Was it a threat meant for you? The wolf cub, I mean –"

No. It was, however, designed to catch my eye. I sensed an energy around it similar to yours.

"Mine?" Merlin frowned. "But I..." he trailed off as realization dawned. "No!"

Yes, those were my thoughts exactly. This has Morgana written all over, meaning she knows of Vivienne.

Merlin was silent for a few moments, as the full extent of his past mistakes threatened to overwhelm. With an effort of will, he pushed it all to the side and asked, "How can we protect her?"

Grace her with your Fae magic defenses, as you did Elaine. It will do in the meantime, while I try to find out more.

Without further comment, Alistair left the dream and awoke by his mistress' side. *No harm will come to you, this I swear. If I have to hunt down that sorceress and her bastard son, I will.*

* * *

Mordred nearly sauntered back to his mother's hiding place, grinning widely.

"Well?" Morgana pressed, stepping out of the shadows.

"Easy as pie, mother," he kissed her on the cheek, then took her hand in his. "The message was delivered, the princess was spooked, and I do believe the demon dog will be contacting my father soon."

"What of the knight? I thought for a moment he might have seen you from her window."

Mordred shrugged off her slightly lecturing tone. "Not a chance."

"Why did you go to Vivienne's room?" Morgana persisted. "There was no need."

"I know, mother," Mordred rolled his eyes, "but I wanted to see Vivienne up close. And, you have to admit, it does have the added benefit they will not believe she is safe in her own castle."

Morgana pondered the words for a moment, then slowly nodded. "I suppose…"

"So now what? How do we get this to Carleigh?"

The sorceress held her cupped palms up, murmuring, "Drop it here."

Mordred lifted his hand and from it appeared a small circle, the color of burgundy. It was no bigger than a cherry and glowed of a darkened aura. When he dropped it in Morgana's palm, it shone brighter for a moment, before stilling.

"Find the one who masters darkness, he goes by the name of Carleigh," she ordered the little orb. "Fill him with the power of this sacrifice, be at my command, and do it so!"

She then threw the circle in the air and they both watched as it flew away.

"Will it really find Carleigh?" Mordred asked.

"Yes. Darkness has a way of finding each other… You have done well, my son."

Grinning, Mordred followed Morgana into the woods,

from where they were to return home.

* * *

A few days later, a ball was taking place at the castle. Despite the recent attack, Vivienne had not seen fit to cancel it.

For hours on end, music filled the ballroom of the castle until Vivienne became quite tired of switching partners. She strode out in the gardens for a breath of fresh air the first chance she got, making sure she was not followed. Of course, within a few minutes, Sébastien came out into the silence as well.

"Are you alright, my lady?"

The royal whirled around at the odd note in his voice, almost tormented. When their eyes met, there was restraint, regret and frustration in his gaze.

"Perhaps I should be asking you this," Vivienne retorted softly.

The harsh glint in the guardian's eyes softened visibly. "I apologize. I did not intend to frighten you."

"What is troubling you, Sébastien?"

"Nothing, my lady," he responded immediately. At her insistent look, he forcefully unclenched his teeth.

"These dancing balls have me on edge. Aside from the security risks, the men are apt at behaving like imbeciles, and one hears things."

"Such as?"

"Nothing suited for the ears of a lady."

"Tell me," Vivienne commanded, guessing where he was going with it.

"Comments about your beauty, my lady..." Sébastien answered, avoiding her eyes. "... and celibacy."

"I see." Vivienne let the words hang in the air for a moment, before sharing, "I appreciate you making an effort to shelter me from it. But I have heard it all before: they deem me unnatural for not letting a man rule me, and yet they all want to bed me."

Sébastien's jaw tightened again at her statement.

The princess could not help from inching closer and running a finger alongside it, watching the muscle jump under her fingertips. "Be at peace, Sébastien, I am alright. Simply weary of the night and wishing it to end. I cannot even enjoy the dancing with all the muttering about."

Sébastien swallowed past the lump in his throat. "Perhaps I can help with that, at least... If I may." As Vivienne frowned in confusion, he added, "A dance with no strings attached."

The monarch paused for a beat while he held his breath, anticipating a rejection. The opposite stunned him.

"I am not stopping you," Vivienne declared.

It was all the encouragement the guard needed. Confidently, Sébastien stepped up to her and slid an arm around her waist. With the music filtering from the ball, he led them in a waltz.

Vivienne gave in to the comfort, relaxed enough to feel the music and enjoy it. Sébastien's strength renewed her vigor and his muscle was the stone she needed to rely on.

When the song stopped, the guardian reluctantly dropped his hand. Vivienne looked up at him, searching his unfathomable gaze for something. After a beat, she inclined her head in thanks and retreated back inside. Sébastien was left staring longingly behind.

CHAPTER 17

"You will recall me explaining enchantments have to come from deep within you. They cannot be used for evil, only for good, and selfless reasons."

Vivienne was tempted to roll her eyes, but knew Merlin would have things to say about such unladylike conduct.

"Yes, master," she agreed instead.

Merlin shook his head at the monarch's antics, the crinkles around his sea blue eyes deepening. "Perfect. Now, it is time. This dove yearns to fly again."

Vivienne fixated on the bird in his hand and its bandaged wing. As she had done many times before, she reached deep down for a well of power and gripped a tiny drop of it. Her entire being centered, as though a chain linked her to the earth, and it to her.

The incantation spread its warmth from the deepest corners within, to the fingertips. Vivienne closed her eyes, at the same time circling a hand above the dove, wishing it could fly again today. She imagined the freedom under its wings, the clouds above, just as the bird itself would.

The wave surged within Vivienne, more than intended, but nonetheless it escaped her fingertips.

"Look."

Merlin's voice caused her eyes to open and watch as tiny gold wisps escaped her palm, enveloping the bird's wing in a halo. It shone brighter for a moment, then dimmed, until the light was completely gone, absorbed within.

The dove tried to flap the wing and upon registering it worked, flew away. Vivienne smiled as it circled them twice, then flew into the distance.

"Well done, Vivienne," Merlin praised, approval evident in his voice.

The princess beamed gratefully, but became distracted by the sound of a horse nearby. She whirled around, pulse beating wildly as Sébastien approached.

"My lady, your father asked for a word," the guardian informed his mistress once he was within hearing distance.

Vivienne inclined her head in acknowledgement, but peered over a shoulder to Merlin. "I have to go."

The speculative glint in the mage's eyes was not lost on her, as he observed the dynamic between her and Sébastien. However, instead of commenting on whatever he perceived, Merlin beamed paternally and waved Vivienne away.

"Tomorrow, then?"

Vivienne nodded in approval, already retreating. Sébastien extended a hand and she mounted behind him, wrapping both arms around his waist. It was then she remembered and glanced behind. "Oh, and Merlin?"

The old man blinked, appearing to disengage from a trance.

"Tomorrow, I would like to meet this Guinevere you keep mentioning to me."

His laugh echoed behind as they left.

* * *

Accompanied by two of her defenders, the loyal Lancelot and the new Sébastien, Vivienne walked over to Merlin's lair. She tried to ignore the guardian's eyes on her, and fixate on the enchantment lessons ahead. When they entered the circle though, Merlin was not alone.

Next to him was a beautiful, young blonde woman with blue eyes. As she faced Vivienne, the two men behind froze at her beauty. The royal, too, was astonished, but soon the glimmer of calculation in Guinevere's eyes caught hers.

"So pleased to meet you, Guinevere," the princess bowed her head in acknowledgement.

The young woman returned the smile and curtsied low. "Lady Vivienne, the pleasure is all mine."

Vivienne's features tightened, barely controlling the reaction to the beautiful maiden – and jealousy it was not. With otherworldly vibes, she could detect something around Guinevere, a web ready to ensnare. When peering at her aura, Vivienne noticed it was of a murky color, like a weed wilting in the sun.

The royal surveyed her two companions. Lancelot could not take his eyes off Guinevere. She was afraid to witness the same thing with Sébastien, but still could not help glancing out of the corner of her eye.

The guardian met her gaze steadily and Vivienne registered with a jolt he never wavered, seemingly immune to Guinevere's beauty – or so she concluded too swiftly. His eyes flickered betrayingly towards the other woman and Vivienne looked away angrily.

She missed Sébastien's frown, as it was not with longing but cold investigation that he looked. The knight was perplexed not only at Lancelot's reaction, but his princess' own uneasiness.

Soon, Guinevere departed back to the castle, accompanied by Lancelot. Sébastien waited by the horses for Vivienne to be done with Merlin. Eyes glued to her pacing form, he noticed the tautness of her shoulders as she spoke with the mage, unaware the stressful demeanor had to do with him.

With an annoyed cry, the monarch stopped pacing and focused on Merlin. The warlock's eyes had never wavered from her countenance during the – rather long – soliloquy.

Except, she observed now, he was busy staring at Sébastien. "I understand they are both enthralled with Guinevere, but –"

"Both, my dear?"

Vivienne narrowed her eyes, wondering what the old man was getting at. Silently, she waited for an explanation.

"I only observed one's eyes on her, Vivienne. And the other's were on you. My dear, Sébastien is quite infatuated with you."

Vivienne's frown deepened, even as she urged her quickening heartbeat to settle. "Lancelot, however, is smitten with Guinevere. We have to be careful, Merlin. She's –"

"I, too, have apprized the situation," he admitted. "She is a trap, yes. But Arthur has fallen in love already. I will shelter him as much I can, and perhaps my presence there will deter betrayal of another sort."

Vivienne inclined her head in assent.

"How about those lessons now?"

* * *

Hours later, Sébastien accompanied an exhausted Vivienne back to the castle. He dropped her off at the main entrance and intended to follow within, when she stopped him.

"Thank you. I will be fine from here."

She departed without a backwards glance and Sébastien could not help following at a distance, despite being dismissed. He convinced himself it was to ensure the princess was not suffering.

The truth was, the guardian had noticed the way she peeked at Lancelot, while the youth gazed at Guinevere, and guessed at her sentiments. He was not surprised when Vivienne used a shortcut to end up at the stables, sneaking in by way of the back door.

Sébastien kept to the shadows, close enough to witness Vivienne walk to where Lancelot brushed his horse.

"Lancelot, we have to talk," the royal declared.

"Lady Vivienne," he bowed with a gallant and confident grin.

"Meeting Guinevere today, I gather you fell to her charms, but she is betrothed."

Sébastien could not help but admire Vivienne's bluntness, as everything else about her person. Lancelot's response, however, shocked him.

"I am aware of that," the man admitted with barely an

ounce of regret in his voice.

"Are you really?"

Sébastien squinted around the corner to distinguish Vivienne touching his arm. "Please Lance, be careful."

Once she departed his presence, Sébastien did not follow.

The pain in his chest was blinding as he walked the opposite way. Illyria waited by the main entrance, and without considering anything else, the knight jumped on the horse and rode far, far away.

Not even the distance between himself and Vivienne was enough to wipe her desolate expression from his imagination. Of one thing, Sébastien was absolutely sure: he was in love with a woman out of his league, whose heart belonged to another.

And the only thing the guardian could do was watch – and suffer – in silence as the other man destroyed it.

* * *

The next day, Lancelot was back in Camelot, at King Arthur's side – and his beloved Guinevere. Though he had tried to stay away from her, he found it harder every minute, as the blonde beauty was a particular drug he could not get enough of.

Arthur had already confided in him that he planned to marry her and Lancelot could do nothing but watch from afar. After all, he was both his best friend and king. Though he shared duties by protecting Vivienne occasionally, Lancelot knew that as soon as Guinevere was crowned queen, Arthur would entrust him with her safety and his days in Elsior would be numbered.

Vivienne's words of warning echoed in his mind when his

eyes locked with Guinevere's, but he paid them no heed.

"Lancelot!" Arthur yelled from across the hall, gesturing for him to join them.

With an easily faked grin, Lancelot approached them.

"Welcome back," Guinevere greeted of her sultry voice, the blue eyes promising a thousand things untold – and forbidden.

Lancelot felt the stir of desire deep within, but squashed it in an attempt at being noble. After all, it was what was expected.

"How was your time in Elsior?" Arthur asked.

"It went well. Vivienne is much grown from the gal I remember," Lancelot murmured, not noticing how Guinevere's eyes flashed at the name. "What did you think, Guinevere?"

"Me?" she wondered, all wide-eyed innocence. "However do you mean?"

Lancelot frowned at her obvious effort to appear unawares, but luckily Arthur was distracted enough by a fight in a corner to not notice. "I will be right back," he muttered to them both, before heading towards the two youths currently going at it.

"Oy!" At his strong command, the two stopped fighting right away, and Arthur's demeanor eased. Engrossed in settling their dispute, he did not register that Guinevere swiftly led Lancelot away from the court and into a deserted hallway.

"I don't understand," Lancelot was saying to the soon-to-be-queen, "why not tell Arthur you were in Elsior today?"

Guinevere turned to face him, twirling a lock of her blonde hair around a finger and pouting. "Can't a girl have some secrets around here?"

When Lancelot only frowned, she realized it was not the right choice of words. The sentiment was further emphasized when the knight said, "I do not feel comfortable hiding something like this from Arthur."

Guinevere barely restrained her scowl. The man was handsome, but boy, was he thick! She needed to think quickly before he went to reveal to Arthur she was already lying.

No... That would not do, at all, she mused.

Instead, she blinked rapidly, forcing some tears in her eyes, and turned away.

"Guinevere!" Lancelot immediately sounded contrite. "I apologize, I did not mean to imply anything by it! I know you care for Arthur, as do I..."

He trailed off when she faced him again, a lonely tear running down her cheek. "I do not want Arthur to know I was in Elsior," Guinevere whimpered, "because I do not want to put him a position to choose."

"What do you mean?" Lancelot frowned.

With a look over his shoulder, she pulled him further into the shadows, their bodies close by. Lancelot took one whiff of her particular fragrance and his head spun, barely able to focus on what she was saying.

"Merlin forced me to go," Guinevere whispered in a scared tone. At his bewildered look, she continued, "I do not think he approves me of me, I always sense his eyes on me, waiting for me to fail."

She buried her head in her hands, sobbing quietly, and Lancelot was lost. He pulled her in his arms – for comfort, he excused the gesture – and murmured soothing words until Guinevere's cries had quieted, and she stilled.

Guinevere then pulled away, just barely outside of the circle of his arms and peered at him. "Oh, Lancelot, what will I do?" she murmured. "I am afraid Merlin will want me gone!"

"Leave the wizard to me, I will ensure nothing happens," he whispered in return, raising a hand to caress her cheek.

Her lower lip trembled and before he knew what was happening, Lancelot leaned closer. His mouth lowered, pressing against Guinevere's softly, barely a taste.

The vixen let the kiss go on for long enough to have him hooked, before pulling away with an audible gasp. Her hand came up to her lips in shock.

"I apologize, Lancelot," she falsely cried, "I do not know what came over me!"

"The fault was all mine," he declared, stepping away, forcefully pushing away the desire to keep on kissing her, regardless of the consequences. "Please do not think less of me, for giving in to baser impulses."

"How could I?" Guinevere whispered, an odd look in her eyes. "In another life…"

Lancelot turned away, breaking the gaze. Before leaving, he stated, "Do not fear Merlin. I promise no harm will come to you."

Guinevere waited until he was gone, then smoothed her gown, her hair, and re-entered the throne room. She joined Arthur once more, the mask firmly in place.

That really was too easy, she reflected with a broad grin. *With Merlin out of the way, Arthur will be mine to control.*

* * *

In the cottage, Morgana turned away from the basin, smiling largely. With a wave of her hand, she had ensured

Guinevere's little tête-à-tête with Lancelot stayed out of Merlin's sights. The silly girl had no idea she was getting outside help, much like Carleigh.

They are all pawns, for a greater purpose.

"Something amusing, mother?" Mordred asked, entering with a hare he had caught hunting.

"Only love, my son."

"How so?" he frowned, having never heard his mother speak of the emotion.

"Arthur, your father's beloved protégé, has fallen prey to love. In its innocence, its seduction will be his doom. I cannot help but find the irony amusing."

Mordred returned the smile, happy to see Morgana in such a good mood. "Shall we celebrate?" he asked, lifting the hare for her to inspect.

Morgana clapped her hands excitedly. "Yes, we shall!"

As she set about preparing the meat, her grown boy took a look at the basin, noticing Guinevere's fading radiant smile. "She *is* pretty," he admitted, before adding, "I cannot understand how Arthur lets himself be ruled by such a base emotion. I will never allow a woman to own me such."

Morgana laughed in her old tinkling way. "My son, if anyone ever dares, I shall ensure they live to regret it."

Content with their day's end, the two set about their dinner.

* * *

Alistair could not sleep. Though the night was quiet, since the close call with the sacrifice he refused to let his guard down. Nights on end, he would stay awake to protect Vivienne – not always understanding the need, but following the instinct within.

One particular such time, Alistair was staring out the princess' window to the grounds below. As he scanned them on the surface, his gaze fell on a shadow crossing swiftly.

With a growl, the demon dog stood up and extended his senses. What he caught made him pause in confusion. *What the...?*

Hesitantly, he glanced at Vivienne's sleeping form, then back down, torn between a need to investigate and the desire to protect her. With a puff of irritation, he blew an extra protective barrier towards his mistress, then took off.

It did not take him long to reach the forest outside. He stepped in, ensuring his paws made no sound, until he found the person he was looking for. Unwilling to extend the courtesy of privacy, he broadened his mind to pry. *What are you up to?*

The cloaked figure turned towards him, blue eyes widened in surprise. "I..."

What did I tell you last, Merlin, about trying to intervene with fate? the demon dog rumbled.

"I was not," the wizard denied, extinguishing the magic in his palms. "If you must know, I was trying to find out more about Sébastien."

Vivienne's guardian? Alistair tilted his head in confusion. *What of him?*

"His emotions are growing, and I sense he will play a large part in Vivienne's future."

And you do not like it.

"Why would you say that?" Merlin enquired, keeping a blank face.

Come now, Merlin, we both know you love being the one in charge of fates and destinies. Was it not what pushed you to ensure Arthur was born by your hand?

Merlin could barely hold back as magic responded to his rising fury, ready to defend. "How *dare* you!?"

It is the truth, Alistair stated, stepping closer. He glanced down at the warlock's shining hands and snorted. *Go on, attack me. I cannot wait to see who will win.*

"You forget, demon lord, I was the one who healed you last!"

And you, wizard, forget who gave you the key to unlock your powers, Alistair retorted. His midnight eyes were once more reflecting the flames of the underworld, even as he stepped nearer.

Merlin's gaze burned in response as he clenched his fists. "What happened between me and Morgana is past."

No. What happened between you two is past, present and future, do not forget that. It is a burden you will always carry.

"What is it you wish of me!?" Merlin lost his patience.

A vow.

Alistair rose to his full height, meeting Merlin's stare unflinchingly. The wizard glared back, breathing hard with the control it took to avoid striking out.

You will not try to intervene between Vivienne and Sébastien, whatever the reason. If you wish to have my continued help, and do not want to be my enemy, you will *submit to this request.*

Merlin gritted his teeth in response and a staring contest ensued. With neither backing down, it was moments before the wizard looked away and muttered, "Fine. I vow to stay out of their romantic life."

Good.

With that, Alistair turned to leave.

"Perhaps you are not so far removed from you old identity, *Atrox*," Merlin spit at his back, but the dog did not dignify the verbal attack with a comment.

CHAPTER 18

The next day during training, Vivienne decided to go observe, convincing herself it was to keep an eye on Lancelot. In truth, it was to stare at Sébastien.

The royal supervised them spar from afar, and could not help herself from stepping in their direction, drawn to the new guardian's vigorous movements as he lunged and parried the other man's blows.

Lancelot, with his childish jabs, was a boy next to him. The way Sébastien covered the ground, with a feral grace, caused the young woman to wonder if he would be the same way in bed.

Vivienne blushed at the thought, and almost as if to spite her, Sébastien's gaze captured hers in that exact moment. It was blazing, whether from the heat of the training or their connection, she could not guess.

At the same moment, Lancelot lunged, and with panic she

observed metal graze skin. In instants, a thin line of blood emerged from Sébastien's shoulder to his abdomen.

"Sébastien!" Vivienne yelled, but he was already moving towards his rival, his strikes much more ferocious, to the point Lancelot was disarmed in the few moments it took the princess to approach them.

By the time she was near, Sébastien was breathing hard, and Lancelot was on the ground, body covered in dust, visage shocked at having been defeated so soundly.

"Sébastien," Vivienne murmured softly, and the knight whirled around.

Ignoring as best as she could the scrumptiousness of his physique, the princess instead gestured for him to join her.

He strode closer, stopping with the fence still separating them. Sébastien did not trust himself by her, thus he avoided eye contact as best possible. He had not intended to come so close to injuring Lancelot, but noticing Vivienne there, admiring the empty-headed knight had caused a full loss of countenance.

"Would you care to join me on a brief stroll by the stream?" Vivienne implored in a softened voice.

When Sébastien met her gaze, there was something there she could not quite grasp. Before she had a chance to probe, it was masked soon enough with an incline of the head. "Of course, my lady."

Dropping the sword still in his hand to the ground, the guardian put the shirt back on and the blood immediately soaked it. He smoothly hopped over the fence and they strode slowly, side by the side, arriving by the stream in a matter of moments.

When Vivienne faced him, Sébastien feared admonishment due to her frown. Instead, she murmured, "Does it hurt?"

He peered down at the blood and shrugged. "It is only a scratch, my lady. I will be fine."

Shaking her head in denial, the princess stepped to him. "Please, let me heal you."

"Why?" His gaze scorched as it plunged into hers, causing butterflies to flutter in the pit of her stomach. Vivienne had the impression he was trying to figure out her very soul, and thus carefully chose a response.

"It was my fault you got hurt. I distracted you and... I do not wish you to be in any discomfort."

Sébastien stared for a beat longer, then bowed his head in assent and she reached for the shirt. He bent over to remove it, watching as Vivienne knelt by the stream to wet it with cold, clean liquid.

When she got back up and cleaned the blood and sweat off his chest, the guardian was surprised at the gentleness of the touch, the patience in her countenance. He could not recall the last time any of his charges had shown much compassion – but then again, Vivienne was special and that was the crux of the problem.

At the first contact of the cool material, Sébastien gasped, but then he settled – though his muscles jumped under the princess' touch.

"I am sorry if the water is cold," she spoke softly.

"It will do," Sébastien murmured, but his voice sounded strained.

Once she had the wound clean, Vivienne peeked at him,

gasping softly upon registering how close their bodies were.

"I –" Vivienne's hand stilled, mesmerized by the blaze in his eyes again.

Sébastien felt the magnetism, tilting towards Vivienne, pushed by a primal need as old as time itself to taste her lips for a single moment – one touch of heaven. He stopped a hair's breath away from her lovely face, and forced some self-control. Leaning backwards, he successfully added some distance.

Vivienne constrained herself to do the same, but her voice came out raspy, through a parched throat. "I was going to ask if it is alright to use an incantation?"

"Yes," Sébastien briskly agreed. Anything to be done with it and get distance from her closeness, before he burst.

Vivienne bowed her head over him, placing both hands on his chest – a very naked, stony and chiseled chest. *Stop it,* she told herself. *Healing is the priority, not jumping his bones.*

"I only ask," she moistened her lips, then continued without looking at him, "because although this heals the wound faster, not everyone is comfortable with me using magic around them."

At the silence that greeted her words, Vivienne peered up. The knight was gazing through half-closed lids, but the intensity was unmistakably there. She had no way to know that at that exact moment, the defender was ready to throttle anyone that made her feel self-conscious.

Sébastien bit down the words of comfort he wanted to speak as a lover, swallowed past the lump in his throat and instead said what a guardian could: "I am not one of those people, highness. No matter what, I am and always will be, on your side."

The princess' lips trembled and she bit down hard to stop it, staring back at the wound to hide the rising emotion. Never had Vivienne felt as connected to someone as she did in that moment with Sébastien.

Focusing back on healing, one palm became ablaze, as did the other. The enchantress held onto the golden glow, rather than letting it escape in wisps. She kept it in her hands as they drifted across Sébastien's bicep, slowly to the side and down the front, following the gash.

Through it all, she surveyed the tough guard from under her lids. She wondered at his closed eyes, the biting of the lip, the neck tendons straining as though tormented.

"Am I hurting you, Sébastien?" Vivienne probed, though her hands kept moving, the glow having closed half of the gash.

"Not in the way you're imagining, my lady," he groaned through gritted teeth.

She could not fathom how to respond.

When the wound was closed, fully mended, Vivienne silently thanked the magic and extinguished it. She backed away, immediately regretting the heat of his body.

"It is done."

Sébastien opened his eyes and admired her handiwork – there was no trace of the blade's cut. "Thank you, my lady," he bowed. "Is there anything else you desire?"

Quite a few things, Vivienne mused. Out loud, she said, "No, that will be all. I can find my own way back."

* * *

Mordred stared in the basin, observing as the knight left

Vivienne alone, and she watched him go longingly. There was something about the young woman, perhaps the fact she was also magical and of the same age as him, that attracted the young man in him.

"What are you looking at?"

The warlock started and with a wave of the hand made the vision disappear, before turning to Morgana. She was already frowning at his odd behavior – he had never hidden anything from her.

"Nothing, mother," Mordred muttered, standing up and moving away in hopes of distracting her.

It was not to be. Like a dog with a bone, Morgana took his place and passed a hand over the water, murmuring, "Show me your last capture."

When the liquid cleared on Vivienne's face, Morgana narrowed her eyes. "Why were you watching the princess?"

"No reason. I thought father might have been around," Mordred lied.

Morgana extinguished the image once more, then turned to face her son. Her grey eyes were filled with suspicion. "Has she gotten to you?"

"What? No!" the youth denied, but it was plain as day on his face.

"You are infatuated with her!" Morgana spit. *How have I let this happen!?* She admonished herself, angry as the situation seemed to slip out of her control.

"Mother." Mordred kept his tone firm, as he knew only too well the look in her eyes and needed to defuse the situation before it spiraled out of control. "I am not infatuated with Vivienne. There is, however, something about her that makes me want to keep an eye on her. I assure you it has nothing to do with lust – or love."

Morgana peered past her son's physical form to the aura underneath and registered he was telling the truth. She glanced over her shoulder to the basin, then the realization dawned on her.

"Her birth."

"What?"

"You are drawn to Vivienne because of her birth," Morgana muttered, looking back to her son. *All is not lost, after all.* "Vivienne was born the same night you were, from what I have gathered in my research. She is your exact opposite – whilst nature tried to prevent you from being born, it welcomed her."

Mordred let the words sink in, their truth echoing within.

"So what am I supposed to do?"

"You will continue to be drawn to her, because you are complete opposites. The important thing is you do not let it turn your head, and remain focused." When Mordred nodded in agreement, Morgana continued, "We have to do something further about Carleigh. Vivienne needs to be tested, so we can see exactly what he needs to fight her and win."

"I will take care of that," Mordred promised, before heading out on a hunt for provisions.

* * *

Sébastien was sparring with a young devil, conscious of Vivienne observing him, always attuned to her presence these days. He did not comprehend whether she was around only for Lancelot, but either way, their eyes always met.

Since she had healed him, the guardian yearned for

nothing more than to hold her and erase the other man from her mind. Yet all he could do was supervise the princess, while trying to ignore the tightening in his chest each time her eyes went to Lancelot, and failing.

The sound of metal clashing and an abundance of noise broke his tumultuous ruminations. Sébastien turned around, immediately remarking two younger pages battling, close to where Vivienne had been standing.

Before he could react, she marched to the two youngsters, yelling at them to stop. This in spite of the fact one of them had a very real weapon in his hand.

When the page whirled at the sound of the royal's voice, he swung the sharpened sword clumsily around. Sébastien's own blade came to block the blow, only inches from Vivienne.

The youth's hand shook, and the sword clattered to the ground. He fell to his knees, his face a mask of shock and angst. "Lady Vivienne! I am so sorry!"

"What do you two imagine you're doing?" Sébastien snarled between clenched teeth, unmoved by their youthful appearance. The anger – and fear – that hit him at the idea of Vivienne being injured was staggering.

Even the young woman cringed at the fury in the guard's voice. She clasped his shoulder, ignoring the way heat permeated her own skin and traveled through. Sébastien inhaled deeply at the soft touch, inclining his head to her.

"I am unharmed, Sébastien. It was my fault, I should not have gotten so close."

The battle was still clear in his eyes, as he had not yet calmed down. Vivienne disregarded him, kneeling instead by the younger youth, who was bleeding.

"May I heal your wound?" she enquired softly, with a warm expression.

The youth nodded, awestruck by the royal's beauty and kindness. Sébastien knew only too well how he felt – Vivienne's face was stuck in his mind, never able to sleep without it, since first laying eyes on her.

Blissfully unaware, the princess healed the young boy in mere moments. She then turned to the still kneeling boy, himself with a cut, barely breathing in fear.

"What is your name?" she requested gently.

"W-W-William," he stuttered.

"You will not be punished, William. But I would like to understand what happened here. May I heal you in the meantime?"

Enthralled by Vivienne – and with a nervous peek at Sébastien – the child recounted a silly story about a stupid fight over a girl. He concluded with a contrite, "I'm terribly sorry, my lady."

"It's alright," she smiled. "Off you go."

Sébastien advanced to intervene, but she glared his way. "Follow me, Dubois."

When they had attained a secluded corner, Vivienne whirled around accusingly. "You scared that poor boy to death!"

"Poor boy, my lady?" Sébastien gritted his teeth. "He could have harmed you – gravely so."

"And I could have healed myself!" she continued, eyes blazing. "He is young, and now petrified because of you!"

"My lady –" he begun, but was interrupted.

"I'm not sure how they do things where you come from,

but in Elsior, every single person is treated with kindness and respect! You will do well to register it, and the sooner the better."

Sébastien dropped all pretense of calm, his voice tight with fury as he towered over the princess. "All due respect, your father hired me to safeguard you and that is what I intend to do. Even if it's from yourself."

Vivienne was about to retort, but something in the guardian's countenance alerted her to danger. She registered they were close enough to touch and there was a heat radiating from him, close to magnetizing.

"I—" she tried, but had to moisten her lips with the tip of her tongue at the sudden dryness in her throat.

Sébastien's eyes lowered at the action and the magnetism fortified, scorching eyes meeting hers. Vivienne's body burned with a humming intensity in her bones, even as it leaned towards him.

They were staring at each other, lost in the moment, when Lancelot showed up. "You up for a rematch?" he dared Sébastien, blissfully unaware of what he had stumbled into.

"Aye," Sébastien muttered, eyes still on Vivienne. "My lady," he bowed courteously, and retreated.

Vivienne was still staring into space, when Alistair appeared by her side, nudging one hand quizzically.

Is the new guardian giving you trouble?

"No… not really. He is peculiar, that's all."

Alistair glanced up at his mistress, and back to the defender, now further away. *I would say protective.*

Vivienne bit her lip in deep reflection, unnerved by their connection and the constant dreams she had of Sébastien. It was bad enough he drew her like a moth to a flame whenever they were in the same vicinity, but now tranquility was impossible to find even when dozing off.

Alistair's second nudge to her hand was a jolt, startling from her musings. She smiled down guiltily, realizing he must have come for a reason, yet she was busy daydreaming. Putting Sébastien out of her imagination for good, Vivienne concentrated on Alistair.

As usual, he interpreted the unspoken query, and opened his large jaws in a doggy grin. *I assumed you would be interested in practicing some unrestrained enchantments.*

"Always!" Vivienne beamed, and followed him off the training grounds.

* * *

After they were done with their lesson in magic, Alistair let Vivienne go but remained behind in the forest.

You can show yourself now.

"You always were very good at sensing me when I did not want to be seen," Ardea muttered as she stepped out of the shadows.

Alistair threw her an unimpressed look. *What is it you wish this time?*

"This new charge of yours, I know Aequus has told you what he has seen. But there is more."

Will there be a price for this information? At Ardea's surprised look, he chuckled. *Come now, sister, I do not expect free gifts from you or my brother.*

"Believe what you will, but I tell you this with no strings attached. I am tired of squabbling with you, Atrox."

Alistair.

"As you wish, *Alistair*. I know there was only one event that would have led to your complete stripping of identity as you did. Whether my suspicions are correct or not, I thank you. With Vulper gone, we finally have peace in the pantheon."

I do not know what you are referring to.

"Yes, I thought as much," Ardea said wearily. "What I came to deliver is this: Mordred, the fruit of Merlin and Morgana's toxic love, is of age as well. They are both helping Carleigh and Guinevere. Though your friend Merlin does his best to shield Arthur, it is a lost cause. Vivienne, on the other hand, can be saved."

How?

"Do not let her fall prey to Carleigh, whatever the cost may be."

You have seen something?

"A trickery, before the ultimate battle... Be warned, brother. Your choice may remove you from the equation, but it will give Vivienne a chance to best them all."

Alistair was silent, pondering his sister's words, and filing them away for future use. Finally, he leveled his gaze to her. *Thank you.*

"You are most welcome," Ardea inclined her head. "If we do not see each other again, I wish you luck."

With that, she shimmered away, leaving the demon dog to his thoughts.

* * *

Vivienne returned to the castle from the forest, not quite aware of where she was heading. It was no surprise when she slammed straight into something solid, and lost her balance. The fall was stopped as a strong pair of arms reached out and grabbed at her waist.

"My apologies," she mumbled, "I was not paying attention to where—"

The words got stuck in her throat when her green eyes collided with his. "Sébastien," Vivienne whispered, a blush filling her cheeks.

The guardian peered down, with the intense stare that was his trademark, as though assessing her very soul. When the noise of their surroundings got past Sébastien's scrutiny, he blinked as though dazed, and let go of her waist.

"Lady Vivienne," he bowed.

The princess stood there, missing his heat, and having the most peculiar craving to be closer again. She bit her lip, muttered something non-committal, and retreated before the urge to do something foolish took control.

Sébastien was left staring after her, wondering if maybe – just maybe – Vivienne was affected by his presence as well.

CHAPTER 19

It was night when Vivienne took a midnight stroll, Alistair by her side. She was not aware that a few feet away, under cover of trees and bushes, Sébastien matched her pace, keeping an eye out for danger.

"Lady Vivienne!"

The shout had come from far behind. As she whirled, the princess distinguished Lancelot running towards her. Alistair barked, once, and advanced in front of his mistress, intimidating in his posture with his teeth bared.

"Yes, Lancelot?" Vivienne enquired when he was near.

The younger man hesitated, evidently afraid of Alistair.

"You should not be strolling the grounds alone."

"I dare say I have managed quite well so far." For some reason, that particular night, Vivienne could not stand the knight's sickening sweet demeanor, which previously she might have found charming. Her imagination was occupied with another man altogether.

"My lady –" Lancelot commenced.

Vivienne's eyes narrowed, and her voice came out frosty. "I am not your lady, Lancelot, and it is a lack of respect to be using that term. You will address me as Lady Vivienne."

The confusion in the guard's eyes was not faked. At the exact moment, Alistair telepathically pointed out to her, *Yet you let your new champion call you so.*

Vivienne ignored them both, despite having the distinct impression Alistair was laughing at her.

Lancelot glowered at the dog, mumbled an "As you wish," and left. Vivienne resumed her walk with Alistair.

In the shadows, Sébastien smirked, before Alistair's voice came to him. *Lancelot is irritating. There is something odd I sense around him. You have to keep him away from Vivienne.*

Masking his shock, the guardian became pensive. *It would be hard, considering her sentiments for him.* He did not realize the words thought could be heard, until the dog's reply.

You humans truly amaze me, always missing the obvious, Alistair snorted in response, then went silent as Sébastien pondered his words in confusion.

Sébastien kept an eye on Vivienne from the shadows as she strode around. When she approached the lake and called on her magic, he could not help but gawk at her beauty and grace under the full moon.

The princess had bewitched him without even trying to, and it seemed the entire realm of Elsior was in the same situation.

The moon flashed brighter, and a headache hit Sébastien unawares. Images came to his head – fragments of holding her hand, embraces under the moonlight. His body tightened with the memories, even as he was filled with a desperate longing that nearly crippled him.

Alistair stopped his observation of Vivienne and glanced to the shadows at the tumult he felt coming from Sébastien. He expanded his mind in an invisible mist, until it attained the man's own thoughts. Hesitantly at first, then more boldly, he probed deeper for the notions, capturing them at the surface, and the aura surrounding him.

In this particular case, when their intellects came into contact, the demon dog's entire body tensed in dismay at the images he found there. He was dumbfounded. It could not be... Was there truly more going on with the two lovebirds than they could all discern?

"Come be a good doggie for once, Alistair," Vivienne implored under the moon, and he turned back to her. With a playful growl, the dog splashed in the water at her request.

At the sound of laughter, Sébastien was able to catch his breath. The memories faded away, but the longing within his mind and body remained. He compelled himself to stay in the shadows, and focus on protecting Vivienne.

Despite his best efforts, the pounding headache remained. The silence he forced upon himself tired him further, but the guardian survived through it for the next hours. When Vivienne retreated to her room safely, he got to his quarters and promptly passed out.

Alistair waited until Vivienne was dormant, then returned to the lake and the full moon. He contemplated the midnight sky, opening his mind and soul, and reached deep within where his old deity abilities rested. Finally, he was prepared to voice a query.

The dog's entire being was surrounded by a midnight glow, and he waited until the earth shifted under his feet, nature settling to listen. When the only noise was his breath, Alistair dared to enquire.

What are they to each other?

The lake, previously calm, swirled for a few moments as a vortex would. Once it settled, the reflection of the moon had changed. Alistair watched, transfixed, as the future played out: Sébastien and Vivienne's fates intertwined, and the incoming trouble.

When he peered back up at the moon, the wind whispered, *Salvation or destruction, that is their fate, as it has been for centuries in their past lives.*

With a low whine, Alistair went back to his mistress, pondering the newfound knowledge and what to do with it.

* * *

The next morning, Alistair woke up at dawn and headed over to Merlin's.

"Something important must be bringing you by this early," the wizard assumed as he saw the demon dog near.

Wary gazes met and held, the recollection of their last meeting very vivid in both their minds. They had been friends, but now a wide gap settled between them, rendering the air thick and heavy with tension. After a few moments, Alistair spoke.

What of Carleigh?

"I do not follow…"

Carleigh, your old apprentice that you messed up. Have you heard of him lately?

Merlin gave the demon dog an odd look, before admitting, "No, why?"

I received a warning about him the other day.

Merlin pondered it for a bit, then shrugged. "I really have no idea where he is or what he is doing. What was the warning?"

None of your business, but suffices to say he may have his sights set on Vivienne. I will return if it does come to be.

"Wait!"

Alistair stopped in his tracks, turning back to Merlin. *What now?*

"Have you no warnings of Guinevere?"

Why do you ask?

"Arthur will soon sign a treaty that will make him king of all surrounding lands, not just Camelot. As High King, he will need to take a wife."

Congratulations.

Merlin shook off the sarcasm, and instead continued, "Guinevere is not the best option for a queen. Not one I agree with, at any rate."

For a moment, Alistair considered not telling him of Ardea's words. Then he sighed, *Morgana helps Guinevere unknowingly, that is all I know. Good luck.*

He left without a backwards glance, missing the wizard's stricken expression.

* * *

"You look like crap."

Sébastien blew out an angry breath, wiping the cold water off his face. He forced himself to count to ten, before raising his gaze to be met with Lancelot's sneer.

"Not in the mood, Lance," the knight grunted.

"So I notice. Late night?" the younger man leered with a knowing expression.

"I suppose." *Or more to the point, an agonizingly short night.* After standing guard for Vivienne all evening and part into the night, he had barely managed to sleep for a few hours before the morning sun rose.

"Who's the lucky wench?"

Sébastien whirled around to retort, but the words died on his lips upon seeing Vivienne's frozen silhouette behind Lancelot. He frowned: she looked refreshed, if a little pale, which did not help his mood. Yet there was an odd glint of betrayal in the princess' eyes, which was bewildering to him.

"My lady," he bowed, "anything I can help you with?"

Vivienne tried to ignore the tug at her heart, but could not forget Lancelot's words. Sébastien had been with a woman, of course he had. He was young, gorgeously irresistible and free. He spent all day with her, which implied the nights were his to enjoy alone – and he obviously had.

The royal rapidly scanned the bloodshot eyes and dark circles of her guardian, and came to the same conclusion Lancelot had.

Vivienne urged her expression to remain neutral, even as she answered in an even voice, "No, I am quite fine, Dubois."

Sébastien arched an eyebrow in question. Vivienne only used his last name when mad at him, yet for all intents and purposes, her tone was neutral. Or so he thought.

"And please refrain from calling me 'your' lady," she added as an afterthought. "Lady Vivienne will do just fine."

The knight's expression became a full-blown glower at

her words. Out of the corner of his eyes, Sébastien noted Lancelot's victorious grin, and gritted his teeth. On edge now more than before, he bowed respectfully to Vivienne. "I apologize."

She ignored the gesture, and instead concentrated on Lancelot, "Someone has to accompany me on a horse ride to Merlin's for some supplies."

"At your service, Lady Vivienne."

Before Sébastien could intervene, they were gone, leaving him angry enough to punch a wall. The guard went to the blacksmith's forge instead to sharpen his sword and work off the frustration.

He was unaware of how much time had passed, when the voice rumbled in his head.

When I urged you to keep Lancelot away from Vivienne, I was not referring to a permanent solution. Temporary and with no blood shed will do just fine.

Sébastien whirled to see Alistair sitting down, eyes glowing in amusement.

"You sure about that?" he muttered, then went back to work, his strokes heavier than before.

Quite.

"I cannot understand it. I was fine calling her 'my lady' and now I cannot. And she accepted Lancelot's presence around her. The idea of them together—"

At the sudden growl coming from the demon dog, Sébastien stopped, astonished. Alistair had bared his teeth, red flames shooting from his eyes menacingly.

You had best not be insinuating Vivienne would allow his touch, otherwise I fear my support of you as her champion has attained its limit.

"No!" Sébastien put both hands up as a gesture of peace. "That is not what I implied! I meant..." He ran a frustrated hand through his hair. "Lancelot is a player and he annoys me, and I do not like him around the princess. I can comprehend Vivienne's affection for him, but he is not worthy."

If you dislike it so much, why not figure out how you wronged her, and fix it!

"I don't know how!"

Sébastien could have sworn the dog rolled his eyes, then stared pointedly before declaring, *You look like crap.*

"Not the first time I heard that today," the knight scowled.

No... Alistair stared at him for a beat, then repeated, this time enunciating each word: *You. Look. Like. Crap.*

"Repeating it as though I'm an idiot is not making this any better, demon dog."

Goddess of all— Alistair stopped midway, and tried a different approach. *To an outsider, it would seem you spent all night enjoying extracurricular activities.*

"What?" Sébastien frowned at the notion. "That is absurd, I was following Vivienne. You know it, you felt my presence in the woods!"

Yes. But Vivienne does not.

"So she concluded I'm neglecting my duties? Is that why she is upset?"

This time, Alistair did roll his eyes. *My mistress is not so selfish as to not permit you free time. I believe the reason of her being 'upset' with you is more due to what those activities might have been... Or with* whom.

Alistair peered in amusement at the guardian as reason

dawned.

"But why would she care if I'm with someone?" Sébastien wondered aloud.

Perhaps your perception of her feelings is not quite so on the spot as you believe. At the man's blank contemplation, Alistair gave up and walked away, grumbling, *This is why I do not get involved in human drama.*

* * *

Later that same night, Sébastien cornered Vivienne in the gardens on an evening stroll.

"Lady Vivienne," he called out formally, stepping out of the shadows.

She whirled, disconcerted upon glimpsing him.

The guard took advantage of the surprise and was by her side in two long strides. Before Vivienne had a chance to protest, he bent down on one knee. "I apologize for this morning. I did not neglect my duties last night. I—"

"Dubois, there is no need for details. It does not concern me." Vivienne's tone effectively aimed to end the conversation, but Sébastien was not about to give up.

"But it does. I was out shadowing you."

"You...what?" The princess' eyes widened at the admission.

"Your father commanded me to accompany you at all times. So have Alistair and Merlin. And I have done just that, wherever you have been the last days – and nights."

Sébastien straightened his back, eyes never once wavering from hers. His unwavering stare dared her to scan for the truth.

"You were up all night following me?" Vivienne wondered, gesturing for the knight to stand up, which he did.

"Yes," Sébastien admitted simply.

"Why did you not come forward?"

"Last time I did, I distracted you," he shrugged. "You were enjoying yourself with Alistair, and did not need another companion. I was content being a shadow."

Vivienne blinked in utter shock at the confession, and had the grace to appear contrite. "I do apologize for my behavior. I was incensed for no reason, and lashed out at you. Thank you for clearing it up."

Sébastien acquiesced, but did not leave.

"Was there anything else?" the princess enquired.

"As a matter of fact, yes. Two things, really. First, I would like you to approve of me alone accompanying you when you exit the palace grounds."

"I can do that," Vivienne complied good-naturedly. "And the second?"

Sébastien inched closer, effectively breaking the rules, and clasped her hand. He did his best to ignore the heat generated where their skins grazed. "I do not call you 'my lady' out of presumptuousness or arrogance," he confessed, voice rough with emotion. "I say it with respect, because you are my charge and I intend it as a threat for anyone who would harm you, to make it known you are protected by me."

Searching her gaze, Sébastien took a deep breath, before admitting the last bit, "I have never in my life given an oath as powerful as the one I gave to you when we first met, believe me. If you wish me to refrain from using those two words, I will. But I preferred to explain myself."

Vivienne was too stunned by the champion's words to speak at first, only scanning his earnest look. The way her body reacted at his every caress was distracting, reminiscent of the strange dreams she had been having. With a supreme effort, the royal breathed in deeply.

"It is fine, Sébastien," she allowed, voice slightly unsteady. "I did not mean what I said this morning. Let us forget and move past it."

A shadow of a smile played on the guardian's lips when he conceded, "As you wish, my lady." He bent over her hand, lingering a few seconds longer than necessary, inhaling the skin's fragrance.

When their fingers disentangled, he regretfully departed.

* * *

It was the feast the same night and Guinevere had been invited at the last minute. Her alliance to Arthur was well known, and King Adrien thought it only fair to celebrate, considering he knew both families.

Vivienne nibbled on food the entire night, and Sébastien observed every moment of it, his chest tightening with each passing moment. He glimpsed her furtive glances to Lancelot, whose eyes were glued to Guinevere, over and over.

Like a moth to a flame, the young man was already deep within the siren's clutches, and Sébastien had a hunch it would not be long before their attraction spiraled out of control.

Halfway through the dinner, the princess stood up, whispered something to her father and retreated. The old man's eyes scoured the room, finding Sébastien's. With a curt nod, he indicated him to follow Vivienne to the room.

Sébastien inclined his head in agreement, and subtly left the hall.

Unaware she was being followed, Vivienne headed to her

quarters, her thoughts fixated on Lancelot. She knew come the morning, Merlin had to be warned – yet again – of what she had witnessed. Arthur, according to the old wizard, was to be a great leader, but Guinevere would only ruin him.

Sliding in bed with a deep groan, Vivienne wearily concluded the entire night had only served to confirm her suspicions: humans were treacherous creatures, indeed.

In the hallway shadows, Sébastien waited until the door closed, and the flickering light streaming out was extinguished. He could not guess where Alistair was, but since the princess was out of harm's way, it was time for him to retreat.

The guardian's own heart, on the other hand, was in turmoil at the idea Vivienne would be dreaming of Lancelot. Shaking his head ruefully, he walked around a corner, only to run straight into said devil.

"Hey, watch your step, man," Lancelot grumbled.

Sébastien did not utter a noise, attempting to detour around, but the other guard seized his arm.

"Are you ignoring me?" he slurred, way beyond drunk.

"It is not a good idea to mess with me right now," Sébastien warned.

"Really?" Lancelot drawled. "If I recall correctly, I drew blood at practice."

Sébastien tightened his fists with barely suppressed rage, as Vivienne's countenance at the dinner still flickered in his mind. "And I kicked your ass. You are quite drunk. Go sleep it off."

"What? You imagine because Lady Viv pays you some special attention, you're better than us? Hell, you're probably her boy toy of the month—"

He did not get a chance to finish as Sébastien's fist cut him off, connecting with his jaw forcefully.

The door to Vivienne's room swung open, and she was astonished to notice Lancelot on the ground, unconscious. Sébastien towered over him, breathing heavily, his fist clenched tightly.

"What is the meaning of this?"

Sébastien peered at her, and the heat of the battle still in his eyes expanded into something else as they traveled over the princess. When the burning ardor met her own confused stare, Vivienne realized the nightgown, with the newly lit candlelight behind her, must be transparent.

With a wave of a hand, she got a cape and covered herself. Sébastien's eyes did not waver as Vivienne's approached him.

"I apologize, my lady," his voice sounded anything but. "The noise must have disturbed you. Lancelot had too much to drink and his words were offensive."

"To whom?"

"It does not matter."

Vivienne might have let it slide, were it not for the crackling fury, almost tangible, emanating from him. "Sébastien, I command you tell me."

"Offensive to you," he mumbled, avoiding her eyes.

"I see."

Vivienne glanced at the younger man on the floor thoughtfully. Then, with a motion of her hand, Lancelot was gone, disappeared into nothingness. Sébastien gaped at his mistress incredulously.

"Merlin has been teaching me to dematerialize things – and people," she explained with a shrug. "I sent him back to his room. He should not be privy to this conversation if his drunken intellect does, by chance, recall it tomorrow morning."

Vivienne stepped to the knight slowly.

"May I see your hand?" she asked softly, coaxingly.

Entranced, Sébastien extended his bruised fist to the enchantress. Vivienne caressed the bloodied knuckle, running a glowing palm over it, before letting the enchantment work. "How is it I keep healing your wounds?" she wondered.

The words were out before they could be stopped, in a rushed intensity. "If only I could do to the same to you, my lady."

"Heal me?" Vivienne looked up from the wound, frowning. "From what?"

The intensity was back again in Sébastien's gaze, and this time Vivienne fell prey to the sentiments urging them both on. With a groan, the knight bent his head and grazed his lips to hers.

What should have been a gentle kiss turned into more when the princess inched near, her body melting against his.

Vivienne moaned in contentment at the soft plundering, her innocence and closeness snapping Sébastien's restraint. In one swift move, he had Vivienne pinned between the wall and himself, as the embrace brought them both deeper down a spiral of pleasure.

When his hand drifted under her cape, stroking the bare skin through the thin chemise, Vivienne gasped at the sensations. The small noise broke past Sébastien's red haze of desire, and he froze.

Realizing what he was doing, the guardian let go at once

as though scalded. "I am so sorry, my lady. I had no right. Please forgive me."

Head dizzy from his skillful lips, Vivienne took a moment to register Sébastien was now kneeling at her feet instead of kissing her. As though it was not confusing enough, the fast-drumming pulse in her veins was impossible to quiet.

"I – it is fine, Sébastien," she managed to stutter, stepping back to her chambers and leaving the still kneeling guardian behind.

"I am a fool," the knight declared to the shadows, bowing his head.

CHAPTER 20

In Camelot, Arthur was walking in the gardens when he fell upon Guinevere, sitting sadly underneath the sun. His heart beat faster the closer he got to the young maiden.

"Guinevere?"

She jumped up, startled, then curtsied in his presence.

Arthur immediately grabbed her hand, tugging to stop her. "Do not bow around me, Guinevere," he murmured. Registering the dried tears on her cheeks, he stepped closer. "Why do you cry on such a beautiful day?"

"I miss my home," Guinevere whispered. "But no matter how badly I long for it, I cannot stand to be away from you…"

Arthur's heart skipped a beat, even as he caressed her knuckles softly. "Do not be wary of telling me your true feelings. Do you not know how I care for you?"

When those large blue eyes only stared back at him, Arthur bent down and kissed the beauty, groaning at the touch of her lips. Guinevere's body melted against his as though made for him, and he could not help grasping her closer.

As they kissed, their caresses grew more feverish, until Arthur pulled away, panting. "Marry me."

Guinevere's mouth opened in shock, before she smiled largely. "Do you mean it?"

"I have never desired anything more, Guinevere. Be my queen."

She nodded and Arthur resumed the embrace, missing the glint of victory in her eyes.

* * *

In Elsior, Sébastien was in the stables, busy brushing Illyria and packing provisions. It had been over a week since their kiss and the guardian was tired of envisioning it over and over – and over again. Vivienne had not spoken one word directly to him, other than to ask for companionship wherever it was she had to go.

The knight did not understand her reaction, or whether she was hurt or simply offended. All he was aware of was the deep longing to do it again... And again.

Inside the castle, Vivienne supervised from a balcony as a contingent of men prepared to deploy outside the castle grounds. The door to the room opened, and the king stepped in.

"Father, what is all this?"

"All the guards are heading to the border," the old man disclosed. "There has been a skirmish, and it worries me that it might escalate."

"All of them?" Vivienne frowned, fearing the worst.

"Yes. Can you put a barrier in place to defend the castle in their absence?"

"Of course."

The princess curtsied and ran out to the gates to do it immediately.

Ensuring there was no one around to get hurt, Vivienne positioned herself close to the castle's gates. Two large, ornate metal doors stood as the official entrance to the palace, and from each started a wall of stone, which circled the grounds. In height, it added up to ten men's, and its width was the same. The rock itself – bricks of a pale grey – had been put together by ancestors of the past; each area ensured none could breach it.

Vivienne took a moment to glance up at the wall, then pressed both palms to the stone. She closed her eyes, searching for the incantation within, and forcing it out into the wall itself. At the hotness underneath her palms, she blinked, to glimpse a green glow escaping them and entering the rocks.

The stone vibrated as the spell traveled within it and upwards. It finally escaped past the top, where the sentries were normally posted, and formed a dome.

As the blazing barrier embraced the grounds and protected them, Vivienne looked around the area, searching for her guardian – in vain.

She went to the stables, where Sébastien was adding some items to his baggage, next to Illyria. Both glanced up at her arrival.

"My lady, you heard?"

Vivienne acquiesced, stepping closer. "I do not like the idea of you in a fight."

Sébastien was pleasantly astounded by the admission, and

followed it with one of his own. "And I, my lady, hate to leave you here unprotected."

"I will be fine... But please come back unharmed." Vivienne placed a hand to Sébastien's cheek in a wordless gesture.

The knight searched her gaze, before inclining his head and pressing his lips to her palm. "I vow so, my lady."

The promise vibrated within Vivienne, and they stared at each other for a few moments. She yearned for nothing more than a touch of his mouth, but his own reaction to their last encounter was confusing.

The princess' eyes went to Sébastien's weapon, and of its own accord, a hand extended to its hilt. With a basic wish, a spell flew in it and Vivienne smiled in satisfaction as another green glow entered the metal.

At Sébastien's raised eyebrows, she explained, "It will defend you, and allow me a glimpse of how the battle is going, in case..." Vivienne trailed off, unable to finish.

The anguish in the royal's eyes unsettled the guardian, but he did not dare a single motion, even as Vivienne wordlessly dropped her hand and left.

As Sébastien exited the stalls, he noticed her next to Lancelot's horse. The younger man had bent his head lower, and Vivienne was whispering in his ear. Under the champion's dismayed gaze, Lancelot clasped the princess' hand in his, and kissed it softly.

Sébastien's heart weighed heavy with what he glimpsed. It was apparent Vivienne's concern for him was for a knight, but for Lancelot, it was for a man.

He had no idea that in truth, Vivienne was tasking

Lancelot with watching after Sébastien, and to let Alistair protect them, without intervening, as soldiers frequently did on the field of battle.

Once she was done, the enchantress met Sébastien's melting regard across the distance, waved a goodbye, and went up to her chamber. Alistair was there, pacing impatiently.

"You are leaving as well, I take it?"

Yes, he replied simply.

"Be careful," Vivienne pleaded, now worried for two loved ones.

The demon dog nuzzled her hand in farewell, then departed swiftly.

* * *

The contingent of men made fast work of reaching the border by nightfall. They had barely passed the last of the forest, when they fell into an ambush.

"To me!" Sébastien raised his sword, rallying the men and charging forward.

Once he got in the midst of the fray, he jumped off Illyria and sent the mare away for protection. The knight was immediately surrounded by their enemies: a mix of mercenaries and –

Druids?

Sébastien found Lancelot across the distance and shared a shocked stare with him, motioning to the men dressed in robes akin to priests.

These are no druids.

Sébastien turned to Alistair, whose midnight eyes flared with red specks. It had taken the demon dog all of two seconds to realize they were facing both humans and sorcerers alike.

How to get Vivienne's soldiers out safe, was another matter altogether.

"What do you mean?" Sébastien asked, disposing of a mercenary with a swift strike of the blade.

Alistair lunged onto an assailant, capturing the hex he was throwing in his own jaws and pulverizing him in return.

He faced Sébastien, registering his widened gaze. This *is what I mean. They may have been druids at some point, but believe me when I say they are full of corruption now.*

"Watch out!"

The knight was pushed aside by Lancelot, whose sword clashed with an assassin's sharp knife just in time to block it. He had been trying to attack from behind, evidently trying to take out Sébastien.

"Thank you," the latter said gratefully, realizing how close of a call it had been.

"No need," Lancelot grinned. "Vivienne would have my hide if I let anything happen to you."

What? Sébastien frowned in confusion. In the midst of the battle, his thoughts turned to the princess back at the castle.

Snap out of it! Alistair admonished, destroying another druid. *If we are to survive, you need to think only of yourself, and focus. Now!*

Sébastien gripped the sword tighter and jumped back into the fray.

In the distance, a cloaked figure observed the two men and dog fight. Though the hood covered his features, Carleigh still kept out of sight, taking in what was happening below.

I have seen enough of the knight, he muttered and stepped away. Now he knew who protected the princess, which would make it easier to take them out.

Focused on his lethal ruminations, the sorcerer never sensed the other wave of dark magic that permeated the surroundings.

Morgana, masked on the opposite end of the battlefield, smiled coldly. Carleigh was the perfect pawn to help her plan. Darkened grey eyes lowered to Sébastien, Lancelot and the Alistair.

Now, to get you three out of commission…

* * *

When night came, Vivienne tossed and turned in bed, unable to rest. She gave in and went to a basin of water. Due to her connection with the water, the liquid was prepared to show her whatever she wished. The princess dipped an index in it, and whispered at the ripples, "Show me Sébastien."

Influenced by the enchantment, the water swirled for a moment before smoothing into a mirror, where she could see the battle itself.

Sébastien valiantly fought for hours against assailants, and Vivienne even caught glimpses of Alistair. But then something struck the guardian, and he went down. There was nothing afterwards, as though the connection had been broken. Worried beyond words, all she could do was pace until her feet hurt.

Within the hour, Vivienne tried again, impatiently tapping her fingers against the basin. This time, she witnessed a moving sky, as if Sébastien was being dragged. She restlessly waited until the group of knights returned to the castle, unsure of how long it would take them.

It turned out to be two more days and nights, then a knock

woke Vivienne up in the middle of the night. She ran and yanked the door open before the third knock came again.

"Sébastien!" Without thought of anything but relief, she jumped in his arms, burying her head in his chest. "I was afraid you were harmed."

The knight's answering moan of discomfort alerted her that he was, indeed, hurt. Vivienne backed away, and Sébastien glimpsed for the first time the tears in her eyes.

"My lady, why are you crying?"

She wiped at her cheeks, embarrassed. "Of relief. I was afraid…." Vivienne trailed off before she could admit to more. "Come in. You are harmed, and I can heal you." She reached for Sébastien's hand, but he would not budge.

"I appreciate the offer, but I only came to ensure you were alright. It is not a wise idea for me to be in your bedchambers."

Vivienne ignored the strained note in Sébastien's voice, and tugged him in regardless. "Do not fight me over this. I care not if anyone notices you, when I can mend you better than any healer."

Sébastien gave up and allowed himself to be dragged in and settled on an armchair. The princess drifted around, lighting lamps, while he tried to manage his breathing and reaction to her. It was a lost cause, as his eyes never wavered off her enticing silhouette.

"Can you remove your amour?" Vivienne asked once there was light, critically inspecting what she could see of the wounds.

Sébastien tried to draw the protective shield up, but the anguish shooting up his arm had him groaning. Vivienne was by his side in an instant, her hand gently restraining.

"Stop, I can do it."

Vivienne used air to help get the armor off the guardian, leaving him in a shirt stained with the battle's grit. She could not help a gasp at the amount of blood.

"It looks worse than it is," Sébastien tried to smile confidently, but it came out as a grimace.

Rolling her eyes, Vivienne grabbed the bottom of the shirt and gently peeled it off him, then over the head. She conjured up a bowl of cold liquid from the lake and a cloth, and got to work wiping off his chest and back, all to better observe the wounds.

Sébastien's shoulder had an awkward angle and developing bruise, and one side of his body had a few deep gashes, which could become infected rapidly if left untreated.

When the clean-up was done, Vivienne announced, "I will use magic for the rest. If you have any objections, now is the time."

Sébastien inclined his head in assent, gritting his teeth as the princess' glowing hands progressed across his body. While Vivienne's powers mended the wounds, the knight's entire world narrowed on the healing angel.

Dark hair cascaded down her shoulders, framing features filled with worry. Biting her bottom lip, green eyes narrowed in concentration, the princess was completely unaware of the effect she had on him.

"Does it hurt badly?" Vivienne asked after a moment, noticing his tension and expression of torment.

"No," Sébastien gave out a strangled groan. The injuries were not the problem – Vivienne's closeness was.

As soon as she was done, he tried to get up but the room

spun warningly around him. Without another option, Sébastien had to settle back down on the armchair.

"Where are you trying to go?" Vivienne enquired, already reaching to restrain him, both hands resting on his chest.

"To my chambers."

"You are still weak from the loss of blood."

"I have to go," Sébastien gritted out, clenching his jaw against the unreasonable desire heating his blood. A few more moments, and he would utterly lose control.

"No, you do not," Vivienne frowned, not understanding the odd behavior. "Let me bring you something to drink, and you can rest. You could even sleep here until mo—"

Sébastien gripped her wrist, a warning to his seriousness. Vivienne peered down at him, noting his rigidity. It was impossible not to also observe the rippling of his muscles, lighted by the fire, and something inside her badly craved to touch the guardian – and not as a healer.

"Please don't," Sébastien pleaded as Vivienne's emerald eyes darkened, and a smoldering rapture resonated within her – similar to the one in his own blood.

Her gaze lingered on his eyes, darkened to coal with barely restrained passion, then moved to his broad shoulders. All Vivienne wanted was to run her hands up and down his back, and feel that strength pressed against her.

"Do not look at me that way, Vivienne, or I will lose control."

The enchantress could not fathom which of Sébastien using her name, how it sounded from his lips, or the actual admission unsettled her more and fueled fascination.

Her lips parted in bewilderment, both at the crackling

excitement and a memory from months back. She had once eavesdropped on guards speak about the thrill of battle and how afterwards all they longed for was to come home to their ladies and bury the newfound ardor in lovemaking.

The yearning for Sébastien's hands on her body was enough to make her dizzy. Throat dry, Vivienne moistened her lips and watched as the knight's last shred of restraint snapped.

In one motion, Sébastien tugged on her wrist, and then Vivienne was in his lap. His heat surrounded her like a scorching furnace, seeping through the thin chemise and warming her entire body.

His hands cupped her cheeks, even as he begged, "Please send me away. In the state I am in, this is not something I can control."

"But I can," Vivienne assured him, then closed the distance between them, pressing her lips against his. She had been dying to do it again – and Sébastien did not disappoint.

One hand went to her waist to gather her closer, whilst the other angled her head so he could better plunder her mouth. The fierceness of the kiss continued, and Vivienne could sense Sébastien's last bit of restraint as he tried to rein it in. She was not sure stopping was an option any longer, with the way her own body was close to combusting.

Vivienne got closer, and Sébastien deepened the embrace, mercilessly taking over. Both hands slid to her hips, pulling her down on him, pressing against his manhood. The growl that escaped him was more animal than man.

His lips drifted with intent down her jaw, then her throat, and back up again with an eagerness Vivienne registered from faraway. She had one instant of clarity, that if things progressed too far – no matter how much she wished them to – Sébastien would feel guilty in the morning.

With a repressed moan, the enchantress let both her hands roam across his back. Much as she enjoyed the feel of steely muscles, Vivienne pushed past her own desires and sent small jolts of warmth to relax them. Before long, Sébastien's lips gentled, and the pace changed from feverish to more tender, until the princess slowly withdrew away.

Sébastien rested his head against her shoulder, drawing in deep breaths as if he had run a long distance.

"I had no right," he muttered shamefully. "But I appear to be making a habit of it."

Vivienne grabbed his chin, forcing him to meet her gaze. "I initiated it, Sébastien. And I did not object to it – nor did I the last time." His disbelieving frown threw her off. "You doubt my words?"

"No, but... Are your affections not taken by someone else?"

Vivienne raised an eyebrow, disconcerted at the query. "Of course not."

Sébastien sighed – he was too tired for affection games. "Please let us finish this conversation at a later time, my lady. I should retire to my chambers now."

"Rest," Vivienne murmured, taking pity on his fatigued state of mind. "I will ensure you sleep in your bed tonight."

With a single hand gesture, the enchantress dematerialized him, as she had Lancelot not long before.

I do thank you for the concern, a grumble came from the shadows.

Vivienne whirled around to Alistair, and ran to hug her

protector. "Of course I was concerned! How are you? What happened in the battle?"

The usual: blood, human against human, and sorcery involved.

Vivienne frowned at the description, but Alistair jumped on her bed and laid his head down, putting an end to the conversation. She would talk to him tomorrow about taking a bath, as he seemed ready to doze off.

She got into bed, careful not to shake it, presuming the demon dog was dormant. It was only after she was settled that Alistair conveyed his particular brand of wisdom once more.

Much as the battle was exhausting, observing you two dance around each other is even more so. Please settle Sébastien's heart before it ends up out of his chest, Vivienne. The man loves you.

Vivienne gaped in shock at the obscurity for a long moment, Alistair's gentle snore the only background noise. With an inhuman effort, she forced herself to sleep, but dreamt of onyx eyes, stony muscles and soft lips on hers.

CHAPTER 21

On the way to Merlin's lessons, Vivienne had to make a conscious effort to ignore Sébastien's presence behind her. Following the night they had so thoroughly kissed, she had not been able to look at him without yearning to do it again. Which, it was obvious he was not interested in, as per the hasty apology.

Nevertheless, she was slowly losing her sanity by being around him as he sparred shirtless, as he escorted her around... Vivienne fantasized day and knight of the knight's eyes, hands, body, and it was fast becoming tedious.

"My lady," the devil himself said from behind, interrupting her musings.

The enchantress schooled her features in an impassable mask, before facing him.

"Lancelot is running this way – with news."

Vivienne peered to where the guardian pointed, noticing

the young man rapidly advancing towards them. She acknowledged him with a welcoming nod and missed Sébastien's scowl.

"What news, Lancelot?"

"Your father declared there's to be a hunting party in an hour, and he requires all his men in on it. I was sent to enquire whether Sébastien will be joining."

"I will be fine without you," Vivienne glanced at Sébastien, "once you drop me off. Merlin can accompany me back, if anything."

He held her eyes for a moment longer, before nodding in agreement to Lancelot. "You can inform the king I will take part."

As the blonde man left with the news, Sébastien offered the princess his arm. "I will at least drop you straight with the mage, before I leave. Would you object?"

"Not at all," Vivienne replied, her fingers tingling as she grasped his extended forearm. At the slight dizziness hitting her, she had to hold on tightly as though her life depended on it.

The rest of the trip to Merlin's was pure torture: thighs brushed as they strolled, hips occasionally bumped each other... A myriad of movements made Vivienne all the more mindful of his presence. And throughout it all, Sébastien seemed unbothered.

Except when they arrived, as she peered up at him, the flame was back in his onyx eyes. The look he levelled on her before departing warmed her up from tip to toes.

* * *

All the bustling around the castle finally got on Vivienne's nerves, and she stopped a panicked servant. "What is going on?"

"The men were attacked by a boar. Sir Lancelot was almost impaled alive, but one of the new guardians saved him."

The princess' heart dropped at the news.

"The new guardian. What is his name?"

"I do not know my lady, my apologies. I believe he might one of your daily guards."

"Sébastien!"

Vivienne did not stop to consider how it might appear. She picked up her skirts and ran for the great hall where they must have arrived, bursting past the doors. The group of men gathered around all gaped at her, but she only had eyes for one.

In their midst, laid down on one of the benches, was Sébastien. He was ashen, with a shirt full of blood, his stomach having been cut open by the animal. The king was at his head, Lancelot by his side.

"Get out of my way," Vivienne uttered in such a glacial voice that the men in her way edged away without a single word.

Her father looked up at the sound of her voice. "Darling daughter, can you save him?"

"Yes," was all she responded, kneeling next to Sébastien's unmoving form.

Vivienne lifted the bloody rag which covered the gut wound, and gasped at its severity. She had never attempted healing on such a scale, especially on a human. But if there was a chance to save him, the enchantress would give it her all.

"My lord, it's not good for the lady–"

Disregarding Lancelot's words, Vivienne announced in a deadly tone, "If you attempt to remove me from Sébastien's side, I will petrify you all to hell."

She did not have to look up to confirm the men's shocked expressions, as the dead silence surrounding her spoke volumes. Vivienne was not one for threats – at least she had not recently been. She had absolutely no idea where the words had even come from, aware only of the longing to save Sébastien.

"There is so much blood," Vivienne uttered to herself in quite a different voice. With a muttered incantation – one of Merlin's own – some clean linen and fresh water materialized by her side. She got to work cleaning the wound, until only fresh blood seeped.

Once that was done, the enchantress placed both hands above the wound and reached deep inside for the healing capacity, much as Merlin had taught her. She could experience the enchantment at work, but could not help noticing Sébastien's slow breathing. Healing the wound would only be part of the problem; he would have to handle the rest himself.

In an effort to block away the astounded and frightened faces – not everyone at the castle was accepting of their mistress' magic – Vivienne closed her eyes. The spell escaped her palms in pale golden wisps, entering Sébastien's wounds, healing the torn flesh and piecing it back together. His features remained of marble during the entire operation, breathing still as weak.

When it was done, Vivienne examined him for any other wounds, but none were apparent. She stood up, and the men in the immediate vicinity backed away a few feet – all except the king. The princess could not tell whether they did so in awe or fear, but she was too numb to bother caring either way.

"He will require transport to a room where he can rest and get about easily. Or be overseen by a servant. Father?"

King Adrien noticed the pleading glint in Vivienne's eyes, and announced loudly to everyone, "Sébastien displayed great courage today. I will have him placed in one of the guest bedrooms in the East Wing. He will have everything."

Vivienne kept her counsel, silently content as the East Wing was on her side of the castle. As she moved away from Sébastien, a few of the men dared to inch closer. They gently grabbed the guardian for transport, and stepped away.

The monarch went back up to her room and fell on the bed, exhausted and in tears. One thing was clear now to her more than ever: if Sébastien had died, she would have been devastated.

* * *

Later in the day, Vivienne went to check on the knight. She was informed he had a fever, and it was worrisome. As the princess stayed by Sébastien's side, using cold compresses to cool him down, he shifted restlessly whilst sleeping.

"Vivienne."

Startled, Vivienne peered up from the book she was reading, but Sébastien was still dormant – with her on the mind, apparently.

"Lancelot, he is alive," the champion mumbled again.

She frowned in confusing, wondering, *What is he on about?*

"I would rather you be happy with him than sad without, my love."

With a gasp, understanding dawned on Vivienne. Sébastien's words from before, of healing her pain, and having feelings for another: he presumed she liked Lancelot! And the reason he saved him...

"You did it for me, putting yourself in the path of the boar..." Vivienne whispered, incredulously staring at the knight. He had almost died, all for her happiness.

Uncaring who saw her, Vivienne gripped Sébastien's hand, and his restless motions stopped. "I do not like Lancelot," she declared, voice raspy with emotion. "It is you my heart yearns for. Please get better soon."

Though he did not answer, the hand she clasped gave a gentle squeeze. The enchantress remained by his side until the fever dropped and only then retreated to her own chambers.

* * *

Guinevere stepped out of the room and headed down to the grand hall. She had heard Lancelot returned and wished to see him, if only to ensure he was enchanted by her.

The walk down was quick and quiet, as the castle was asleep. She found the knight staring into the large fire, a sad look upon his face.

"Lancelot," she murmured, and he turned around. Guinevere could see in his eyes the unanswered desire and had to hide a satisfied smirk. Instead, she forced just as sad an expression on, whispering, "I know I should not be saying this, but I have missed you."

She stepped closer to him, until only a few inches separated them. Lancelot lifted a hand as if to touch her, then dropped it back down. "I have missed you as well, Lady Guinevere."

Listening to her impulses, the young woman jumped in his arms, ensuring her body was glued to his enticingly. She then moved her lips to his ear. "I cannot stay away from you."

"But we must," Lancelot urged, gently peeling her off him – at a huge cost to his own longings. "Has the wizard bothered you again?"

Guinevere looked at him blankly, before recalling the lie from before. "No," she admitted, "but I still fear Merlin."

"Do not. I am here now, and soon Arthur will sign this peace treaty. Once he does and becomes High King, he will rule the entire land, you will be queen, and I will become your protector. No one will harm you."

"Oh Lancelot…"

"I must go," he forced the words past gritted teeth and departed her presence, before baser impulses took over and he was no longer master of his actions.

Guinevere watched Lancelot leave, smiling widely. "What a lovesick fool," she muttered aloud.

"Indeed," the voice came from behind and she whirled around to face none other than Merlin, stepping from the shadows. "Well played, Guinevere."

"I do not know what you are referring to," she retorted, lifting her chin defiantly.

Though cold, Arthur's love interest was no fool. Fury emanated in waves off the wizard, and it was enough to make her aware of how impressive an opponent he could be.

"What did you tell Lancelot, hmm?" Merlin bared his teeth, barely holding back the urge to throttle her. "That I threatened you? All in order to ensure his undying loyalty and push me aside?"

Guinevere lost hold of her countenance and scowled in answer. "And if I did?"

"Nothing you do will get Arthur to cast me aside," Merlin stated, his blue eyes glowing of an unnatural fire. "Be careful which enemies you make, young one. You may regret it."

"As if!" Guinevere laughed, and Merlin could not help but wonder what in hell Arthur saw in her icy demeanor. "Once we are married, Arthur will do anything to keep me happy. *Anything*. Keep that in mind."

Guinevere walked past him, about to depart, but Merlin grasped her arm tightly.

"You foolish girl!" he growled, his face close by. "Do you really think you can get away with this? What makes you think I will not tell Arthur tonight what I have witnessed?"

"What, and ruin his poor morale?" Guinevere snickered. "You can tell him... but he will not believe you. There is a stronger chance he will trust me over you."

"Will you take the risk?"

"I think the better question is, will *you*?" Guinevere countered mockingly.

Merlin's grip on her arm tightened and magic glowed underneath his palm. His control slipped, and the power hummed underneath the surface, lighting his eyes of a blue hue so pale, it was almost white.

The Fae in him, which Merlin always sought to keep at bay, was no longer responding to his silent urging to calm down. Instead, it wanted to control, to possess, and to bend to his will.

Guinevere dropped the arrogant act and fear showed in her eyes, even as she struggled to get out of his iron hold. She had pushed too far, and now could not go back.

"What are you doing?"

"I am ensuring you will forever be at my command," Merlin declared without an ounce of emotion. Already, the magic was seeping into the young woman, blurring the lines of her will and curbing it to his.

Enough!

Merlin snapped out of the angry daze to see Alistair in a corner. It was apparent from Guinevere's glazed expression that she was oblivious to his presence, but the dog had only eyes for the warlock.

Let her go this instant, before you make a bigger mistake than with Morgana!

Scowling, Merlin dropped his hand and Guinevere walked away. She would not remember the last instants, only leaving with a vague feeling of having concluded their conversation with the upper hand.

Once she was gone, the mage turned to Alistair. "Why did you stop me?"

As I said, you would have made a bigger mistake. There will be a time to get Guinevere away, but this is not it.

"Arthur is to be crowned king of the entire land soon, and he has asked her to marry him. I cannot let this come to pass."

Listen to me this once, wizard. If you intervene and try to change Arthur's mind, you will lose him. You need to wait until he doubts Guinevere, and then swoop in.

With the wise words, Alistair departed, leaving Merlin to his dark musings.

* * *

In her cottage, Morgana's gaze lingered on the mage,

before she ended the connection. Guinevere had more gut than she gave her, but I was past time Morgana stepped in to seal the deal.

For a moment, before the demon dog intervened, she had almost rejoiced that Merlin was stepping to the dark side. Then he had not…

She knew why Alistair had stepped in. If Merlin had used light magic to bend Guinevere's will, not only would he have been a step closer to darkness, but it would have made him more easily influenced by her hand.

The dog must have foreseen it, damn him!

Ruefully shaking her head, Morgana set about preparing the next step of her plot.

* * *

It had been two days following the hunt, and Vivienne was worried for Sébastien. She had been told he had awoken, but was still weak. That night, she finished dinner early, barely eating anything as it was, and left the great hall.

As the princess wandered the hallways, she sensed a presence behind and whirled around.

"Sébastien!"

"I did not intend to frighten you, my lady. I was attempting to ensure you got to your quarters safely."

"What are you doing awake?" Vivienne inched towards him, and stopped before reaching the handsome knight. "You should be resting."

"I have had all the rest I could without being able to see you."

Vivienne's lips parted in surprise, and she glanced hopefully into Sébastien's rapt expression. His eyes were devouring her, taking his fill as if she had not been within his sight in ages.

"I–" the princess stopped, unsure of how to go on. The intensity in the guard's gaze was even a bit worrisome, and she backed away instead.

"I had a strange dream while I rested," Sébastien divulged, his stare never once wavering off hers. He advanced, one step at a time, even as Vivienne kept moving backwards. "I dreamt you healed me, and revealed that it was not Lancelot your heart pined for."

"That is a nice dream, indeed," the princess replied faintly past her throat dry. She was afraid of what would happen when they came into contact, knowing her body had no discipline whatsoever around him – truly a chilling notion.

"It was," Sébastien agreed, inching near some more. "I dreamt of your healing touch and kept convincing myself I had to wake up, and tell you in person..."

He was now in front of her, barely a hair's breath away. Vivienne had run out of room to back away, and now they found themselves in a deserted part of the hallway, behind a pillar. Cold stone was at her back and Sébastien's warmth at her front.

The enchantress tilted her head back to meet his gaze, unaware of how inviting her parted lips were.

"Tell me what?" Vivienne whispered, an almost daring inflection in her voice.

Sébastien placed both hands on the wall on either side of her, effectively caging her in. His body moved, closing the last gap between them as he confessed, "I love you. Not as a knight to his lady, but I have fallen for you as a man for a woman. I cannot stay away from you. The only reason I lasted away is because I presumed your affections belonged to another. If I am overstepping, now would be a good time to shut me down."

Vivienne stared into onyx fire, unable to speak, only shake her head in denial. The small victorious gleam she noticed spoke volumes, before Sébastien gathered her close and his mouth descended on hers. As before, it commenced slowly and tenderly, but soon escalated into more.

The only thing that mattered, in both their minds, was getting closer after the days spent apart. As he embraced his beloved, Sébastien captured her moans, and her lips opened at his gentle prodding. With a barely suppressed growl, he deepened the kiss, grabbing her waist and lifting her up in his arms.

He nearly dropped to his knees when Vivienne wrapped both legs around his hips, pulling him closer. And still the defender's mouth plundered hers, tasting sweetness and innocence.

It was only Sébastien's keen listening skills and years of training that alerted him to the guard patrolling the hallway.

Immediately, he froze. If Vivienne was caught, her reputation would be ruined. Blissfully ignorant of it, she still kissed him, and he did not want it to stop – damnation and all. With a huge effort, Sébastien drew back from the princess' eager lips.

"Open your eyes, love."

He smiled at her glazed, satisfied expression, planning to continue as soon as the threat was eliminated.

"There is a guard," Sébastien murmured, his voice barely above a whisper.

Vivienne's eyes widened at the implied message, but Sébastien placed an index on her mouth for silence. "Shh."

He slowly let her feet get back to the ground and angled his body to hide hers, just in case. They waited with bated breath, but the guard's footsteps drifted further away rather than closer.

"Well. That was ..." Sébastien peered down at the grinning royal, chuckling softly at her sheepish expression. "I truly apologize, Vivienne. I should have known better than to let it progress this far in public."

"How about in private?" she whispered, and his heart beat faster at the invitation in her eyes. Before he could stop her, Vivienne captured his hand in hers and dragged him to her room.

Once inside, she locked the door and waved a hand for a sound proof barrier, ensuring they would have complete privacy.

When she circled back to him, however, Sébastien was already retreating, palms held up – to keep her away, or him from getting closer, he could not say. "Vivienne, I cannot in all good conscience take your virtue."

The enchantress could not help a small smile, as his loyalty and principles made him that much more endearing. "Then spend the night with me, and keep me company. I cannot bear to be parted from you now."

"That, I can do," Sébastien agreed.

As the princess stepped away to change, the guardian removed his boots and left only his breeches and an undershirt on. He hesitated for a moment, glancing at the large bed, but was saved from making a decision by Vivienne's soft curse.

Sébastien raised his eyebrows as she stepped out of her private room, and turned her back to him with an annoyed sigh.

"Would you object to unlacing my corset? My handmaiden usually does it, but for obvious reasons, I would prefer not to call her…"

Her timid tone was his downfall.

Sébastien shifted behind Vivienne and slowly unlaced the corset with expert fingers. Each time his fingertips grazed the bare skin of her back, little electric jolts tingled them both. When he was done, the knight had an impossible time recalling why it was he could not bring the situation to its inevitable conclusion.

And then, Vivienne spun in the circle of his arms, her green eyes wide and innocent, and he remembered. He bent down for a light goodnight kiss, but kept a tight leash on the passion still stirring underneath the surface.

Sensing it, Vivienne retreated once more to the private room to change, before joining him in bed. It was the first night in a long time that Sébastien slept soundly.

CHAPTER 22

"My lady," a different voice than the one in her dreams woke the princess up. "Your father wishes to speak with you. There is someone here to see you."

Vivienne groaned, but got up nonetheless.

King Adrien waited in the throne room, smiling reassuringly as she entered. Vivienne managed to return it, despite the sour mood she was in already.

"Dear daughter, I am aware of our understanding that you will focus on the supernatural, and not marriage, but the son of one of my oldest friends has dropped by to visit. As a favor, could you please show him around? And be pleasant."

"Of course, father," Vivienne rolled her eyes. "Might I get an escort, though?"

"Yes, yes. Bring Sébastien. He is protective of you."

Vivienne dipped into a curtsy, lowering her lashes to hide her joy. Showing a stranger around would be bearable so long as Sébastien was there as backup.

The man himself was scrawny and awkward, about her height, but respectful and polite. Vivienne could not put her finger on it, but something in his countenance – a glint in the eyes, the way he smirked – was disturbing.

"We have to get my guard," she announced and headed towards the training grounds, the suitor following far behind.

As they neared, Vivienne noticed Sébastien disappearing around a corner. For a moment, she could have sworn glimpsing a flash of blonde hair right ahead.

With a bad presentiment in the pit of the stomach, the royal gestured for the suitor to wait. She went towards the stables, following the voices. One was Sébastien's deep tone, and another was a more melodious one. Vivienne did not have to see its owner to identify Guinevere.

She rounded the corner just in time to see the young woman step into Sébastien's embrace, and his arms go around her waist, much as they had with her. The cold bite of betrayal was harsh on the enchantress' heart.

Vivienne was about to retreat to nurse her wounds, but was held back by something. The hesitation was enough to notice Sébastien was not gripping Guinevere lovingly, but rather to drive her away. When he finally did so successfully and backed away, he gave the young woman a wide berth.

"What is the matter with you!?" Even Vivienne cringed at the tone of Sébastien's voice, the disgust and scorn more than apparent. "You are promised to Arthur! Does it mean nothing to you?"

"It is precisely why I have to enjoy my freedom while I still can."

"Well, go enjoy it with someone else. I am not interested."

Guinevere's expression contorted in an ugly pout, but she caught sight of Vivienne and sneered. "Oops! We have a witness. Lady Vivienne," she curtsied in a mocking bow.

Sébastien whirled around, and the princess noted in his eyes the realization she must have witnessed everything. "My lady, I–"

Vivienne waved a hand dismissively, cutting the guardian off, and instead marched straight to Guinevere.

The royal had not intended it, but her words came out as glacial as with the men of the hunting party. "Lady Guinevere – and I do use your title only out of politeness, as no lady behaves this way – you will do me the honor of staying the hell away from my guards, unless you wish your fate to not be so pretty after all."

Guinevere paled in front of her anger, but Vivienne was not done. "Sébastien is off limits. As is every man on these grounds. You belong to Arthur and it is to him you shall swear fealty and loyalty. Are. We. Understood!?"

The dreadfully calm voice, with the ice underneath, gave Guinevere goose bumps, and she dropped in a curtsy so low, her knees almost grazed the ground. This time, there was no mockery as she acquiesced, "Yes, my lady."

"And, Guinevere?" Vivienne let an enchantment imbue the words, enthralling. "Lancelot is not for you. You will stay away from him, as well."

Guinevere nodded blankly, and retreated.

"Vivienne?" Sébastien's voice came questioning, as if he was unsure it was truly her. The princess whirled to him, ignoring the bewilderment in his eyes.

All the guard could glimpse was the reined in lightning of her magic reflected in her green gaze. He knelt in front of her, in awe of her powers, and in shame of what had taken place. "Please forgive me; I had no idea she would –"

Vivienne stopped him with a raised hand. "I need you to escort me. There is a suitor here to speak with me, and I have been tasked to parade him around the castle."

Sébastien nodded, though he yearned to add so much more. Vivienne's words only truly sank in as he followed her. The fact that his beloved had a suitor already courting, this only the day after they had spent the night together, was disturbing, to say the least. And so it was with a heavy heart that he did his duty.

Neither of them distinguished the shadow of the visitor in a corner, having witnessed everything. Now he knew Arthur's weakness, and all he had to do was ensure Guinevere did betray him, as he had foreseen. The little charm Vivienne had set, imbued with his shard of the occult, would be enough to unravel Camelot and its king.

* * *

Vivienne was not mad after the incident with Guinevere – not really, and definitely not at Sébastien. She was, however, extremely confused at her reaction towards him. The princess had not expected the all-encompassing hurt when she had witnessed him with Guinevere.

Still with the visitor, she was conscious of Sébastien's presence behind them – and of his taciturn emotions swirling about. Vivienne yearned to speak with the knight, but knew it would be a conversation better suited for the evening, when they were alone.

As they approached one of the armories, the suitor surprised her with a request. "Lady Vivienne, I rather hoped we might have a word, in private?"

She nodded, and ordered Sébastien, "You can wait here."

At the panic in the guardian's eyes, Vivienne tried to reassure him, but could only send a whisper to his mind, "Listen to my call. I will be fine."

Sébastien assumed he was losing all sanity when Vivienne's voice echoed mentally, without the words being spoken out loud. It then dawned on him that Alistair must have shared his skills with his mistress.

As Vivienne stepped away and the door closed behind them, he forcefully relaxed his fists, trying to wipe off the bad taste the suitor left in his mouth – and it was not jealousy speaking.

It was as he was pacing back and forth, moments later, that Vivienne screamed in his head. "Sébastien, I need you now!"

The knight rushed in the armory, and his eyes fell on the princess pinned to the wall, the visitor attempting to make a pass at her. With a roar, Sébastien launched himself on the man, aiming only to inflict pain. The thought of his hands on Vivienne was enraging, fueling him as one fist, then another pummeled the man into the ground.

Lost in the need to deliver justice, Sébastien did not notice Vivienne leave momentarily, then return with three guards.

Moments later, Vivienne's gentle tap on his shoulder and her calm voice managed to break past the red haze. "I am fine, Sébastien. He did not have a chance to hurt me. Let him go."

Glowering, the champion noted the man had a bloodied

nose and lip, and his hands were wrapped around the ashen throat to choke him. With a snarl, he released the suitor, whirling to Vivienne instead. His ardent gaze raked over her form, examining for injuries.

Sébastien craved to wrap his arms around her, to comfort her, but observed instead the royal's countenance was calm – much too calm considering what had transpired.

Vivienne saw the frown, and her explanation tumbled out. "He is magical," she pointed to the man. "Quite probably an impostor, too. Merlin taught me how to interpret auras, and since I met him, I registered there was something odd about him. I knew once we were alone, he would show his hand. And now I have learned what he wishes."

"You know nothing!" the man spat from the ground.

"I have gathered enough," Vivienne retorted, before flicking a wrist to imprison him. One of the ropes pending came and wrapped itself around his wrists. She added an extra spell for strength, so her attacker could not remove it. "As for this Carleigh you speak of, he will realize soon enough you failed in your attempts to hurt me."

With finality, she nodded to the guards and they grabbed the man, dragging him to the prison tower.

Vivienne waited until they were gone, then faced Sébastien, her eyes softening. "The guards will handle him now. Please, come with me to speak to my father."

They strolled in silence to the throne room, though Vivienne was conscious they were both bursting with words unspoken.

As expected, when they filled the king in on the events, he was outraged.

"How dare he put his hands on my daughter!" the old king rumbled. "Sébastien, if you had not been there, I shudder to guess what could have happened. How can I repay you?"

Sébastien knelt at Adrien's feet, and bowed his head. "All I wish is to defend your daughter with all my might."

The king peered at the young champion, and his daughter. Something passed between them, something he knew would be impossible to refuse Vivienne.

"Very well," nodding slowly to himself, Adrien spoke out loud. "You will have quarters next to Vivienne to defend her from this new peril. It appears she is not as guarded as we assumed, even in this castle."

Vivienne managed, only barely, to hide her astonishment at Adrien's gratitude. To let Sébastien have quarters nearby was a measure of the trust the king put in him. In such a brief time, it was quite an accomplishment.

After the champion exited the room, Vivienne approached the king.

"Sweet daughter, are you truly alright?" His kind eyes were full of concern as he clasped her hand in his.

"I was never in any peril, father," the princess reassured him. "I knew the stranger was magical and I lured him away to find out his true purpose. Sébastien was there when I needed him to, for witnessing. Now the man can have a trial, with a guard to give testimony that he was seen assaulting me."

"Yes, so I gathered. What about this Carleigh? Is he a real portent of evil?"

Vivienne hesitated, preferring not to cause worry, but also not liking to lie to her father. "I will go speak to Merlin about him, perhaps he has more information. For myself, I have no idea who he is; only that he sent this man here to hurt me. To what purpose, I cannot fathom."

King Adrien was silent for a moment, before leveling an imposing stare towards his daughter. "Do you have feelings for Sébastien?"

"I–" Astounded, Vivienne could not formulate a response.

"I know you promised yourself to the learning of magic," Adrien continued in a voice made wise by age, "and you allow yourself no distractions… But not even Merlin can deny you true happiness. While you might not have a conventional marriage, please have faith I will support whichever man you choose."

"Thank you." Vivienne managed to smile past her tears, choked at her father's kindness, and hugged him close. "I do care for him."

"Good, especially considering I presume he returns the feelings for you." At her bewildered gaze, the old king added, "I have been observing Sébastien for a while and not once does he let you stray from his sight. I am happy you are surrounded by the same love me and your mother had, Vivienne, as it will truly shield you."

"That is what scares me, father. Where my future is headed, there will be plenty of dangers no normal man can chase away... I have so little to offer him, since I will not have a family of my own to speak of."

"My dear daughter," the old king took both her hands in his, "you are everything to him, and that is more than enough. Give Sébastien a chance to prove it."

Vivienne assented and, pecking him one last time on the cheek, went to her chambers.

* * *

In the prison tower, the visitor's simple disguise fell and in his place appeared Mordred. The sorcerer rubbed the side of his jaw, where Sébastien had pummeled him. His palm glowed faintly, healing the forming bruise.

"Fool of a knight," Mordred growled, still annoyed at having gotten badly beaten. It was to be expected that the knight would attack, and now his mother had informed him the ultimate fight would be with Arthur.

Mordred would not have minded it being with Sébastien, seeing as the guardian was his nemesis' soul mate, and all.

Oh well. Time to go.

Mordred headed to the window of the tower. He looked down – twenty feet of distance separated the cell from the ground.

Grinning widely, he got onto the window sill, then jumped. He screamed in exhilaration, enjoying the wind hitting his face. The warlock waited until the last minute, right before his body made contact with the unyielding earth, before throwing his mother's pouch of powder – the portal exploded open with the spell contained, engulfing him.

Mordred appeared on the outskirts of Elsior, in a camp near an old power place. He could sense the ancient energy in the earth, but it had nothing to do with the purpose of his visit.

He donned a disguise and headed to Carleigh's encampment. The sorcerer, having felt his presence, was already up and expecting him.

"Who are you?" Carleigh asked off the bat.

"A generous donor," Mordred replied, masked under the features of a homeless man. "I came to give you the piece of information you are missing. I know you are aware of what Sébastien and Lancelot can do, but Vivienne still eludes you."

Carleigh's suspicious face smoothed into a look of interest. "Continue."

"She can wield the elements, and has a very good perception of the auras. Her light magic is incorruptible – the guardian's is not. Oh, and they are old soul mates."

"What do you mean his is not? Sébastien is not magical."

"By association with Vivienne, his abilities are much more than a mere mortal's. I would suggest you use weapons poisoned with dark magic going forward. If anything, by reaching Sébastien, Vivienne will suffer as well."

They shared a grin, then Mordred turned to leave.

"Why help me?"

"Evil sticks together, brother."

With that, he was gone and Carleigh was none the wiser to his true identity. Now, at least, he knew what awaited him ahead.

* * *

As she bathed and changed for bed, Vivienne was acutely conscious of Sébastien's chambers being only on the other side. Excitement tumbled in her stomach, to the point she could not wait anymore and headed for the secret passage that connected both rooms.

She entered the barely lit room, and for a moment feared to have chosen wrong. Then she noticed Sébastien in front of the fire. He was sitting, naked except for a towel hung low on his hips. The champion must have just finished washing, as droplets of water still glinted in his hair.

However, the tortured demeanor emanating from him was

confusing: he had his head in both hands, seemingly deep in reflection.

Vivienne knew it was bad to spy on Sébastien, but rarely did she have a chance to truly observe him. She took her fill of the only thing visible: his broad shoulders, stretched with whatever burden he carried around, flexing almost in anger.

As the princess stared, a warm feeling spread through her, and her throat became dry, her body aflame.

"This is ridiculous, I have to explain!"

Vivienne jumped when Sébastien spoke, but before there was a chance to make her presence known, he whirled around and saw her standing there.

They stood apart, staring at each other, each afraid to start first, until both spoke.

"I did not mean –"

"It was not your fault –"

They both stopped talking. Vivienne offered a tiny smile, and inched closer. Sébastien was frozen, hands clenched as though to stop from reaching out, his regard burning brighter with each step she took.

Within instants, Vivienne was only a small distance away.

"I know Guinevere threw herself at you. I did not intend to keep you at a distance today, but I was confused." At his small frown, the royal continued, "I experience too many feelings around you, and I am not used to it. The incident today affected me, and I was trying to understand the emotions it caused."

Vivienne paused, before admitting, "I long to be with you, Sébastien, but I cannot offer you much. I will never be a wife or mother. My life is dedicated to guarding my realm, and it is such a big price to ask you to pay."

The guardian still did not voice anything aloud, and she chewed on her bottom lip nervously. "Please say something," Vivienne pleaded in a small voice.

That snapped Sébastien out of his reflections. In one fluid movement, he wrapped an arm around his beloved's waist, pulling her close, lips descending on hers in a new kind of embrace. This one was not restrained, rather possessive and hungry, and the young woman gave in gladly.

Vivienne wrapped an arm around his neck, and placed the other on his chest, close to his fast-beating heart. With a groan, Sébastien deepened the kiss until her knees wobbled. Only then did he slowly draw back, never breaking the intimacy of the hold nor adding space between them.

"Never say please to me again, Vivienne," he implored hoarsely. "I am the one person you never have to ask for anything. As for this price you mention, I gladly pay it for even one more moment in your company, one more taste of your lips. But I cannot compromise your virtue –"

"My father gave us our blessing," she interrupted, chuckling softly at the shock in Sébastien's eyes. "I was as amazed as you. It appears his wisdom is beyond compare."

"When you say he gave his blessing…"

"He instructed me to take whatever makes me happy, and if that is you, he stands behind me."

One of Sébastien's hands rose to cup her cheek, and she nuzzled it. "We are free to do as we wish," Vivienne resumed.

"And what is it you wish, my lady?" The blaze in his eyes was now a full-blown fire.

"You."

"In that case… Your wish is my command."

Then his lips caught hers again, this time gentler, slower. Sébastien planned to tease her with the kiss, but when Vivienne insisted for more, he matched her pace. They could not get close enough, and so he picked the princess up, and carried her to the bed. There, he worshipped her like the goddess she was for the entire night, until they both fell asleep.

* * *

It was still dark outside when the door to Vivienne's room opened. A shadow stepped in and moved closer to the bed, making no noise.

The enchantress jumped awake, immediately aware of someone in the room, just as…

"Alistair!" she whispered furiously, then frowned noticing it was dark outside. "What is going on?"

Who was here?

"What are you talking about?" Vivienne rubbed at her eyes sleepily, wincing. "It is the middle of the night, would it kill you to be clearer?"

Highness, I apologize, but I was off cleaning Merlin's mess and am in no mood.

"Merlin's –"

Ignore that. Who *was here?*

"Some son of my father's friend, who turned out to be magical and in league with someone named Carleigh. Apparently, he wishes me harm."

Vivienne stopped at Alistair's growl, throwing him an odd look. Sébastien turned in his sleep, his arm tightening around her waist.

Carleigh, another one of Merlin's messes, Alistair finally revealed. *Whoever that person was, he was much stronger that Carleigh, majesty. It is the same scent I felt during the blood moon attack.*

A shiver ran up Vivienne's spine, and Sébastien's arm tightened around her waist as though sensing it. "What are you saying?" she whispered weakly.

The man is gone, escaped from the tower with no trace.

"But…"

Alistair stepped closer, nudging her hand with his muzzle in reassurance.

Do not worry, princess, and go back to sleep. There is nothing to be done at this point. In the morning, go to Merlin and tell him everything. I will attempt to find out more.

Vivienne wanted to stop him, keep him close for comfort, but Alistair was gone as silently as he had entered. She snuggled back in Sébastien's embrace, and the safety his arms provided.

* * *

"Carleigh?" Merlin's features betrayed shock, staring first at Vivienne, then Sébastien, who had accompanied her.

"Do you know him, Merlin?" the pupil questioned.

"Yes."

The old wizard snapped out of his daze, and sat down on one of the boulders, clasping his staff as was his custom. Vivienne sat on another rock in front of him, and Sébastien, after a rapid going over of the landscape to ensure they were alone, joined her.

"You both have to listen to this," Merlin commenced in a weary voice. "Carleigh was an apprentice of mine – an incredibly cunning and competent young man, but also obscure. He dabbled in the black arts and I refused to teach him further. On the other hand, you, Vivienne, I kept as an apprentice. I believe him targeting you is due to his belief you usurped him."

"Be that as it is," Sébastien interrupted, "we have to stop him before these attempts escalate."

"I am afraid it is much too late for that," Merlin admitted. "I have captured his damnable aura lately, but now I am most sure he is past salvation. He will keep trying to attack." Merlin leveled his expression with Vivienne's and continued, "You have to be careful. Do not underestimate him. However, let him underestimate you."

"What are you implying?" the princess frowned.

The old wizard got up, and motioned for the youngsters to do the same. "From your mother, you have inherited great powers. But now you have grown into a young woman, and they have multiplied. Let me show you."

Merlin clasped one of Vivienne's soft hands in his older one and advised, "Reflect on your magic, and your love for Sébastien. I want to reveal to you what the force of love can do."

Vivienne did as the wizard bid, closing her eyes to better concentrate. A blinding blaze escaped past her eyelids, and she blinked in astonishment, gasping. Her entire being radiated from within, and from her palms emanated a pure, golden glow.

Despite the blinding radiance, the royal studied Merlin and his sparkling blue eyes. "This power is tangible. You can transform it into a healing light, or into a harmful one. You can have rays to scorch anyone who opposes you, or soft glows to heal the deepest of wounds. I will teach you how to sharpen and use it wisely. But now, you must let it retreat back to the earth. Gently."

Vivienne had to focus on the enchantment again, reining it in as one would an overeager puppy, until the exuberance was gone. The glow retreated from her being, flowing into the ground beneath her feet, imbuing the earth with ancient power.

When the enchantress opened her eyes again, her skin was back to its normal tone. She met Sébastien's awed gaze, her heart singing with joy.

* * *

In the encampment, Carleigh waited until the sun was setting before gathering his druids. He placed them in a circle, with himself in the center.

Unaware he was being watched from the shadows by Morgana, he started the chant that would tie their powers to him, constantly fueling the dark magic.

Morgana waited until the spell was ongoing, before touching his mind with hers and instilling one more suggestion.

Tie them to you even in death... Forever in your duty.

* * *

It was past sunset in Camelot and Guinevere was brushing her hair, preparing for sleep. She looked at the ring on her finger – an engagement gift from Arthur – and grinned widely.

Earlier that day, Arthur had signed the famed peace treaty, and a feast had been held in the honor of the new High King of Britain. Their marriage was to follow soon after.

She thought back to Merlin's astonished stare, and Elaine's... The woman annoyed her, she was much too close to Arthur. Once Guinevere had him in her claws, it would be time to get rid of her.

The best way is to seduce him...

Guinevere started at the voice in her head, which had been growing stronger every day. Everything it suggested to do ended up working in her favor. Some may call it conscience, but the soon-to-be queen knew it was not – after all, she had none.

I cannot, she thought back. *Arthur expects me to be pure...*

He is only a man, he will not refuse you nor think less of you. If you want Elaine gone, it is time you stake claim to what is yours.

Guinevere looked at the reflection in the mirror. Her hair glowed softly, framing her face where the blue eyes shone brightly, the red lips full and alluring. She sprayed some scent around her neck, then stood and headed to Arthur's chambers.

The king was in bed, covered with nothing but a sheet, when Guinevere stepped in. He stood up, startled, and thought he saw an angel.

"Guinevere..." Arthur whispered, not knowing whether it was a dream or reality.

Like in his fantasies, she walked over, the light of the moon bathing her and showcasing the body underneath the nightgown. Arthur felt himself stir, but still the gentleman in him warned, "You should not be here..."

"Shh," she stepped onto the bed, and he rose to meet her halfway. "I could not sleep, Arthur," Guinevere entreated in her exotic voice. "I burn for you..."

Arthur inhaled deeply, and his hand rose to caress her cheek. "Guinevere..."

The invitation in her eyes was his undoing. Something more than desire was pulling him to Guinevere, an inkling within him that he had to possess her – now.

Arthur gave in to the impulses, dragging her mouth to his. Once her body was molded against his, he rolled over and kissed down her throat, to her breasts, and lower.

Soon, Guinevere's moans filled the chamber, her cries of ecstasy spurring him on. Arthur got up and moved the sheets out of the way, then buried himself inside her with a groan. The fact she was not a virgin never registered in his passion-filled mind.

As he rode out his own ecstasy, Arthur did not notice the glow that surrounded them both, then left their skins and traveled down the ground like a dark red mist, in search of its prey.

* * *

Elaine had an urge to go by Arthur's room, to speak to him of the final coronation and the upcoming marriage to Guinevere. She could no longer remain quiet.

As she headed over, a flash of blonde hair caught her eye, entering the king's room. By the time Elaine reached it, she heard whispers, soon followed by the sounds of lovemaking.

The maiden lifted a hand to her mouth, stifling her horrified gasp. *I have truly lost him, then.*

Tears filling her eyes, Elaine ran back to her room, crashing on the bed and letting the sobs take over. She soon fell asleep, exhausted and in pain.

Moments later, the dark red mist covered the ground and climbed over the sheets. It crawled over her skin, and was absorbed by it.

Morgana's eerie shape appeared by the bed, translucent in its essence like a ghost. "Sleep, beautiful Elaine… Listen to the voice of this spell, and rest easily, knowing your king is well taken care of."

Her eyes glowed with Fae-like quality, and the charm was completed. "Sleep," Morgana hissed once more, "and stop interfering with my plans."

When she was gone, Elaine was in a deep slumber, a light sheen of sweat on her forehead as the affliction took over.

CHAPTER 23

Merlin captured the presence long before the dog approached him, and exited the cave to meet him. "Old friend, what brings you here?"

The dog paused and sat down on his hind with a peculiar glint. *Vivienne and her champion – they are being pulled together and it is not normal.*

"You suspect witchcraft?" Merlin enquired politely. He had not forgotten their meeting, when Alistair had forced him to vow to stay out of the romance.

No. But there are outside forces involved. I am of the impression they are soul mates. Ignoring the dismay in the old wizard's eyes, he carried on. *From the strength of their bond, more than a few lifetimes before this one.*

Merlin's only response was a furrowed brow.

There is a way to find out for sure, Alistair continued. *We should bring them here and have them perform a ritual.*

"Why is this important?" Merlin wondered. "If they do not yet perceive it, maybe we should stay out of it. Would this not harm, more than help them? What if they prefer to ignore the past?"

I know you keep your secrets, old mage, and there are things in the future you have foreseen. But this is one you have not, and I have. I had a vision: Sébastien can be Vivienne's salvation or her doom, if he turns to darkness.

"Then it cannot be ignored," Merlin agreed, brows narrowed in concentration. "Bring them here at the earliest opportunity."

* * *

Vivienne jumped awake at the insistent knock on the door. She wrapped a cape around herself quickly, and approached it cautiously. Sébastien was there, his entire body coiled with tension.

"We have to go."

"What is happening?" the princess demanded, moving so he could enter the room.

"Your father was hurt. Carleigh ambushed us on our way back from the hunt. Alistair came in time to deflect the worst of it, and the king is unharmed for now. I am to bring you to Merlin, as per Alistair's orders."

With a swift nod, Vivienne rushed to put on a thicker cloak, and followed Sébastien out the chambers, and down the empty hallways to the entrance doors of the castle. Once there, she paused, tugging on his hand.

"Wait. Let me conceal us with an enchantment to avoid detection."

Sébastien acquiesced briskly, and Vivienne placed both

hands on his. A soft glow enveloped them both, sank into their skin, and disappeared – they were now invisible to anyone's eyes but each other's.

The lovers kept their hands joined as they rushed across the gardens, past Vivienne's usual spot of learning with the mentor, and the large prairie separating them from the forest where Merlin's lair resided.

When they passed the barrier to the mage's grounds, Sébastien looked around, then murmured to Vivienne, "You can uncover us now. I do not wish for it to tire you."

Vivienne was about to disagree, but at the glint in his eyes, shrugged and removed the cloaking spell. They started again, rushing now to get to Merlin's as rapidly as possible. Sébastien kept his body shielding Vivienne, alert, scanning the surroundings, even whilst never slowing his strides.

They had exited into a meadow, which Vivienne knew to be close to Merlin's, when there was a hiss in the air behind. She whirled around, and noticing the arrow coming her way, lifted a palm to stop it in time with a barrier. It plummeted to the ground, inert.

The princess peered over one shoulder to Sébastien to alert him, but it was too late as he was hit with an arrow in the shoulder.

He let go of her hand and unsheathed his sword, moving in front of her. "Stay behind me!" Sébastien ordered. He advanced to the two men from the shadows, in warlock cloaks, chanting incantations aimed at the two lovers.

From behind Vivienne, leaves rustled, and she confronted two opponents as well, starting with a barrier of protection. Thankful more than ever for Merlin's insistence to learn both defensive and offensive techniques, the enchantress conjured small balls of magic, and concentrated their assailing strength towards the druids.

As Sébastien cut one of the adversaries in two, there was an odd crackling in the pit of his stomach. The world around him evaporated, nothing except the rage of the fight left behind.

By means of their bond, Vivienne also perceived the rippling energy, and tasted the bitterness of evil. She looked over her shoulder, distracted from her own fight, to witness Sébastien swiftly disposing of his assailants, but at the expense of his own strength.

"We have to get the arrow out!" Vivienne yelled to her lover.

The champion did not react, instead moving towards the next challenger.

"Sébastien," Vivienne linked to his mind, warning telepathically, "you have been poisoned by the arrow. I can detect it obscuring your aura and sapping your strength."

With an annoyed cry to her opponents, she blasted orbs towards them and they disappeared into nothingness. Now free, the princess went to Sébastien. As if sensing her close, the knight whirled around with the blade held high, almost cutting her.

Alistair materialized out of nowhere between Sébastien and Vivienne, and the metal hit the barrier he had erected between them, inches away from his mistress' head.

"Alistair!" Vivienne's cry did not deter the demon dog from his defensive stance.

Stay away! he commanded, tilting his head a little to the

side, but not letting Sébastien out of his sight. *Carleigh did a number on him. The arrow had a rage-inducing spell, and he could gravely hurt you, if you get close. I can tolerate the darkness, and remove it from him.*

"No," the enchantress pleaded. "You have done enough for my father, and you have your limits. I can get him to listen."

Vivienne— the demon concentrated fully on the royal, and noted her determination. With a sigh, he bowed his head. *Not here, though.*

He dug his paws in the ground, and a translucent panel covered them. It shimmered and, in a blink, they found themselves in front of Merlin's cave.

Alistair ran in to get Merlin, while the young woman headed to Sébastien.

The guardian was on his knees, breathing heavily, when Vivienne inched closer. He stood up and gripped her hand insistently. Though she winced at the discomfort, the princess did not draw away. Instead, she stared into his eyes and begged softly, "Come back to me."

With her other hand, Vivienne yanked the arrow out of his shoulder, following the action by pressing a glowing palm to heal. The tension of the fight left Sébastien, until the knight sagged in her embrace.

Sébastien blinked, eyes no longer glazed, but fixated on Vivienne. At the pain etched on her features, he glanced down and released his tight grip. The bruise forming on her wrist was visible to his horrified look. "I am so sorry."

"No harm done," Vivienne smiled reassuringly, clasping his hands in hers. "You are unharmed, and it is all that matters."

The guardian did not appear it though: pale and covered in dirt, eyes haunted by the guilt of what could have happened. By means of their connection, Vivienne captured his shock, and a remnant of the darkness that had entered him.

Alistair came back with Merlin in tow. His staff was ready for action, believing the royal was still in danger. The demon dog was the first to comprehend Sébastien was no longer under the curse's dominance, as he noticed the clear aura surrounding him.

He tilted a satisfied grin to the wizard, and declared for all to hear, *I told you I was right.*

"Not now," Merlin hissed.

Now is a good a time as any, Alistair rumbled.

Vivienne surveyed them both, as did Sébastien. "What are you two talking about?" she demanded.

With a scowl to his canine friend, Merlin explained Alistair's theory of them being soul mates. When he was done, Vivienne peered at Sébastien and read his shock, mirrored only by hers.

"How do we learn for sure?" the guardian enquired.

"It is a simple thing of unlocking your past memories, and reconnecting you with your old lives." Merlin paused, searching both their expressions. "Are you quite sure you would like to witness this?"

Vivienne hesitated, but Sébastien gripped her hand in his, and squeezed it reassuringly. His gaze was still not quite right, haunted by what had transpired, but he murmured, "We want to know."

The princess' eyes landed on Alistair and Merlin, nodding

for both of them. "Yes. We want to learn it – all of it."

"Hold hands," Merlin recommended.

They did as they were bid, and the wizard approached the staff over their joined hands. The crystal on top of it shone brightly as a sun for a moment, before it extinguished. Merlin then touched the air surrounding the hands, and under the lovers' stunned gazes, ripped a transparent piece out, as though from a book. It would be the gate which would let the two lovers see into the past.

The cloth, if it could be called such, took the color of whatever it was cast over. When the mage set it over their joined hands, it became tan, blending in. Alistair came closer and breathed on it, a faint white fog that surrounded the clasped hands, hovering and immovable. This would be the essence grounding them, to not lose track of the reality.

Observing the handiwork, Merlin peered at Vivienne, then Sébastien, and finally uttered, "Let it be remembered, all that was forgotten."

The cloth shone softly as a glow enveloped their joined hands, and a blinding radiance escaped. Recollections hit them both: a life in the desert, one in the mountains, and another in the glaciers.

It was as though the couple was surrounded by a bubble of light, with the memories swarming, assailing them: all the lifetimes, the love and agony, losing each other because of calamities and enemies.

It was always the same pattern: they met, fell in love, and lost one another due to a hidden, nefarious energy which followed them across time and space, forever haunting and stealing away their happy ending.

Among the flashbacks, Vivienne saw herself in a vibrant garden, and witnessed Sébastien dying in her arms. Another memory was of when he came to warn of danger in the chambers. On and on it went, until they had both born witness to their entire past together.

When it was over, the glow evaporated, and Vivienne turned to Merlin, her cheeks bathed in tears. "Are we to be always doomed?"

Alistair advanced before the wizard could respond, having glimpsed it all through their minds. The potent vitality of love had imbued the couple, to the point the demon dog had been dragged in the memories despite his better judgment.

No, he answered truthfully. *Whatever happened in the past does not have to repeat itself. Whoever hunted you, threatened you, can be thwarted. It means nothing. We can rewrite your fate, highness.*

Merlin did not join in the conversation, lost in his own reflections. Not even visions had prepared him for the strength of their love, let alone the extent of their shared past. He could not help the thought that if only Arthur had fallen in love with Vivienne, she could have been his and Camelot's salvation.

At the growl by his side, the wizard noticed Alistair's black look.

Do not listen to my thoughts if you do not like hearing them, Merlin advised mentally, and the dog broke his stare.

Overwhelmed by emotions, Vivienne went to Sébastien's arms for safety and comfort. The guardian leveled a discouraged gaze to the dog and wizard, comprehending now what the flashes in his head had been all about.

We will find a way, Alistair reassured, meeting his regard steadily.

* * *

Vivienne strolled in the castle's garden, the moon high in the sky, waiting for someone – Sébastien, her heart conveyed.

There were footsteps behind, and she whirled around eagerly, but the smile died at the apparition.

"Carleigh," the royal greeted, her voice firm and unshaken.

How he had passed the guards, was a mystery. Though Vivienne's first instinct was to engage him in a supernatural duel, the shadows surrounding him were enough to give her pause.

"What are you doing here?" she asked instead.

The sorcerer ignored the question, instead glancing at the flowers. "Not quite who you expected, princess?" She cringed at the voice, so raspy to her ears.

"Not sure what you are alluding to."

"Your lover, Sébastien." Cold eyes narrowed at her, well aware of the risk taken, coming alone, and apparently not caring. "That is who you were expecting, is it not?"

The royal training took over, and Vivienne's voice was icy as she met the sorcerer's disturbing stare. "That is none of your business, nor do you have the right to defy your princess."

"Oh, but you will not be so for long. Enjoy your reign, highness," he sneered malevolently, "while you still can."

Vivienne watched as Carleigh skulked out of the gardens, blending with the obscurity, until his presence was gone.

Sébastien entered a few minutes later, but his grin faltered at her worried frown. "What's wrong?"

"Nothing."

The guardian's regard, though he tried to mask it, displayed his hurt. Contrite, Vivienne bit on her bottom lip, before murmuring, "I did not intend it that way. It was a poor attempt not to worry you… Carleigh was here."

The fury in Sébastien's expression was unmistakable.

* * *

Vivienne woke up in the middle of the night to an empty bed. She got up and joined Alistair by the window of the chambers. He was standing guard, ears pricked forward, fixated on something. Glancing outside, she noticed Sébastien by the lakeshore, pacing restlessly.

"How long has this been going on?" the princess wondered.

The demon dog squinted up at her, and admitted, *A few nights. He feels guilty for hurting you, and succumbing to Carleigh's influence. I tried to explain to him that he did not fail in his duties, but…*

Vivienne petted him gently, and grabbed a shawl. When Alistair went to follow, she shook her head. "I have to do this myself."

The dog watched as his mistress left the room, then turned his gaze back to knight. *You cannot give in to your despair, he* warned. *It will eat you alive, and Vivienne has need of you.*

The knight stopped the endless pacing and looked up, as though guessing the demon lord was watching. It was not long before Alistair caught an echo of his thoughts.

Perhaps she would be best off without me.

Never say that, knight!

Despite the encouragement, Alistair could still sense much doubt in Sébastien. What Carleigh had done, with the arrow and darkness, seemed to have shaken the guardian more than either of them had realized.

With a sigh, the demon dog sat down, still looking out the window. *It is out my hands, unless Vivienne can get through to him...*

* * *

Going by the servant's tunnels, the royal was soon outside in the crisp air. She approached her lover, speaking only when she was by his side. "Sébastien?"

The guardian whirled around, eyes haunted. The minute he recognized it was Vivienne, his body froze.

"You should not be here alone," Sébastien advised, then turned away from her.

"With you, you mean?" Vivienne finished for him. "Yes, I should. I can help."

"I do not anticipate you can, my lady. I failed you in this, and hurt you."

"You did not fail me. On the contrary, you used your body as a shield, and without you, I could have been the one hurt." The enchantress moved around him, and caressed his cheek gently. "Please let me help you."

"I can refuse you nothing," Sébastien murmured, inclining his head in assent.

Vivienne beamed, letting the shawl fall off her shoulders, and entered the lake. It was not cold, as it warmed with her basic wish. Sébastien stared after her, mesmerized, until the water was up her waist.

"Come join me," she invited, extending a hand towards him.

Sébastien hesitated for a moment, before removing his

boots and following in, until he was by her side. He was pleasantly surprised at the warmth of the liquid, until he realized the princess was dominating it.

"Do you trust me?" Vivienne asked him.

"Always."

She immersed her hands in the water, always maintaining eye contact. It bubbled at her touch, until two jets of clear liquid splashed up like a fountain. They rose in height on either side of the guardian, then joined on top of Sébastien's head. Through it all, he held her gaze.

Vivienne's green eyes flamed with power as her soft, melodious voice, imbued with an enchantment, recited a spell from deep within. "With this water, I cleanse you. Let the remnant shadows be expelled, your spirit be purified, and your soul lightened. You are, and will be, untouched once more. I, keeper of this realm, so cleanse you."

As the liquid poured over him, Sébastien closed his eyes, allowing it to sink into his clothes, under his skin, and into his very soul. A warm, gentle wave flowed within him like a torrent, taking away the remnants of the darkness and weight on his soul.

When he blinked, Vivienne smiled at him, eyes an emerald green once more. He bent his mouth to hers and pulled her into a soft kiss, thanking the fates for his luck.

Up in Vivienne's room, Alistair surveyed the moon, recalling the prophecy he had foreseen. "They really are soul mates," he muttered, and knew it was time for Merlin to keep his end of the bargain.

CHAPTER 24

The royal was out riding Shadow across the castle grounds, when Sébastien caught up with her at sunset at one of their favorite spots. He hopped off Illyria, moving until he was next to Shadow, smiling up at his beloved.

"My lady," the knight extended a hand in invitation. Vivienne slid off the horse, against his body, and straight into his arms.

"Where have you been all day?" the princess beamed at Sébastien, dizzy from her tumultuous sentiments, yet aware of the shivers running up and down her body.

"Your father had me running errands."

Vivienne laughed, then wound her arms around his neck, pressing closer. Sébastien's mouth descended in a sweet and tantalizing embrace. It was a slow dance of yearning, a promise of what was to come later.

When the champion drew away, she smiled. "Are you all

done now?"

"All yours, yes."

Sébastien captured her hand in his and walked to the shore. They had no sooner reached it, that in a fit of silliness, he pretended to fall to the ground and dragged the princess with him. They tumbled on the soft grass, nearly landing in the lake, but the knight stopped them at the last minute.

Hovering over Vivienne, Sébastien dropped his enamored gaze to hers. She lifted her hand, caressing his chin and stubble, confessing, "I love how secure I feel in your arms, like nothing can get to me."

Sébastien's gaze softened, and he buried his head in her neck, inhaling her citrus perfume until he could not get enough. "You always will be. I will always keep you safe, at any cost. It is what makes me worthy of you."

When he lifted his head again, Vivienne was beaming, gorgeous in the sunset's light. Unable to hold back any longer, Sébastien bent his mouth to hers, needing a taste like he needed his next breath.

* * *

Absolutely not! Alistair bellowed.

"You cannot stop me if I am attempting to put an end to this feud!" Vivienne yelled back.

Like hell I can't, majesty. I will go to your father and he will have you locked up in an ivory tower before you can act on this madness!

"Alistair—"

No! he shook his massive head, eyes flashing. *It is much too perilous!*

"What the hell is going on here?" All the yelling had

attracted Sébastien. He took in their defensive postures, subconsciously already angling his body to defend Vivienne.

Relax, knight, I am not the danger here. If you want to protect Vivienne, protect her against herself!

Sébastien focused on the princess, frowning. "What is he referring to?"

Vivienne avoided his look.

You will not even tell him? the dog growled, and advanced to Sébastien. *Vivienne received a message from Carleigh, to meet for a so-called parlay. That lying bastard pretends it is in order to call a truce and work out terms.*

Vivienne saw Sébastien tense out of the corner of her eye, and glowered at Alistair. "Now you've done it."

"He is absolutely right," the champion agreed. "It is much too dangerous to meet him. And I assume, on top of that, he expects you to go on your own?"

Of course he does! Alistair snarled. *This has gone on long enough, and is Carleigh toying with us. I will involve Merlin, maybe he will be able to talk some sense into her.*

"No!" Vivienne protested. "He has enough on his plate with Arthur and Guinevere. Please let me do this. If I can avoid more attacks, it is worth an attempt. Alistair, you always say I have untapped potential... Let me try."

The dog walked towards Sébastien, rolling his eyes. *I give up. Your turn.*

The defender faced Vivienne, cupping her cheek in his palm. "Love, if you go and get hurt, I will never forgive myself. But I also cannot restrain you. What I propose is you let me come with you."

"No!"

"Then you will not go," Sébastien clenched his jaw at the refusal. "I agree with Alistair. We can go to your father and Merlin."

"Fine," Vivienne scowled at them both. "You can come."

I as well, then, the dog jumped in.

"Alistair–"

No negotiating, princess.

"Alright!" She glared at both of them, annoyed at having lost her ground. "But we depart now."

They saddled only one horse, Vivienne's Shadow. Sébastien rode behind her, one arm wrapped around her waist the entire ride. It was a reassurance for the enchantress, giving her strength for a task she was not quite sure she could accomplish, despite all the bravado portrayed.

Alistair followed them on foot, more than able to keep up with the horse.

They had no sooner left the castle grounds – and Vivienne's safeguard – when a grey sphere materialized in front of their eyes. It hovered in mid-air, before heading down a path into the forest.

Fascinating. Now we follow a glowing orb. This is a great *idea, Vivienne,* Alistair muttered in their heads, and pursued the sphere with an annoyed bark.

After a few hours' ride, they arrived at a clearing, and the orb evaporated. They were long past Elsior's grounds now, having delved deep into unfamiliar territory.

"You brought guests, despite my warnings?" Carleigh walked out of the shadows abruptly.

Vivienne dismounted, with Sébastien doing the same. He placed himself next to her, prepared to step in at the slightest provocation to remove the princess out of harm's way.

"Sébastien is my most trusted knight," Vivienne declared. "My father would have been suspicious and dispatched an army if I had left without him. I can enchant him to sleep if it would put you at ease."

Carleigh was annoyed at her defiant tone, implying he was fearful of one mortal man. "Your lover can stay awake," he snickered, not fooled in the least. His spies had informed him about the monarch's tryst with the horseman. "To witness and report back to his king."

Alistair bared his teeth, stepping in front of Vivienne, and Carleigh levelled a dismissive stare to him. "Nice dog."

The demon's body shook with coiled tension as a thunderous barked escaped him.

Carleigh lifted his palms and made a come hither motion to the woods behind him. Seven corrupt druids strode out, dressed in mantles the color of midnight.

"You promised this was a meeting for a truce!" Vivienne gasped.

"I lied." The sorcerer smirked. "Or are you so naïve to believe everything you hear? You truly have led a sheltered life, Vivienne. But that is about to change."

"I highly doubt that," she hissed, and Sébastien was proud at the strength in her voice, not even remotely afraid.

Vivienne backed away, one palm glowing for a mere moment, before an invisible bubble escaped her and surrounded Shadow. It was done subtly, and neither the druids nor Carleigh noticed the new protection the horse had acquired.

Then, she elevated both hands in front of her. In full view

of the warlocks, a spell formed between her glowing palms, and she hurled it towards Carleigh without further ado.

Sébastien unsheathed his sword, and went back to back with the princess, facing the conjurers surging behind them, as well.

In the midst of the battle, they got separated, but Alistair's bark could be heard above all noises as he jumped from one warlock to another.

It was only a few moments later, as they each faced different opponents, that Sébastien heard him warn, *Vivienne, no!*

He whirled around to notice the young woman facing Carleigh. The sorcerer gathered dark magic in his palms, in the shape of a coated ball, and flung it towards Vivienne. Just as it would have hit her, Alistair lunged with his jaws wide open and absorbed it all.

Carleigh's stupefaction would have been worth a laugh, had Sébastien not caught the slight wobble in the dog's paws when he landed. Focusing on him, he saw Alistair bend a paw to the ground as if unable to stand following the heroic action.

"I see it is not a dog after all you have there. A demon, Vivienne? How intriguing." Carleigh cackled, then continued, "If only my magic was not overpowering him with the new poison I have created."

"Alistair!" Vivienne knelt by the dog's side, checking for injuries, and leaving herself completely exposed. By means of their unbroken bond, she realized the damage came from the spell Alistair had inhaled, and its poisonous tendrils that paralyzed both his powers and body.

Get out of here, Alistair's voice came in her head, weaker than before, yet he got up and defied Carleigh.

"No, I will not leave you here!"

Get out, princess! For once, listen to me. This is no game.

Vivienne froze at the authority in Alistair's tone, and turned her gaze to Sébastien. Across the distance, he read the indecision in her mind as clearly as if he had been by her side.

Get her away! Alistair yelled in the guardian's head, whilst remaining fixated on the sorcerer.

Sébastien whistled to Shadow, who galloped towards him. He snatched onto the saddle and jumped on the horse, racing to Vivienne. The exigency in Alistair's tone was not feint. He bent down, captured the princess by the waist and yanked her on the horse as well.

With a nudge, the defender rode Shadow in the direction they had come from, leaving the dust and chaos of the battle behind. He glanced behind only once, and was met with Alistair's gratefulness.

Keep her safe.

Then, the massive demon dog turned away, confronting Carleigh and the remaining conjurers alone.

"Why did you take me away!?" Vivienne twisted in the saddle to Sébastien and lashed out, hitting her closed fists against his chest. "We should have stayed and fought by his side!"

"I was only listening to Alistair's orders, beloved."

Sébastien's soft voice got past her outrage, and Vivienne collapsed against him, sobbing.

* * *

Asleep in the cottage where Sébastien had stopped for the night, Vivienne dreamt of her last meeting with Merlin and

Alistair – the dear protector, whom she might not see again.

"I must leave the kingdom before it gets worse," Vivienne declared, standing before them. "My father has been hurt once, and I fear my staying here will only further incite Carleigh to keep attacking."

"I disagree," Merlin said, ignoring Alistair's dark look. "You are a lady of light. You should stay and fight," the wizard advised.

"You trust that I am strong enough?" Vivienne demanded.

"Yes, I do."

The princess peered at Alistair for confirmation, but he remained silent.

"Alistair?" she prompted.

I cannot intervene further than I have. The decision is your own. For what it is worth, you do have pure magic, highness, and that in itself is a gift.

Vivienne woke up from the recollection at the sound of a door closing. She stood up in bed as Sébastien headed towards her.

"Where have you been?" the enchantress whispered drowsily.

She knew something was wrong when he knelt by the cot. In the dim light, Vivienne could see Sébastien's shoulders were hunched, his head bowed as he grasped her hand in his.

"I rode ahead to scan the surroundings and ensure there were no traps. I got up to the riverbank, from where we could see the castle. Vivienne—"

Sébastien choked on the words, unsure of how to announce the news.

With a hand movement, Vivienne lighted the candles

around them, illuminating his pain-ravaged face. "What happened?"

"Carleigh took his revenge," the champion revealed, maintaining her gaze.

Vivienne swallowed the despair threatening to overcome, and instead stood up. "Show me."

With a heavy heart, Sébastien helped her mount Shadow and led her to the destruction site.

* * *

Sébastien watched, helpless, as Vivienne faced the ruins of her castle, her silhouette ramrod straight, the fragile girl in her crumbling. The entire building was in flames, with no sign of any survivors – least of all her father.

"This is not your fault," the guardian declared.

He could feel the princess' – now queen – heart breaking into a million pieces by means of their bond, and his own clenched in pain.

"It is," Vivienne's voice answered hollowly. "I called this despair upon my realm. Carleigh wanted me, and when he could not attain his goal, he sought an easier way to bring me pain."

"We will ensure he pays."

The young woman only shook her head, tears streaming down her cheeks. "They deserve a proper burial, more so than vengeance."

Pushing past her despair, Vivienne waved her hand towards the mass of rocks. From the earth, a blaze was born. It was not the usual orange, but rather a cold, icy color and it grew in height, washing over the castle. In mere moments, the entire structure, and its grounds, glowed faintly with the incantation.

With a stifled scream, Vivienne clenched her fist. In front of her eyes, the once majestic towers wavered, before the foundation shattered in tiny pieces. The towers were next, crumbling to the ground, and the rest of the structure followed in a domino effect.

When it was all only a mass of ruins, the enchantress attacked the grounds. The earth itself vibrated, groaned, then split into two with a sigh. With her free hand, Vivienne called forth the lake, swirling a palm to raise a wave high up, before dropping it onto the ruins.

The leftovers of her kingdom were submerged underneath, buried and obsolete. Under their gloomy regards, the chaos was smoothed out, the lake now larger than before – a tomb worthy of the realm.

Vivienne fell to her knees, barely holding herself together. Her back was rigid with the strength it took her to avoid crumbling, when all she wanted was to let go and fall apart. Sébastien helped his beloved up, attempting to comfort her to the best of his ability.

It was not long before someone appeared behind them. The guardian whirled around, and his eyes fell on Merlin surveying the lake's depths.

"I gather it is not what you hope to hear," the old wizard revealed, "but fate cannot be changed. In the end, all of this furthers you becoming the Lady of the Lake, as you were intended to be."

Vivienne backed out of Sébastien's embrace, her beautiful features distressed with anguish. "Answer me truthfully. Were you aware of what would happen?"

"I foresaw it, yes."

"So when I came to you wanting to leave, and you advised me otherwise, you knew this would happen."

Merlin did not respond. Vivienne clenched her fists in anger, his betrayal cutting deep.

"You lied to me!" she accused. "You knew what would happen, even foresaw that Carleigh would go as far as this!"

"The future is not clear," Merlin admitted. "What it predicted, to my eyes, was a tragedy. I realized it could not be stopped, but that it would drive you to new challenges." He glanced at the ruins underneath the water. "This never should have happened."

"So what did I do wrong?" Vivienne's voice broke.

Sébastien advanced to her, glaring at the wizard. Could he not see the guilt he was adding to with his rash words?

"Nothing, my dear," the old mage retorted. "It was Carleigh's sorcery that over tipped the balance, and my fool mistake that cost you, in the end."

"You had no right! *No right* to hide this from me!"

"You are correct," the wizard agreed. It was the first Sébastien saw of his remorse, but Vivienne had already turned away from him.

"Get out. Please leave me alone. I do not wish to set eyes on you again."

"Listen to me, just this once," Merlin pleaded. "Do not give in to revenge, otherwise this will have been for nothing."

Vivienne tilted her head to him and met his eyes blankly. "I have no strength for revenge. I will build Aisling Caisleán here, my own 'castle of dreams', in memory of the shattered innocence you helped cause."

When she gazed back to the lake, Sébastien shook his head to Merlin and with a dark look invited him to leave. Once he was gone, he gathered Vivienne back in his arms, taking her sobs as they came. In the queen's mind, the dam was breaking, and she fell to pieces as the extent of her loss crashed down on her.

* * *

"Is it true?"

Merlin made an effort to wrench himself from his thoughts and turned around at Arthur's question, his face a blank mask. "Sire?"

"I heard an odd story of Elsior disappearing overnight. Is it true?"

Of course, the rumor had reached even Camelot. It had been merely a day since he had left Vivienne in front of the ruins of the castle...

"I am afraid so, my king."

"But... how? Is there anyone we can help there?"

Always good of heart, the king truly meant well with his intentions, Merlin realized. Yet it was not something he wanted to linger on. The last thing he needed was Carleigh to fixate on Arthur the same way he had with Vivienne.

"No, sire, they are all gone," Merlin lied. "It was a great curse, and it wiped everything out."

"And... Lady Vivienne? Her father?"

"Them, too," Merlin continued the trickery, unwilling to disclose the princess was still alive, but not looking to see anyone. If word got out to Guinevere, she would use it to her advantage and it was not a chance the mage could let happen at the moment.

Arthur looked away, oddly touched at the loss. Though he did not have tight relations with Elsior, Lancelot spoke only well of the princess and her father.

"Lancelot has no kingdom now," Arthur mumbled, already thinking his longtime friend had earned the stripes to be a full knight by his side.

"Sire?" Merlin frowned.

"I will knight Lancelot here, in Camelot, and name him protector of the queen," Arthur declared.

Merlin was about to voice his doubts, but sighed – what was the point?

"There is something else, my king. Elaine is sick."

That finally got through to Arthur and he rushed to her bedside.

* * *

Arthur returned to his chambers, weary of the day. No one knew what had happened to Elaine, only that she was not waking up. The best healers had been called, to no avail.

And he had been so engrossed in Guinevere, he had not registered that one of his best friends had lost his home, and the other was sick.

The king pinched the bridge of his nose, sighing heavily.

"You look like you need some relaxing."

Arthur turned around to see Guinevere enter the room, but this time not even the sight of her uplifted his mood.

"I have had some terrible news of Elsior going under, and Elaine is not well," Arthur muttered, rubbing his face.

Guinevere took him by the hand, bringing him to the bed to sit down. She moved behind to massage his neck. Arthur relaxed in the soft touch, and soon all thoughts of the outside world left him.

Sensing it, Guinevere stood in front of him and let her robe fall at her feet. "Now, my king, let me truly remove those worries from your mind…"

All it took was a touch of her lips, and Arthur was lost.

* * *

Sébastien entered the solarium where Vivienne was seated on a chair facing outside.

Following the destruction of Elsior, she had used an enchantment to build a smaller version of the castle on the lake, envisioning and creating it from nothing. She had hidden it to mortals' eyes, baptizing it Aisling Caisleán – Castle of Dreams.

Only the queen and Sébastien lived there, along with a few servants found in adjoining villages. For the most part, they were outcasts and work at the new castle provided them with a purpose.

Anyone who required an audience with Vivienne could get it, and would be shown a way to Aisling Caisleán if their intent was pure. More often than not these days, the lady kept her sorrowful eyes away from peers, and Sébastien was running out of options to help her.

Thus, it was with a heavy heart the guardian observed Merlin arrive, and headed to announce it to his beloved. He gravitated past the entrance of the sun room and approached the queen, resting a hand on her shoulder.

It took her a few moments, but Vivienne eventually looked up at him, her eyes bloodshot and with dark circles underneath. She was still gorgeous to his eyes, but he felt helpless at her devastated expression.

"Love," Sébastien whispered in a soft voice, "Merlin is here."

"I do not wish to set eyes on him." Vivienne's voice was devoid of emotion, her eyes blank as she twisted away.

"Please. It is for Arthur," Sébastien pleaded.

The enchantress wearily shifted to him, as if each movement took all her energy. Tiredly, she ended up nodding. She appeared frail, so unlike the strong and exuberant royal he had first met.

The mention of Camelot's king moved Vivienne, only due to the fact she felt all realms representing the golden age should be defended as Elsior had not been.

Sébastien glanced over his shoulder and motioned to the valet who kept to the shadows. Merlin was let in within the minute. As the mage observed Vivienne, the knight noted the sadness in his eyes.

Always the cunning wizard, Merlin masked his emotions and instead declared, "You were right about Guinevere and Arthur. He is losing faith, and her affair with Lancelot has already commenced. I would not ask if it was not absolutely necessary, but only a weapon will restore him when the time is right."

"Why come to me?" Vivienne enquired blankly. "I am no blacksmith."

"You are pure of heart. A weapon forged by you would trump all others, Lady of the Lake. Please."

A flash of anger hit Vivienne's eyes at the wizard's manipulations. It was soon gone, replaced by a vacant look.

"Do not call me that. I have listened to your query, and have no response to give. Now get off my grounds."

The old wizard looked to Sébastien for help, but the champion only shook his head. Merlin's back hunched over and he departed, unfulfilled, wondering if he had mistakenly meddled this time.

EPILOGUE

Alistair stumbled into Vivienne's solarium that same evening, bursting the large doors open with a push of his magic.

The queen, lost in ruminations, jumped up to her feet immediately. "You're alive!" she exclaimed in surprise, unable to believe her eyes.

The demon dog met her shocked gaze for a beat, before collapsing on the marble floors with an audible thud.

"Sébastien!" Vivienne yelled, and ran to Alistair's side, kneeling down and running her glowing palms over to heal him.

The champion rushed in, alerted by the noise. He joined the queen on her knees, immediately noticing Alistair's weakness and labored breathing.

I do not have much time left, his voice rumbled in both their heads, his eyes still closed. *I escaped Carleigh's clutches, but could not yet come back to you. I was busy on the damn sorcerer's trail and it led me to Arthur. He is still out there, Vivienne, planning to do the same to Camelot as he did to your realm. Do not let him.*

"How can I help Arthur when I failed my own people?" the enchantress cried.

Trust in yourself, Lady of the Lake, Alistair nuzzled her hand. *Own your title and your spirit, open yourself up to the old and the new. Listen to the song of my mourning tonight, under the full moon by your element, and you shall understand. It will come to you.*

The dog blinked, focusing on Sébastien one final time. *Defend her. At all costs.*

Then his eyes closed, the massive body exhaled its last breath, and he became still. Vivienne dug her hands into his fur, sobbing quietly. She was startled when the fur became dust, raising her head in horror. Under her distressed stare, Alistair's body crumbled apart, until there was nothing left.

She picked up a handful of the ashes, and clutched them to her heart as the sobs shook her. Sébastien picked the queen in his arms, holding her close, unable ¡to hold back the tears streaming down his cheeks at the loss of his friend.

A gentle breeze picked up, sweeping away the remaining ashes until it was as though Alistair had never existed – except for the memories in their subconscious.

Later that night, when Vivienne was done crying, she stepped out by the lake with Sébastien training behind. The guardian stayed back, watching as she let her head fall back, surveying the moon.

When it was at its apex, nature stirred in unity, and the

wind picked up a beautiful song of mourning and loss, as the leaves joined in. The rustling was the tempo, the howling a crescendo. The water sloshed back and forth, forth and back, and the moonlight shone stronger, illuminating Vivienne's radiant features.

Sébastien registered as he never had before just how much their lives intertwined. After having shared such a major loss with his beloved, he was more attuned to their own mortality than he had ever been. Having lost each other multiple times before, the defender dreaded their own fate, at times. The song stirred him deep, with an irresistible longing to have the queen in his arms and never let go.

The guardian was distracted from staring by the glow coming from the lake. Vivienne walked in, and it seemed to part for passage. And there, in the middle, something glistened.

The enchantress crossed her arms and bowed her head, and when she blinked, her eyes shone with the force of the magic she weaved. Sébastien could detect its pale glow filling each fiber of her body. Through their bond, he could experience its vibrant murmur.

The light in the middle grew stronger. Vivienne extended her hand and the water parted. From its midst, a sword floated forward, the metal shining strongly under the moon.

As the creation approached, the monarch was breathless at its beauty. An exquisite dragon design shaped the hilt, of both gold and silver nuances depending on how the radiance touched it. The sharp edge of the blade effortlessly cut through the surface of the liquid, barely creating a single ripple in its journey.

When it got to her, the blade hovered in mid-air, pointing

its hilt towards the royal. The grip was adorned by highly refined leather, wrapped around the strong neck of the beast. The pommel was where it stood: an impeccably designed head, scowling viciously at all those unworthy to wield it, its ruby eyes shining menacingly. Glorious wings substituted the cross guards, superbly constructed for strength and speed without sacrificing the grace of the mythical legend.

The sword seemed filled with a life of its own, as though it would viciously tear apart armies of evil with or without a mighty warrior to wield it.

When Vivienne gripped the weapon by the hilt, the beam shone blindingly, and Sébastien had to shield his eyes with one hand.

The young woman, attuned to the sword already, heard the name whispered clearly in her subconscious, and voiced it out loud. "Excalibur. So shall you be named."

When she walked out the lake, the queen was renewed. Vivienne's every step was confident and determined, wafting past on sure footing. Her shoulders, long having slumped and turned inwards for protection, now straightened into a regal posture. The chin was raised up, eyes shining brightly with newfound magic and an iridescent gleam within.

After a moment, Sébastien was able to look at her directly, once the radiance behind and around her softened. He was immediately enthralled by the sudden changes in his beloved.

Vivienne's face was no longer the deathly pale he had grown used to, but glowing instead, her joy fully visible. Her entire body, approaching him, did not simply radiate power; it was as if the royal had become the sun itself, banishing evil and returning hope to anyone in her vicinity.

She was no longer the fragile person of the last few months. Rather, an enchantress, sure of her abilities and realm – indomitable, unstoppable.

Before reaching him, the queen stopped and studied the treasure in her hand. "Go find Arthur," she softly commanded, "wherever he is. His quest should be hard, but not too much. He needs you at his side."

Excalibur shimmered, then evaporated altogether, to reappear much further away, embedded in the stone from which Arthur alone could withdraw it.

Back in Elsior, the couple embraced under the moonlight. And for the first time in what seemed like forever, Sébastien sensed Vivienne's passion in her caresses. She ran a finger across his jaw, smiling wickedly as the muscle jumped under her fingertips.

"You have been patient, my love," she whispered, her voice husky with forbidden temptation.

Sébastien gulped, attempting to rein in the stirrings of his desire – and failing. He let his forehead drop against Vivienne's, inhaling her sweet fragrance.

"I have missed you," the defender murmured back.

Vivienne threw her head back, lips invitingly parting for his. With a groan, Sébastien dropped his mouth to hers, unprepared for the response of their bodies – clutching, gripping, and melting beyond closeness.

Aflame with desire, neither noticed the glow slowly surrounding them as the union of their spirits sanctified their soul mate bond. When their garments came off, the only thing that mattered was the scorching flame driving them both, rising always higher, until they found heaven together.

* * *

Alistair's deity form shimmered, then appeared in front of a large door. He looked around at the empty space, then his human body, and scowled.

"What now?"

"You came seeking peace." The voice echoed all around, followed by laughter.

Alistair whirled around, but could not notice anyone. "And if I did? I would think I earned it after the last centuries of punishment."

More snickers answered, then, "Earned? You have not *earned* anything. You are here at our command, for us to toy with as we wish."

Alistair growled, then took his wolf form. *You can try...*

* * *

In Camelot, the night was of rejoicing. Arthur had married Guinevere, and they were off to consummate their marriage. Everyone was happy, drinks and food flowing widely – all except for Lancelot. The knight stood in a corner, morose, his gaze fixated on the bedroom window of the king.

The fact the woman he loved was there, currently in his bed, was enough to make him crazy. Sighing, he downed the last of his drink and went to his chambers.

Merlin, too, was focused on Arthur's window, but for different reasons. He dreaded what Guinevere would do now that she was queen and, even more so, what would happen to Elaine.

The only woman who could have thwarted the little witch was now sick, and not appearing ready to wake up anytime soon.

Merlin finished the mug of ale, his thoughts drifting off to Alistair. The previous night, he had a dream, and knew his old friend was gone from the world. *Now who will stop me from making stupid decisions?*

To top it off, Carleigh was nowhere to be found. Merlin had tried to go after the sorcerer to exact vengeance for Vivienne, but the sleazy man had truly disappeared – undoubtedly helped by Morgana.

Heavily exhaling, the mage got up, unwilling to stand by and watch the hypocrisy taking place. Merlin lifted the cape over his head and went to the stables. If he could not control the outcomes, then perhaps he could find some peace in the meantime.

Upstairs, Guinevere waited until Arthur was asleep, then slipped from the warm sheets. She stepped into the bathtub, washing herself quickly, then headed down the stairs.

In his room, Lancelot turned to the door that opened, eyes widening in surprise. "You…"

"I have come to the one I love," Guinevere whispered, then threw herself in his arms.

Lancelot, drunk on love and pain, was not about to deny her. He made quick work of Guinevere's clothes and laid her on the bed.

End of Part II

PART III

LOYALTY

CHAPTER 25

Arthur looked out the window of the study, his gaze falling on Guinevere with her handmaidens. His gorgeous wife was all he could wish for, he could not complain. By day, she was at his side making him smile and at night she met his every fantasy.

Despite this and his completely enamored state, the monarch felt something was missing. The grin froze on his lips as he glanced down and that ache spread inside again. He rubbed his chest absentmindedly, then turned away from Guinevere's enchanting form.

It was time he went to visit Elaine.

Arthur passed through the corridors and stepped into the maiden's room. It had been months since Elaine had fallen asleep to never wake up, but Arthur still hoped she would open the blue eyes he missed so – and soon.

The king stepped by the bedside and held her hand in his,

eyes roaming over her features. Elaine was pale, her cheeks hollow as she had not eaten. Merlin had used magic to keep her as healthy as possible, but nothing could snap through whatever haze had captured her mind.

Arthur had called onto the best healers in the realm, with no luck. Every day that passed, he despaired Elaine would ever wake up. The thought alone was enough to cut off his air supply, and he had to force it back into his lungs.

Steeling himself against her frail appearance, Arthur squeezed her fingers, trying to ground her when she seemed ready to take off.

"Elaine, if you can hear me, I need you back here. Please."

The king did not bother to hide the pleading in his voice. Here, in Elaine's room, he could be himself as he never was on the outside. She understood him and though she could not speak, he could still draw comfort from her presence.

But I miss her laugh… Her smile…

Arthur shook his head, attempting to clear it. Yes, he yearned to hear Elaine be alive once more, he could not deny it. A part of him felt absent and not even his wife could fill the void.

The monarch stayed behind for a few more hours until the door opened and in walked Guinevere.

"Why so sad, my king?" she asked softly, attempting to entice his senses.

Arthur glanced up, surprised at the slight irritation coursing through him. Elaine's room was his sanctuary, and somehow it felt as though Guinevere was intruding.

Stop being foolish! he admonished, forcing a weak smile.

"I wished to stop by and see Elaine. I miss her so…"

Eyes glued to the young maiden's sleeping expression, Arthur did not catch the flash of anger that crossed Guinevere's features. She opened her mouth to speak accusations, but managed in time to bite her tongue, and take a calming breath.

Only once she was sure not to say anything rash, did Guinevere continue, "I understand, my love. But all this time indoors is not doing you any good. The people need their king healthy. Come join me outside for a picnic."

When Arthur did not move, gaze lost in thought and locked on Elaine's unmoving form, Guinevere stepped closer. She lifted his chin and kissed him, pressing closer. In the embrace, Arthur found himself forgetting the anguish…

Shortly afterwards, he followed Guinevere out and into the forest. With the moon out, they made love under the stars, until Arthur's undivided attention was fully hers again.

* * *

Merlin was helpless – and it was killing him. He stopped by Elaine's room, knowing full well Arthur was with Guinevere.

For months on end, he had cursed and cajoled the deities and his own elemental powers for help – all to no avail. Whatever held Elaine in its grasp was not quick to let go. And the more she lay dormant, the more the blonde witch overwhelmed Arthur's wits.

The mage had no Alistair to turn to and Vivienne was deaf to his calls. He was alone with this problem, and though he had a hunch of who was at its source, he could do nothing.

What use are all these powers, when they cannot do anything against this!?

The wizard neared Elaine's bed and knelt by her side. "If you hear me, Elaine, you truly need to wake up. Guinevere has Arthur under a spell and he does not see past her charms. Only a true, pure love like what you have for him can break something that has been started by sorcery."

He paused, before whispering, "Please return. Camelot needs you – as does its king."

Once Merlin left, Guinevere stepped from the darker corners of the room, where she had hidden. She had followed the warlock knowing full well he would attempt – once again – to release Elaine from the clutches of the spell.

"The fool!" she scowled at the mage's retreating back. Merlin was a thorn in her side, one she needed to figure out how to remove.

But first…another problem arose.

Guinevere turned her wrath to Elaine, lips curled disdainfully at the young woman. "You will not wake up," she ordered, hissing straight into her ear. "Forget about Arthur, he is *mine*. Mine until death does us part, you little wench."

Guinevere stood up, and with a straight back headed out of the room. When the door closed behind her, Elaine's body gave a little shiver, then was immobile once more.

* * *

Merlin was out of options and it was thus he headed to the lake where Vivienne resided once more. He tried in vain to call for her, but was answered with resolute silence.

Unwilling to give up, he fell asleep on the grass, prepared to remain there for as long as it took – even if it meant giving up the comforts to which he had gotten used thus far.

A noise in the night woke Merlin up. He stood up slowly,

scouring the surroundings and expanding his senses. He had an eerie feeling of déjà-vu as he recalled another similar night, and another presence that had shadowed him.

"Who goes there?" Merlin asked.

There was no noise, then a woman stepped out from the forest. Her long hair dropped to her waist and she had bi-colored eyes that stared right through him. For the first time since Morgana, Merlin was struck speechless.

"I am Ardea," she murmured, and her voice carried on the wind, a sound so pure his ears trembled.

Merlin took in the ancient robe, the brooch clasped on her shoulder, and the aura of power he caught emanating from her. "You are of Atrox's kin," he stated, already standing up from the ground and lifting his staff in protection.

"Very good," Ardea smiled, though it did not warm her expression. "You are wasting your time here, wizard, as you are wasting your energy with that toy."

Merlin was not about to be fooled. Though he lowered the object of power, he kept a tight rein on the elements at bay. "What is it you wish?"

"No need to be so wary, I come here in peace."

"Right," he snorted. "That is not what I heard from Atrox over the years."

"My brother speaks too much," Ardea retorted in a slightly menacing tone.

Brother!? Merlin succeeded in keep his face impassable, but just barely. For all the years they had been friends, the demon had never mentioned the extent of his lineage to the gods – only that they had shunned him. It was shocking information to find out in the wake of his death.

"As for what I wish," the magician had to focus once more on Ardea, "it is more what *you* wish. You still burn for Morgana."

Merlin did not know which of the goddess' inflection or words made him blush, but he looked away, embarrassed.

"Would you like to know where she is?"

Merlin peered closely at Ardea, trying to figure out what game she was playing.

"What is your price?" he asked warily.

"None," Ardea answered.

"I find that hard to believe. You must have some purpose to helping me."

The goddess pursed her lips, surveying him with a very familiar stare for a few moments. In the end, she sighed in annoyance. "Your former lover intervenes even now with Arthur's fate, controlling Guinevere. By having the object of his affections in her grasp, Morgana grows more powerful daily." Ardea paused, unwilling to reveal too much. "She must be stopped."

"I am not a pawn," Merlin declared fiercely. "And neither is she!"

"Fool!" Ardea scoffed. "You have been too long amongst humans, Halfling. You forget you are not one of them."

Under his bemused gaze, Ardea shimmered, then disappeared. Merlin was left to wonder if he had made a mistake – yet the part in him that still loved Morgana refused to strike against her at the behest of a manipulating deity.

Despite this, Ardea's words had given the warlock an idea. Dropping the idea of enlisting Vivienne's help, he rushed back to the castle and Elaine's chambers, already conjuring the spell.

* * *

Guinevere was brushing her hair the next morning when the voice came in her mind.

You need an heir... Give Arthur a child... To secure your throne.

"My position is already safe," she scowled at her own reflection. "I do not need a crying baby."

Foolish! Do not be so proud and blind... A child settles your future.

"Arthur is besotted with me," Guinevere smirked proudly.

Beauty fades... His lust will wane... An heir is the only way.

Guinevere scowled, her pretty features twisting into something ugly. Then she nodded, knowing the voice had never strayed her wrong.

That same evening, when they were done making love, she awoke Arthur and started anew. He was left exhausted, but fell asleep with a smile on his lips.

* * *

While the royals were otherwise occupied, Merlin was waiting in Elaine's bedroom. He had sensed Morgana's energy in the castle, now that he knew to search for it. It surrounded Guinevere like a cloak, bathing her.

Keeping a tight connection with the queen's vibration, he felt it when the time had come. Turning to Elaine, Merlin spoke the counter-spell. "Guinevere is doing damage, Elaine. But she knows not what forces she is playing with. The life she wants to conceive requires a price. Whether or not it succeeds, I beg the elements to take their payment in the spell that surrounds you, thus freeing you."

Merlin pressed his index and middle finger to Elaine's forehead, resting them on the clammy skin until a soft, white glow enveloped the maiden. Only then did he step back, and allow himself to rest.

Hours later, Guinevere lay dormant by Arthur's side, sated in what she believed had been created. In that instant, a magic older than time itself went to work. The Fae energy surrounded the blonde woman, then Elaine, until the glow disappeared.

In Elaine's chambers, the young woman's eyes fluttered open, and she inhaled deeply.

"Arthur," she whispered aloud.

* * *

The next morning, Merlin happily strode into the king's bedchambers.

"Merlin, what is it?" the king grumbled groggily, whilst Guinevere glared from the bed.

"Elaine is awake," Merlin announced, grinning widely.

Arthur stared at him in shock for a moment, then jumped up and pulled on his clothes, uncaring of his half-nudity in the haste to run to Elaine.

"Darling, I thought we would visit the villagers today," Guinevere whispered, dimly trying to find a reason to hold him by her side.

"It can wait!" Arthur paused a beat at his own abrupt tone, then appeared contrite. "I apologize, sweetheart, but I have waited too long for Elaine to wake. I need to see her."

Without as much as a kiss, he was gone out the door. Merlin lingered behind, unable to keep the smug expression off his face.

"You think you have won?" Guinevere bit in anger.

The wizard leveled his gaze to hers, calmly retorting, "No. But I am on my way there. With Elaine awake, you will no longer have a monopoly on the king."

Merlin turned and left, but Guinevere's words followed him. "We shall see about that!"

In Elaine's room, Arthur already had gathered her close, holding onto her frail body tightly. "I was so afraid to lose you," he whispered, inhaling her sweet fragrance.

She held onto him, hands roaming his broad, bare back, sensing the muscles shift under her touch. The net of darkness that had fallen over her was lifted, and Elaine inhaled deeply into Arthur's neck, taking in his woodsy scent to ground herself.

When Elaine pulled back and her eyes locked onto his, Arthur felt a click of something, a shifting of an axis. He was aware of her every breath, and even more so of her touch on his back. His body craved closeness, not wanting to allow even the breath of distance between them.

Elaine is no longer just your best friend, but a part of you. Arthur gulped at words from his conscience, entranced by the soft curves pressing against his hardened body, the gentleness in her eyes, the rapidly beating pulse of her wrist.

Shaking his head to break the spell, Arthur stood and forced a smile. "I... I should let you rest, I do not wish to tire you," he mumbled sheepishly.

"Never, Arthur," Elaine beamed.

How I missed that, Arthur thought, but said nothing. He was already acting too peculiarly, and noticed the confusion in Elaine's gaze. With a last thin smile, he left the bedchambers, before he did something stupid.

It was only after Arthur left that Elaine turned to Merlin, eyes filled with questions.

"What happened? The last thing I remember is seeing Arthur with Guinevere…"

"Some spell was thrown on you, and you have been asleep for months. The king has married Guinevere. There was nothing either of us could do to stop him."

Elaine looked away, blinking through the tears.

"Then what was the point to me waking up?"

"I think there was more than one reason you returned to us, Elaine. Arthur needs you, and that must have shattered through the spell itself."

She seemed unconvinced, but nonetheless said, "How can I help, then?"

"We have to break him of Guinevere's spell. The more time you can spend with him, the better."

"I will do my best."

"Thank you," Merlin hugged her. "I will let you rest, as well."

* * *

In the next few weeks, Merlin's plan succeeded. Arthur spent most days with Elaine, not neglecting – per se – his wife, but definitely no longer setting her as a top priority. As Guinevere continued to fume, Arthur found peace around his friend.

One such day, as they walked in the gardens, Elaine took a deep breath and asked, "Arthur, may I speak freely?"

The monarch stopped in his tracks, looking down at her with a gentle look in his eyes. "Elaine, you and Lancelot have been my most trustworthy friends. You may always speak freely."

The young maiden paused even further at the mention of the knight's name. For the last days, she had noticed Guinevere skulking around at night with Lancelot, unable to do anything to stop their betrayal.

Part of her wanted to show Arthur in the most brutal way, to ensure he had no doubts about them. But the larger part of her that cared deeply for his feelings did not wish him to crumble under the weight of truth.

"There is more to Guinevere than meets the eye," Elaine carefully chose the words.

"Yes... there is," the king grinned, beguiled.

"Arthur..."

At the look on his face, Elaine bit her lip. "I do not wish you to be hurt."

"Why do you think I would be?" he asked quizzically, tilting his head. "Guinevere makes me happy."

"That is all I can ask," Elaine forced a smile, and they continued their walk.

* * *

Guinevere was close to bursting as she watched the two friends from her room's window. That same night, once Arthur was sated after their lovemaking, she began, "I want to speak to you about Elaine."

"Hmm?" Arthur asked sleepily, drawing lazy circles over her hip.

"She is in love with you."

The blunt announcement had the effect of cold water being thrown on Arthur. He shot upright in bed, eyes narrowed in confusion. "What?"

"You heard me! Elaine loves you, and I want her gone."

"But, Guinevere..." Arthur was taken aback at the cold tone of his wife. "She is my oldest friend!"

"And *I* am your wife." The imperious, self-sufficient tone Guinevere used was not lost on Arthur. He could not believe such words were coming from his sweet, loving queen.

Arthur searched her expression, hoping this was some joke. The queen's cold features left no room for interpretation, yet the king surprised himself by flatly saying, "No."

"You would prefer her over me?" Guinevere switched tactics.

"That is not what I said, darling," Arthur tried to reach for her, but she pulled away. "You make no sense!"

Guinevere only stared at him expectantly.

"I do not know who put these ideas in your head," Arthur grumbled as he got out of bed, pulling his clothes on, "but you are being ridiculous. We will talk in the morning."

As he walked away, Guinevere yelled, "If anything happens to me, it will be your fault!"

Arthur shook his head, finding solace in the night surrounding him.

* * *

A few days later, Elaine was walking the corridors at night and heading to her bedroom. The queen had been absent from dinner and she had enjoyed spending time with Arthur. Having recounted to her Guinevere's accusations, Elaine had been shocked – but kept her mouth shut on the truth she desperately wanted to divulge.

"Elaine!"

The young woman froze, turning around to see Guinevere headed towards her swiftly. She had a crazy look in the eyes, and Elaine took a step back.

"What can I do for you, my lady?" she murmured. Glancing around, she noticed they were alone – no witnesses.

"You can leave my husband alone!" Guinevere shrieked.

As she kept moving closer, Elaine backed away until her back was to the wall atop the stairs. Behind her was the narrow staircase that reached to the lower deck.

"I do not know what you are referring to," Elaine tried to reason.

"Oh yes you do, you wench! And I am telling you, Arthur is *mine*!" With that, Guinevere flung herself towards Elaine.

Out of pure reflex, she edged out of the way and the royal went tumbling down the stairs. "Guinevere, no!"

Elaine reached the top of the stairs just as Arthur, Lancelot and Merlin stepped from the hall below. The king looked at her, then Guinevere's body on the ground, and whispered, "What have you done?" before rushing to his wife.

Lancelot had to clench his fists to forcefully keep away, whilst Merlin only stared at Elaine's shocked expression. He took her away from Arthur before the king did something he regretted.

"She threw herself, didn't she?" the mage whispered, accompanying Elaine to her chambers.

"How did you know?" she peered up in surprise.

"Guinevere fears you. Only a move such as this could grant her Arthur's unconditional support."

"What am I to do?" Elaine sobbed quietly.

"I will speak to Arthur."

Merlin left Elaine to head to the queen's chambers, where he found Arthur by her bedside table. As he entered, the castle healer was leaving the room.

"I told you!" Guinevere was crying. "I warned you that she would harm me... and now our child..." She turned her face away, burying it into the pillow.

Merlin had to clench his fists to avoid throttling the witch. Arthur's next words confirmed he had lost.

"I shall send her away at once, my dear. I am sorry, so sorry, for not seeing it sooner."

The king stood to his feet, moving numbly. Merlin tried to intercept him, but all Arthur said was, "Move."

The warlock watched as he strode purposefully towards Elaine's room. He turned to Guinevere, noticing the lack of tears as she was now grinning – the proverbial cat that ate the canary.

"There was never any child."

"Of course not!" Guinevere scoffed, then laughed. "But now there will be no Elaine, either."

"So you bribed the healer?"

"People will do anything for some gold, Merlin. Have you not learnt that yet?"

The mage walked away, disgusted by her actions.

At the same time, Arthur reached the room where Elaine was pacing back and forth, and kicked the doors open violently.

"Arthur –"

"You are to leave at once."

"No, you don't understand –" Elaine tried to move closer, but Arthur was quicker.

"You lied to me!" he got up in her face, snarling in rage as he pushed Elaine against the wall. His features were twisted in terrible anger, his entire body taut with tension. "You hurt the queen, and thus me. I cannot believe I did not see it before."

"Arthur, please!" Elaine sobbed. "It's all lies! Guinevere will betray you, and make a fool out of you!"

"Leave at once."

It was only once Arthur was back to his study that the broad shoulders slumped with the weight of the betrayal, and the oppression of the choice he had been forced to make. A part of him in exchange for the love of his wife. Only time would tell if it was worth it.

CHAPTER 26

Merlin watched from afar as the once boisterous monarch slowly turned into himself. Since Guinevere had succeeded in driving Elaine away, Arthur was not the same.

He went about his duties as though in a daze. Though he was still as gentle with the people, he was prone to bouts of morose silence, falling into deep, dark thoughts. Finally, rumors had started that Guinevere would not let him into the matrimonial bed since the miscarriage.

Merlin narrowed his gaze as one of the council members tried to get the king's attention, but he seemed to be focused on Lancelot. The two shared a look, something unspoken passing between them, then Arthur turned away.

"Leave me." At the abrupt silence, he realized his less than normal tone and rephrased, "We will return to this topic tomorrow."

Everyone departed the room, throwing wary looks over

their shoulders, but Merlin stayed within earshot. He watched as Lancelot stood and walked to Arthur, whispering low.

To his utter surprise, Arthur snapped and grabbed the knight by the scruff of the neck. He did nothing else, just stared at him with a look of such utter pain across his face, that Merlin wished nothing more than to erase it.

Then Arthur let him go. Lancelot backed away, swaying from the sudden release. He hesitated, but the royal was not to be contested.

"Leave. Now."

Without a glance to the warlock, Lancelot obeyed.

Merlin waited for a few moments, observing Arthur in silence. When the monarch took a seat on the floor by the window, dropping his head onto a bent knee, he could no longer sit by doing nothing.

"Sire, what ails you?" Merlin asked, stepping closer.

Arthur answered nothing at first, but ultimately glanced up. "Have you ever felt something so strong, it tears you up inside?"

Merlin nodded, thinking of Morgana, and Arthur looked away, avoiding his gaze. *Could it be Arthur finally realizes his feelings for Elaine, and that is the reason behind the sorrow I sense?*

"Guinevere will not let me near her," Arthur confessed, shattering the mage's hopes. "I cannot take back the child we lost, but… Merlin, I know not what to do to save our love."

The wizard knelt next to Arthur, placing a hand on his shoulder. "Sire, there is something you must know. I cannot remain quiet any longer."

Alistair's warning from long was very much present in

Merlin's mind – to stop intervening. But even more so was a desire to get Arthur back to his former help. Interfering or not, the warlock felt the need to do something.

When Arthur remained unfazed, Merlin continued, "It is Guinevere, sire. The child you mourn never existed."

There was a pause, as though air itself slipped away, then Arthur raised a confused stare to Merlin's. "What?"

"She lied to you, Arthur. Guinevere was never pregnant."

The mage trailed off at the anger burning in the king's eyes. "That cannot be truth!" Arthur contested.

"I have always been honest with you, sire."

Arthur grasped his shoulder, searching his expression as though willing him to take back the words. When Merlin did nothing of the sort, he stood abruptly and turned his back to him.

Merlin paused, trying to read his emotions. Past Arthur's aura and the trembling of his muscles, he could register the distraught. In spite of it, logic was getting through.

Arthur swam through the current of chaos in his mind, until the furious shaking subsided and he was calm once more. He whirled around, and though his expression was closed, his voice maintained the respect that had always been there.

"I cannot believe this, Merlin, not of Guinevere. But I will find out if it is true."

He stepped away resolutely, walking back to his chambers – and Merlin let him.

Later that same evening, Arthur stepped into the queen's room. It took only one look to register Guinevere was not there, and the bed was made. In some deep corner of his heart, the royal was none too surprised by her absence.

Nonetheless, he took a seat on an armchair by the shadowed corner of the window and waited. It would be hours until the creak of the door startled him awake, and in walked Guinevere.

Gorgeously bathed in moonlight, she stepped towards the bed in a silky, pale blue robe. The hair cascading freely down her back gave her an almost blonde halo, somehow drawing attention even more to Guinevere's flushed cheeks and bruised lips – as though she had spent hours being kissed.

Over the hours he had reflected, Arthur believed Guinevere spent her days alone, mourning the loss of their child. This siren revealed to his eyes was not the image he had despaired over for the last months.

With a sensuous shrug of the shoulder, Guinevere let the robe fall at her feet. She was about to slide into bed when she noticed him – and jumped.

"Arthur! You gave me a fright," she accused.

The king stood from the corner and watched Guinevere from a distance without saying anything. His eyes roamed over her naked body, but not with desire, rather cold inspection.

"What is it you wish?" Guinevere murmured, getting antsy. *He cannot have guessed where I was... Could he?*

"Is it true?" Arthur asked point blank. He felt no remorse at putting the queen on the spot, not after what his instincts whispered.

"I do not know what you mean."

"The child. *Our* child. Is it true that you faked it, that you were never pregnant to begin with?"

Guinevere blanched, then caught herself and threw back, "How *dare* you accuse me of such a thing!?"

Arthur frowned, fighting off the guilt creeping for asking the question. Guinevere was good – he was only now realizing just *how* good she was at acting.

"Is it true?" he pressed.

"Of course not!" Guinevere sputtered.

Something in her tone hit Arthur in the gut, convincing him of the lie. The next words left his lips before he could stop them. "What of tonight, where have you been?"

"How *dare* you!?"

In a few steps, Arthur was by her side, towering over and clenching his jaw. A fury the likes he had never felt boiled underneath the surface, and he had the clear urge to throttle his dear wife.

Instead, he willed his fists to remain at bay, even as he hissed, "I dare because I am your husband! And king, in case you have forgotten."

Guinevere raised her chin defiantly and refused to respond. Her blue eyes sparkled with malice, not love, and for the second time that night, Arthur realized he did not truly know her – nor had he ever.

Arthur assessed Guinevere as though he was seeing her for the first time. A veil lifted off his eyes and he could see the coldness in her gaze, the façade hiding behind the smile. Her beauty was no longer entrancing, rather something he could stare at unfeeling.

How have I been so blind?

Without any further comment, he walked away, not even bothering to force an answer regarding where Guinevere had been. It was written all over her.

Arthur returned to his own bedchambers and slammed the

door behind. In rage at the situation, he shoved everything off Guinevere's vanity to the ground, then turned and punched the wall, roaring in pain when his fist passed through.

Alerted by the noise, a guard entered immediately, fearing the king was in danger.

"Sire, are you –"

"I am fine. Leave me!" Arthur ordered, keeping his back to the soldier. When the door closed, the king inhaled deeply, willing himself to think clearly. In the end, all he could do was peer out the window to the moon waning outside.

Now *what do I do?* Arthur scowled.

* * *

The rumors were getting to him. A kingdom on the verge of upheaval, a wife who did not let him in her bed, a brother in arms who warmed it in his stead…

"Sire?"

Arthur turned to Merlin, seeing the newly pronounced lines on the wizard's face. It had been a week since the showdown with Guinevere, and he had not addressed the queen since. She had tried coming into his bed the next night, and he had coldly refused.

The monarch had revealed to Merlin some of what had taken place, but not all. Now, for the first time, he was finally aware of his surroundings again. His old friend seemed sadder these days, as though the world had caught up. Then again, it had definitely caught up with him.

Arthur got lost in his thoughts, thinking to the previous night, to Guinevere and Lancelot and what he suspected of them… There was nothing worse than the flame of betrayal he felt licking at his heart. Though whatever emotions he had for his wife had died the moment she admitted the horrible lie, his pride suffered.

Even more so, what cut deepest was having lost the one person who truly understood him – Elaine.

The king wanted nothing more than to go crawling to her to apologize, but was afraid she would turn him away. That was a risk he could not take, if only because it would destroy him. In the deepest corners of his heart, Arthur now understood just how much he had forsaken – and for how little.

Guinevere was never worth it.

Arthur exhaled heavily, focusing back on his advisor and friend. He answered the query with a question of his own. "Is something the matter, Merlin?"

"What do you mean, sire?"

"Only that you seem sadder these days," Arthur stated. He turned fully to face Merlin, before murmuring, "I may be drowning in my own dark ruminations, but I have noticed you spend more time here."

"I…" Merlin paused, unwilling to reveal he dreaded the loneliness of his cave, where his own regrets awaited. Instead, he continued, "I lost a dear friend, and made some choices that were not beneficial for a loved one."

Arthur's eyes glazed over as he recalled a different time, a different woman by his side… "Yes, that seems to be the case with loved ones."

Merlin used magic to look beyond, registering for the first time the toll on his king. He had known Guinevere was manipulative and that it would eat at him, once he learned the truth. What he saw now within Arthur was a true loss of hope, a weight the size of the entire universe pushing down on the broad shoulders.

The mage knew no spell could ease the burden Arthur had placed upon himself. For a man such as him, the only thing that would was the realization that the things in life that sapped strength were the ones he had to fight, and turn his anger towards.

And only one person could help with that particular quest.

It is time.

* * *

It took Merlin longer to get to Aisling Caisleán, Vivienne's domain. This time again, no matter how much he pushed at the charms hiding the place, he was not allowed entrance.

With no other options, the wizard made camp by the lake, waiting until he was either granted an audience, or someone came to kick him off. He made sure to let loose enough bursts of energy to ensure his presence was not missed.

On the eve of the second day, the waters stirred. It was barely perceptible, but his Fae senses caught it. Merlin rose to his feet, eyes trained on the lake for what he could not see.

After moments of silence, he stated, "I know you are out there, Vivienne."

Quaintness was the answer, as though nature itself lay in wait. Then the fog split into two and a shape stepped closer.

The Lady of the Lake emerged from the mist. She wore a simple white dress, scintillating under the moon's radiance like a diamond. The material flowed over her like rippling liquid and a pendant attracted the moon's rays like a magnet.

Vivienne's long, dark hair was wavy to her waist, held back by a small leafed tiara. Her green eyes shone with steely strength, another change from their last meeting. This was no longer a child, but a true enchantress. Though she held no staff or object of power, Merlin could feel the magic emanating from her – a purity not even he could touch.

In spite of his better judgment, the mage was kneeling before she had even reached him. "Highness…" he murmured, recalling he was now in front of a queen.

"Rise, Merlin," Vivienne's voice sounded strong, not like the frail creature he had last laid eyes on. Behind her, a shadow moved – Sébastien, always watchful. "What is it you wish, wizard?"

Merlin's gaze locked onto hers, noticing the fire within. Whereas before it only appeared when she used magic to its fullest, now it was reflected in the emerald depths as though part of her.

"Vivienne, I –"

"It is not Vivienne who you call to," the enchantress interrupted in a firm tone. "The young princess you refer to is long gone, Merlin. You made sure of it." She watched as he flinched, then continued indifferently, "Thus, I repeat: what is it you wish?"

"Nothing for myself, great lady," Merlin murmured. "I come for Arthur, king of Camelot. He bends under the weight of his destiny, to this day broken by those around him."

"I warned you long ago," the lady retorted. "It is not my mess to fix."

"Vivienne, please –"

"No," she cut him off.

The green eyes flashed, even as the queen pursed her lips. Nothing else in her countenance gave indication of turbulent emotions, but Merlin knew Vivienne well enough, having seen her grow before his very eyes.

"You do not get to beg," Vivienne continued. "You do not get to ask anything of me. Do you know, only, what the last sacrifice I had to see was?"

When Merlin did not respond, she divulged, "I had to bury Alistair. Watched him turn to dust in front of my eyes."

"I…" *How did I not see it?*

A stabbing pain hit the wizard at the recollection his longtime friend had perished. In his cave, for the last years, it had been a fact he could ignore, one less regret he could push away from his mind.

Now Vivienne forced Merlin to relive emotions he much preferred to forget. He had simply not thought it possible for demon lords to disappear, believing the entity forever protected despite the warnings that had come. In the end, it seemed the warlock did not understand as much as he would have liked of the laws ruling their world.

"You do not see everything, wizard," Vivienne taunted, oddly echoing his thoughts.

Merlin tried to step closer, but was stopped by an invisible wall not even his staff could pass.

"You are not welcome here," Vivienne warned. "There is nothing you can say that will change my mind."

Then she turned and walked away.

It truly registered, in that moment, that Merlin had no power over her. Vivienne was out of his bounds, and nothing he said or did could change her mind.

Once again rejected, Merlin could only stare as the evasive queen retreated, the knight by her side. With Fae sight, he could still see the bond between them, and recalled everything he had helped out with.

"You can lie to me," Merlin accused, annoyed at having lost and being dismissed so easily, "but we both know this is what you were meant to be! Do not turn against me for having made you who you are!"

Vivienne stopped moving, and Sébastien threw a look over his shoulder. Irritation emanated off him in waves.

"You owe me!" Merlin threw as a last resort.

The mist swallowed them both, but behind them movement arose. Merlin watched with widened eyes as the lake rose into a wall, as threatening as a bulldozer ready to rip him apart.

Waves curled high above, slithering like creatures ready to pull him in. The mage took a step back and raised the staff in a defensive gesture.

Then Vivienne's voice came, as unmovable as the waters she held the key to. "You should be happy, Merlin. You got your wish, made me who I am. Nonetheless, I will never be of use to *you*."

Then the wall dropped, and the lovers disappeared from his sight as well.

* * *

In a parallel realm, Alistair was back in deity form, glaring at the same door he had been staring at for what felt like ages.

He sensed a shift behind and turned to see a figure step out of the darkness. She had wavy red hair, startling blue eyes and a petite figure. What most surprised him were the two wings protruding from her back, thin and shiny like a butterfly's. Only the tips were visible from where he stood, and only under a certain light.

"What now?" Alistair half-groaned mockingly. "So this entire time, I have been kept at bay from my peaceful slumber by Faes?"

The woman laughed – tinkling bells – before settling an amused gaze on him. "Nay, wolf. It is your own kin that keep you away."

"And why would my brethren do so?"

"For sport," she shrugged, and it moved the barely there gown she had on ever so slightly. The blood-red material wrapped around her body like a second skin, somehow setting off the freckled skin and brilliance of her eyes.

Alistair's senses stirred, something he had not felt in ages – not since Deasa. There was something alluring about the woman... "What is your name?" he asked hoarsely, then cleared his throat to hide it.

"I am Catriona," the Fae responded.

Something in her tone had Alistair stop his inspection to meet her eyes – at a huge cost to his self-control – and he noticed the mocking glare. Then it dawned on him: she was playing him!

"Enough of your tricks," he growled, folding his arms across his chest. "What is it you wish?"

Catriona answered nothing, instead the blue gaze roamed suggestively over the muscles of his arms, down his chest, and lower still. As Alistair cleared his throat, she looked up sheepishly.

The former demon lord was befuddled at the odd behavior. Yet as they squared off like adversaries, he recalled one thing about female Faes: they were ruled by instinct and baser impulses. The purer the Fae blood within, the more those desires took over.

When Catriona's gaze darkened, her lips parting in response to his own racing pulse, Alistair bared his teeth. "Enough!" he thundered, wanting to put a stop to whatever it was between them. "Your answer, now!"

"You are being further punished because you intervened," Catriona murmured distractedly, stepping closer. "That, and you helped one of ours while on Earth."

"And if I did?"

"Help him again... Merlin needs guidance."

Alistair could not help snorting. "He always was a handful."

"Yes," Catriona smiled, finally giving him her undivided attention. Ironically, Alistair found it did not calm his body's reactions any further. "Since he was a child."

Alistair tilted his head, then wondered, "Why is it you care about him?"

"Merlin is my half-brother. Though I can never see him, unable as I am to enter the earthly realm since my father blocked the entrance... I wish him well."

With that, she turned to leave back into the nothingness.

"Wait!" Alistair took a step forward, but only tinkling laughter answered him. In a flash, Catriona was gone.

"Just how in hell am I supposed to help that annoying Halfling, anyway?" he growled. "As if I can get out of here!"

A burning on his chest had him look down, where a pendant now hung around his neck. Alistair picked it up, noticing it was a fairy's wings. Then a voice whispered, *You can reach him in dreams, simply use this as a channel...*

* * *

Merlin rode back to Camelot and was back within its walls in the half-day it took him to travel. On the way back, he had analyzed Vivienne's words and come to one conclusion: she may not give him help, would not refuse Arthur.

The warlock barged into the king's study, a huge grin on his face.

"Merlin, you have come back!" Arthur greeted and moved to pull him into a hug.

The mage returned it, then pulled away and clapped him on the back.

"You seem happier."

"I am. Sire, there is something you should do... Someone to see." At Arthur's confused look, Merlin continued, "She lives in a palace, Aisling Caisleán. She is called the Lady of the Lake."

Arthur pulled away, shaking his head in amusement – and slight shock. "Merlin, I will remain faithful to my wife." A shadow passed in his expression as he continued, "No matter what *she* does."

Merlin could not help laughing. "You misunderstand, Arthur. It is not for love you are to see her. The Lady of the Lake can help with an ultimate hurdle."

"And what is that?"

"Get you to be the ruler you are meant to."

At the monarch's still bemused stare, Merlin grasped his shoulder firmly. "You may not understand what I am saying, but you have lost your way, dealing with all this betrayal. The Lady is light personified. She can help you in a way no one else can."

"Not even you?" Arthur had a hard time believing it.

"Not even me," Merlin confirmed. "Please trust me on this, and go to her. You have nothing to lose."

Arthur pondered the words for a few moments, before nodding slowly. "Very well. I will make arrangements."

* * *

"Stupid fool!" Morgana raged at the basin.

Arthur was supposed to be cowering by now, under her damn spell. But the blonde queen had all but ruined her plans, becoming so engrossed with Lancelot she paid no mind to the rumors started.

Morgana turned away from the bowl of water to pace, clenching her fists. If only there was a way to hurt Merlin worse... Mordred was already working towards helping Carleigh grow in strength, and the sorcerer's numbers were rising.

Arthur was losing faith – but now Vivienne would help restore it. No, she needed something more. Some weakness of the great king, something to truly bring Merlin to his knees.

It came to her in a flash: this entire time, she had been focused on using Arthur to hurt Merlin...while he was alive.

My half-brother could prove much more useful dead... Especially considering my dear Merlin's task is to keep him alive. And it would not hurt to get that little enchantress out of the way...

Content, Morgana turned back to the basin. Watching, always watching, for the moment when the balance would shift...

CHAPTER 27

Sébastien had left the safety of Aisling Caisleán, pushed by a nagging feeling that something was afoot. He had no sooner gotten off the shores of Vivienne's lake, that ten mercenaries attacked him.

He jumped off Illyria, sword in hand and straight into the fray. Ten was not a small number to fight, but Sébastien got lost in the feel of the blade and clash of metal.

He did not notice one of the attackers skulking behind, ready to deliver a killing blow. When he raised his axe to strike, it met another sword.

Sébastien turned around in surprise, noticing another man – not much older than himself – wielding a blade with the same skill he did.

The guardian quickly sized him up as an ally and, with a nod of accord, they went back to back, raising their steely weapons. The mercenaries struck them that much harder, but both knights worked as a team and dispatched them within moments.

Scoffing, Sébastien turned to the newcomer. He noticed the hazel eyes and gentle demeanor almost immediately. There was a force radiating off the man, but it was muted by the slightly haunted look in his eyes.

"Thank you," he said gratefully, sheathing his weapon and extending a hand in greeting.

The other man gripped it by the forearm and Sébastien had his doubts confirmed. The stranger went by the same code he did – of knighthood and honor.

"Forgive me for asking, but what brings you here?"

"I could ask you the same," the man replied with a wry smile.

Sébastien grinned in response, "Fair enough. I was out for a walk."

"A *walk*? In these parts?"

The enchantress' companion had to laugh. "I happen to live nearby."

"Then perhaps you may help me…" The stranger trailed off, hesitating for a beat, then finished, "I am looking for a Lady of the Lake."

Sébastien's grin widened. "You have come to the right place. There is but one, but she is fair enough for all."

Something about the man's tone put Arthur at ease, and he nodded in return. "Take me to her, please," he begged. "I come from Camelot, my name is Arthur."

"*King* Arthur?" Sébastien corrected.

The man looked away, then with a shrug admitted, "Yes, though I do not feel very kingly at the moment."

The guardian took a longer look at the monarch, sizing him up once more. Yes, there was definitely strength in him, but also sadness. Whatever was burdening the royal, perhaps Vivienne might be able to help.

"Follow me," Sébastien said, then whistled for Illyria. The mare trotted to his side with Arthur's stallion, and together they headed out.

It took them a fair hour before reaching the lake's shore once more. "Are you at ease with magic?" Sébastien asked the king.

Arthur had to chuckle, recalling Merlin's tricks from childhood. "Quite, yes."

"Good."

Then Sébastien faced the lake and called out, "I seek entrance to Aisling Caisleán."

His voice carried across the water, echoing in a way that should not have been possible. Only silence answered at first, but Arthur kept a narrowed stare onto the water. Even one as non-magical as him could feel the power lurking underneath its surface.

Soon enough, a mist rose from the water, moving across as though blown by an invisible breeze. When it neared them, a female voice whispered, "Who asks?"

"The enchantress' companion."

There was silence, then a soft chuckle, before she answered, "You may enter, Sébastien. Welcome home, beloved."

Arthur turned a surprised look to the man, noticing his wide grin. "You *do* know her."

"Oh yes," Sébastien laughed. "Your time coming here has

not been wasted, sire."

Then the fog engulfed them, and all was quiet. Arthur felt as though the world itself faded, and then they were floating. He looked under Aryan's hooves, but could see nothing past the mist. Nonetheless, the sensation of not touching ground remained.

Despite this, the horse was ever calm, following Illyria's lead and standing perfectly still. Moments later, it felt as though they had landed and Aryan stepped out of the mist.

For once, Arthur was left speechless at the sight.

"Enter, sire," Sébastien offered. "I will go find whom you seek."

And then he was gone, leaving the king to stare at the immense structure that was Aisling Caisleán. When Merlin had suggested he come here, Arthur was far from believing the tales of an enchantress living in a similarly charmed castle.

And yet, facing him was a sight that proved him wrong. The castle was white, with two towers. In the light of day, with the slight mist surrounding it, it scintillated like it had diamonds across the stone. When Arthur entered, he noticed the marble flooring, stark white against the dark oak of the furniture decorating every piece.

He stepped around staring at everything, unwittingly getting closer to where he was meant to be.

* * *

Vivienne was strolling in the gardens when Sébastien came to get her.

"Arthur is here."

It had been months since the queen had forged Excalibur. She had never expected the king of Camelot himself to come, but then again…

"Let him in," she commanded, following Sébastien back to the throne room.

The enchantress had barely sat down when the large doors opened and the young leader entered. Vivienne noted the strength of the knight's shoulders, but his weary eyes stirred her soul.

"Arthur, welcome."

For a moment, she feared he might recognize her as the girl that had once crossed his path. Though it meant nothing to Vivienne, she much preferred to entertain the legend that had started of her life, and not let the outside world know she was still alive when Elsior itself had perished.

"Lady of the Lake," Arthur bowed in her direction, not a flicker of recognition in the eyes, and nodded to Sébastien. "I come to seek your counsel."

"I am flattered, and hope the journey was not for naught. How can I help?"

Arthur's request was swift, though bewildering. "Do you believe in soul mates?"

"Yes," Vivienne admitted, glancing to her own love for confirmation.

"Is there… Do you suppose it is possible that soul mates are incompatible in a second life?"

"I am afraid not." Thought Vivienne softened her voice, she could tell her words had dealt Arthur a blow. "I can only speak from my own personal experience, but soul mates always meet up, and live another life. The true significance of the term is that they complete each other, live in harmony with one another."

Arthur sighed heavily, having realized as much.

"If I may be blunt… What ails you?"

"My wife, Guinevere, and Lancelot, my best man… I believe they are betraying me, breaking their vows."

Damn you, Merlin, and your meddling. With all your powers, and you could not save Arthur the hurt? Vivienne pushed away the distracting rumination, then got off the throne.

She approached Arthur and raised a hand to his cheek, imbued with a tiny spell to boost his spirit. "Soul mates do not hurt each other. She is not yours, only borrowed. Guinevere follows her own path, as do the ones who trail behind her. You, dear king, have a kingdom to rule. Do not let this destroy you. What you require is something to bring back your faith, both in yourself and in the world."

Arthur peered in her green eyes, dazed at the wisdom of the words and the odd sense of familiarity. There was something about the enchantress…

Smiling, Vivienne placed a glowing palm on his chest, and Arthur lost his train of thought. "Follow your heart on a quest. Rediscover your strength and forge ahead, Arthur. With or without Guinevere."

"Will it be enough?" he asked.

At the lady's confused stare, he continued, "Enough for me to be leader I am meant to be. Merlin said seeking your counsel will help set me back on the path."

Vivienne glanced down at the magic in her hand, then up into his eyes. "You are already on the path, sire."

Nodding, Arthur prepared to leave. Sébastien, after a look to Vivienne, followed him out to the lake's shore.

"You are lucky," Arthur murmured.

With a side-glance to him, Sébastien agreed, "Extremely. But Arthur, you cannot count yourself less so. After all, if Guinevere is not your soul mate, that means your chance at true happiness is still out there, waiting for you to seize it."

Arthur mused over the words, ultimately murmuring, "Perhaps."

"I will tell you this…" Sébastien hesitated, but at the man's unconvinced look, had to finish, "Anything truly worth it has to be fought for."

The wisdom of the statement was not lost upon Arthur. He had much to decide once he was back onto regular land.

When the fog rose once more, Aryan stepped within it and the king was gone.

"He will be fine," a voice whispered from behind.

Sébastien turned to Vivienne, pulling her into his arms. "I believe you, my love. Thank you for helping him."

"How could I not? After all, he is the future."

Hand in the hand, the two headed back within the palace.

* * *

"You have not acted on my suggestion," Catriona's voice startled Alistair out of his musings.

He turned his wolf head towards the Fae, glaring. *I do not take orders.*

"Tsk, you really should learn to behave more," she chastised, stepping closer.

This time, she was wearing a dark green sheath that wrapped her body, stopping barely at mid-thigh. Alistair could sense her particular fragrance much better with the animal nose, and it was turning his head.

He transformed back to his human form, scowling. "Are you *bored*?"

Catriona tilted her head to the side at the question, laughing, "Perhaps. The Fae realm tends to drive even the best of us slightly insane. Why, is my presence annoying you?"

"Much."

Catriona chuckled again at his darkening expression and moved nearer still. Alistair was surprised she did not fear him, this Fae that was half his size. She affected him, yes, but also provided a welcome distraction.

"I am in no mood to be playing games, child," he spit in an effort to get Catriona to back off.

Her pretty blue eyes shone and sparked lightning, much as Merlin's did. Except in this particular case, the hunter within Alistair rose to the surface. Something about the Fae urged him to stake claim.

"If I am such a child," Catriona whispered seductively, "then why is your body so eager to claim me?"

"Get *out* of my head!" Alistair ordered, towering over her.

Catriona threw her head back, but kept her eyes locked onto his defiantly. "I was not in your head, wolf. Your body is doing all the talking."

Alistair's nostrils flared in anger, even as they squared off. Then, before he could tell himself it was a bad idea, his arms snaked around her waist and pulled the Fae closer.

His mouth descended on Catriona's brutally, even as her body pressed against his. She reached both arms around his neck, wrapping them tightly. For the first time in eons, Alistair felt a lick of desire, a flame of passion burning within.

He managed to put a stop to the madness just as Catriona

was removing all breathing space between them. "You need to leave."

She smiled mockingly, as though sensing the true depth of his desire. Her blue eyes sparkled, her mouth swollen by the kiss. "You can deny it all you want, wolf, but the man within you wants me."

"Regardless, it does not mean I will act upon it."

Catriona's gaze changed, almost regretful. "Too bad."

She turned to leave but right before flying away, threw over a shoulder. "*Do* consider helping my brother."

Alistair was glaring at the spot he had last seen her in for a long time afterwards, his body nowhere close to cooling down.

* * *

On his way back to Camelot, Arthur was dragging his feet, so to speak. He did not feel ready yet to join his wife, nor did he want to see the betrayer Lancelot. And yet…where else could he go?

Stopping for the night, he made a fire and slept under the stars, his gaze lost beyond them. *Somewhere out there, someone waits for me…* The thought was more hopeless than it was encouraging. How was he to find her?

Without even noticing it, he fell asleep… And was dragged into a dream. He was in a meadow, where a stone stood. In it was embedded a sword, much like the one he had once yanked free to become King of Britain.

The moon shone on the sword, and Arthur was attracted to it, pulled by a magnetizing force.

"Where am I?" he whispered around.

Where you belong, King Arthur…

He looked around, trying to find the source of the voice,

before realizing it was coming from the sword.

"I have an uncanny feeling that I need to find you."

Yes, sire. I am waiting, as I always have been, for your just hand to find me.

"Where are you?"

Here.

Arthur frowned, puzzled at the riddle. Since Merlin had taught him well, he rephrased, "How can I find you?"

'Tis only from a place of happiness you will be able to find me.

Then the dream ended, and switched instead to a woman kissing him. Right before Arthur woke up, she pulled away and her sparkling blue eyes stared into his. On his arm cascaded long, brown locks of hair – not blonde.

The next morning, Arthur's heart knew him better than anyone. It seemed his horse, Aryan, did as well, as he took the way to Elaine's manor.

Arthur reached the place by the end of the night. He left Aryan in the stables and walked to the main door, knocking on it. To his utter surprise, it was Elaine that opened. Her sleepy expression glanced over the stranger, not recognizing him with the two days' beard, and his features hidden by a cape. Then their eyes met and held, and she froze, eyes widening in surprise.

The years had made her more beautiful, yet sadder. The soft blue eyes that had always been smiling were wary, and everything in Arthur wanted to wipe away the hurt he had caused. Something inside him longed to bring back the sparkle that was missing.

After a few moments, Elaine stepped out of the way and

allowed him into the home.

"A stranger in the night, my king?" she curtsied, keeping a level tone.

Arthur dropped the hood down, searching her gaze. "There is no king here, Elaine. Just an apologetic fool."

His tone was soft, conveying the regret he felt. Still, the wariness remained in Elaine's stance as she folded both arms over her chest, hugging herself.

"Where is your queen?"

"I am not here to speak of Guinevere," Arthur shook his head. He then did the only he could under the circumstances: dropped to one knee, taking her hands in both of his, hazel eyes looking up into blue. "Forgive me. I have no right to come ask this of you, and you have no obligation. I come as your once friend to admit you were right. And I miss you."

Elaine was silent, eyes locked onto his for a moment, before tears started streaming down her cheeks. Whimpering, she dropped in his arms and clutched him tightly.

Since she had been sent away from Camelot, her heart pined for the man, despite her best judgment. There was no way she could forget Arthur, and many a sleepless night had been spent going over the lines of his face she could recall.

In Arthur's arms, Elaine could let go of all the emotions of the past months. She could not fault the king for having been under a spell. Not now, when he had finally returned to her.

Arthur held onto Elaine as a rock in his world, realizing he felt at peace in that moment, as though a missing piece had been given back to him. The encounter with the Lady of the Lake replayed in his mind, how her guardian had looked at her, and the strength she seemed to gather in his presence. It was the same he sensed by Elaine's side.

The monarch pulled back from the embrace, peering at his friend with new eyes. It was as though a veil had been lifted off – again.

Guinevere's face was gone from his mind, replaced by this beauty that had been his from the beginning, though he had not known it. He recalled his wife's accusations, and as he searched her gaze, Arthur could see the unsaid emotions in Elaine's expression.

Arthur's palm cupped her cheek, caressing its softness and marveling at his own slowness.

"How did I not see it before?" he murmured wonderingly.

Elaine's eyes grew wide and she trembled in his arms, afraid of what he was saying, afraid to hope. But it was there, in Arthur's eyes: a wonder – love.

Gently, carefully, he leaned closer for a kiss, but Elaine pulled back.

"I am not Guinevere," she murmured.

Arthur searched her features, uncomprehending, until he noticed the hurt and it registered what she meant – he was still married.

"I know, I… Forgive me," he pleaded. "I have missed you so, and I cannot believe how much of an idiot I have been, I—"

The monarch stopped, frowning as something else clicked into place. "You knew? About Guinevere, and Lance…" He trailed off as Elaine broke the stare, bowing her head in shame.

"I did not tell because I did not want you hurt. I hoped against it all that Guinevere would change… Besides, would you have believed me?"

At the hurt in her voice, the pain he had cause unwittingly, Arthur's irritation fell away. Elaine had not betrayed him, she had been trying to protect him despite his own foolishness.

"You are probably right," Arthur admitted, and Elaine glanced back up at him. "I was too far gone to listen to any advice. But darling... Dear Elaine, please believe me, I have not come here to dishonor you. Your friendship means everything to me."

Elaine sized him up, this king that was on his knees in front of her, and pushed her conscience away. She allowed her body to do what it wished. Like an elastic being released, it pulled towards Arthur, and their lips grazed.

When their mouths touched, Arthur could not help but close his eyes in pure relief, as though he was finally whole. They pressed closer and Elaine fell against him, surrendering to the kiss.

There was a softness in there Arthur had never felt, and he could not help but want to be careful. Her heart was a gift, one he intended to appreciate to its fullest. When they pulled apart, he blinked out of the daze.

"All this time, what I sought was right in front of me.... Thank you, Elaine."

Elaine smiled, reading everything else he wanted to say in those few words. Then she stood up and pulled him by the hand. "Come eat, my king. You must be famished."

CHAPTER 28

In the multiple basins, Morgana could see Vivienne and Sébastien, Arthur and Elaine, Merlin...

Merlin!

Their happiness was disgusting, but at the same time filled her with envy. She had been stolen the chance at a love so great it could transcend time, space and everything else.

In the existence Morgana had chosen, she had no one but Mordred to confide in. Nothing else mattered except vengeance, a line she could not wait to cross.

For years now, she had watched them all, had manipulated Guinevere, done her best to offset the balance. She could feel the darkness rallying around Carleigh, her one chance at striking twice.

The Fae blood got off on the chaos caused, but some part of Morgana still wished for the life she could have had – if Merlin had not made his mistakes, and caused the loss of their baby.

The sorceress's hand moved to her womb and for the first time in ages, Morgana allowed tears to fall. It still hurt, despite the years that had passed. The life she had not been able to birth, the boy or girl that had never seen the light of day.

She recalled how happy she had been to find out she carried Merlin's child, thinking that together, their baby could have the power to truly influence the world. *All the dreams, the hopes, for what?*

Morgana scowled at the basin, feeling the familiar burn of hatred in her chest towards the wizard. Merlin had bought her, repaid her unconditional love and devotion with betrayal and deceit. For years she had waited, but no longer. Her unborn child's death would be avenged, as would be the loss of the inheritance.

Once Arthur and Vivienne were gone, and Merlin destroyed, Morgana planned to not hold back whilst delivering the final blow. Only then would she be truly happy, knowing she had succeeded and had the kingdom at her fingertips.

Her beautiful face was frozen, no expression showing except within the eyes. They burned with anger in an ashen face. She looked to Mordred, the son that was now a man. At least one good thing had come out of the failed romance with Merlin.

Mordred was bright, with her quick spirit, and his father's eyes. It pained Morgana, excruciatingly so, that every time she looked upon him it was a memory of what she could not have. And yet…

Morgana sighed, turning her attention back to the water bowls. Vivienne's glowing face, Sébastien's eyes shining with love, achieved to infuriate her.

"Mordred, wake up! We have work to do."

* * *

Alistair, from his place in the other realm, turned away from the image. The surrounding mist took pleasure in tormenting him by showing what was happening outside – a world he was forever barred from.

In truth, he knew what Morgana was up to and could do nothing to stop her. Unless... Alistair's hand rose to the pendant around his neck.

Am I willing to do it?

His thoughts turned to his own death, and how it had come to be. Pride had stopped him from thinking of it in ages...

Alistair watched as Sébastien, listening to his urging, took Vivienne away to safety. He then focused on the necromancer facing him and growled.

"You are a stupid mutt," Carleigh warned. In his hand rose an orb, which he aimed towards Alistair.

The demon dog took one look at it and prepared to swallow it as he had done with the other. The sorcerer lifted the spell, ready to launch, but a voice came from the forest.

"Leave us."

Carleigh stopped as though in a daze. His eyes glazed and like a puppet, he turned and walked away, the remaining druids following in his steps.

Snarling in confusion, Alistair turned in a circle, sniffing...

"Morgana!"

Laughter echoed all around, then the Halfling entered into his view. "Yes, demon dog. We meet again."

It took one look to realize Morgana had come for vengeance and nothing else.

"*I figured it out, you know. What Merlin was hiding, about Arthur. I will control his fate, whether my former lover wants me to or not.*"

"*You can do as you please,*" Alistair rumbled.

"*So long as I stay away from your precious Vivienne?*" she cackled.

"*What have you done!?*" Alistair grunted, body tensing with fury as he moved closer.

"*Me? Nothing.*" Her innocent look did not fool Alistair. In the once-laughing grey eyes was a calculating, cold glint he knew well. "*Carleigh, on the other hand... Is even now on his way to destroy what is left of her realm.*"

"*No!*" Alistair glanced to where Vivienne had disappeared with Sébastien. He stepped as if to follow, but Morgana was quicker.

"*Not so fast!*" With a flick of her wrist, she erected a barrier and imprisoned them both. "*Answer me this: where is Merlin? No matter how I search for his place of residence, it is hidden to my eyes.*"

Alistair stood to his full height, paws spread onto the ground and canines bared ferociously in response.

"*Very well,*" Morgana muttered, registering he would not say anything. She lifted a palm and threw a force field towards the demon.

Despite Alistair's barrier, the Halfling's power, being Fae, burst right through it and made contact. He flew in the air, landing further.

"*Shit,*" Alistair muttered, recalling the old wars between

Faes and gods – and the fact he did not have even half of his regular powers.

Despite it, Alistair stood once more and smacked his front paws onto the earth, forcing it to vibrate. The energy he amassed slid under and went to strike Morgana – shattering on her barrier.

"Tell me now," the sorceress ordered, "before I finish you off."

Alistair opened his jaws to lunge, but found himself immobilized.

"You can play dirty as much as you want, witch," he rumbled. "I will not tell you anything."

"Have it your way!" Morgana shrieked, then threw an orb of darkness. It hit Alistair full force and he crumbled to the ground, unmoving.

Satisfied, Morgana turned and left, muttering, "What a waste of time."

She did not see the dog raise to his feet weakly, nor his pitiful crawling away. A pain the likes of none he had ever felt spread through Alistair as the Fae magic slowly stripped him of the shell he had called body. Despite it, the demon knew he had to try and stop Carleigh and protect Vivienne one last time.

The god Alistair shook his head, coming out of the dark ruminations. "I suppose if I do not warn the blasted wizard, no one else will…"

Sighing heavily, he touched the pendant and fell into a deep sleep.

* * *

Merlin was dreaming when he was dragged in a field.

"Feels odd to have this done to you, no?"

The warlock turned to see a man smirking knowingly. He was as tall as Merlin, with broad shoulders, a thin waist, black hair and onyx eyes.

"Do I know you?"

There was something about the newcomer that set the wizard off, but he could not pinpoint it. Noticing Merlin's quizzical expression, the stranger laughed heartily, his booming voice echoing in the distance.

Merlin's eyes widened as he met pitch black ones in shock, the laughter having clued him in. "Alistair!"

"That would be me, yes. The name Vivienne once attributed to me." The man's face became nostalgic, and Merlin went on.

"What are you doing here? I thought you were dead... Vivienne told me she had seen your ashes."

Alistair tilted his head to the side, sizing the wizard up. "She still talks to you?"

"No, not since the loss of her realm."

"Your games finally caught up to you? I warned you they would."

Merlin scowled, not in the mood for a lecture. "Yes, you did. Will you tell me how you are here?"

"I cannot die," Alistair shrugged. "They can ban me from the skies, throw me to the underworld, remove my powers, and still I cannot be eliminated."

"Ever?"

"Faes could, once upon a time, kill us deities." Alistair threw him a long look, then continued, "They have lost the art to do so – luckily for us."

"What about your godly squabbles?"

"The Cardinal Rule prevents a god from killing another, unless he wishes to give his own life afterwards."

"Interesting." Merlin's tone left doubt to the fact it truly was. "So for you being here…"

"That can be blamed on you, wizard," Alistair's look darkened. "I followed Carleigh and came upon Morgana. It is she who ended up hurting me, poisoning my shell so that I would not live past it."

Merlin was silent, absorbing the shock. No matter how much he was faced with it, the fact Morgana had turned to the darker side was not something he could fully comprehend, nor come to terms with.

"You had best believe it," Alistair warned. "It is a truth you should accept by now."

"Stay out of my thoughts!" Merlin growled.

"Careful, mage, we are in my domain right now." With a meaningful look to the staff flaring in response with magic, Alistair continued, "Be at peace."

Merlin took a deep breath, before finally saying, "So Morgana was the one who defeated you."

"Yes. Afterwards, I went back to Vivienne. I am unsure how much good it did, but I believe she found some semblance of peace."

"Why do you not call to her, as you did me?"

"Believe me, I wish I was dealing with her rather than you," Alistair muttered under his breath. Louder, he stated, "Because Vivienne cannot action this request. You can."

"And that is? What truly is the purpose to this?"

Alistair paused, before admitting, "Warning you: Morgana

is out of control."

"I gather as much from what you have told me."

"This is worse. The pain you caused her has truly twisted her mind, and she is determined to destroy not just you, but Vivienne and Arthur as well."

"If she goes near either of them, I will be there to stop her," Merlin vowed.

"Truly?"

"Yes. What makes you contest that?"

"Morgana is your biggest weakness, Merlin. I have not forgotten. You two were fated to be together in the same way as Vivienne and Sébastien, but much, much worse. And now that it has fallen apart…"

"My romantic life is none of your business!" Merlin scowled.

"Fair enough… But heed my warning, Merlin. Do not let Morgana get to you – again."

"I will not!"

Alistair sized the mage again, then nodded pensively. "Let us hope so. You have much to deal with, but you should start with Morgana. At this point, with me gone, you are the only one who can put an end to her. The sooner the better."

Merlin sighed, for once showing the weariness this was costing him. He recalled Alistair's words from a long time ago, warning that only another of their kind could kill a Fae, otherwise they were practically immortal.

"Yes, I promise I shall. Morgana will not see the day when her powers overthrow mine enough to hurt Vivienne and Arthur. Count on it."

"I will." And with the final statement, Merlin was returned

back to his dream.

* * *

Mordred followed his mother deep into the neck of the woods, as did the animals. Her Fae nature attracted all creatures, even the most innocent. Though he did not know what she had planned, he could guess it would mark the beginning of a new phase in their joint vengeance.

Once they reached a large enough meadow, Morgana stopped. In its middle was a massive circle of stones, the boulders being twice to three times the size of a human being. Mordred stepped closer, pulled despite himself to the power lurking underneath the surface.

"What are these, mother?"

"Power stones," Morgana muttered, walking around and inspecting each of them. "Do not touch them!" she warned when Mordred lifted a hand towards one, and he quickly yanked it back. "These stones have been used since the beginning of dawn to recharge magic. For a Fae, there is no better spot."

"How did you find out about it?"

"Your father. He was well-versed on the subject and, if nothing else, he did impart his knowledge onto me."

Looking back to the circle, she missed Mordred's look of speculation. Waving to the animals, Morgana stepped inside the sanctuary and they all followed.

Disregarding everything else but the pure energy she felt, Morgana let it bathe her. The magic flowed out of her hands into the stones, then back to the sorceress. She threw her head back, filled with euphoria.

Carleigh could never understand what it felt to have this

much strength to command. She was an elemental and, unlike Merlin, unafraid to let the power control her.

Morgana opened her eyes, and they shone unnaturally bright, almost white. The animals cuddled trustfully towards her, unmoved by the coldness in her gaze. The energy flowing from her extended to the beasts, hitting each one of them like silvery rays of lightning.

They all became immobile, staring in surprise and fear at their master. There was a loud vibration, the stones themselves shaking, then the animals screamed in pain. Within moments, their vital force had been sucked clean, and their shriveled, lifeless bodies littered the circle. They turned to ash as the energy, now red the color of blood, returned back to the sorceress.

Mordred gaped in amazement as Morgana inhaled everything out of the animals' innocent bodies. The amount of power wielded was more than he could grasp presently, but he yearned to be able to match it. Eagerly, the son watched as the energy balled up in front of Morgana, placing itself in her hands.

"I gift this sacrifice to Carleigh. May it add to the darkness he serves and give him full potential for destruction."

Morgana watched in satisfaction as the orb disappeared, to be absorbed by Carleigh – wherever he was presently.

* * *

Guinevere was walking back to her room after a particularly enjoyable session with Lancelot. She was still smirking at the fool's pathetic love declarations, and did not register that the door was open.

Once inside, she jumped up when the door banged closed

behind. The queen turned around, gasping, to see a woman step out of the shadows.

She had long, dark hair to her waist and grey eyes that glowed like silver, an unnatural occurrence. Guinevere felt a shiver cross her spine: the stranger was powerful – and dangerous.

"Guinevere," her husky voice greeted, "How are you?"

"I… Who…" Guinevere paused, cleared her throat then tried to imperiously ask, "Who are you, and what are you doing in my chambers?"

"You know me," the woman smirked. "I am Morgana. And do drop the airs, dear, you are not in front of an equal, here."

Guinevere paled. "*You*'re the one. In my head, whispering…"

"Yes, that is true," Morgana admitted. "And as such, I have every right to be here, since I put you on this throne."

The queen gulped, but could not – would not – let herself be intimidated. "What is it you wish?"

"To lay eyes, face to face, with the foolish woman who threw everything away."

"What do you mean? I did no such thing, I followed your every advice!"

"And failed." Morgana looked around, sneering. "Enjoy the luxury while you can, o queen. Your reign will soon be over."

"What do you mean!?" Guinevere shrieked.

Morgana paid her no attention, instead moving past her to exit.

"I demand you answer me!"

Morgana lifted a hand towards the queen and Guinevere felt the air around her throat close. "I answer to no one! *You*, least of all."

Before leaving the room, as Guinevere lay on the ground, panting to regain her breath, Morgana could not help snidely throwing over a shoulder: "Arthur will soon hand out your punishment. You have pushed your limits, Guinevere – and his."

Then she departed, not once glancing back, unrepentant of the chaos caused.

* * *

Vivienne woke in the middle of the night. Something was calling out, the water near her castle rumbling with sounds only she could hear.

She slid out of bed – and Sébastien's warm embrace – and headed down the staircase to the outside.

The enchantress knelt by the water, burying one hand within its cold depths. "What is it?" Vivienne murmured, frowning at the agitation she could sense. In tune with nature now more than ever before, the currents she perceived were unsettling.

Eager to communicate, the water swirled until it became a mirror. On its limpid surface, Vivienne observed her mother. Vevila was screaming, giving birth to her. The scene shifted, showing a comet crossing the sky – the good omen she had been told about all her life.

A lump formed in Vivienne's throat at her parents' happy faces, a sight she would never see again. "Why show me this?" she choked.

The image shifted again, blurring before it stopped above

a cottage in the middle of a forest. Inside it, another woman was giving birth. On the outside, nature was rebelling, furious winds, thunder, darkening clouds and then pouring rain.

Vivienne watched, uncomprehending. Then a boy was born, and the mother picked him up. Her face, beautiful despite the sweat, softened looking at the baby.

Then a name passed her lips. "Mordred."

Vivienne froze. She had heard the name before whispered in the shadows, a warning to keep an eye out for. The enchantress backed away from the water in shock, realizing the man had been fated to be her nemesis from the beginning. Born the same night, yet a complete opposite.

As if on cue, a wind rose and beat against her cheeks. Vivienne stood, her gaze hovering uncertainly towards the other shore. In the distance, she could almost distinguish a shape, staring back, unmoving.

Shivering, she turned and walked back into the safety of her castle, analyzing what to do with the information given.

* * *

Across Aisling Caisléan, Mordred stood watch. He could perceive on the other shore Vivienne's presence and it called to him. He wanted to throw magic at the barriers and shatter everything in his path to get to her.

Mordred wanted to face Vivienne. It was a need ingrained in him since he had been a child and first seen her face in Morgana's basin.

Now, a young man, the yearning was eating at him. He could not get Vivienne's face out of his mind. Obsessed, Mordred paced back and forth, even as her presence disappeared.

Soon...

CHAPTER 29

With Elaine, Arthur spent the next few weeks at peace. Their friendship renewed, and they spent most of their time together, taking long walks, talking about everything and nothing. And through it all, there were the looks, the small touches.

Arthur did not want to, for the first time, return to Camelot. Not to the toxic presence of Guinevere, nor the regretful one of Lancelot. In short, he did not want to go back, period.

A message came from the queen through Merlin that she was worried. There was even a slight rumor that something had happened to him. Aghast at Guinevere's manipulations, Arthur sent word back: a letter, signed by his hand and using the royal crest.

Merlin showed it to the advisors, who were thus convinced of Arthur's wellbeing. In the instructions, the monarch advised he would be away from Camelot for a short time on a quest. He sent no such information to Guinevere.

It was through Merlin, as well, that Arthur received an answer. It did not take long for the wizard to report that Guinevere was making no effort to hide the affair with Lancelot, and that more than one advisor was speaking of treason. Furthermore, they wanted Lancelot punished for betraying the king.

It was that letter, detailing the situation, which Arthur was reading on a fine morning. His marriage with Guinevere, the happiness he had felt long ago, was a distant echo. Removed from her, he could now perceive whatever sorcery had ensnared and made him do things he never would have – such as cast aside a perfectly loyal friend.

Morose, he stared out the large French windows onto Elaine's grounds. Arthur had spoken at length with her about the so-called attack on Guinevere and the miscarriage that never was. He had apologized profusely, and Elaine had been kind enough to forgive him. Still, the memory of the lie left a bitter taste in his mouth.

He glanced back down to the paper and, with a disgusted sigh, crumbled and threw it in the fire, watching it become ash. With every passing second, Arthur was picturing burning his ties with Guinevere the same way – for good.

It was time to face a choice he had made long ago, before stepping any further with Elaine. There was unfinished business with Guinevere, and Arthur needed that chapter to be closed, before moving on to the person he truly wished to be with.

Arthur moved once more to the window, observing Elaine

for a few moments. He wanted nothing more than to forever be by her side, but not yet. He scribbled a note hastily, then left, returning to reality.

He could not bear to see Elaine face to face. If he did, Arthur gathered he would never leave her side. And she deserved better – much better.

The note lay on the table for Elaine to find:

Sweet Elaine,

I must return to Camelot, but I will come back. The time spent with you has cleared my head in a way that has not been so for ages.

Please wait for me.

Yours always,

Arthur

The king straddled Aryan and pushed on to Camelot. The closer he got, the more determined his features became. He did not intend to lose more time than had already been wasted.

Steeling his heart against any magic, Arthur galloped through the doors of the castle. Leaving Aryan in the stables, he marched through the halls straight to his bedchambers – or rather, Guinevere's.

Bursting through, he caught an eyeful of her naked back and Lancelot's blonde hair underneath.

They turned to him in shock, freezing like does caught by a hunter. As Guinevere registered who was standing there, she jumped off Lancelot and covered herself with the bed sheet.

"Having fun, my queen?" Arthur smirked derisively.

Guinevere gaped in surprise, then attempted to stutter an explanation. The king lifted his palm to stop her, features darkening.

"No. I want no more of your lies. I want you *gone*." Arthur turned behind and motioned for two guards that were posted at the end to get nearer. His unflinching stare settled on his former wife. "You have until the morning to pack up and leave."

"You cannot do this!" Guinevere shrieked, while Lancelot watched on, helpless. "I am your queen, you vowed –"

"As did you!" Arthur interrupted, dangerously stepping closer. When Lancelot made a move to get out of bed to protect Guinevere, he scoffed. "Do not bother. She is all yours."

Arthur walked past the guards, throwing over a shoulder, "I will draft you papers for a monastery, where you can be safe from my subjects' wrath. Or you can take Lancelot with you, if you prefer to live with him. I could not care less."

Addressing the guard, the monarch barked, "Make sure she does not roam around the castle." To another, he added, "Her majesty is to be relieved of her duties and out of my sight by morning."

Then Arthur stepped out of the room, letting the guards handle the two betrayers. With the distance between them, he felt like a huge weight had been lifted off his chest. *I am free...*

Heading to his study, Arthur set about drafting a royal decree to his advisors and people. As a last thing, he wrote a letter ensuring Guinevere's safety and gave it to the guards to pass on to her.

* * *

In the midst of the night, Arthur watched with satisfaction – and a certain amount of sadness – as two horses left the grounds. One carried the former queen, the other his previous head knight.

"How was I such a fool, Merlin?"

The wizard had joined him shortly after the letters had been dispatched, having found out in his own way what had occurred. They had been sipping ale, passing time for the last few hours, when noises had attracted their attention towards the windows.

Arthur shook his head at his own foolishness. "Sorcery or not, I was truly gone and easily manipulated by her."

"Love makes fools of the best of us," Merlin responded.

Arthur turned to him, alerted by his inflection. "Were you ever in love?"

"Once, my king. Long ago." At the unspoken question in Arthur's eyes, Merlin revealed, "It did not end well." His tone implied there was much more to the story, but being newly scarred himself, the monarch did not pry.

Instead, he nodded and turned back to the two betrayers. Once their silhouettes were gone from the horizon, he announced, "I will be gone for a few weeks."

"Might I ask where, my king?"

"A quest. Given by the Lady of the Lake."

But first, someone I must see.

Arthur had not forgotten the enchantress' wise words, nor his dream of the sword hence. However, his heart demanded first that he go to the one he craved.

Merlin used his Fae sight, and smiled. Finally, he could breathe at ease that the burden was lifted and Guinevere's influence was truly gone from Arthur's life.

"As you wish, sire. I will keep an eye on the realm," he promised.

Arthur clasping him in a manly embrace for a minute, then withdrew to leave.

"You will not wait until morning, sire?"

"No... It is much too far away."

Arthur then went straight to the stables, where he saddled Aryan. Merlin watched them from the window and lifted a hand in blessing. "Keep him safe," he ordered, and a shred of magic went to surround the king for protection through the voyage.

Within moments, Arthur was gone, disappearing in the night with his black stead. Merlin turned his thoughts toward the kingdom. A quick sweep of the senses assured him no danger was about, and thus he allowed his body to rest to replenish forces. The day when they would be sorely needed was fast approaching, he felt.

* * *

The night was dark, rain pouring outside when the king of Camelot arrived by Elaine's estate. An elderly man by the stables moved to block his way, seeing only a stranger with a hood drawn up high across the face, obscuring it from sight.

The poor man nearly had a heart attack once Arthur hopped off Aryan. His eyes widened at the monarch's determined request. "Fetch your mistress."

Arthur was let into the house and went by the fireplace to warm his hands, waiting on Elaine. Soft footsteps soon alerted him to a presence.

He turned to see the wariness in Elaine's eyes – being woken up in the middle of the night to see a stranger in her quarters was not a normal occurrence. Arthur threw off the cape impatiently, and surprise lit her features.

"I did not think to see you again, my lord." Elaine's tone was soft, almost wondrous.

"Yet here I am," Arthur paused. "Think, or wish?"

At Elaine's perplexed look, he continued, "Did you think you would not see me, or wish you would not?"

Understanding lit her features, and Elaine smiled softly. "I thought you got what you came for."

It was his turn to frown, until she clarified, "Your apology accepted."

Arthur shook the rain out of his eyes and stepped closer. He was nervous, something that never happened even with Guinevere. Elaine's eyes teased him, a smile tugging at the corners of her lips.

All Arthur wanted to do was pull her into his arms, and claim her. But first, he had to clarify another matter altogether.

Turning away, he cleared his throat. "Did you get my letter?"

"Yes…"

"I had to return to Camelot. To Guinevere."

Part of him wanted to turn around to see her expression, but could not. He missed the look of hurt crossing Elaine's face, as she thought his purpose there was to tell her goodbye – again.

"While I was away, she made no secret of her affair with Lancelot. I had to go back to ensure the people of Camelot do not kill her." Arthur whirled around, unable to keep his eyes off Elaine anymore. "You understand, do you not?"

"Of course, you care for her. She is your wife."

Arthur was silent, trying to see if this was Elaine's way of asking him to return to the life he had. With a resolute shake of the head, he announced, "Not anymore."

Elaine's eyes widened at the statement, and the urge to kiss her was that much more imperious. "You misunderstand me. Yes, I care for Guinevere as much as any of my subjects. But the betrayal, the lies she put me through…it destroyed whatever was between us. I went back to end things."

"I am not sure I follow…"

"Guinevere is gone from Camelot, Elaine. I gave her safe passage papers to a monastery, or wherever else she wishes to go with Lancelot. They are both exiled, returning here only upon pain of death."

"But she is still your wife."

"No." Arthur stepped closer, slowly grinning. "I issued a decree, then put it to a vote. No one contested me – they all wanted her gone." He paused, then said the words he could not take back: "I am free."

Elaine lips parted, and she searched Arthur's expression as though she could not believe the words.

"You said my apology was accepted…" At her soft nod, he could not hold back anymore and leaned forward, pressing eager lips to hers. When she responded, Arthur deepened the kiss.

He pulled away shortly, pushed by a need to hear her say the words.

"I wish much more than that, beautiful Elaine," he cupped her cheeks, earnest in the declaration. "I must have fallen in love with you since I first saw you, but was too young and blind to see it. These last months, without you at Camelot, it was like a part of me was missing. I cannot be with you any longer… I want your heart to guard, and give you mine in return. Please say you accept."

Elaine blinked away the tears and bowed in curtsy. "I am at your service, my lord."

Arthur pulled her out of the bow with an impatient tug, breathless to feel her in his arms. "Never bow to me again," he ordered huskily.

Then his mouth descended on hers passionately, and the time for talking was gone. Clothes fell from their bodies as though by magic, and after worshipping her, taking his time, Arthur finally claimed Elaine as his. When all was said and done, he brought her upstairs to the bedroom and tucked her into his side.

The king of Camelot fell asleep beaming widely, finally at peace.

* * *

Morgana woke up from the vision, sliding out of bed to the window. She could see the rain pouring outside, but her mind was on what she had witnessed.

Arthur and Elaine...

In removing her help to Guinevere, she had been well aware the queen would soon be gone. However, she had not foreseen the strong bond between Arthur and Elaine. So much time away from love had blinded her to its existence.

The enchantress pressed her lips together, mulling over the events and how she could use them to her advantage.

"Mother?"

Morgana turned to see Mordred rubbing sleep from his eyes, frowning. "What is it?"

"I woke up from a vision," she revealed. "Of Arthur and his new lady love."

"Elaine?"

Morgana was surprised at his perceptiveness, then recalled he had spent the last few days in close watchfulness of not only Arthur, but Vivienne as well.

She nodded to his query. "Yes...."

"Is it something we can use?"

"Indeed, my son. Finally, a weakness we can exploit. One your father cannot guard him against."

Mordred rolled his eyes. "It is always love that weakens them so."

"Why do you suppose that is?" Morgana wondered, curious to see his take on it.

"It makes fools of all of them," he shrugged, then continued, "They get so taken in by protecting their loved ones, they forget to be ambitious. Then they lose track of what is truly important and start believing in fairytales. And trust... Look at Arthur, he was so taken with Guinevere, he trusted the wrong woman."

Morgana nodded pensively, lost in thought. Soon, Mordred's soft snoring came to her ears.

Perhaps he is right. Love had also made a fool of her, made her give credence to Merlin's words, and that had not turned out well. And yet, without it, she would not have Mordred... Either way, the power itself was not one she could ignore.

Morgana would use love and Arthur's weakness against him. She would do the same with Vivienne, until Merlin would come to realize that all was truly lost.

Satisfied with the resolution, Morgana went back to bed. It took her hours to fall back asleep, and when she did, she dreamt of the past – and her own affair with the wizard.

* * *

Alistair turned away from the images, knowing full well there was nothing more he could do. He had warned Merlin, as per Catriona's request. *If he is stupid enough not to go after Morgana, that fault lies on his shoulders, not mine.*

"Thank you."

He whirled around, gaze falling on Catriona's form. She smiled beguilingly, dressed in a purple sheath this time, with gold spirals.

Alistair gulped, even as the primal needs within him rose to the surface.

"You have no need to thank me," he shrugged. "You were right. Your brother needed some prodding...not that it will do much good."

"Why do you say that?" Catriona asked, inching closer.

"Come now, Catriona," Alistair glared, "they were both half-Fae. Mutual destruction is assured."

She laughed again, but already was only a hair's breadth from him. "Kiss me again."

"No."

"Why refuse yourself the delight?" Catriona smirked. "Are you afraid...Atrox?"

"I no longer go by that name," Alistair scowled.

"Perhaps not... But your wolf does."

Catriona touched his chest with one hand and the tiny flicker inside him that desired her burst into a flame, scorching through.

Alistair pulled the Fae closer, dropping his mouth to hers. At the back of his mind, the demon tried to push past the haze of desire, but it was to no avail. Catriona's body felt too good against his.

His hands roamed under the material of her gown and she arched her back, pressing closer. Alistair yanked her closer and she gave a guttural sound, close to a purr. As the kiss deepened, Catriona gave in with a whimper of surrender.

What man can resist this?

Hours later – or so it felt – Alistair came out of the desire-induced daze. He was naked, lying on the ground, and Catriona was getting ready to leave.

"What exactly was the point of that?" he grumbled, unhappy to have been used – though his body was not complaining.

"Come now, Atrox," Catriona mocked, "do not pretend you did not enjoy that. The point was pleasure, which we both took. I have to say…" She trailed her fingers over his chest, before giving him a quick peck. "I could not be more content."

The god gripped her wrist, eyes flashing warningly. "I told you, I do not answer to that name anymore."

"But I much prefer it," Catriona giggled, then pulled out of his grasp.

Blowing him a kiss, the Fae flew away and left the god to groan against his own weakness.

Before Alistair could even compose himself, a form shimmered by him, then dissolved into two. Ardea and Aequus leveled their annoyed stares on their brother.

"Will you tell me what I did now to upset you, or am I to guess?" Alistair muttered.

"Even stuck between worlds, you cannot help yourself!" Aequus started.

Alistair rolled his eyes, then turned to Ardea. "What is he going on about?"

"The Fae that was here," his sister started, "what are you doing dallying about? They are not to be trifled with!"

Alistair looked back and forth between them, trying to gauge their seriousness, then burst out laughing. His booming voice echoed around them, even as the gods' faces darkened in response.

"Oh, I see now," Alistair chuckled, addressing his brother, "you're jealous she came to me and not you!"

"You arrogant mutt!" Aequus growled, stepping closer with his fists clenched. Ardea put a restraining hand on him, angling her body between them.

"We did not come here to squabble," she reminded Aequus.

"Sure you didn't," Alistair mumbled under his breath.

Ardea turned the force of her bi-colored eyes to him. "If you intend to keep this new identity as Alistair, you best stop acting like your old self, Atrox."

The warning words shut the former god up, and he folded his arms defiantly. "What is it you wish?"

"To grant you entrance to your peaceful ever after."

Alistair narrowed his eyes on the two, then looked behind at the door that had been closed since his arrival.

"To what end?"

"Get you to stop meddling!" Aequus burst, glaring at him. "You have done enough."

Alistair mulled the proposal over for all of two seconds – then realized he still had Catriona's pendant. No matter what, it was a link to the outside world, thus a way to help out

Vivienne if needed.

Grinning, he looked to Ardea and nodded. "I accept. Open it!"

Aequus and the goddess shared a look, then shrugged in response. Ardea lifted her palms up to face the door and murmured in the ancient language of divinities. The large oak panels squeaked in protest, then opened to allow Alistair entrance.

"Now go."

Alistair did not wait, stepping into the paradise that had awaited this entire time. Satisfied, the remaining siblings waited until his form disappeared in the light, then turned their backs to it and left.

"Let that be the end of it," Ardea muttered.

CHAPTER 30

For the next few weeks, Elaine and Arthur enjoyed their budding romance. They spent hours in bed, and many more so talking and simply being together.

Arthur planned to bring her to Camelot, but first he had to finish the quest. Like a nagging at the back of his mind, it turned from a vague thought into something imperative to do.

One night, the king dreamt of the sword embedded in stone calling out to him: "It is time. You have to claim me."

When he woke up, Arthur turned to Elaine, sleeping by his side. He caressed her naked back, then overtaken by a passionate urge, kissed her. She woke up with a moan, melting in his arms. The royal enjoyed the feel of her so close by, where she should have always been.

Groaning, he rolled them over until he was hovering above Elaine. Gently, with utmost tenderness, Arthur then slid inside and took her on pinnacles of pleasure until they both fell back asleep, entangled.

The next morning, Arthur was first to wake up. He touched Elaine's cheek, whispering softly, "Beloved, wake up."

She blinked sleepily, smiling at him. "It is not fair you wake me so early after the night we just had."

Arthur chuckled, then tugged on a lock of hair to grab her attention. "I need to leave for a few days. Perhaps a week."

Elaine was instantly awake, sobering up. "Where?"

"There is a quest I have been putting off... It is necessary for the survival of my kingdom, and my own."

Elaine searched her lover's gaze, then slowly nodded. "Might I come with you?"

Arthur kissed her softly, then said, "I do not know what dangers I would face, thus it is best I go alone."

Elaine buried her head in his chest, whispering, "Please be careful. I could not bear it if anything happens to you."

"Nothing will," Arthur reassured, tightening his arms around her. "The Lady of the Lake herself tasked me with this."

Elaine frowned, pulling away. "She sounds like an enchantress."

"She is, but a good one. I helped her consort a few weeks back, and it was she who put my mind at ease... Beloved, trust in me. I will return safe and sound."

At a loss of words, Elaine could only press her lips to his. She wanted to give Arthur a good memory for the nights to follow, one to always remember. With his murmured encouragements, she pushed the king to his back and straddled his hips.

She then moved against him in an invitation he could not refuse. Groaning, Arthur grabbed her hips and slid back inside her, watching as Elaine's expression flushed with desire. The young woman rode him slowly, taking her time and savoring the last moments of peace.

When they both reached ecstasy together, she collapsed onto Arthur's chest and hid the tears. At the back of her mind, Elaine knew she had to be strong for the monarch.

Much later, once Arthur was packed, they stood by the stables with Aryan. Elaine's angel eyes looked into his, brimming with unshed tears.

"Do not be sorrowful, my dear," Arthur urged.

Elaine willed away the bad feeling in her chest. After all, this was a quest given to Arthur by the Lady of the Lake. Surely a lady such as her would not hurt a man for no reason.

And yet, doubt lingered. A nagging presentiment warned Elaine the journey would not be as simple as Arthur believed and that true danger would court him.

She watched, heart constricting, as the proud, gentle king hopped onto Aryan and rode away.

Arthur looked back one last time, waved, then took off. Aryan being a powerful horse, within the hour they had long passed Elaine's manor lands. He tried to shake off the sensation of being watched, but it eluded him.

It had started shortly after leaving Elaine, and persisted through the distance. Yet Arthur heard no hooves behind and could see no one around.

Within a few more hours, Arthur reached a forest. Aryan did not hesitate, going straight in and Arthur had no choice but to let him lead.

The environment quickly became unfamiliar, but Aryan seemed to know where he was headed, trotting through at a leisurely pace. Large trees loomed the path, crossing high above and blocking the light. Had it been days, or only hours? Arthur could not tell the sun from the night.

Eventually, Aryan paused. Even more peculiarly, he knelt one leg to the ground, as though bowing. Arthur jumped off, frowning at the new surroundings. The trees were even more closely drawn together, causing everything to be bathed in a pitch-black mist. He pushed through to a clearing, bare except for a large rock in the middle.

In the stone, as Arthur had dreamt for the past months, was a sword. Not just any blade, though: it had a grip made of refined leather, a dragon's head designing it, ruby eyes shining menacingly. With the wings of silver as cross guards, the blade should have been a work of art.

Yet it seemed its beauty was hidden, as though dulled. Remembering the words in his dream, Arthur walked over, wrapped his palm around it, and pulled.

Nothing.

He frowned, then tried again with both hands. Still no result. A snort behind made him glance to Aryan, who was shaking his head furiously. It took Arthur a minute to realize the horse was laughing at him.

"Glad you find this amusing," Arthur muttered under his breath, before turning back to the sword. With no other option, he knelt by the rock, bowing his head in prayer.

Though *what* he prayed for, not even the king knew.

* * *

Arthur was dreaming – he realized it was a dream, but was

helpless to stop it. In it, he was facing a panel of two judges. One was a man, the other a woman. The monarch peered closer and felt the power coming off them in waves.

"Where am I?" he asked them when it registered they would not stop chatting amongst themselves.

The two did not answer. They did not even look his way, instead continuing their conversation. Arthur shrugged and stepped away, inspecting the large room he was in.

Large posts held the high ceiling up, and the floor was made of pure gold, as were the thrones they sat in. The two speakers had dark hair and there was a faint familiar resemblance to them.

Arthur lost his patience and snapped, "Who are you?"

Again, there was no response.

Annoyed at wasting time, the royal marched forward. "I demand you answer me!"

The two stopped talking and turned to him. The woman's eyes surprised him the most: one green, one black.

"Watch your tone, mortal. You are in front of Ardea and Aequus, heads of the deity pantheon that governs your Earthly realm. Why should *we* listen to *you*?" she enquired.

Arthur opened his mouth to retort, then thought better of it. Mulling over a respectful way to get his point across, he finally mumbled, "I never asked you to... I simply want to know what it is I am doing here."

"Very good question. What *are* you doing here?" Aequus repeated.

Arthur glanced from one god to the other, at a loss. "If this is a joke..."

"We do not have time for jokes."

"Neither do I!"

"Oh, so you are in a rush?" Ardea taunted.

"I said no such thing. I simply wish to get back to my quest!"

"A quest you are currently failing at…" Aequus pointed out mockingly.

Arthur could not help his scowl. "It takes time."

"No, it does not. We have been watching you, King of Camelot. It started with your mentor, who was tightly intertwined with someone we are interested in."

"And then," Ardea continued, "we believed your energy to be unique. Yet you seem to have lost yourself."

"I disagree," Arthur retorted, thinking of Elaine. "I have recently *found* myself."

"Then why can you not pull the sword? You had no issues with your first one."

Arthur was at a loss.

"Who are you?" Ardea tilted her head, defying him.

"I am Arthur," the monarch answered automatically.

Aequus stood up, the same height as the king, though bulkier if that was possible. "Who *are* you?"

"I am Arthur!"

"That sword you seek was forged by a powerful enchantress and fueled by our brother's ashes," Ardea revealed, joining her brother in his stance. "You cannot have it if you see yourself unworthy."

"I *am* worthy!" Arthur raged.

"Says who?" Aequus taunted.

Arthur was at a loss of words for a few instants. Then he thought of all he had accomplished, everything he had gone through, even his mercy towards Guinevere and Lancelot, despite their betrayal. Something in him snapped, and he met the gods' gazes unflinchingly.

"I do not have to defend myself to you," he stated.

"As a matter of fact, you do, High King," Ardea smirked. "If you do not believe yourself –"

"Enough!" the royal roared. "I am Arthur, King of Camelot, leader of the new world, and I *am* worthy. I have always ruled justly, and endeavored to do well. The sword will be secure in my safekeeping."

His voice had thundered with conviction, but as soon as the last of the words were out of his mouth, Arthur paused. Somehow, he doubted that was the way to speak with deities. Half-expecting to be punished, he maintained a defensive stance.

The two siblings shared a look, then Aequus grinned, "You are free to go."

Arthur was about to argue with them, find out more of who they were, but his form in the dream shimmered and disappeared into nothingness.

As soon as he was gone, Aequus turned back to Ardea. "Well, that was fun."

"I thought you were going to hit him for a moment," Ardea laughed.

"For a moment, so did I. Humans can be very obtuse, would you not agree, sister?"

Ardea chuckled, and Aequus held his arm up for her to take. "Now that we have taken care of this little thing you held so dear, let us go enjoy some food."

* * *

Arthur woke from the dream, blinking sleepily at the ray of light hitting him square in the face.

Light!

The monarch jumped up from the grass, staring at the same boulder – with the same sword. This time, it was encompassed in brilliance, shining and attracting his eye. Arthur got up and walked towards the angelic-looking place. His hand, of its own accord, grabbed onto the hilt and pulled. There was a slight resistance, then the sound of metal scraping stone.

Arthur gaped at the weight of it and the radiance it emitted. Fine golden runes were on the blade, spelling a name: Excalibur.

As the king stared in astonishment, they faded away to nothingness and the sword was his. All that it had taken was a path down an odd dream, facing some judges, and convincing himself he was worthy.

Not bad for a day's work!

Arthur swooshed Excalibur in the air, enjoying its light weight and the way it cut through the air. The sword was truly forged for him, a perfect fit in his palm. It did not feel like a weapon, but as an extension of his arm.

A scoff behind had the knight turn to Aryan, who was once more shaking his mane in obvious laughter.

Arthur grinned in response, then jumped on the horse. He was eager to return back home to Elaine and, eventually, Camelot.

Arthur was lost in thoughts as Aryan trotted forward, dreaming of the future that was his for the taking now. He only snapped to when they came to an abrupt stop. They had barely gotten back on the road and Aryan shifted under Arthur, uneasy.

The king tightened the hold on the reins, shushing comforting noises. The horse snorted fiercely in response, refusing to listen. Though he did not try to throw Arthur off, it was evident in the tightening of his muscles and the overall agitation that he was unwell.

Something was spooking Aryan, and that same something caused Arthur to get the nagging feeling in the pit of his stomach again.

Then the breeze shifted and a child walked onto the road. He wore a cape, covering his thin but lithe frame. He raised pale cerulean eyes in an angular face, framed by black curls, towards him.

"Best not lose your way, my lord."

Arthur frowned, distrust seeping through him despite the inoffensive appearance of the boy. That, and he had an uncanny familiar sensation, as though the stranger had somehow crossed his path before.

"Beautiful sword," the boy murmured, eyes falling onto Excalibur. They lingered briefly, then met Arthur's one last time. With a curt nod, he then went about his way.

As soon as he cleared the road, Aryan jumped forward. His hooves pounded the pavement, breath panting, and he did not stop until miles had passed between them and the little boy.

Left behind, Mordred's lips twisted in a sneer.

"Well, Mother, that is a king I will take pleasure in killing."

Then he shifted his appearance back to his adult body and

walked away.

* * *

Merlin stopped the herb picking, his entire body freezing at the gust of darkness emerging from behind. He stood slowly, deliberately keeping his back to the necromancer.

"Turn and face me…master."

Carleigh.

Merlin did not deign to reason. He felt the man's wrath despite the distance, but was not about to give in and be bullied.

Instead, he curled his lip, and remained still. "Will you stab me from behind like a coward, pupil of mine? Will you bite the hand that fed you?" Merlin taunted, knowing full well he was poking at things he should not. His voice was cold, laced with rage but still in control.

Carleigh's was not when he answered. "You starved me into seeking the black arts."

"No," Merlin scoffed derisively. "Do not blame me for a decision you were solely responsible for!"

"I want her *back*!"

Merlin finally turned, pity showcased on his features. Carleigh's face was further inflamed in anger by what he could read in the warlock's expression. "Do not dare pity me!"

"How can I not?" Merlin whispered. "You lost your mother at a young age and have found only contempt on your path since then. Despite what you may think, learning the dark arts to bring her back from the dead is no use. Nothing can return the dead to life."

"You took me away from her!" Carleigh pointed an accusing index towards the wizard. "I remember you, as a child, coming to tell me to find you in a few years' time. Had you left us alone, I would still have my mother!"

"Do you really believe that?" Merlin shook his head, wondering how he had been so far off in his predictions – again. "Then you truly are a fool."

"You know nothing!" Carleigh spit. "Thinking you're holier than thou, because you never made a mistake!"

"I have made plenty," Merlin answered, thinking how one such error was now in front of him. *I should have killed you when I had the chance.* "But I never took the easy way out," he finished.

Carleigh jabbed a finger his way, scowling. "You wait, Merlin. The day will come when your shortcomings will be revealed. And I shall be there. In the meantime, your protégée best beware!"

"Leave Vivienne out of this!" Merlin yelled, but already Carleigh was turning to leave.

As the darkness swallowed him, Merlin could catch a faint scent of something he had long ago forgotten. *Morgana...*

He stepped to where the necromancer had been and touched the earth, seeking a clue. It revealed what it could: a vision of Morgana in a circle of stones, of a sacrifice, and gifting the power to Carleigh.

The realization she was helping him was the last thing the mage had expected. Despite the years, it was a blow hard to swallow.

Merlin sighed in the empty forest. "The day of my shortcomings might come sooner than even *you* imagine, Carleigh," he muttered, then left as well.

* * *

Alistair was in paradise. Rather, the gods' version of it. He existed in a meadow, far from the outside world, and could do as he pleased. He ate, slept, frolicked and took advantage of all the pleasures offered.

All for the benefit of his siblings, whom he knew would keep an eye out for him.

At night, however, he latched onto Catriona's pendant and looked beyond, keeping an eye on Merlin and Vivienne. It was thus he bore witness to the warlock's encounter with Carleigh, and caught the implications.

As he was returning from the dream, Alistair knew he had no other choice. He needed to contact Vivienne, much as he had Merlin. Even with her powers, the enchantress would be in danger if the sorcerer decided to go on the offensive.

His way back was suddenly blocked and instead of returning to paradise, Alistair was by a waterfall. Frowning, he glanced around, trying to see who had brought him there. The former god knew there had to be a person, as the realm he currently existed in was not accessible to mere mortal magic.

"It's just me, lover," Catriona's voice came from behind.

Alistair turned to see her fly down from above the waterfall. As her bare toes touched the ground by his feet, the scintillating wings folded onto her back and were absorbed within. Catriona's only response to his glare was a grin, even as she stood on tiptoes to kiss him.

"No need to look so sour. I thought you might enjoy the freedom."

Alistair inspected the surroundings, noticing the beauty of the place they were in. A lake was next to the waterfall, and all around them was a large, majestic forest. The colors were vibrant, unlike what he had seen onto Earth, and more like…the godly pantheon.

"Where are we, exactly?"

"My little piece of heaven," Catriona shrugged. "My father gave me a kingdom, and I created it to my fashion."

That had Alistair's attention. "You're a *queen*?" Catriona's laugh only annoyed him further. "This is not funny!"

"Oh, but it is. Does it matter if I'm royalty? I would have thought you enjoyed our encounters either way," she smiled flirtatiously.

Alistair wanted to growl, punch something, be mad at her, but already his body was heating up under the inviting blue gaze.

"Come join me," Catriona whispered, stepping closer and pressing her body against his.

Alistair inhaled deeply, in a semi-attempt to regain control – and lost it the minute the Fae placed a hand on his chest. His mouth descended on Catriona's vengefully and he crushed her body closer. When his hands descended to her lower back, then continued further down, she pulled away.

Catriona shook her head in mock chastising and jumped in the water below. Alistair had no choice but to follow her. His body broke the lake's surface smoothly and he dove under, enjoying the smoothness of the water.

When he came back up for air, Alistair saw Catriona's form nearby. Her red hair was wet from the water, plastered to her head, and those cerulean eyes shone ferociously with a need that was only matched by his.

The Fae opened her mouth to say something, but Alistair

stroked the water and arrived by her side, kissing her once more. He made quick work of their wet clothes, then pulled Catriona to him, wrapping her legs around his waist. Heated, unable to wait, he plunged inside her. Pure male pride surged through him at her moans of delight.

"You…" Catriona tried, but lost her train of thought when Alistair hit a particularly sweet spot inside her.

"I?" Alistair teased, nibbling on her earlobe.

"You…really…deliver…Atrox," she finished on a gasp, then succumbed to his powerful strokes, and let herself be taken by the pleasure.

"*Not* my name," Alistair growled.

Catriona's glazed eyes found his in the throes of passion, and she smirked. "Yes it is."

Snarling ferociously, Alistair gave in to the need within and lost control until they found the pleasure they sought.

Much later, after their heartbeats had calmed down and they were lounging on a flat stone, he caressed her naked back. "What was the point of this? Is it even real, or happening in my dreams?"

Catriona laughed. "That would be too cruel, would it not?"

"Then it *is* real."

"You tell me, lover," Catriona teased as her hand drop from his chest, following a one-track path down.

Alistair gripped her wrist, putting a stop to the distracting exploration. "How can your powers be a match for gods?" he enquired.

"You know how," Catriona shrugged. "We both come from the same sources, Atrox. Only, you guys are the rule makers, and we are the breakers."

Her smile was enticing, but Alistair willed himself to get back on his feet. "I need to return. Will you send me back?"

Catriona gracefully stretched, then stood slowly. Her beautiful, naked form faced him, alluring and unashamed. "Is this payback for last time?" she pouted. "For how I left you?"

"Maybe," Alistair grinned, and dropped a swift kiss on her lips. "But I do need to leave."

"To warn Vivienne?"

Alistair froze, then peered down at his lover. There was no malice in her, nor jealousy, simply interest. "How did you know?"

"The pendant is a gift from me, remember?" Catriona chuckled. "I am tied to it and thus, to you. I do not blame you for wanting to use whatever you can to warn Vivienne. I have noticed her light, as well. Only, be careful… There will be a price to pay."

At the sad tone of her voice, Alistair stepped closer. "Have you seen something?"

Catriona stared back as though wanting to say something, then shook her head. "Their fate is already sealed. Yours, not yet."

"My fate is tied with theirs," Alistair countered.

Catriona said nothing, only continued gazing at him in that mysterious way she had. Then she lifted a hand in goodbye and Alistair's form shimmered to disappear. Within moments, he reappeared inside the paradise of the gods.

CHAPTER 31

The moon was brighter than normal that night as Vivienne stared out the bedroom window. She felt an inexplicable urge to go by the lake, and so followed her heart. As soon as she took a spot on the grass, the enchantress fell asleep.

"It has been a long time, princess."

Vivienne turned around, eyes widening as they fell upon a dark haired man. He was clothed in only a toga and smiled paternally at her.

"Who are you?" she questioned in the same breath.

When he grinned, followed by a booming laugh, Vivienne gasped in recognition.

"Alistair!"

"Yes," he barely had time to acknowledge when Vivienne hurled herself in his arms for a tight hug. Her mind was grasping to comprehend this man, her companion... But to have him still alive!

Alistair returned the embrace, inhaling the fragrance of her hair. "I have missed you."

"And I you! How is this even possible?" Vivienne enquired, pulling away.

"My soul continued on, but lingered betwixt the worlds for a bit. I eventually was let in."

"Let in?"

Alistair rolled his eyes. "The deities which banned me were having fun at my expense, denying me entrance to the underworld."

"Why?"

When he only stared in response, realization dawned on Vivienne. "Because you helped me," she stated flatly.

In the same breath, a wave of rage filled her at the unfairness of it. Alistair had been her protector and friend, and while he may have gone against the rules that were set, his actions had saved her.

Vivienne whirled around, yelling at the empty space. "His decency is more than I have seen of you all, so called deities. When all you do is watch evil succeed, it does not make you free of guilt!"

Silence only answered.

She turned back to Alistair and his twinkling eyes. "Oh, I really have missed your enthusiasm, highness."

Vivienne smiled, but sobered up as another thought struck her. It was evident Alistair would not have risked the encounter unless there was something important at stake. "What is it you wish of me?"

"Nothing, highness. Only to help you."

"Not at your own detriment!" Vivienne vehemently

rebelled, unwilling to see him punished again.

"They cannot touch me now," Alistair declared in a voice that left no room for questioning. He laid his hands on Vivienne's shoulders for emphasis, before darkly revealing, "There is a battle coming to Arthur. Merlin will beg you to interfere, to aid the king. Please do not."

"This is not the first time you asked me to step back," Vivienne murmured.

"No. But this time, your very life is in danger."

"Why?"

Alistair hesitated, unsure of how much to divulge. At the stubborn glint in the queen's eyes, it registered she needed to comprehend everything, otherwise she would ignore the threat.

"Merlin was in love, once. Morgana was her name, a half-Fae like him. She is as evil as you are good. She is the one bringing the fight to Arthur, to destroy Merlin."

Vivienne recalled the vision she had at the lake of the child. "Mordred," she whispered. When Alistair froze, it was proof she was on to something. "The waters of my lake showed me something the other day... My birth and his. Mordred is my complete opposite, is he not?"

"Yes," Alistair admitted. "And dangerous. Morgana has set him like a rabid dog onto Arthur. Mordred will not stop until he succeeds, for he knows only chaos and destruction. You will do well to say out of his way."

"Should I not help Arthur, at least?"

"Highness," Alistair held onto her shoulders firmly, "please. Morgana does not fight fair. She is too much of a wild card, too damaged to comprehend. The vengeance she wants to wreak onto Merlin will be enough to destroy the worlds, if she triumphs."

Vivienne understood the threat, but what was being asked of her, she could not in all faith agree to. If it came to pass, the enchantress knew very well she would end up helping Arthur, if only to ensure his legacy remained.

Aware of Alistair's heavily worried gaze on her, Vivienne sighed and forced the lie past her lips. "I shall stay away. I promise."

Alistair nodded and, with one last hug, let his previous charge return to regular dreams. Once she had disappeared, his sister shimmered in her place.

"Will you never stop?" Ardea admonished softly.

"Helping Vivienne?" There was no point denying it, having been caught red-handed. "Never."

"No matter what we do, we cannot keep you from seeking her out." Ardea shook her head, bemused. "How are you to find your own peace, if this goes on?"

Alistair met her gaze frankly, stating, "I will not until Vivienne is safe. If you do not like it, you will have to kill me."

"There is no need for such drastic measures," Ardea rolled her eyes. "You truly have changed, brother... Will you join your sister for a walk, like we used to?"

Alistair hesitated for a split second, then followed Ardea. Despite her attempts at conversation, his mind remained on Vivienne.

* * *

Merlin had not seen the king this happy in too long. Since he had returned to Camelot with Elaine in tow, Arthur was a changed man. Everyone was content to have the young woman back and they gave her the respect she deserved.

Though they could not marry until Arthur's separation of Guinevere was finalized in a year's time, she was nonetheless given the exact same respect and treatment as a queen. It only helped their cause that Elaine, so gentle and kind, was well seen by everyone.

As for Arthur, a newfound peacefulness had settled over his shoulders, one that gave him more strength and bettered him as a man and a king. Since he had retrieved Excalibur, the monarch could truly believe in the potential everyone else had always told him he possessed.

Merlin did not wish to ruin such a good mood, but it was time to warn Arthur of what was coming. For the last few days, nightmares had assailed his once peaceful nights, as well as visions of Camelot afire. One face kept coming back, over and over: his son's.

Sighing, the wizard stepped into the library where Arthur was spending time writing.

"My king, a word?"

Arthur looked up from the letter, a smile tugging at his lips. He folded the piece of parchment and gave it to a valet with instructions. "Make sure Lady Elaine gets this before supper."

Little things he did, like sending her a simple love letter, brightened Elaine's day, and he loved going to bed and her radiant smile. She had adapted extremely well to her new role and the people's acceptance of her warmed Arthur's heart.

He massaged his chest, where the happiness bubbled, amazed he could feel this way. Once upon a long time, Arthur had thought the most he could feel was the lust for Guinevere.

Now, he knew that with the right woman at his side, he could soar to new heights.

Out of the corner of his eyes, Arthur registered Merlin's stillness and focused on him. The mage's serious expression and pale features were enough to wipe the smile off.

"What happened, Merlin?"

To his utter surprise, the warlock fell to his knees, holding onto the staff for support. His head hung low in shame, shoulders curved inwards.

Alarmed, Arthur quickly stepped to him, wanting to raise Merlin to his feet. The words he mumbled low made him pause.

"I have to ask your forgiveness, sire."

"Forgiveness?" Arthur tried to pull him up. "There is no such need to humble yourself, Merlin. You are my friend. Whatever it is, we can fix it together."

When the mage only shook his head in desperation, Arthur felt his heart constrict. "Is it truly this worrisome?" Only silence responded, and it was enough for the king to kneel as well. "Look at me... What is it?"

Merlin took a deep breath, then met Arthur's gaze and revealed everything. About Morgana, Uther, his conception, and Mordred. The monarch's face went from bemused, to shock, to horror, and finally settled into resignation.

"So my half-sister wants to kill me, both to avenge the past as well as to hurt you? And Mordred, my nephew, is to be the tool?"

Merlin nodded sadly at the summary. It had not been easy to divulge the entire truth, especially as he feared it could change Arthur's view of him. It was not the first time he had been proven wrong. The monarch was only worried for the future, and for what this news would bring to Camelot.

Arthur got up and paced to the window. He leaned his too hot forehead against the cool glass, watching the rain fall outside. Though he was still exhilarated at having Elaine nearby, now there was a suffocating fear of losing her. Of having found happiness, only to see it slip past his fingertips so quickly.

Arthur could not fault Merlin for what he had done, not when he had fallen for Guinevere. After all, love made fools out of the best of men.

"Will nothing change Morgana's stance on this?" Arthur enquired. "Perhaps if I met her, offered her the throne she was denied…"

Merlin tried to keep the horror from his expression. He was no fool to realize that Morgana would kill Arthur the first chance she got. The only reason she had not yet, was because she fully intended to create as much suffering as possible.

"No, sire," he answered firmly. "Morgana is set on this vengeance and her heart will not budge."

Merlin did not divulge the last of the information. That he and Morgana were half-Fae, and that the reason she would not change was because of their powers. He did not wish Arthur to fear that he would turn against him in the future.

Instead, he sighed and stood from the ground. Merlin was about to leave the king to his ruminations, when he spoke.

"It is not your fault, Merlin," Arthur sighed, facing the wizard who had advised him thus far. "Fate has had it in for me since I was born, something I have always been dimly aware of. The real irony is that I met Mordred." A bitter laugh escaped him, of hopelessness rather than humor.

"What? When?" Merlin probed.

"When I found Excalibur," Arthur revealed, recalling the scene and the cerulean blue eyes. "He was on the path there, but as a child. I recognize now why his features were so familiar. They reminded me of you."

My son looks like me? Merlin wondered, then pushed the thought out of his mind, replaced by another. Morgana contributed to hiding Mordred, which was why he had no visions about him and could not figure out what their next move would be.

As the rest of Arthur's words registered, the wizard whispered, "Mordred must have changed his appearance to appear more innocent... So he knows you have Excalibur."

"Yes. Does it matter?"

"If Mordred does, so does Morgana. It gives them ample time to find a way to fight the strength of the sword. Luckily, as it was a weapon forged in light, they cannot use it against us."

Thank you, Vivienne, Merlin whispered mentally, though he knew the enchantress would ignore it.

They were both silent, lost in regrets, before Arthur declared, "I stand by what I said. We will fix this, together. But I have one request of you."

"Anything, sire."

"Do not tell Elaine. She is to be shielded from all of this."

Merlin nodded, understanding the need that was driving this. For his king's happiness and fulfillment, he would do anything.

* * *

Sébastien woke up in the night to find his beloved gone. It was not the first time in the last few weeks when his only companion was an empty bed. Something was bothering Vivienne, and he knew not how to help out.

The knight got off the bed, pulled on a pair of trousers and walked down the marble staircase. He found the enchantress buried in an armchair in front of the fireplace, her gaze lost in the flames.

"Beloved," Sébastien murmured, then kissed the top of her head.

Vivienne stirred at the gesture and looked up at him. For a moment, he saw the shadows haunting her, swimming in her green eyes, before she blinked and smiled.

"Why are you awake?" Vivienne asked, trying to keep a light tone.

Sébastien caressed her cheek, then knelt by the chair. "Please let me help you. Whatever burden you have been carrying for weeks, let me share it."

Tears filled the queen's eyes, even as she denied, "There is nothing."

"Do not lie to me, Vivienne. I can feel it in every bone of my body. Something is coming. I wish to know what it is, so that I can defend you."

Vivienne's heart swelled with love for this man who had stood by her through thick and thin, protecting her with his own body when necessary. So much time had passed since they had first met, yet their love had only strengthened.

Through all that had come their way, Sébastien had been there, always strong, a rock to rely on. Vivienne needed to give him some of that protection in return. "It is not I that needs it," she murmured.

Before Sébastien could probe further, Vivienne bent over and kissed his lips forcefully. His body responded in keen, even as his mind tried to reject the distraction. When Vivienne slid off the armchair and fit so perfectly in his arms, body melting against his, Sébastien was lost.

He captured her neck with one hand, angling her to better take control of the kiss. When she sighed in satisfaction, his free hand roamed under the cloak, lifting the chemise up to her hips and finding her moist center.

Vivienne gasped in his mouth and surrendered to Sébastien's touch, submitting to his skillful fingers. Lost in passion's embrace, all thoughts of a menace left both their minds.

The only existing truth was Vivienne's sighs, Sébastien's groans, and the crackle of the fire. Heatedly, he claimed her on the carpet, over and over, until she fell asleep in his arms.

* * *

"You cannot keep intervening."

Alistair turned to see Catriona in the paradise land. His eyes darted around quickly, half-expecting his siblings to rain down hell and fire.

"They cannot perceive my presence here," she answered the unspoken question.

"How is it you can do all this?" Alistair pressed, not for the first time. The Fae was a mystery.

Catriona hesitated, then decided honesty was her best bet. "There is a reason everything Merlin does has such an impact on people's lives. Our father is not *just* a Fae, Atrox. He is *the* Fae."

"What do you mean?" he narrowed his eyes, for once not bothering to correct her on the use of his past name.

"Merlyddus is the oldest and wisest of our kin. He is, for lack of a better word, first of our race. Because of this, his magic is the most potent – and so is the one of his children."

Alistair let the words sink in, then looked anew at his lover. "You truly *are* royalty."

Catriona paused for the briefest of moments, then nodded. "Yes. And because of that, anything that I do – or Merlin does – has the potential to cause even more havoc than regular Fae magic. But it also lets us break most rules with ease, hence my apparition here."

"That explains a lot," Alistair muttered, thinking of all the times when Merlin's good intentions had gone haywire.

"This fight that is coming," Catriona continued, "this ultimate showdown between Merlin and Morgana, you cannot be part of it. No one should, really. But you know as well as I do that Vivienne will not stay away."

Alistair could not help his scowl – yes, he was well aware the enchantress was stubborn and wanted to help out, regardless of the danger to her own life.

"Two half-Faes such as them fighting will upset the balance between worlds," Catriona added urgently. "You cannot do anything other than what you have already done, otherwise the vortex of that will take you in, too."

"But you will be alright, regardless, because you are Merlyddus' daughter." Alistair tilted his head to the side, observing the Fae – and mulling over her warnings.

Catriona nodded, believing he would shy away after her revelations. After all, her kin had not long ago battled

Alistair's. And the most powerful of them had been feared even by the gods. She had known it going into the romance, but something about this man was too alluring to resist – even for a fully-grown Fae.

Instead, Alistair surprised her. He stepped closer and distracted her with a kiss. When he pulled away and she was no longer frowning, he smiled. "Good. That means I do not have to worry about protecting you, as well."

Catriona chuckled, pleasantly amazed at how well he was reacting. Then she recalled the original reason of her arrival. "I meant what I said, about intervening."

"I only go to them in dreams."

"Alistair, your siblings do not like it. They can see some things. Though they know not how you go about it, sooner or later they will act. And plus, it is useless."

"Why do you say that?"

"Because you cannot change what will happen. Vivienne is a champion of light in the same way Carleigh is the chosen pawn of darkness. Their destinies were written the moment of their birth."

"You know more than this," Alistair accused. "Tell me everything."

"No." Catriona stepped away from his embrace, shaking her head. "I refuse to be a part of this, of you falling from grace – again."

"You are Fae. Are you not supposed to enjoy meddling?" Alistair scowled.

Catriona masked the hurt his words brought, but not before the god saw a flicker of it in her gaze.

"I did not mean it," he tried to apologize, but the words

tasted bitter in his mouth and he could not give her the proper apology she deserved.

Catriona shook her head, mumbling, "This was a mistake."

Alistair took a long look at her, realizing she did not mean just the current visit, but rather their entire relationship – if it could be called such.

Avoiding his piercing eyes, Catriona disappeared.

Well, damn. I do believe I have been dismissed.

Alistair tried to remain indifferent of the fact, but emptiness spread within that he did not like. In an effort to get his mind off the Fae, he clutched the pendant in his hand. His mind searched for one who was asleep, so that he could warn them.

Sébastien...

* * *

It was hours later the guardian awoke from a dream, confused. Sébastien could only to remember a man's dark midnight eyes, and a warning:

Keep Merlin at bay. The menace threatening Vivienne comes from him, and Mordred is its name.

CHAPTER 32

Sébastien watched distressingly as Merlin walked past the oak doors until he was a few feet away.

After his dream of a few days back, he had been none too surprised when the old wizard came to ask Vivienne for an audience. He had been, however, taken aback she granted it.

As Merlin stepped nearer, Sébastien moved. "Close enough," he ordered coldly, dark eyes shooting off warning flames.

Is everything alright? Vivienne asked mentally, sensing his odd behavior through their bond.

Sébastien gritted his teeth, but answered back with a curt, *Yes.*

Vivienne focused on Merlin, who was watching the two with knowing eyes.

"I come in peace," the mage started, fixating his gaze on Vivienne. "And warning."

Vivienne ignored Sébastien's rigidity and instead schooled her expression. "What kind of warning?"

Though she expected her former mentor to mention Mordred, it was another name that passed the Merlin's lips.

"Carleigh."

Vivienne almost breathed a sigh of relief, but caught herself in time. The necromancer would be easier to deal with than the man who was supposed to be her opposite – especially if what Alistair had divulged would come to pass.

"This does not seem to be new information to you," Merlin observed.

Vivienne shrugged, almost tempted to be indifferent. When the blue eyes shone with a brief hint of despair, she softened her tone ever slightly. "It was to be expected. I did not think Carleigh destroying my realm or threatening Camelot would be the last we saw of him."

"Then be wary. He has accumulated more darkness, as of…" Merlin paused, shifting on his feet in contrition. It was the first Vivienne had seen of the uneasiness in him.

"As of when he eradicated all of Elsior and sacrificed my people."

Sébastien was surprised at the factual tone of Vivienne's voice. It had become an event she could speak of without raw pain in her voice, something he was thankful for.

Merlin nodded at the words, then cleared his throat. "I truly am sorry, more than I can say."

Vivienne observed the warlock past his aura and noticed the real regret shining through. The words were past her lips before she could stop them: "Then show it."

"What do you mean?" Merlin's brow furrowed.

"Prove your remorse by telling me what else you know. You cannot have come all this way only to deliver a warning about Carleigh."

Merlin glanced to Sébastien, noticing his expectant gaze – and the hand on his sword. Settling back on his former pupil, he could feel the power of Vivienne's magic surrounding him. She was ready to force the truth out of him, if need be.

That, more than anything, convinced Merlin to be honest. Not because he was afraid, but because if Vivienne had gotten to a point where she could challenge him, then she did not need him stepping around eggshells and protecting her anymore.

Abruptly, Merlin agreed before he could change his mind. "Very well. Carleigh did not get powerful only from sacrificing Elsior to darkness. Morgana also aids him."

"Your former lover?"

Merlin gaped in shock. "How did you know?"

"You *did* make me Lady of the Lake, Merlin. If I did not see this coming, I would not be deserving of the praise lavished upon me by the people."

Though Vivienne's tone was sarcastic, the mage could not fault her. "Yes, that same Morgana," he answered in return. "She is half-Fae, like me, and the magic she is supplanting Carleigh with acts of its own."

"Elemental," Vivienne murmured and, though he was puzzled at the depth of her knowledge, Merlin nodded in assent.

Vivienne held his gaze for a moment, then inclined her head. "Very well. Thank you for your honesty, Merlin. I cannot forgive nor forget, but in the best interests of this fight,

I cannot knowingly hold a grudge against you. I will not go back to trusting you as before, however I believe I can be of help in my capacity as Lady of the Lake."

Merlin stood frozen for a moment, staring in amazement at the gracious woman before him. In the back of his mind, he had never expected Vivienne to be so magnanimous. Ultimately, he bowed low and murmured, "Thank you, highness."

"I am no longer that," Vivienne smiled wryly.

Still bent over, Merlin whispered, "To me you always will be, now even more so."

Then he was gone, walking down the marble stairs and out the door. The wizard barely reached the shore of the land, when a voice stopped him.

"Merlin!"

The warlock turned to see Sébastien heading over, his features set in stone, jaw clenched. It was evident he was in no good mood.

"Will you tell me now what I have done to upset you?" Merlin lifted an eyebrow.

"Your games put Vivienne in danger, wizard. I do not particularly enjoy having her in the midst of an incoming tornado."

"I do not know what you are referring to."

Sébastien took him unawares, grabbing the front of his cape and pulling him closer. His gaze glinted in cold anger as he hissed, "I would give my life for Vivienne. And though you may not understand this, I would kill for her if it would keep her safe."

Merlin's blue eyes softened, the lightning that had been

rising disappearing in a flash. "You can let me go, knight. I know full well what you mean. I, too, loved once."

Sébastien let go of the cloth and Merlin stepped back, putting a distance between them before continuing. "I do not willingly bring Vivienne into this fight, only because I need her help."

"You are half-Fae," the guardian growled. "Why can you not handle this yourself?"

Merlin pursed his lips, turning away to the lake. "You would not understand."

There was a pause, then Sébastien said, "I think I do. You are afraid."

Merlin whirled around to the guardian, frowning at his perceptiveness.

"You are afraid of how powerful you could be, if you let yourself. Do not look at me like that, old man. I may not be magical, but I have common sense. Morgana is the same as you, yet her abilities are heightened. It has nothing to do with light and dark, as the elemental magic that powers her is not prone to it." He paused in the tirade. "Tell me I am wrong."

When Merlin could only grit his teeth in response, Sébastien's features darkened. "I thought as much. Heed my words, Merlin. If any harm comes to Vivienne, I will hunt you to the ends of the Earth!"

With the warning delivered, Sébastien watched as Merlin left into the mist, disappearing. Once he was convinced the man was truly gone, he returned into the castle to Vivienne.

Sébastien knelt by the throne, grasping her hand. "You are truly the most inspiring person, for being so…accommodating."

Vivienne focused on him absentmindedly, causing Sébastien to re-think his words. "What is it, my love?"

"Carleigh draws close. I try to see his next move, and find it blocked." She frowned in frustration. "Something has to be done to put him out of use, once and for all."

"Vivienne –" Sébastien started, then stopped as she stood to pace, deep in thought. "Be careful," was all he finished with.

"I will." The enchantress stepped to him, holding his cheek. "I would never put us in jeopardy."

That is what scares me so, he ruminated darkly.

* * *

Merlin was on his way back from Vivienne's place, less burdened now that they were on civil terms. The pain he had caused her was the one regret that haunted his time mentoring her.

The cracking of a branch was his only warning. The mage turned around, eyes widening as they fell on –

"Morgana!" The name escaped him half in awe, half in horror, even as his treacherous heart skipped a beat.

The sorceress was still as beautiful as she had always been, but there was a new iciness in her expression he did not remember. What most surprised him were the silver eyes that once looked at him in wonder, now burning with a hate he could feel on his skin.

Morgana looked feral with her hands clenched as though ready to gauge his eyes out. Her dark, long hair was flying about her with the force of the elemental power within. And yet Merlin wanted nothing more than to hold her.

That was when he realized he was truly lost.

"Darling," Morgana sneered, unaware of his inner turmoil,

"fancy running into you here!"

When Merlin was silent, she chuckled bitterly. "Cat got your tongue?"

"Morgana, I –"

"No!" she lifted a palm in a gesture of silence, snarling and imperious. "The time for talking is over. You had no thought of betraying me, of tearing me apart in the past. Now is not the time to fix things."

"Then what are you here for?" Merlin questioned warily.

"Revenge."

The answer, delivered with such precision and indifference, achieved to stun the wizard. Before he could do anything, Morgana hurled a ball of air towards him. Merlin did not protect himself, rather flew into the closest tree and fell to the ground with a groan.

Another attack followed. And another. Morgana was more than he could have expected, unleashing the full extent of the elements against him. She used them all recklessly, fueled by anger and a profound need for vengeance. Merlin opposed no resistance, powerless against the emotions that had him tied in chains.

He was recovering from the latest attack, faintly thinking, *If I let Morgana have her revenge, then perhaps Arthur can be saved, after all.*

"Is that all you are planning to do?" Morgana taunted. "Stay and take it, penance for what you did wrong? It does not work that way!"

Like a force of nature, she struck again with a ball of fire. Merlin was thrown once more into the air, then landed and rolled over on the ground, extinguishing the fire on his garments. Though left panting, Merlin still did not go on the offensive.

"I will not fight you."

"Why not?" Morgana pressed, almost shrieking.

"You robbed our son of a father. I will not rob Mordred of his mother, as well."

Morgana seemed stunned for a brief moment, silver eyes clashing with blue. Then rage took over once more. "Mordred has no father. He hates you."

"Why?" Merlin could not stop the question, no more than he could his love for the sorceress.

"He loathes you," Morgana smirked, "because I told him you abandoned us both for royalty. That you discarded us and gave his inheritance to Arthur. That you betrayed me and broke my heart... and killed his brother."

Merlin was shocked for the longest time, staring at the woman who had once had his heart. It was one thing to have spent all these years away from Mordred, but to learn now the child detested him because of Morgana's deceit... The wizard's fists clenched onto the ground, but he willed himself to calm down.

Then Sébastien's words came back to his mind. The knight had been right: fear *did* stop him from fully accessing the full potential at his fingertips.

Since he had been a child, then a teenager, Merlin had been afraid to let go completely and hurt the people around him. Forever prisoner to the angst, he had become his worst enemy. Morgana, on the other hand, once she had discovered how powerful she could be, had dived head in.

Merlin's eyes landed on the gorgeous sorceress and an

untamed wrath fueled him at the lie she had told their son. The magic that normally animated the warlock pushed for more access and, for the first time, he allowed it.

Body aflame with a surge of energy the likes of which he had never felt before, Merlin started to fight back. A burst of magic slammed into Morgana's barrier, then pierced through and flung her into a tree.

She stood back up, smiling triumphantly. "It was about time!"

Their magic met and burst, trees flaming in response, the earth shaking beneath their feet. Like two giants, they faced off and every living creature in the vicinity scurried off to a safer place.

Nothing in the world of men compared to a Fae battle. The closest that could describe it would be a fireworks display, though even that would be an understatement. Both the sorceress and the wizard were soon panting, but still the attacks increased, escaping them both mercilessly, unchaining the elements and destroying everything in their path.

Flares of different colors escaped their fingertips, bouncing off their barriers and sometimes going straight through. More than once, both ended up flung into trees with such force the trunks broke. Yet still the Halflings stood up, unharmed.

In a stroke of luck, Merlin gained the upper hand. Before Morgana could strike again, he moved up close and wrapped his hand around her throat. He pinned her against the tree, lifting the free hand to finally do what he had sworn to long ago.

Alistair's words echoed in his mind: *You need to start with*

Morgana.

There was his chance to put an end to it. All Merlin needed to do was clench his fist tighter against Morgana's pale throat, and squeeze the life out of her. Or he could destroy her with the burst of magic that was at his fingertips.

Many thoughts went through Merlin's mind in those few seconds as he stood lingering, on the precipice of the most important decision of his life.

And then his eyes locked onto Morgana's, desperately seeking something – anything. There was only hate reflected within, and a different rage consumed Merlin. *How can she have thrown away what we had so easily, when we could have healed together?*

The fury filled him whole, further egged on by the elemental energy flowing around them. It stirred Merlin's primal instincts like long ago, and their bodies leaned closer as though pushed by an invisible force. Growling, Merlin gave in and his mouth descended on hers in a bruising kiss.

Morgana froze, then latched onto him like he was a rock in the midst of a tornado. She opened her mouth under Merlin's, allowing entrance, craving more.

Neither was in control of their faculties as they gave in to the embrace, wanting nothing more than to get closer. Merlin pushed his body nearer, pinning Morgana to the tree. His hand dug into her scalp, grabbing a handful of her hair and angling her for better access.

Morgana groaned into the kiss, even as their pulses raced. Fire in both their veins, there was no rationale to the embrace. Only a need to assuage their despair, their hurt, their broken past into each other. An escape – it was all they wanted.

The magic they generated slammed together and the elemental force escaped in a flash. Unseen by them, it inflamed the surrounding forest. Still, Merlin and Morgana continued to kiss through it, unaware of the danger courting.

It was a branch breaking, falling nearby with a loud thud that snapped them out of the craziness. They froze, then Morgana pushed Merlin away. Her eyes shone with desperation, hate and love all in one.

Her slap resounded in the forest, but all Merlin could do was stare back despite the stinging in his cheek.

Everything they could have had crossed the warlock's mind in a flash. Unable to do what he needed to, and unable to get what he craved, Merlin did the only thing he could: disappeared, returning to Camelot.

Morgana fell down, crying at the pain coursing through even as the forest around her continued to burn.

* * *

Sébastien watched Vivienne as she, once more, snuck out bed. This time, he was done waiting.

He moved quickly and grasped her hand, ignoring the gasp as she met his burning gaze.

"I will not," Sébastien growled, "stand by and watch as you court danger, trying to protect me. I made an oath long ago, one I intend to keep." The knight tugged on the wrist, pulling the enchantress back to bed and rolled over to cover her with his body.

"Let me in, beloved. Tell me the truth."

Vivienne's green eyes flashed in frustration, but she ultimately inclined her head slightly in assent. Unwilling to allow room to change her mind, Sébastien remained hovering over through her revelation. He listened as Vivienne explained about her dream with Alistair, about Mordred, Merlin, Carleigh, and the connections she had made.

It was only towards the end that the rigidity he tried to keep at bay took control of him. Fear froze Sébastien's heart at what they were facing – dread of losing what they had fought so hard to maintain. Now that he comprehended the extent of the danger surrounding them, he realized it was a battle beyond their own love and survival.

"I wish I could tell you this is not your fight."

The enchantress smiled softly at him. "But it is."

Vivienne had realized that, if nothing else. Whereas Merlin had manipulated everyone to the point of causing messes, she had this one chance to set everything right. To restore the balance. It was not something she could turn her back on.

Sébastien knew he could not change her mind by the stubborn glint in those green eyes he loved so. He could focus on only one thing: enjoying their last time together before all hell broke loose.

With a frustrated groan, he bent his head and brushed their lips together. It took only the slight graze for Vivienne to arch upwards, meeting his yearning for closeness with desperation.

After, sated in each other's arms, Sébastien ran a finger across Vivienne's naked back. *I will regret this,* he mused darkly. Inhaling deeply, he murmured, "Tell me how I can help."

Vivienne lifted a gaze shining with gratitude towards him, and in that moment, the terror gripping his heart at what lay in wait was worth it. Holding his beloved tightly, Sébastien listened to her plan – and hid his despair.

* * *

Since Merlin's confession, Arthur had taken to having long runs with Aryan across the plains of Camelot. He did it as much to calm his mind as to try to find a solution. A part of him refused to believe there was no option except waiting.

On the day Merlin was battling Morgana – unknown to the king – Arthur left Camelot to ride as he normally did, and was gone for hours.

As he stopped by a stream, noises could be heard in the distance, like thunder and lightning coming together. He scoured the surroundings until his eyes fell on a display of magic further in the distance.

Dark and light, the different colors hit back and forth. Arthur watched in consternation, then a dread like no other gripped his heart. Though the attack was far from Camelot, Elaine was still there.

He hopped onto Aryan and pushed the horse back home. Leaving him at the stables, Arthur ran through the castle and barged in the bedchambers like a madman.

Elaine jumped from the bed, a sword ready to attack at the noise. Upon seeing him, she dropped it to the ground.

"Arthur!"

Her stomach clenched painfully at the ravaged look on his face. But all the king did was gather Elaine in his arms, cupping her cheeks. He looked in her trusting blue eyes for the longest time, trying to reassure himself she was well and nothing would happen to her.

Elaine placed her palms over his, staring back in confusion. She was well aware of the force he held back and the turmoil within. When she opened her mouth to ask what was wrong, Arthur pulled her closer for a kiss.

Unable to do anything else, Elaine gave him everything. She returned the embrace ardently, hoping that whatever Arthur needed, whatever solace she could provide, he could get it from her.

The knight, tormented by the panic of losing Elaine, felt every aspect of their lovemaking that much stronger. Her skin was softer under his hands, her moans of content were music to his ears, and her soft gasps spurred him on.

Arthur completely surrendered to the heat of Elaine's body and the radiance of her soul. That night, their bodies truly became one, in a way they never had before.

As he lay after, trying to fall asleep, Arthur could not help his roaming thoughts.

He had come home to the one person who could help him find the light, the hope in this day of darkness. Elaine was all that and more, loving him through the night, giving him everything to assuage the yearning she felt growing in her lover.

In the end, Arthur fell asleep, still haunted by the fear of not having Elaine next to him in the morning – and the time he felt slipping away.

CHAPTER 33

Arthur woke up mid-day to an unnatural stillness, as though nature itself was holding its breath. He looked at Elaine sleeping peacefully in his arms – where she belonged.

The young woman stretched and, eyes still closed, smiled sleepily. "I can feel you staring."

For all response, Arthur kissed her naked shoulder, lingering for a longer moment. The urge to leave, to face whatever was out there lying in wait, was stronger. It felt as though if he did, Elaine would be safe.

Still, there is one thing I must do before leaving.

Arthur waited until Elaine opened her eyes, then grasped her hand in his. The words came naturally: "Marry me."

Elaine's eyes widened. "What?"

"Once this year is over and I am fully separated from Guinevere, I want you to be my queen. I want to commit to you, forever, as I should have done long ago."

Tears streamed down Elaine's cheeks as she nodded, "I am yours."

A surge of happiness unleashed in his heart, and Arthur pulled her closer. Their kiss was arduous, passionate, and their bodies soon became a tangle of limbs and sighs of ecstasy. They spent most of the day in bed, relishing each other's presence, savoring the pleasure.

It was much later, once she was asleep, that Arthur left Elaine a note begging her to stay safe. It was time for him to meet his fate – and he wanted to do it as far away as possible to avoid the repercussions from getting to Camelot.

As he left their bedchambers, dressed in his best clothes and holding onto Excalibur, Arthur had the nagging feeling of going to meet his doom.

At the back of his mind, the monarch knew he should get Merlin. But he did not know whether the wizard would be able to face Morgana and Mordred and still come out unscathed. As afraid for him as for Elaine, Arthur chose to take the risk of facing them alone.

He glanced up at the skies, noticing the full moon, which somehow seemed more threatening than ever. "Keep Elaine from harm," he begged deities he had never prayed to.

The king lingered for a longer moment in the courtyard, musing over lost time as he gazed at the stars. *If only I had known back then...* With a deprecating sigh, he went into the stables to saddle Aryan.

The horse was still, as though guessing the turmoil in his master's heart. Once all was said and done, Arthur left at a trot from Camelot, exiting the doors of the castle – and, unknowingly, Merlin's protection – in the midst of the night.

He could only pray against it all that he would see Elaine again in this lifetime. Whether it was a vain hope, or something he could truly hold on to, only time would tell.

Arthur was only sure of one thing: as leader of Camelot, it was his duty to protect the kingdom against everything.

* * *

Mordred lay in wait, the anticipation of the fight bubbling under the surface. Around him, everything was immobile in the darkness. The moon loomed high above and his eyes kept being drawn to it, even as he jumped on the balls of his feet.

"Patience," Morgana urged, her sweet voice low. Underneath it, he could catch the excitement scraping the surface.

They had chosen this night, the last full moon of the equinox, and they had chosen well. The changing times charged the earth itself with power, strengthening them both.

"Here he comes…"

Morgana stepped back into the shadows, letting Mordred take the lead. She could see in the far distance Arthur nearing and could almost taste the vengeance within reach.

Mordred threw her one last excited look, then moved away. He stepped until he was at the very edge of the forest, from where he had a perfect view of his incoming opponent.

* * *

Aryan was galloping when suddenly he slowed down and came to a full stop. He neighed nervously, shaking his head and refusing to budge further.

Arthur glanced at the trees facing them, then back to Camelot.

So it is time. Not even far away…

With a repressed sigh, Arthur jumped off Aryan and let the beast go. The horse tried to stay behind, eyes wildly widened, but Arthur smiled wryly.

"No, Aryan. Go home, and be free. Return to Elaine." When the horse still lingered, Arthur raised a hand and touched his muzzle gently. "This is my fight alone, dear friend. Your life should not hang into the balance. Please, go and give Elaine the same service you have given me."

With one last look at him, then at the forest, Aryan edged away and took off like lightning.

Arthur waited until he was out of sight, then turned and unsheathed Excalibur.

A young man stepped out from behind the trees, with black hair up to his shoulders and cerulean blue eyes similar to Merlin's. He swaggered with every step taken, arrogant in his youth. In one hand, he held a sword – its metal glinting dangerously in the moon, casting odd shadows on the ground.

"Mordred, I presume?" Arthur inquired, gripping Excalibur tighter. He could perceive the darkness emanating from the young man even from the distance, and despite his non-magical senses.

"My liege," Mordred bowed mockingly, before meeting Arthur's gaze with his fiery one. "Good day, *uncle*."

May the gods help me, Arthur pleaded.

* * *

Elaine woke up to insistent banging at the door. She quickly pulled on a robe and a cloak, then ran to it.

Before she could reach for the knob, it burst open and Merlin staggered in, pale as ash.

"What is it?" she asked.

"Where is Arthur?" the mage questioned instead, looking around wildly. As he feared, the king was nowhere to be seen.

"I –" Elaine stopped, realizing she must have fallen asleep longer than she thought. Her eyes scanned the room until they fell on a note by the bedside table. She reached for it with a trembling hand.

My beloved Elaine,

These last few months with you have been paradise. My only regret is not having had all the time we could have, by my own foolishness. I love you with all my heart, and hope to return back to you.

I meant what I said this morning: I want to marry you and spend the rest of our lives together. I want to make you smile every morning, and hold you in my arms at night. You are everything I could have wished for, and more.

My darling, this night I know I have to meet my fate, whatever it may be. I hope to do so and come out a victor... If I do not, please do not mourn me, but remember the good times we had.

With all my love,

Arthur

The letter dropped from Elaine's hand as she stared in horror at Merlin. The mage grasped the falling piece of parchment and read it quickly.

"He must have left while I was asleep," Elaine murmured. "The note says he will be back, but it sounds like... Merlin, what is happening?"

The wizard crumbled the paper angrily, furious with himself for having missed it. "Damn Morgana and her tricks!"

"What is going on?" Elaine demanded, grabbing hold of

his hand.

"Arthur left to face an enemy," he divulged, then froze. In the distance, he could hear thunder. His Fae senses caught a ripple in the air, then a vision hit him.

Sword against sword, they went at it. One for light, one for darkness. The fate of the world hanging in the balance as blue eyes met hazel, and magic met strength.

When Merlin snapped to, it was to see Elaine's slightly panicked look. Then he realized the clash of swords was real. The warlock ran to the window, from where he could see dark clouds gathering in the distance by the edge of the forest.

"It is them, is it not?" Elaine whispered.

Merlin absentmindedly muttered an agreement and turned to leave, not even noticing that Elaine followed him.

Just as they exited the castle, Aryan galloped into the courtyard. Disregarding the stables, the horse went straight to the mage, shoving his muzzle in his face and snorting nervously.

Sparks appeared in the distance, further adding onto the already charged atmosphere. Merlin lifted a trembling hand to Aryan's neck. "Will you take me to Arthur? I will need all the magic I can for this."

In response, the horse bent to the ground to let Merlin hop over, which he did without a second thought.

"Take me with you!" Elaine begged.

Merlin was about to refuse, in order to keep her safe as he knew Arthur would have wanted. Another clash had him jump, and a shiver ran down his spine. *We are running out of time...* As if on cue, a vision assaulted him once more.

Arthur lay on the ground, blood seeping from the corner

of his lips. The gentle eyes were glazed as death tightened its grip. He focused on someone and the angle shifted to show Elaine, crying over him. Arthur smiled one last time, then gave his last breath.

Merlin blinked and glanced to Elaine. Her pleading expression and the image he had just seen achieved to decide him. The wizard extended a hand to help her mount, then they took off.

If Arthur is fated to die, I cannot deny him happiness in his last moments.

* * *

Arthur was meeting Mordred's parries with effort, as though his arm was filled with lead, almost dragging. Every time their swords met, sparks flew. He noticed clouds gathering above, as though nature itself was witnessing their battle.

Little did he know how right he was! In the skies above, the gods themselves peered down, following the battle with interest.

When he barely blocked Mordred's last attack, Arthur growled and grasped Excalibur with both hands. "What sorcery are you using?" he spat through gritted teeth.

Mordred merely smirked, renewing the blows. Right, left, he struck over and over, and Arthur grunted under the effort. The boy was younger and had a strength few possessed.

In spite of the odds stacked against him, Arthur had something to fight for. Elaine's face shone in his mind, as well as the certainty that if he lost, Camelot itself would be gone from the face of the earth. It was not something he could allow to happen – not while he could stop it.

With renewed vigor, Arthur parried back. Taking advantage of his opponent's arrogance, he swung Excalibur high in the air and managed to nick Mordred on the shoulder. The surprise at the blood drawn was enough to make him lose focus and trip over a tree root.

As he tumbled to the ground, Arthur felt Excalibur become smoother to handle. Panting, he lifted it and pointed the tip at Mordred's throat.

"This ends here. This vendetta against your father and me."

"Not quite."

The voice came from behind, alluring like a siren's, yet the hair at the back of his neck stood. Arthur turned slowly, positioning himself to keep an eye on both Mordred and the newcomer.

A woman faced the king clad in a black, silky dress that wrapped around her form and a dark green cloak. Her jet-black hair moved around as though agitated by an invisible breeze, and the silver eyes burned cold iron.

"Morgana."

Arthur had no trouble recognizing the sorceress. The familiar features were reflected on Mordred's face, and it oddly made sense that the woman who had wounded Merlin was as beautiful as an angel.

Morgana only smiled in response and raised a thin, elegant hand. Excalibur flew out of his grip, landing a distance away. Arthur's focus shifted to Morgana's other raised palm and he saw his life flash before his eyes.

"NO!"

No!

Recognizing Elaine's voice, Arthur tried to turn, to command Elaine to run away. Before he could, air became a necessity and his vision blurred.

* * *

Merlin jumped off Aryan, ordering Elaine to stay behind – and throwing an incantation to protect her. He marched straight to Morgana, staff aimed menacingly.

"How *dare* you intervene?" he growled, then launched an attack.

Whereas before he had hesitated, now the warlock was faced with the reality Morgana really did plan to hurt Arthur. Without a glance to his son, Merlin focused on the duel at hand.

The full extent of his Fae magic hit her, interrupting what the sorceress was doing to Arthur. The king fell to his knees, inhaling deeply, on the brink of losing consciousness.

As he tried to regain his countenance, Mordred stood up, picked his sword and inched towards the monarch. Merlin saw the gesture out of the corner of his eye and extended one hand to immobilize him, whilst the other was still deflecting Morgana's offensive strikes.

Mordred's gaze rose to his father's, and they both froze. Morgana watched as, for the first time, father and son met face to face.

"Hello, father," Mordred smirked. "How unsurprising you take *his* side."

Merlin lowered his hand – the instinct was too strong. The young man in front of him was both him and Morgana. He had the sorceress' fair features and dark hair, but his blue eyes and build.

The wizard's gaze roamed over the son he had not seen growing, even as he stepped closer. He longed to both protect Arthur and be nearer Mordred – flesh of his flesh, blood of his blood.

From the new vantage point, Merlin could now see both Mordred and Morgana – one to his right, the other to his left. Arthur was straight across from him, and Mordred was inching closer.

"Leave the king alone," Merlin warned, but his voice lacked strength.

Shaken at seeing Mordred, the mage could not decide on the best course of action. Then the last time he had seen Morgana flashed through his mind and he turned to her. "You lied to him all this time. Tell him the truth! Tell him it was a mistake!"

Morgana only shook her head, smiling coldly in the way he hated more than anything.

Merlin gave up reasoning with her, and instead pleaded with Mordred. "Please, my son. You have to know there are two sides to the story!"

"Oh, I do," Mordred chuckled. "I simply do not care to hear yours."

Merlin's hopes crushed as he registered the icy glint in his son's gaze. There was nothing there, no emotion whatsoever for him, except a brutal need to inflict pain and destruction.

And with every spoken word, Mordred got within striking distance of the semi-conscious Arthur.

Inhaling deeply, Merlin lifted his hand again, magic shining within. "Step away from Arthur."

"What will you do, father?" Mordred grinned madly.

"Hurt me?"

With a mocking scoff, and a wink to his mother, he lifted the blade in his hand above Arthur's head. Nothing in Merlin would allow anyone to hurt the king, not after all the time he had spent trying to keep him safe.

The elements in his hand, reading the intention – though it was not fully formed – reacted of their own accord, and slammed into Mordred. The force sent him flying backwards into the nearest tree.

"How could you!?" Morgana shrieked, before launching a new barrage of attacks onto Merlin.

Mordred, rising to his feet further away, lifted a palm as well and started blasting magic towards Merlin. His face was twisted in fury, the brilliance in his eyes reaching an unnatural shine.

Struck from two sides, the light mage could only hold his ground, unable to bring himself to hurt the two. He threw a barrier over Arthur, ensuring at least none of the magic would harm him. In spite of it, nothing could keep him safe from Mordred and the newly approaching sword.

"Arthur, get up!" Merlin shouted.

The monarch, shaking his head to clear it, managed to push himself to his knees. He scanned the surroundings, but Excalibur was out of his reach.

Elaine, who had been staying away up until that point, jumped off Aryan. She had been observing the battle, afraid to intervene for fear of distracting either Arthur or Merlin.

Her heart clenched painfully as she registered the danger her beloved was in. Despite it, she had the right mind to realize it would be foolishness to jump into the fray and end up being used as a bartering tool.

However, noticing the situation Arthur was in, she stepped around the duelling warlocks, aiming for where Excalibur lay forgotten in the grass. Easily dismissed by the Halflings, Elaine managed to grasp Excalibur.

She turned to Arthur, who was a few feet away – too close to the wizards for her to get to him.

"Arthur, catch!" Elaine threw Excalibur and the monarch lifted his hand, where the hilt slid smoothly.

He pivoted on a knee, raising the weapon to block Mordred's attack just in time. Now distracted by the sword fight, the younger sorcerer had no choice but to cease the attack onto his father – though seeing him lose would have pleased him immensely.

Annoyed at Elaine's provided help, Morgana screamed in anger and lifted a palm towards her. The burst of air hit the young maiden full-force and she flew in the air, landing near Aryan.

"Leave her *alone!*" Merlin growled, doubling the charge towards Morgana and forcing his former lover to focus on him alone.

When Elaine came to, she observed the scene before her, holding onto her ringing head. She did not know what to do to help, but she knew *something* had to be done.

As she tried to get closer, however, an immobile wall blocked her progress. Though she had no magical powers, Elaine figured out that it had been erected by either of the two attackers in an effort to stop anyone from intervening.

The barrier stopped her from entering the circle surrounding Merlin and Morgana, Arthur and Mordred – all engaged in a duel to the death.

Elaine bit her lip, heart constricting as she watched them fight for their lives. Just as she thought there was nothing she could do, she recalled one person who had helped Arthur in the past.

Please, Elaine bowed her hand, joining her hands in prayer. *Lady of the Lake, they need your help. I beg you,* please *come to Arthur's aid.*

* * *

At Aisling Caisléan, Vivienne was absent-mindedly looking for a cape. In the morning, she had woken up to a clear thought: *Carleigh will attack tonight.* She had been unable to shake off the presentiment and was debating on sharing the news with Sébastien.

It was then she heard Elaine's call as clearly as though the woman was next to her. *Please, Lady of the Lake, they need your help. I beg you,* please *come to Arthur's aid.*

The plea was so passionate, Vivienne caught onto its lingering emotion and traced it back to Arthur's love. Through her eyes, she could see the barrier and the four people engaged in a battle.

The cloth dropped from her hand and Sébastien stepped to her, feeling the change of mood. "What is it?"

Vivienne turned to him, her green eyes searching his darker ones. She knew what Sébastien would say, but could not stop him. "It is time," she revealed. "Mordred and Morgana have attacked, and Arthur is in danger."

Vivienne was already halfway down the stairs when Sébastien snapped out of his stupor enough to follow, and grab her hand. "Vivienne, Merlin can help him."

"He cannot alone, I saw it. He is faced with both Morgana and Mordred, something that cannot be handled alone."

"Yes, he can!" Sébastien denied vehemently. "Merlin has the strength, if only he is willing to tap into it!"

The enchantress' eyes softened, understanding the worry in her lover. Nonetheless, her duty demanded she act, something that could not be refused in order to safeguard her own life. "I cannot take the chance, my love."

"Vivienne…"

She raised an index to his lips, then removed it to kiss Sébastien softly. "I have to go to their aid."

"Alistair warned you not to."

Vivienne smiled sadly, looking at this man that had always protected her, watching her grow and loving her. "I have to," she murmured, then headed out to the lake.

With a wave of her hand, the waters swirled until a portal opened, similar to a vortex. Just as Vivienne was about to step in, Sébastien stopped her again.

"Let me come," he pleaded.

"I cannot, my love." A swift kiss, a caress. "One of us has to stay here, for I have a feeling Carleigh will decide now is an opportune time to attack. Protect Aisling Caisléan, it is our home. I will return."

Sébastien shook his head in denial, but there was nothing to do. He crushed Vivienne to his chest, kissing her arduously one last time, trying to give her strength he knew she already had.

When she pulled away, he whispered hoarsely, "Come back to me unharmed."

"I will," Vivienne vowed, knowing full well it was not a

promise she could uphold.

The enchantress jumped into the portal and emerged on the other side, in a pond by the forest.

CHAPTER 34

Vivienne took in the sight before her: Elaine on her knees, Arthur fighting Mordred, Morgana with Merlin. She was overpowering the stubborn wizard because he refused to attack in order to injure her.

"Love truly can be blind," Vivienne muttered. *Forgive me, Alistair, for breaking a promise. I cannot stay out of this.*

She let the cape fall to the ground, in a gesture meant to shed herself of all that could become a burden during the fight. Underneath it, Vivienne wore a white dress, with long sleeves and a V-neck. The garment shone of an angelic glow.

Merlin saw brilliance out of the corner of his eye and was about to turn to it when he felt a stab. He glanced over his shoulder in time to see Mordred withdraw the tip of the sword from his side to parry Arthur's attack.

The wizard felt pain radiate from the laceration, but it was not that which made him stagger. Rather, the realization that his son had gone so far as to stab him. *Does he truly hate me so?*

The question was answered when he had to duck another assault, as Mordred managed to evade Arthur and get closer to Merlin once more.

"I *will* make you pay, father," he hissed, even as Arthur struck again.

"Leave Merlin alone!" the king ordered, then slammed Excalibur against the youth's own sword in faster blows, in an effort to distract him.

Blocking one of Morgana's attacks, Merlin slid a hand to the open cut and managed to shoot a burst of healing energy towards it. Though it was not enough to close the wound, it would at least stop the bleeding until the end of the fight.

Another shine towards the left had Merlin turn around to see Vivienne step through the barrier as though walking through liquid. In her trail, slithers of water followed like obedient pets, and her eyes shone of all fires.

"Vivienne!" Merlin breathed in disbelief.

Go heal yourself, Vivienne entreated mentally, even as she positioned herself to face Morgana in Merlin's place.

The sorceress' face contorted in rage recognizing the champion of light. "You *cannot* intervene!"

"Vivienne, no," Merlin protested weakly, but had to shake the dizziness out of his eyes.

Mordred being a half-Fae as well, his blow had the potential to be fatal unless the warlock took the proper time away to cleanse his system. Already, Merlin was feeling drained from the force of his son's rage that seeped through him.

"And yet I have," the enchantress responded to both.

You need to heal, otherwise Morgana will win. Go!
Vivienne ordered mentally again.

When Merlin made a move to step by her side, she lifted a palm towards him. The emerald gaze gleamed almost mockingly, and Merlin was forcefully pushed out of the barrier. It closed around the two women, and Arthur and Mordred once more.

Morgana pursed her lips, not liking that Merlin was out of her reach. "Your own realm will be lost," she threatened.

"It was already."

"I mean your *new* one," Morgana taunted.

"I know all about your planned strategy with Carleigh," Vivienne revealed, enjoying the look of shock on the sorceress' face. "I have ensured my palace remains protected. You should worry about yourself, Morgana. Merlin may have been afraid to use his full strength against you, but I do not cower in fright of my magic."

With that, Vivienne let the shine from within radiate to its full extent. She became a beacon and Morgana had to look away, the radiance hurting her eyes.

Light magic clashed against elemental as they sparred. Despite Morgana's Fae heritage, Vivienne had the advantage of dueling with a clear head. Morgana was angry and, in her wrath, she did not think things through, rather used bursts of energy at random.

Vivienne, on the other hand, used the magic from within only when needed. She created a shield for protection and cajoled water to tangle Morgana up into a web she could not escape.

Behind the enchantress, Mordred tried to intervene a few times, eager to square off with his nemesis. The only thing he achieved was to get the pitiful attempts bounced back to himself. Scowling, he paused in order to finish off his uncle.

Arthur continued striking, and as the better swordsman of the two, quickly gained ground. Determined to put an end to it, Mordred tried to throw magic at the king again, but found it unresponsive.

The young sorcerer, as though pushed by a sixth sense, looked across the distance to where his father was healing. The man's blue eyes were glued onto his, lips moving in a spell to block the elements from functioning properly.

"Damn you!" Mordred yelled at Merlin, then resolutely focused on the sword fight.

Hearing her son yell, Morgana glanced around and also noticed Merlin's intervention. Angry with Vivienne for ruining her plans, the sorceress took out a pouch of powder from within her robes.

I had intended to use this on Merlin, but even the best-laid plans unravel...

Without hesitation, she threw the sachet towards Vivienne. Surrounded by Fae magic, it passed through the enchantress' barrier and hit her straight in the face. Black powder escaped it and surrounded the young woman in a mist.

Vivienne coughed, inhaling it all. Mere moments later, she fell to her knees, panting and trying to breathe in air.

Merlin, having passed through the barrier anew, rushed to her. His Fae senses could already feel Vivienne's heartbeat slow down, her vital energy at risk.

"Yes, Merlin," Morgana laughed evilly, "poison."

The warlock looked up at his former lover, scowling. "Human poison can be healed!"

Merlin lifted a palm, about to absorb it from Vivienne – puzzled as to why she was not doing so herself.

"Uh uh," Morgana taunted. "You might want to rethink that. This is Fae poison, darling."

The wizard looked at Vivienne, then back to Morgana. "How did you get it?"

"Did you think all these years I waited around, moping after you?" Morgana chuckled darkly. "You were wrong. I managed to gain entry to Fae realms you can only dream of, Merlin. That poison comes from one such place, and cannot be healed except by elemental magic, wielded by a full Fae."

As his face fell, Morgana had to laugh. "Yes, since you are half – and not even that, as you are afraid to use your powers – you cannot do anything for her." Addressing Vivienne, she hissed, "You should have stayed out of it."

Merlin grasped Vivienne's arm, ordering, "Get out of here! Go to your place of power, it should slow this sorcery down enough to buy us some time. Let me handle this, it was my fight to begin with."

Vivienne shook her head in denial, then raised an incensed gaze to Morgana. "Elemental magic, you say?" she whispered weakly.

With a trembling hand, she reached out to the water nearby. The slithering snakes crawled over the ground, closer and closer, until they wrapped around Vivienne's arms, then neck.

The element itself cleansed her, much like it had done with Sébastien long ago. It was not enough to fully heal,

Vivienne was aware of it. But it would gain her more than enough time to continue.

Morgana gaped as the young woman stood panting, but alive and unharmed. She realized, in that moment when Merlin gazed at her proudly, that she had underestimated the enchantress.

Then a cry behind made them turn to watch in horror the events unfurling.

Arthur did not block Mordred's blow and the younger man's sword slipped off his, then plunged straight into his chest. The king froze, looking down at the blood seeping out.

In a last attempt, Arthur lifted Excalibur and drove it through Mordred's chest. Since the young man's blade was still embedded in the monarch's body, he had no way to block the attack. Both men fell down, the swords dropping out of their grasps and landing on the grass.

"No!" Morgana screamed, running to Mordred. He should not have been fatally wounded, but the fact his fate and Arthur's had been tied, broke all the rules on Fae mortality. With a sinking feeling, the sorceress sensed her son's pulse slow down.

Merlin rushed to Arthur, followed closely by Vivienne.

"Elaine," Arthur gasped.

Vivienne glanced behind and with an impatient hand gesture, shattered the barrier. Elaine, who had been at the very edge observing, hurried towards Arthur. Tears were running down her cheeks as she cradled the king's head in her arms.

"Do not leave me," she sobbed. "You promised!"

"My beautiful…queen," Arthur lifted a hand slowly to her cheek. "It should have been you and I from the start. All these years wasted…"

Elaine shook her head vehemently, grasping his hand in hers. "It always has been you and me, Arthur. Even while we were apart. Stay with me, my darling, please!"

Arthur choked, then coughed out blood. His lids closed, the hand landing limply on the grass as though he no longer had the strength to keep it up.

"No, stay!" Elaine bent low and whispered in his ear.

Arthur's eyes opened, widening in surprise, then joy. "How truly wondrous!" he whispered. The hazel eyes latched onto Elaine's one last time, memorizing the lines of her face. "Until we meet again…" he whispered, then his gaze went blank.

Elaine buried her head in his chest, crying all the tears in her body. After all this time, they had had such a short happiness…

Vivienne glanced behind, but Morgana and Mordred were gone. She walked past a stricken-looking Merlin to the spot Mordred had fallen. It took only one touch of the blood that tainted the earth and she had confirmation of his death.

"Mordred is dead as well," she informed Merlin.

"How?" the mage asked, unable to comprehend. "He is half-Fae, like Morgana and me, only another Fae or god could have harmed him fatally. I…"

"You forget, Merlin," Vivienne interrupted softly, "that Morgana made it so his fate and Arthur's were tightly linked. Much as your magic acted out of turn many times, causing havoc, hers must have as well."

Pain crossed the warlock's features, for his king as well as the son he had never had a chance to know better. *All is lost…*

"Let me take Arthur," Vivienne pleaded with Elaine, shaken by another presentiment. "Let me send him where Morgana can never find him."

Elaine looked at her, then nodded. "Take Excalibur, too."

"No... It was Arthur's, and should be kept by you."

Vivienne levitated Arthur to the lake, where a boat miraculously stood waiting. She laid the king in it on a bed of flowers, then lifted both her palms towards it. With muttered incantations, it moved away and disappeared into the morning fog.

The enchantress turned to Merlin, noticing his odd expression at the words she had whispered.

"Avalon," he murmured. "The land of forgotten dreams... That is where you sent him?"

It occurred to Merlin, not for the first time, that his previous pupil now much surpassed him in all aspects of things. To reach Avalon, it was not enough to be a wielder of light magic. One had to have a pure heart, incorruptible and just.

The island was said to have been created by the gods and Faes after their last wars, a place to send their fallen. To the present, no regular human had ever entered. Yet Vivienne had managed, with a single spell, to gain Arthur entrance to the holy place.

Not only is she powerful, but no barrier can withstand her purity...

The enchantress' next words snapped Merlin out of his thoughts.

"Avalon is the only place Morgana can never desecrate Arthur's body," Vivienne declared, then turned to Elaine. "If you need help, call to me."

Before the young woman could answer, Merlin froze and landed in a trance.

Sébastien was fighting druids with magic and a sword. Behind them, Carleigh was waiting for the chance to ruin it all. Vengeance would soon be his, with the Lady of the Lake not there to stop him.

The scene shifted, and a young boy gazed upon the ruins of Camelot. His hazel eyes shone with unshed tears as he walked away, to a better future.

"Your castle!" Merlin warned, and Vivienne's eyes glittered with anger. "You need to go, Sébastien needs you!"

The enchantress glanced to Elaine, then Merlin, hesitating. In the end, she nodded and jumped into another portal.

Merlin wrapped an arm around Elaine, who fell in his hold, sobbing. The wizard let the tears he held back run down his cheeks, at all that had been gone awry.

Then he recalled something and pushed Elaine away to peer down at her face. "What was it you told Arthur?"

"I carry his child," Elaine murmured past the tightening in her throat.

"Truly a wonder!"

Now the prophecy makes sense. Arthur's legacy is not lost at all!

Merlin put a hand on Aryan, who had neared. "I have given him instructions. He will take you far away from here, to a safe place. There are druids there who will care for Arthur's heir the way he – or she – deserves. "

Elaine was too tired to speak, and simply inclined her head in assent. Camelot would no longer be safe for her, not with Arthur gone. It would take the lords mere days to start their squabbles over who should replace him.

Shoulder curled inwards, Elaine let Merlin help her onto Aryan, and clutched the horse's mane as though her life depended on it.

"I will join you as soon as I can," Merlin promised, then watched as Aryan took her away.

* * *

Back at Aisling Caisléan, Vivienne arrived in the midst of the druids on the shore. She found Sébastien sporting some minor wounds, but otherwise alive. Her spell had thankfully worked and saved him from the brunt of their magic, and protected the entrance to their castle.

"Let me help," she announced, blasting a few of them away with fire.

The knight turned to her with a grin, but it fell away as he noticed how tired the enchantress looked. "What happened?"

"Morgana was a powerful opponent," Vivienne revealed, unwilling to worry him more. "Arthur is dead."

"I am sorry to hear it," Sébastien whispered.

"I, as well, my love. He was a good leader, but at least his legacy will be safe." With a glance to the druids heading closer, she clasped their hands together. "Let us try to ensure ours remains behind, as well."

Sébastien nodded in agreement. Never had he loved Vivienne as much as he did in that moment.

They fought side by side, him with the enchanted sword, Vivienne using her magic, for hours on end. For each sorcerer that died, another took his place until the entrance to the castle was littered with bodies.

Vivienne lifted a palm, commanding a strong wave to wash her shores clean. The water did its mistress' bidding, avoiding her and Sébastien. Still, she could sense more attackers approaching, their nefarious energies rippling across the lake.

And somewhere between them was hidden Carleigh – a wolf in the midst of the sheep.

Vivienne knew the moment he stepped onto her land, as the island rebelled, earth vibrating loudly. She was about to head to him, but a wave of dizziness drained her energy.

The enchantress leaned against one of the castle walls, hiding from Sébastien's gaze. Morgana's poison had left her weak, *too* weak to fight Carleigh – and win.

As Vivienne had no time to recharge in the lake, the cursed poison would keep eating at her strength until there was nothing left. In such a vulnerable state, a properly aimed strike from Carleigh could mean the end. Ultimately, attacking him would be suicide.

The enchantress looked to her nemesis, then her lover. *There is no choice here, I must do what I can.*

She stepped to Sébastien after he finished the last druid and pressed her lips against his fervently, knowing it might be the last time. Pulling away, Vivienne's gaze locked onto his, "I love you."

Before Sébastien had a chance to grab her and keep her by his side, Vivienne turned away, heading towards Carleigh. More druids attacked the knight, and he had no choice but to fight them.

As a ray of darkness shot past him, he glanced towards Vivienne. She was involved in a duel with Carleigh, their magic flying everywhere.

* * *

Vivienne was dying, and Sébastien was helpless to stop it. He had taken his eyes off her and the dueling sorcerer for a mere moment, to kill off his final opponent, and turned back to see an orb of darkness hit his beloved full front.

She flew into the air and landed closer to him, but this time, she did not get up. He ran to her side, pulling her into his arms, but Vivienne was unresponsive.

"Merlin!" the guardian roared in need, holding her close. "Help me! Do not let her die!"

"She is too far gone," a voice snickered behind mockingly.

Sébastien kissed Vivienne's forehead, then lunged for his sword and stood up to confront Carleigh.

"You will pay for this!"

"I highly doubt that," the malicious sorcerer smirked.

He flung a sphere of dark magic at Sébastien, which the defender deflected with his weapon.

The duel went on, and the knight held his ground. He managed to injure Carleigh, but could tell by means of their bond that Vivienne was slowly slipping away.

Noticing he could not win by pure blade skill alone, the sorcerer sent a wave of witchcraft to attack Sébastien from behind, causing him to drop to the ground. Deep, bloody gashes spread across his back, even as he screamed in agony.

Carleigh strode towards Vivienne, his midnight robes – and the shadows at his feet – trailing him like a second skin.

"Get away from her!" Sébastien roared.

Helpless, he saw the warlock approach Vivienne and

whisper in her ear. He could not hear what was expressed, but the enchantress' eyes fluttered open and he perceived a sudden burst of hate through their bond.

"I said," Sébastien croaked, "get *away* from her!"

There was a blinding flash, and Merlin appeared. Sébastien let the wizard handle the fight with Carleigh, being far more concerned for his beloved than the fate of the world. He crawled to Vivienne, desperately searching for a pulse.

Her hand was cold, almost translucently pale. "Please stay with me," Sébastien pleaded.

Vivienne opened her eyes and smiled weakly, tears streaming down her cheeks.

"I will always love you, remember that," she whispered.

When shouts clamored from behind Sébastien, he could not help but glance, torn between a need to help Merlin, and a longing to save the queen. It was the idea of Carleigh running free, after all the damage he had inflicted, which helped the knight decide.

"Please wait for me, beloved, do not give in just yet," Sébastien implored, squeezing Vivienne's hand.

He waited for her weak nod, and only then got up one last time to help Merlin, despite the loss of blood he had already suffered.

With the defender blocking the attacks with his sword, Merlin was able to use the staff's concentrated power to fatally wound Carleigh. They managed to get the warlock down, pinning him to the earth, where the old wizard's power captured him.

His evil no match for Merlin's acute abilities, the sorcerer gargled blood, choking on his own viciousness. Before perishing, Carleigh smirked at Merlin. "You are too late. Your precious is already cursed."

Sébastien grabbed him by the throat. "What did you do?" he snarled.

"Keep your strength, pretty boy, or else you shall join her in the grave."

"Speak!" Merlin commanded.

"I cursed her. She will not be reborn until her dear champion's heart turns to darkness."

With a furious snarl, the champion picked up the blade to end him. Yet it was Merlin who gave the final blow, sending a wave of spirit so strong into Carleigh, it caused the execrable sorcerer to turn to ash.

The mage then helped Sébastien get to where Vivienne lay dying. "Please save her," he begged. "I will give my life in exchange if I have to."

"I cannot. You have no idea how much I wish it, but it is too late."

At the words, Vivienne gasped, as though running out of breath. Sébastien gripped her hand, sobbing hot tears of shame and regret, having been unable to save her life.

"Please don't leave," he cried.

The enchantress' beautiful green opened one last time, and her gaze locked onto Sébastien's, love shining through. Then they fluttered closed, and Vivienne exhaled her final breath.

Merlin's sorrowful eyes turned to Sébastien, barely keeping his own sorrow in check. "Listen to me well. Did you hear Carleigh's curse?"

Concentrated on Vivienne's last few breaths, Sébastien pleaded, "Let me die of my wounds, so I may join her in the next life. You explained soul mates find each other."

"Yes, they do. But you heard what he said: only when you turn evil, will she be reborn. If you let it enter you, the darkness of the curse will affect Vivienne, as well."

At the words, the guardian peered up at Merlin, realizing their meaning. "You mean to say if she is reborn, I cannot be with her, as it would taint her?"

Compassion shone in the old man's eyes, but he did not disagree. Sébastien knew his fate was sealed. He contemplated Vivienne, her beautiful features frozen forever in death.

"The world cannot be denied her radiance. Let me die of my wounds, Merlin, and I will wait for her, and defend her from afar when she is reborn. I give you my oath. I would die a million deaths if it helped her."

Merlin acquiesced, and pressed both hands to Sébastien's forehead. "Then be at peace, good knight."

The flame was blinding, entering his forehead, and Sébastien felt himself slipping away. "See you soon, beloved," he murmured, tightening his grip on Vivienne's hand one last time, before letting go.

EPILOGUE

In the midst of a village, in a hut in the middle of nowhere, a woman screamed.

An elderly woman wiped her brow, then whispered, "Push, my lady. You are almost there."

With one last agonizing shout, a baby's cry was heard and the young woman smiled.

An older man stepped in, relying on a staff. He had grey, almost white hair, and a beard. "A boy, Elaine," he murmured. "How truly wondrous, indeed."

"I will name him Arthur, after his father," Elaine whispered, smiling at the child in her arms. He would be her world, the only connection to Arthur she still had left.

She then glanced up to the newcomer. She had been surprised at first, not recognizing him, but then he had explained the need for the disguise. With the fighting happening on Camelot's old lands, if anyone was to recognize him, realize who he truly was, they might try to follow him to Elaine's safe haven.

"Thank you for being here, Merlin," Elaine murmured. Their eyes met, the pain they both felt not lessened – Arthur had taken a part of each of them, with him in death.

Merlin smiled weakly, and lifted a hand to bestow a blessing upon the child. Then, he left Elaine to the care of the druids. A strong protection had been placed around her to ensure the baby could never be found – and neither could Elaine.

As for himself, he walked miles upon miles that night, lost in thought, until he reached a different cave and the portal within. He stepped in, and sealed the entrance with a crystal wall. In his little alcove of quiet, Merlin decided to let go of the rest of the world, and to watch the tides of time turning.

Sometime in the future, Arthur would be reborn. And when he was, Merlin would be there to guide him and succeed where he had failed this time around.

* * *

In the gods' palace, Alistair walked around as though in a daze. When Vivienne had died, he had felt a part of him being yanked out, never to be filled again.

He did not notice, lost as he was in memories of his former mistress, that the ground underneath his feet became more vivid, and the surroundings changed.

"Atrox."

Only her voice pulled him out of dark thoughts. Alistair glanced up at Catriona, mere feet away from him. The look in her eyes, the regret in the cerulean gaze, hit him full force. There was a lump in his throat, then the proud former god fell to his knees, letting the tears fall.

"I failed," he stated hoarsely.

Catriona rushed over, hugging him to her. "You did not!" she whispered fiercely, knowing it would do no good.

The wolf-god let his sorrow out, knowing only the Fae could understand how much he had tried to change the course of events, and how little impact he truly had.

Eventually, he pulled away, wiping at his face to remove all trace of weakness. Catriona kissed him softly and Alistair let the healing she tried to communicate wash over, welcoming it. When he opened his eyes, she was gone and he was back in the gods' paradise.

In the distance, he could sense Ardea's presence and followed it with wooden steps.

The goddess was standing next to a small pond, looking within. When Alistair was near enough, she lifted a hand and the water twirled.

Alistair peered within, seeing Vivienne's peacefully sleeping face.

"What is this?" he growled.

"I know it has hurt you to lose her, brother, but Vivienne will be reborn. If you so wish, you can join her in the next life."

Alistair tried to gauge whether it was a trick or not, but not sensing anything, he nodded. "I wish to return in her service."

"And so you shall."

With a wave of the hand, Alistair became a glowing orb, which Ardea dropped into the pond.

Aequus appeared around the corner after he was gone. "You forgot to tell him one thing."

"He will figure it out," Ardea laughed, then stepped away. "Besides, being a canine may suit him better than we think."

* * *

On the earthly realm, Morgana appeared by the circle of stones. It had taken her close to nine months to recharge her magic, as she kept using parts of it to keep Mordred's body intact.

Originally, she had planned to find Arthur's body and use his link to the light to bring Mordred back. But that had failed when Vivienne had put him in Avalon – and then went and got herself killed.

Without other options, Morgana had willed herself to be patient.

Now, she levitated Mordred's body within the circle of stones, and stepped in herself. The moon was high in the sky and it was the perfect time.

Morgana let the energy flow around her until it created a beacon around the rocks. Inside the circle, a portal was created. She stepped within, entering the realm of the unknown.

She had not lied to Merlin. Over the years, as she had dwelled further into the Fae powers and how to use them, Morgana had discovered they were surrounded by different Fae realms. Amongst them was the one where the dead of her kin went to rest in peace – and where the final judgment was passed on each one of them.

It was there she aimed her thoughts to this time. The only place that could help out and bestow upon her what she wished.

Morgana lost sense of time as she floated around on her knees, cradling Mordred's head in her lap. After what seemed like hours, she came to a stop. There was nothing surrounding her, only the thickest of fogs.

Through her senses, she could feel them there – elder Faes that had passed on, that could still wield powerful magic.

"I ask for my son to be restored," Morgana enunciated.

Nothing answered at first, then a whispery voice came close to her ear – though there was no one there.

"And what do you give in return?" it whispered.

Morgana lifted her silver eyes, shining with determination. "My Fae immortality."

There was silence, murmured words all around her. Faes alone were not afraid of dabbling with death, and the rules that would be broken. To them, some chaos was a price to pay in a world of light and dark.

"How did you know to contact the underworld of the Fae?" another voice asked.

"Those who do not know, seek," Morgana whispered.

Another silence, then, "Granted."

A glowing golden orb shone into the darkness and struck the sorceress full force. Morgana felt a drain of energy, as though something was being torn from her. Then, before her stunned gaze, Mordred inhaled anew and his eyes opened.

"Mother!"

She hugged him close, whispering, "All is fine. You are alright."

He pulled back, pushing away the memories of the world he had stepped into for the last nine months – the darkness, the unknown, the nothingness.

"What happened? I should not be alive."

Instead of an answer, Mordred heard a voice in the midst.

"The price has been paid. You are free to leave, Halflings."

Mordred look at his mother, a foreboding sensation in the pit of his stomach. For the first time ever, he was afraid. "Mother, what is it talking about? What price?"

Morgana caressed his cheek lovingly, then kissed his forehead like she used to when he was a child. "Do not worry about it."

"What did you do?" Mordred pressed, grasping her wrist in his.

The blue eyes demanded an answer and, unlike his father, Morgana had sworn to be truthful to him – as much as she could.

"I did what I had to, in order to get you back. We are in the underworld of the Faes, they were the only ones who could help."

"Mother…"

Ignoring the horror in his gaze, Morgana rapidly divulged, "I gave away my immortality in order to get your life back."

"You… No!" Mordred looked around helplessly. "Undo it! She cannot be allowed to do this!" Morgana was now mortal, meaning though she still had magic, she could be killed by non-Faes as well.

"What is done cannot be undone," the bodiless voice stated.

"Mother…" Mordred turned to her with tears in his eyes. "Why?"

"I could not bear to be without you," the sorceress admitted, then wiped his cheeks – and hers. "Besides, now we can continue."

"How?" he asked. "We lost."

"Not quite, darling. I have placed a spell upon them all – they will not remember us, nor the trouble they had to go through to fight us."

Mordred nodded at her wisdom, then rubbed his chest in the spot he had been stabbed. Somehow, though he had been brought back to life, Mordred doubted it would ever go away.

"But the magic, it will not work on father... No Fae can spell another directly."

"True. However, knowing Merlin, he will not tell them the full truth unless it suits him. And it will not."

Mordred looked around. "What then?"

"Now, we do what your father does," Morgana smiled coldly. "We stay within the confines of space, until it is time for us to step back into the fray."

Mordred's blue eyes met hers, then he slowly nodded determinately. This time, he would face Vivienne herself – and win.

Mother and son stood from the fog and joined their palms. With their free hands, they opened a portal into their new home – and jumped in.

This may be the End of Part III
but it is The Beginning...

...of The End

Stay tuned for Book III
The final installment of *The Avalon Chronicles*
"Avalon Nightmares"

(Flip the page for a sneak peek)

Preview

"Avalon Nightmares"

Vivienne woke up gasping, unable to shake off the feeling. She turned to Sébastien's arms, but after hours trying to fall asleep, gave up.

She slid out of bed, moving instead towards the window. The moon was high in the sky, and she had an odd feeling about tonight.

What is it, highness?

She turned to see Alistair watching her warily. These days, her companion kept to himself, and though she did not want to be overprotective, something felt off.

"A bad dream, is all," she murmured. "What about you?"

What do you mean?

"You feel odd lately...preoccupied. Is everything ok?"

Alistair did his doggy grin and woofed happily. *Of course, majesty. Go back to sleep.*

Once Vivienne was back in bed, the demon dog curled up onto himself, whining dejectedly.

Good job, the voice murmured. *Now I need you to get the knight out of the equation.*

I will not hurt Vivienne!

But you are not really hurting her, mutt. You are helping her.

Morgana, this is really pushing it!

There was silence and for a brief moment, Alistair almost thought he had peace. Then her voice came back.

Do you wish me to release Carleigh, and start this all over again for Vivienne? Or do you want to help her, and in exchange return to your deity self? The choice is yours.

Alistair growled, but ended up saying, *What is it you wish me to do?*

Kill Sébastien.

Alistair managed to nod. Once he felt the presence leave, he raised his head. Blocking mind and thoughts, he went to the knight and shook him awake.

"What is it?" Sébastien whispered, rubbing the sleep out of his eyes.

Morgana wants you out.

"Not surprising, she needs Vivienne weakened." The guardian glanced to his beloved, fast asleep in the security of his arms. "What should we do?"

I think we give in. I will pretend to kill you, and instead throw you into a coma.

"I don't like this. And who will protect Vivienne?"

Me. And you. At his confused look, Alistair explained, *Your former self. When Morgana and Mordred break through the portal here, I can get you through, as well.*

Sébastien mulled it over, then nodded. "Alright. I trust the me back then to do an even better job at protecting Vivienne."

Alistair gazed at him, thinking all may not end of so easily. Still, it was the best chance they had.

Good, it is settled. Get some sleep.

Continue reading!

ABOUT THE AUTHOR

Alexa Whitewolf was born in Romania a little after the fall of Communism, 1992 to be exact. Growing up in the Transylvania region surrounded by epic mountains and a never ending stream of legends and stories was bound to create an overactive imagination. From a young age, she started rescuing pets–abandoned dogs in warehouses, kittens about to be drowned–and spent her childhood talking to animals. This devotion to the furry creatures shows up in her writing, as most of her series will have one–or more–pets involved (think Alistair if you read _The Avalon Chronicles_, Tyr in _The Sage's Legacy_).

The move to Canada in her teens was a sometimes rough adjustment, and Alexa overcame it by burying herself in books–both reading and writing. She started her young adult series at that time, and continued with the fantasy of Avalon in university. Nowadays? She's working on a few other upcoming series, among which a werewolf paranormal romance.

Alexa currently lives nearby picturesque Ontario, where Starbucks locations abound. When not at home writing–or awake in the middle of the night trying to put her characters to sleep–Alexa can be found enjoying walks with her husband and two masters of mischief, Zeus and Achilles. Her social media feed is always inundated with animal posts, so if you're looking for some sunshine in your day, you know where to find it: Facebook, Twitter or Goodreads, so don't be shy!

When the mood strikes, Alexa also dabbles in handmade jewelry and stationery for special occasions, as well as the occasional website creation for friends. And if that's not enough to keep this night owl busy, she's still trying to convince her husband to get another puppy–sadly, a work in progress.

You can read more on her books, enter giveaways and follow her blog on travel, dogs and life in general at www.alexawhitewolf.com

Be sure to sign up for Alexa's mailing list for exclusive perks!

ALSO BY THE AUTHOR

The Avalon Chronicles series
Avalon Dreams
Avalon Wishes
Avalon Nightmares

The Sage's Legacy – YA series
The Dragon Medallion
The Dragon Manuscript
Relics of the Underworld

Moonlight Rogues series
First to Fall
Second to Surrender
Third to Tumble
Last to Love

Standalone novels
Blood Ties, Love Binds
Unconditional Love
Blazing in a Storm of Ashes (Coming Soon)
More novels coming soon!

Sign up for my readers' group at
www.alexawhitewolf.com/contact and
receive a copy of *Unconditional Love* for **FREE,**
as well as first dibs on cover reveals,
discounts, giveaways, prizes **and more!**